A HALF-CENTURY OF SF CLASSICS!

This stellar selection spans the career of the world-renowned master of science fiction—Edward E. "Doc" Smith. From his debut in 1928 until his death in 1964, E. E. Smith thrilled fans and fellow authors alike with his insightful treatments of science and space exploration.

Opening with an epic passage from his first great achievement, THE SKYLARK OF SPACE, and including several stories never before collected, THE BEST OF E. E. "DOC" SMITH contains the inimitable mixture of suspense and scientific speculation that the Doctor has prescribed for 50 years. It's sure to cure every SF reader's fever for adventure and sheer cosmic exuberance.

THE BEST OF E. E. "DOC" SMITH

A JOVE/HBJ BOOK

Printed in the United States of America

Library of Congress Catalog Card Number: 78-71874

First Jove/HBJ edition published March 1979

Jove/HBJ books are published by Jove Publications, Inc.
(Harcourt Brace Jovanovich)
757 Third Avenue, New York, N.Y. 10017

LIST OF CONTENTS

PREFACE

When "The Skylark of Space" was published in AMAZING STORIES in 1928 it gave the science fiction fraternity the road to the stars. It also had a profound effect on other writers, notably John W. Campbell, who took their cue from Smith.

TO THE FAR REACHES OF SPACE, a complete-in-itself excerpt from the famous novel, records this initial leap beyond the solar system. Told with verve and gusto, the narrative admirably shows Smith's panache in handling vast distances and strange alien worlds.

As "The Skylark of Space" shattered the confines of the space story in 1928, so ROBOT NEMESIS widened the frontiers of the robot story when it first appeared (under another title) in 1934. Robots in the early days of science fiction were usually clanking monstrosities who threatened their scientist creators. In this story Smith's illimitable imagination postulates a future wherein robots actually threaten to supplant mankind as the Lords of Creation.

Smith's writing was never better than in the opening chapters of "Triplanetary." The complex structure of the pirate base, a self-contained world in space, comes across with absolute credibility in the complete segment PIRATES OF SPACE.

THE VORTEX BLASTER is definitive Smith, with its skillful intermingling of super-science and human interest. The tragedy of Neal Cloud immediately grips the reader who easily identifies with Cloud in his fight against the atomic horror responsible for his wife's death.

In TEDRIC (1953) and LORD TEDRIC (1954), the reader is offered two lost gems which were originally published in two of the rarest magazines in the field. Here one finds a fascinating blend of sword and sorcery and the paradoxes of time travel, in the inimitable Smith style.

SUBSPACE SURVIVORS (1960) is a compelling novelette written in the modern tradition which marked Smith's triumphant return to the pages of ASTOUNDING SCIENCE FICTION after a thirteen year absence.

THE IMPERIAL STARS (1964) marks the high watermark of the final phase of Smith's work. Whilst presented in the slick, modern manner, it evokes the old magic of the Lensman series, with its galactic agents and star-spanning intrigues. Intended as the first in a new series, later parts are said to exist in outline and may yet appear in some form or other.

That is something to look forward to. Meanwhile you will find encompassed here the best of "Doc" Smith, eight stories spanning an incredible *five decades* of science fiction history, by its best-loved pioneer.

Philip Harbottle,
Wellsend,
March 1975.

FOREWORD

EDWARD E SMITH, PhD—CIVILIZATION'S HISTORIAN

Dekanore VI—A non-Tellurian planet inhabited by immensely ugly, spider-like beings, to whom Kimball Kinnison was a shuddersome sight.

Adams of Procia—Commander-in-chief of Procyon's armed forces; appointed general of Procyon by Roderick Kinnison in the formation of the Galactic Patrol.

Croleo's—A bar in the city of Ardith, on Radelix.

Slasher-worm—A Venerian creature which Herkimer threatened to use in torturing Jill Samms.

Thought-cap—The Jelm version of the thought-transfer helmet, or mechanical educator.

"Tail high, brother!"—The Vegian war-cry.

Devoted followers of those doughty heroes Richard Seaton, Kimball Kinnison and Neal Cloud will be able to make good sense of these items from *The Universes of E E Smith*. They are typical of hundreds of entries in a unique concordance to the eleven best-known novels of the late Edward Elmer Smith, Ph.D., which took two of his disciples four years to compile.* Its 270 pages from a complete reader's guide to the complex webwork of imaginary worlds and fantastic creations which earned the beloved "Doc" the title of "Historian of Civilization;" a fitting memorial to one of the most inventive and influential writers to leave his mark on the popular literature of science fiction.

* By Ron Ellik and Bill Evans. Advent Publishers, Chicago, 1966.

Few others have made such an impact as he did at his first appearance in 1928, or continued so long to delight a host of fans most of whom remained faithful even after his work had been dismissed as artless and juvenile. That his first novel, *The Skylark of Space*, opened the door for the most extravagant excursions of super-science into the remotest regions, and led the way for "space opera," has been held against him in recent years where once it was deemed a vital spur to the development of the genre. Yet, despite their undoubted limitations on the literary level, the sweeping "epics" of "Skylark" Smith are still relished for their sheer exuberance.

The pioneering *Amazing Stories* magazine was in its third year when it serialized what it described as "one of the outstanding scientifiction stories of the decade," predicting that it would be "referred to by fans for years to come." The prediction proved perfectly valid. Nearly twenty years later, when the first of several enterprising specialist book publishers began to resurrect "classic" tales from the magazines, the much-vaunted *Skylark* was an obvious choice— and sold out so quickly that the firm had to be reorganized to cope with the demand. Since 1946 it has seen publication in several forms in many parts of the world, and it is still being reprinted, like the other "Doc" Smith serials that followed at intervals through the years. Yet, before *Amazing Stories* accepted it, *The Skylark* had gathered what the author cheerfully claimed was "probably the most complete collection of rejection slips in America."

In a pleasant correspondence which we conducted in the late 1940s, he told me how he had begun to write the story after starting out as a chemical engineer in 1914 and did not complete it until 1920. For two years Mrs. Lee Hawkins Garby, the wife of an old classmate, helped him with the romantic interest that readers found so treacly but which hardly interfered with the high-geared action. But she didn't have the staying power of the determined Smith, who by the time he was 25 had held down a dozen different jobs from millhand and stevedore to street-car conductor.

Born 1890 in Sheboygan, Wisconsin, E. E. Smith was raised on a riverside homestead in northern Idaho, where he worked as a lumberjack until his eldest brother and sister helped him get to the university. By 1915 he was earning

10

enough as a food chemist with the U.S. Bureau of Standards to marry a girl from Idaho and settle down in Washington, D.C., where his wife went to work as a stenographer to enable him to get his Ph.D. This is why the book version of *The Skylark of Space* is dedicated "To Jeannie" —though Mrs. Garby got her name in the by-line—and her share of the 125 dollars he was paid for the magazine serial.

In spite of the college-boy dialogue and the melodramatic exchanges between heroic Dick Seaton and his scheming rival "Blackie" DuQuesne, *Amazing Stories* readers, whose ranks I had recently joined, clamored for a sequel. So, in *Skylark Three*, which followed in 1930, Smith took his atom-powered voyagers out again to the rescue of the people of the Green System who faced annihilation by the marauding Fenachrone. This "tale of the galactic cruise which ushered in universal civilization" presented a stupendous panorama of alien life-forms, mile-long spaceships, traveling faster than light, devastating ray-weapons, and frightful battles in the void ending in inevitable triumph for the visiting Earthmen.

To keep him in tow, *Amazing* paid Smith more generously for this three-part serial, to which he wrote an epilogue suggesting that his readers had heard the last of the all-conquering Dick and his musical sweetheart. By way of a change, in 1931 he came up with another story, *Spacehounds of IPC*, which confined his new heroes of the Inter-Planetary Corporation to the solar system. This, he insisted, was true scientific fiction, not pseudo-science, and he planned to make it the first of a series—but it wasn't what his fans wanted. "We want Smith to write stories of scope and range. We want more Skylarks!" was the cry. And *Amazing*'s 80-year-old editor Dr. T. O'Conor Sloane, who still had seven years to go before he retired, pointed a lean finger out towards the Milky Way.

But whatever the critics said about the results of his labors, Smith was never a "hack" writer. He planned his stories with care, and took his time writing them. Invariably he would plot a graph to help him in developing his plot, the reactions of his characters to the situations they encountered and the background atmosphere he weaved into the story. "Not that I ever managed to stick to one of

11

them all the way," he confessed. "Somehow my characters always break loose and take the yarn out of my hands—which is a good thing, I guess."

As science fiction advanced into the 1930s there were other editors, too, who wanted to get hold of his stories. Competition had set in—but so had the Depression, and if it had not suffered a temporary setback in 1933, *Astounding Stories* would have featured *Triplanetary*, the story which gave rise to the "Lensman" series. In any event, it went to enliven four issues of *Amazing* in 1934. It was this story that introduced the concept of the "inertialess drive" by which, it was assumed—since it could neither be proved nor disproved—spaceships might traverse the impossible gulfs of Smith's literary cosmos. When asked about the scientific probability of such a device, Smith responded: "It is not probable at all, at least in any extrapolation of present-day science. But as far as I can determine, it cannot be proved absolutely impossible and that is enough for me. In fact, the more improbable a thing, the better I like it—so long as it cannot be demonstrated mathematically impossible. I got the idea of inertialessness from a lecture given at the University of Michigan in 1912."

So, this time, the eight-limbed amphibians of the far planet Nevia, who were greedy for iron rations, were properly frustrated by Conway Costigan and his colleagues, and obliged to sign a Treaty of Eternal Peace. And thirteen years later, to make a book of it, Smith wrote six new chapters to precede the *Amazing* story, harking back to the dawn of creation, recalling the end of Atlantis and the fall of Rome, and drawing on his own experiences during two world wars. All history is seen as a titanic struggle between two races of super-beings, the Arisians and the Eddorians, who influence human-kind for good or ill as civilization advances to the era of the Triplanetary League.

When the book appeared in 1948, even Smith's gentler critics had difficulty in digesting this turgid mixture of cosmic imagery and rip-roaring adventure. Nevertheless it was accepted as a useful prelude to the "Lensman" saga—most of which had already run its course in the revived *Astounding Stories*. The missing link was *First Lensman*, which Smith wrote specially for book publication in 1950 to bridge the gap between *Triplanetary* and *Galactic Patrol*, first serialized in 1937–38. By that time *Astounding* readers had claimed "Doc" Smith for their own. Prodded by editor F. Orlin Tremaine, he had produced a third "Skylark" story which the magazine presented with a fanfare in 1934 and ran through seven issues. With the first installment of *Skylark of Valeron* the magazine's sales soared, and at the end the author had increased his fans by thousands. He had also put what seemed to be an irreversible end to the luckless DuQuesne by reducing him to a capsule of pure intellect and flinging him into the fourth dimension. But good villains die hard, and he was still immortal . . .

That *Astounding* was in its most expansive conceptual period at this time lent power to Smith's imagination, and thus Dick Seaton's mental capacity, his new spaceship and his area of operations were all enlarged to maximum proportions. After *Valeron* it seemed there was nothing left to explore, nor any more possible variations on the familiar themes which had made Smith's tales so popular. And he was still a part-time writer; he had business problems to wrestle with. For seventeen years he had been employed as chief chemist with a Michigan firm concerned with the specialist art of compounding doughnut mixes. In 1936 he moved to a new firm in which he had a financial interest, and it left him little time for science fiction. Yet, within a year, Smith was busily plotting the "Lensman" series, which began in *Astounding* at about the same time that Olaf Stapledon's *Star Maker* appeared, which outdistanced Stapledon's previous work *Last and First Men*.

To equate the beloved "pulp" writer Smith with the equally genial philosopher Stapledon might seem almost profane; yet, though their methods and literary styles are poles apart, in the final analysis their works are essentially similar, especially in the scope of their projection and their concern with the eternal struggle of good and evil which, in Smith's stories, is reduced to its simplest elements. The idea of an interstellar police force protecting a community of worlds against piracy and insurrection was familiar in American science fiction when Smith devised his *Galactic Patrol*. But he used it to better effect against a more elaborate background in which the ancient Arisians, who had sown the seeds of life throughout the galaxy, enlisted the

Lensmen in the struggle to subdue the power-crazy rulers of Eddore, a planet in another space-time continuum.

The Lensmen and their ladies, selected from many worlds for their superior qualities, are so-called because they carry a device enabling them to communicate with any form of sentient life their creator can dream up, and which brings quick death to unauthorized users. Their leading heroes are *First Lensman* Virgil Samms, who extended the Triplanetary League to embrace the entire solar system; *Grey Lensman* Kim Kinnison, whose exploits range over two galaxies, and his mate Clarissa MacDougall, the red-headed nurse who made good as a *Second Stage Lensman.* Not until many tyrants have been overthrown on as many planets are Kim and "Mac" able to get married and complete the ages-long breeding program culminating in the five *Children of the Lens,* who are destined to succeed the Arisians as the Guardians of Civilization.

In all, the "Lensman" series helped to fill out eighteen issues of *Astounding* over a ten-year period ending in 1948, during which that exacting editor John W. Campbell held sway. In between times the number of science fiction pulps had multiplied, but few of the newcomers survived the war years; the real boom came afterwards. One of the casualties was *Comet Stories,* edited by Tremaine, for whom Smith agreed to write new series featuring "Storm" Cloud, a nuclear physicist and spaceman whose job is to snuff out atomic power plants when they run wild like oilwells. Only one story appeared before the magazine was extinguished in 1941, leaving *Astonishing Stories* to feature two more before it too folded. Because of their loose connection with the "Lensman" tales, in 1960 the three stories were combined in a book titled *The Vortex Blaster,* published here more recently as *Masters of the Vortex.*

The war hit Smith hard, too. He found himself redundant and was forced to live on his savings until, at 51, he went to work in an ordnance plant. Only when he was back in the cereals business in Chicago after the war did he essay *Children of the Lens*—with an eye to his own three children and their offspring. "This," he informed me, to settle arguments between his fans over the proper sequence of these stories, "is the *real* Lensman story, to which the other three are merely introductory material." This led up to something he especially wanted to say about his endings (and which he repeated elsewhere): "It's a darn hard job to write a book which is part of a series and yet have it end clean, without a lot of loose ends dangling. Many authors—Edgar Rice Burroughs, for instance—didn't try. But I *hate* loose ends. Besides, suppose the author should die or something without *ever* finishing the damn thing? In *Galactic Patrol* and *Grey Lensman* I could clean them up without too much trouble, but in *Second Stage Lensman* it was practically impossible. I sweat blood . . ." And how he got over the impasse he told in his essay on *The Epic of Space.**

In 1957 Smith retired to live in Florida—and continue his writing. For he could not ignore the current trends in science fiction, which challenged his powers; especially after his earlier work, which he had spent ten years revising for book publication, had been diminished by relentless critics. For example, P. Schuyler Miller, who, reviewing *Grey Lensman* in 1952, lambasted his "incredible heroes, unbelievable weapons, insurmountable obstacles, inconceivable science, omnipotent villains, and unimaginable cataclysms." And Groff Conklin, in whom it evoked "alternate waves of incredulous laughter and dull, acid boredom" because, he suspected, "science fiction is growing up and leaving these primitive artifacts behind." So, in *The Galaxy Primes*, Smith introduced the sort of concepts that were being encouraged in *Astounding*, deriving from what editor Campbell termed 'psi phenomena": Smith's pseudo-living, telepathic Lens, he instanced, was "essentially a psi machine." But Campbell didn't care so much for his new story, which *Amazing* found more acceptable and serialized in 1959 before it emerged, finally, as a paperback.

Undaunted, Smith contrived to make his last appearance in *Astounding* the following year with *Subspace Survivors*, a short story paving the way for a novel—which Campbell found wanting. It reached Smith's devoted fans in 1965 as a hardcover book entitled *Subspace Explorers*. And towards the end he found a more receptive market for his

* In *Of Worlds Beyond: The Science of Science Fiction Writing*. Fantasy Press, Reading, Pennsylvania, 1947; Dobson, London, 1965.

work in the magazine *Worlds of If*, which in 1961–62 featured *Masters of Space*, a two-part tale which also carried in its by-line the name E. Everett Evans. Of all Smith's army of admirers, this one-time secretary of The Galactic Roamers fan club was the most constant, and when he died leaving this novel unfinished, Smith revised it completely.

The affectionate regard in which "The Doc" was held by the science fiction fraternity was demonstrated when, in 1963, at the 21st World Convention in Washington—where *The Skylark* was hatched—veteran fans presented him with their Hall of Fame award. By then he was having trouble with his eyes, but he had still not done with writing. The following year he reappeared in *If* with *The Imperial Stars*, in which he tried to recapture some of the atmosphere of the "Lensman" stories. This tale, too, gave promise of a series featuring a troupe of circus performers involved in sabotage in a galactic empire. Then editor Frederik Pohl, having egged him on, surprised Smith's old-time followers by presenting *Skylark DuQuesne*, in which the legendary villain who had been dispatched thirty years before was reincarnated, and compelled to join Dick Seaton in resisting another grim menace from afar. The serial had hardly ended when the news reached his friends, in August 1965, that "Skylark" Smith had died of a heart attack. It was the end of what *If* had called "the most famous science fiction saga of all time."

WALTER GILLINGS
Ilford, Essex, 1975.

TO THE FAR REACHES OF SPACE

Hair-raising explorations and strange ventures into far-away worlds as Man breaks the light-speed barrier and heads into the black depths of interstellar space.

For forty-eight hours the uncontrolled engine dragged Du-Quesne's vessel through the empty reaches of space with an awful and constantly increasing velocity. Then, when only a few traces of copper remained, the acceleration began to decrease. Floor and seats began to return to their normal positions. When the last particle of copper was gone, the ship's speed became constant. Apparently motionless to those inside her, she was in reality moving with a velocity thousands of times greater than that of light.

DuQuesne was the first to gain control of himself. His first effort to get up lifted him from the floor and he floated lightly upward to the ceiling, striking it with a gentle bump and remaining, motionless and unsupported, in the air. The others, none of whom had attempted to move, stared at him in amazement.

DuQuesne reached out, clutched a hand-grip, and drew himself down to the floor. With great caution he removed his suit, transferring two automatic pistols as he did so. By feeling gingerly of his body he found that no bones were broken. Only then did he look around to see how his companions were faring.

They were all sitting up and holding onto something. The girls were resting quietly; Perkins was removing his leather costume.

"Good morning, Dr. DuQuesne. Something must have happened when I kicked your friend."

"Good morning, Miss Vaneman." DuQuesne smiled, more than half in relief. "Several things happened. He fell

17

into the controls, turning on all the juice, and we left considerably faster than I intended to. I tried to get control, but couldn't. Then we all went to sleep and just woke up."

"Have you any idea where we are?"

"No . . . but I can make a fair estimate." He glanced at the empty chamber where the copper cylinder had been; took out notebook, pencil, and slide rule; and figured for minutes.

He then drew himself to one of the windows and stared out, then went to another window, and another. He seated himself at the crazily tilted control board and studied it. He worked the computer for a few moments.

"I don't know exactly what to make of this," he told Dorothy, quietly. "Since the power was on exactly forty-eight hours, we should not be more than two light-days away from our sun. However, we certainly are. I could recognize at least some of the fixed stars and constellations from anywhere within a light-year or so of Sol, and I can't find even one familiar thing. Therefore we must have been accelerating all the time. We must be somewhere in the neighborhood of two hundred thirty-seven light-years away from home. For you two who don't know what a light-year is, about six quadrillion—six thousand million million— miles."

Dorothy's face turned white; Margaret Spencer fainted; Perkins merely goggled, his face working convulsively.

"Then we'll never get back?" Dorothy asked.

"I wouldn't say that—"

"You got us into this!" Perkins screamed, and leaped at Dorothy, murderous fury in his glare, his fingers curved into talons. Instead of reaching her, however, he merely sprawled grotesquely in the air. DuQuesne, braced one foot against the wall and seizing a hand-grip with his left hand, knocked Perkins clear across the room with one blow of his right.

"None of that, louse," DuQuesne said, evenly. "One more wrong move out of you and I'll throw you out. It isn't her fault we're here, it's our own. And mostly yours—if you'd had three brain cells working she couldn't have kicked you. But that's past. The only thing of interest now is getting back."

"But we can't get back," Perkins whimpered. "The

power's gone, the controls are wrecked, and you said you're lost."

"I did not." DuQuesne's voice was icy. "What I said was that I don't know where we are—a different statement entirely."

"Isn't that a distinction without a difference?" Dorothy asked acidly.

"By no means, Miss Vaneman. I can repair the control board. I have two extra power bars. One of them, with direction exactly reversed, will stop us, relative to the earth. I'll burn half of the last one, then coast until, by recognizing fixed stars and triangulating them, I can fix our position. I will then know where our solar system is and will go there. In the meantime, I suggest that we have something to eat."

"A beautiful and timely thought!" Dorothy exclaimed. "I'm famished. Where's your refrigerator? But something else comes first. I'm a mess, and she must be, too. Where's our room . . . that is, we *have* a room?"

"Yes. That one, and there's the galley, over there. We're cramped, but you'll be able to make out. Let me say, Miss Vaneman, that I really admire your nerve. I didn't expect that lunk to disintegrate the way he did, but I thought you girls might. Miss Spencer will, yet, unless you . . ."

"I'll try to. I'm scared, of course, but falling apart won't help . . . and we've simply *got* to get back.'

"We will. Two of us, at least."

Dorothy nudged the other girl, who had not paid any attention to anything around her, and led her along a handrail. As she went, she could not help but think—with more than a touch of admiration—of the man who had abducted her. Calm, cool, master of himself and the situation, disregarding completely the terrible bruises that disfigured half his face and doubtless half his body as well—she admitted to herself that it was only his example which had enabled her to maintain her self-control.

As she crawled over Perkins' suit she remembered that he had not taken any weapons from it, and a glance assured her that Perkins was not watching her. She searched it quickly, finding two automatics. She noted with relief that they were standard .45's and stuck them into her pockets.

In the room, Dorothy took one look at the other girl, then went to the galley and back.

"Here, swallow this," she ordered.

The girl did so. She shuddered uncontrollably, but did begin to come to life.

"That's better. Now, snap out of it," Dorothy said, sharply. "We aren't dead and we aren't going to be."

"I am," came the wooden reply. "You don't know that beast Perkins."

"I do so. And better yet, I know things that neither Du-Quesne nor that Perkins even guess. Two of the smartest men that ever lived are on our tail, and when they catch up with us . . . well, I wouldn't be in *their* shoes for *anything*."

"What?" Dorothy's confident words and bearing, as much the potent pill, were taking effect. The strange girl was coming back rapidly to sanity and normality. "Not *really?*"

"Really. We've got a lot to do, and we've got to clean up first. And with no weight . . . does it make you sick?"

"It did, dreadfully, but I've got nothing left to be sick with. Doesn't it you?"

"Not very much. I don't like it, but I'm getting used to it. And I don't suppose you know anything about it."

"No. All I can feel is that I'm falling, and it's almost unbearable."

"It isn't pleasant. I've studied it a lot—in theory—and the boys say all you've got to do is forget that falling sensation. Not that I've been able to do it, but I'm still trying. The first thing's a bath, and then—"

"A bath! *Here?* How?"

"Sponge-bath. I'll show you. Then . . . they brought along quite a lot of clothes to fit me, and you're just about my size . . . and you'll look nice in green. . . ."

After they had put themselves to rights, Dorothy said, "That's a *lot* better." Each girl looked at the other, and each liked what she saw.

The stranger was about twenty-two with heavy, wavy black hair. Her eyes were a rich, deep brown; her skin clear, smooth ivory. Normally a beautiful girl, thought Dorothy, even though she was now thin, haggard, and worn.

"Let's get acquainted before we do anything else," she said. "I'm Margaret Spencer, formerly private secretary to His High Mightiness, Brookings of Steel. They swindled my father out of an invention worth millions and then killed him. I got the job to see if I could prove it, but I didn't get much evidence before they caught me. So, after two months of things you wouldn't believe, here I am. Talking never would have done me any good, and I'm certain it won't now. Perkins will kill me . . . or maybe, if what you say is true, I should add 'if he can.' This is the first time I've had that much hope."

"But how about Dr. DuQuesne? Surely he wouldn't let him."

"I've never met DuQuesne before, but from what I heard around the office, he's worse than Perkins—in a different way, of course. He's absolutely cold and utterly hard—a perfect fiend."

"Oh, come, you're too hard on him. Didn't you see him knock Perkins down when he came after me?"

"No—or perhaps I did, in a dim sort of way. But that doesn't mean anything. He probably wants you left alive—of course that's it, since he went to all the trouble of kidnapping you. Otherwise he would have let Perkins do anything he wanted to with you, without lifting a finger."

"I can't believe that." Nevertheless, a chill struck at Dorothy's heart as she remembered the inhuman crimes attributed to the man. "He has treated us with every consideration so far—let's hope for the best. Anyway, I'm sure we'll get back safely."

"You keep saying that. What makes you so sure?"

"Well, I'm Dorothy Vaneman, and I'm engaged to Dick Seaton, the man who invented this spaceship, and I'm as sure as can be that he is chasing us right now."

"But that's just what they want!" Margaret exclaimed. "I heard some Top Secret stuff about that. Your name and Seaton's brings it back to me. Their ship is rigged, some way or other, so it will blow up or something the first time they go anywhere!"

"That's what *they* think." Dorothy's voice dripped scorn. "Dick and his partner—you've heard of Martin Crane, of course?"

21

"I heard the name mentioned with Seaton's, but that's all."

"Well, he's quite a wonderful inventor, and almost as smart as Dick is. Together they found out about that sabotage and built another ship that Steel doesn't know anything about. Bigger and better and faster than this one."

"That makes me feel better." Margaret really brightened for the first time. "No matter how rough this trip will be, it'll be a vacation for me now. If I only had a gun . . ."

"Here," and as Margaret stared at the proffered weapon, "I've got another. I got them out of Perkins' suit."

"Glory be!" Margaret fairly beamed. "There *is* balm in Gilead, after all! Just watch, next time Perkins threatens to cut my heart out with his knife . . . and we'd better go make those sandwiches, don't you think? And call me Peggy, please."

"Will do, Peggy my dear—we're going to be great friends. And I'm Dot or Dottie to you."

In the galley the girls set about making dainty sandwiches, but the going was very hard indeed. Margaret was particularly inept. Slices of bread went one way, bits of butter another, ham and sausage in several others. She seized two trays and tried to trap the escaping food between them—but in the attempt she released her hold and floated helplessly into the air.

"Oh, Dot, what'll we *do* anyway," she wailed. "Everything wants to fly all over the place!"

"I don't quite know—I wish we had a bird-cage, so we could reach in and grab anything before it could escape. We'd better tie everything down, I guess, and let everybody come in and cut off a chunk of anything they want. But what I'm wondering about is drinking. I'm simply dying of thirst and I'm afraid to open this bottle." She had a bottle of ginger ale clutched in her left hand, an opener in her right; one leg was hooked around a vertical rail. "I'm afraid it'll go into a million drops and Dick says if you breathe them in you're apt to choke to death."

"Seaton was right—as usual." Dorothy whirled around. DuQuesne was surveying the room, a glint of amusement in his one sound eye. "I wouldn't recommend playing with charged drinks while weightless. Just a minute—I'll get the net."

22

He got it; and while he was deftly clearing the air of floating items of food he went on. "Charged stuff could be murderous unless you're wearing a mask. Plain liquids you can drink through a straw after you learn how. Your swallowing has got to be conscious, and all muscular with no gravity. But what I came here for was to tell you I'm ready to put on one G of acceleration so we'll have normal gravity. I'll put it on easy, but watch it."

"What a *heavenly* relief!" Margaret cried, when everything again stayed put. "I never thought I'd ever be grateful for just being able to stand still in one place, did you?"

Preparing the meal was now of course simple enough. As the four ate, Dorothy noticed that DuQuesne's left arm was almost useless and that he ate with difficulty because of his terribly bruised face. After the meal was done she went to the medicine chest and selected containers, swabs, and gauze.

"Come over here, doctor. First aid is indicated."

"I'm all right . . ." he began, but at her imperious gesture he got up carefully and came toward her.

"Your arm is lame. Where's the damage?"

"The shoulder is the worst. I rammed it through the board."

"Take off your shirt and lie down here."

He did so and Dorothy gasped at the extent and severity of the man's injuries.

"Will you get me some towels and hot water, please, Peggy?" She worked busily for minutes, bathing away clotted blood, applying antiseptics, and bandaging. "Now for those bruises—I *never* saw anything like them before. I'm not really a nurse. What would you use? Tripidiagen or . . ."

"Amylophene. Massage it in as I move the arm."

He did not wince and his expression did not change; but he began to sweat and his face turned white. She paused.

"Keep it up, nurse," he directed, coolly. "That stuff's murder in the first degree, but it does the job and it's fast."

When she had finished and he was putting his shirt back on: "Thanks, Miss Vaneman—thanks a lot. It feels a hundred per cent better already. But why did you do it? I'd think you'd want to bash me with that basin instead."

"Efficiency." She smiled. "As our chief engineer it won't do to have you laid up."

"Logical enough, in a way . . . but . . . I wonder. . . ."

She did not reply, but turned to Perkins.

"How are you, Mr. Perkins? Do you require medical attention?"

"No," Perkins growled. "Keep away from me or I'll cut your heart out."

"Shut up!" DuQuesne snapped.

"I haven't done anything!"

"Maybe it didn't quite constitute making a break, so I'll broaden the definition. If you can't talk like a man, keep still. Lay off Miss Vaneman—thoughts, words, and actions. I'm in charge of her and I will have no interference whatever. This is your last warning."

"How about Spencer, then?"

"She's your responsibility, not mine."

An evil light appeared in Perkins' eyes. He took out a wicked-looking knife and began to strop it carefully on the leather of the seat, glaring at his victim the while.

Dorothy started to protest, but was silenced by a gesture from Margaret, who calmly took the pistol out of her pocket. She jerked the slide and held the weapon up on one finger.

"Don't worry about his knife. He's been sharpening it for my benefit for the last month. It doesn't mean a thing. But you shouldn't play with it so much, Perkins, you might be tempted to try to throw it. So drop it on the floor and kick it over here to me. Before I count three. One." The heavy pistol steadied into line with his chest and her finger tightened on the trigger.

"Two." Perkins obeyed and Margaret picked up the knife.

"Doctor!" Perkins appealed to DuQuesne, who had watched the scene unmoved, a faint smile upon his saturnine face. "Why don't you shoot her? You won't sit there and see me murdered!"

"Won't I? It makes no difference to me which of you kills the other, or if you both do, or neither. You brought this on yourself. Anyone with any fraction of a brain doesn't leave guns lying around loose. You should have seen Miss Vaneman take them—I did."

"You saw her take them and didn't warn me?" Perkins croaked.

"Certainly. If you can't take care of yourself I'm not going to take care of you. Especially after the way you bungled the job. I could have recovered the stuff she stole from that ass Brookings inside an hour."

"How?" Perkins sneered. "If you're so good, why did you have to come to me about Seaton and Crane?"

"Because my methods wouldn't work and yours would. It isn't on planning that you're weak, as I told Brookings—it's on execution."

"Well, what are you going to *do* about her? Are you going to sit there and lecture all day?"

"I am going to do nothing whatever. Fight your own battles."

Dorothy broke the silence that followed. "You *did* see me take the guns, doctor?"

"I did. You have one in your right breeches pocket now."

"Then why didn't you, or don't you, try to take it away from me?" she asked, wonderingly.

" 'Try' is the wrong word. If I had not wanted you to take them you wouldn't have. If I didn't want you to have a gun now I would take it away from you," and his black eyes stared into her violet ones with such calm certainty that she felt her heart sink.

"Has Perkins got any more knives or guns or things in his room?" Dorothy demanded.

"I don't know," indifferently. Then, as both girls started for Perkins' room DuQuesne rapped out, "Sit down, Miss Vaneman. Let them fight it out. Perkins has his orders about you; I'm giving you orders about him. If he oversteps, shoot him. Otherwise, hands off completely—in every respect."

Dorothy threw up her head in defiance; but, meeting his cold stare, she paused irresolutely and sat down, while the other girl went on.

"That's better," DuQuesne said. "Besides, it would be my guess that she doesn't need any help."

Margaret returned from the search and thrust her pistol back into her pocket. "That ends that," she declared. "Are

25

you going to behave yourself or do I chain you by the neck to a post?"

"I suppose I'll have to, if the doc's gone back on me," Perkins snarled. "But I'll get you when we get back, you—"

"Stop it!" Margaret snapped. "Now listen. Call me names any more and I'll start shooting. One name, one shot; two names, two shots; and so on. Each shot in a carefully selected place. Go ahead."

DuQuesne broke the silence that followed. "Well, now that the battle's over and we're fed and rested, I'll put on some power. Everybody into seats."

For sixty hours he drove through space, reducing the acceleration only at mealtimes, when they ate and exercised their stiffened, tormented bodies. The power was not cut down for sleep; everyone slept as best he could.

Dorothy and Margaret were together constantly and a real intimacy grew up between them. Perkins was for the most part sullenly quiet. DuQuesne worked steadily during all his waking hours, except at mealtimes when he talked easily and well. There was no animosity in his bearing or in his words; but his discipline was strict and his reproofs merciless.

When the power bar was exhausted DuQuesne lifted the sole remaining cylinder into the engine, remarking:

"Well, we should be approximately stationary, relative to Earth. Now we'll start back."

He advanced the lever, and for many hours the regular routine of the ship went on. Then DuQuesne, on walking, saw that the engine was no longer perpendicular to the floor, but was inclined slightly. He read the angle of inclination on the great circles, then scanned a sector of space. He reduced the current, whereupon all four felt a lurch as the angle was increased many degrees. He read the new angle hastily and restored touring power. He then sat down at the computer and figured—with that much power on, a tremendous unnerving job.

"What's the matter, doctor?" Dorothy asked.

"We're being deflected a little from our course."

"Is that bad?"

"Ordinarily, no. Every time we pass a star its gravity pulls us a little out of line. But the effects are slight, do not

26

last long, and tend to cancel each other out. This is too big and has lasted altgether too long. If it keeps on, we could miss the solar system altogether; and I can't find anything to account for it."

He watched the bar anxiously, expecting to see it swing back into the vertical, but the angle grew steadily larger. He again reduced the current and searched the heavens for the troublesome body.

"Do you see it yet?" Dorothy asked, apprehensively.

"No . . . but this optical system could be improved. I could do better with night-glasses, I think."

He brought out a pair of grotesque-looking binoculars and stared through them out of an upper window for perhaps five minutes.

"Good God!" he exclaimed. "It's a dead star and we're almost onto it!"

Springing to the board, he whirled the bar into and through the vertical, then measured the apparent diameter of the strange object. Then, after cautioning the others, he put on more power than he had been using. After exactly fifteen minutes he slackened off and made another reading. Seeing his expression, Dorothy was about to speak, but he forestalled her.

"We lost more ground. It must be a lot bigger than anything known to our astronomers. And I'm not trying to pull away from it; just to make an orbit around it. We'll have to put on full power—take seats!"

He left full power on until the bar was nearly gone and made another series of observations. "Not enough," he said, quietly.

Perkins screamed and flung himself upon the floor; Margaret clutched at her heart with both hands; Dorothy, though her eyes looked like black holes in her white face, looked at him steadily and asked, "This is the end, then?"

"Not yet." His voice was calm and level. "It'll take two days, more or less, to fall that far, and we have a little copper left for one last shot. I'm going to figure the angle to make that last shot as effective as possible."

"Won't the repulsive outer coating do any good?"

"No; it'll be gone long before we hit. I'd strip it and feed it to the engine if I could think of a way of getting it off."

He lit a cigarette and sat at ease at the computer. He

27

sat there, smoking and computing, for over an hour. He then changed, very slightly, the angle of the engine.

"Now we look for copper," he said. "There isn't any in the ship itself—everything electrical is silver, down to our flashlights and the bases of the lamps. But examine the furnishings and all your personal stuff—*anything* with copper or brass in it. That includes metallic money—pennies, nickles, and silver."

They found a few items, but very few. DuQuesne added his watch, his heavy signet ring, his keys, his tie-clasp, and the cartridges from his pistol. He made sure that Perkins did not hold anything out. The girls gave up not only their money and cartridges but their jewelry, including Dorothy's engagement ring.

"I'd like to keep it, but . . ." she said, as she added it to the collection.

"Everything goes that has any copper in it; and I'm glad Seaton's too much of a scientist to buy platinum jewelry. But, if we get away, I doubt very much if you'll be able to see any difference in your ring. Very little copper in it—but we need every milligram we can get."

He threw all the metal into the power chamber and advanced the lever. It was soon spent; and after the final observation, while the others waited in suspense, he made his curt announcement.

"Not quite enough."

Perkins, his mind already weakened, went completely insane. With a wild howl he threw himself at the unmoved scientist, who struck him on the head with the butt of his pistol as he leaped. The force of the blow crushed Perkin's head and drove his body to the other side of the ship. Margaret looked as though she were about to faint. Dorothy and DuQuesne looked at each other. To the girl's amazement the man was as calm as though he were in his own room at home on earth. She made an effort to hold her voice steady. "What next, doctor?"

"I don't exactly know. I still haven't been able to work out a method of recovering that plating. . . . It's so thin that there isn't much copper, even on a sphere as big as this one."

"Even if you could get it, and it were enough, we'd starve

28

anyway, wouldn't we?" Margaret, holding herself together desperately, tried to speak lightly.

"Not necessarily. That would give me time to figure out something else to do."

"You wouldn't have to figure anything else," Dorothy declared. "Maybe you won't, anyway. You said we have two days?"

"My observations were crude, but it's a little over two days—about forty-nine and a half hours now. Why?"

"Because Dick and Martin Crane will find us before very long. Quite possibly within two days."

"Not in this life. If they tried to follow us they're both dead now."

"That's where even you are wrong!" she flashed. "They knew all the time exactly what you were doing to our old *Skylark,* so they built another one, that you never knew anything about. And they know a lot about this new metal that you never heard of, too, because it wasn't in those plans you stole!"

DuQuesne went directly to the heart of the matter, paying no attention to her barbs. "Can they follow us in space without seeing us?" he demanded.

"Yes. At least, I think they can."

"How do they do it?"

"I don't know. I wouldn't tell you, if I did!"

"You think not? I won't argue the point at the moment. If they can find us—which I doubt—I hope they detect this dead star in time to keep away from it—and us."

"But why?" Dorothy gasped. "You've been trying to kill both of them—wouldn't you be glad to take them with us?"

"*Please* try to be logical. Far from it. There's no connection. I tried to kill them, yes, because they stood in the way of my development of this new metal. If, however, I am not going to be the one to do it—I certainly hope Seaton goes ahead with it. It's the greatest discovery ever made, bar none; and if both Seaton and I, the only two men able to develop it properly, get killed it will be lost, perhaps for hundreds of years."

"If he must go, too, I hope he doesn't find us . . . but I don't believe it. I simply know he could get us away from here."

She continued more slowly, almost speaking to herself,

29

her heart sinking with her voice, "He's following us and he won't stop even if he knows he can't get away."

"There's no denying the fact that our situation is critical; but as long as I'm alive I can think. I'm going to dope out *some* way of getting that copper."

"I hope you do." Dorothy kept her voice from breaking only by a tremendous effort. "I see Peggy's fainted. I wish I could. I'm worn out."

She drew herself down upon one of the seats and stared at the ceiling, fighting an almost overpowering impulse to scream.

Thus time wore on—Perkins dead; Margaret unconscious; Dorothy lying in her seat, her thoughts a formless prayer, buoyed only by her faith in God and in her lover; DuQuesne self-possessed, smoking innumerable cigarettes, his keen mind at grips with its most desperate problem, grimly fighting until the very last instant of life—while the powerless spaceship fell with an appalling velocity, and faster and yet faster, toward that cold and desolate monster of the heavens.

Seaton and Crane drove the *Skylark* at high acceleration in the direction indicated by the unwavering compass, each man taking a twelve-hour trick at the board.

The *Skylark* justified the faith of her builders, and the two inventors, with an exultant certainty of success, flew out beyond man's wildest imaginings. Had it not been for the haunting fear for Dorothy's safety, the journey would have been one of pure triumph, and even that anxiety did not preclude a profound joy in the enterprise.

"If that misguided ape thinks he can pull a stunt like that and get away with it he's got another think coming," Seaton declared, after making a reading on the other ship after a few days of flight. "He went off half-cocked for sure this time, and we've got him right where the hair is short. Only about a hundred light-years now. Better we reverse pretty quick, you think?"

"It's hard to say—very hard. By our dead reckoning he seems to have started back; but dead reckoning is notoriously poor reckoning and we have no reference points."

"Well, dead reckoning's the only thing we've got, and

anyway you can't be a precisionist out here. A light-year plus or minus won't make any difference."

"No, I suppose not," and Crane read off the settings which, had his data been exact, would put the *Skylark* in exactly the same spot with, and having exactly the same velocity as, the other spaceship at the point of meeting.

The big ship spun, with a sickening lurch, through a half-circle as the bar was reversed. They knew that they were travelling in a direction that seemed "down," even though they still seemed to be going "up."

"Mart! C'mere."

"Here."

"We're getting a deflection. Too big for a star—unless it's another S-Doradus—and I can't see a thing—theoretically, of course, it could be anywhere to starboard. I want a check, fast, on true course and velocity. Is there any way to measure a gravity field you're falling freely in without knowing any distances? *Any* kind of an approximation would help."

Crane observed, computed, and reported that the *Skylark* was being very strongly attracted by some object almost straight ahead.

"We'd better break out the big night-glasses and take a good look—as you said, this optical system could have more power. But how far away are they?"

"A few minutes over ten hours."

"Ouch! Not good . . . *veree* ungood, in fact. By pouring it on, we could make it three or four hours . . . but . . . even so . . . you. . . ."

"Even so. Me. We're in this together, Dick; all the way. Just pour it on."

As the time of meeting drew near they took readings every minute. Seaton juggled the power until they were very close to the other vessel and riding with it, then killed his engine. Both men hurried to the bottom port with their night-glasses and stared into star-studded blackness.

"Of course," Seaton argued as he stared, "it is theoretically possible that a body can exist large enough to exert this much force and not show a disc, but I don't

31

believe it. Give me four or five minutes of visual angle and I'll buy it, but—"

"There!" Crane broke in. "At least half a degree of visual angle. Eleven o'clock, fairly high. Not bright, but dark. Almost invisible."

"Got it. And that little black spot, just inside the edge at half past four—DuQuesne's job?"

"I think so. Nothing else in sight."

"Let's grab it and get out of here while we're all in one piece!"

In seconds they reduced the distance until they could plainly see the other vessel: a small black circle against the somewhat lighter black of the dead star. Crane turned on the searchlight. Seaton focused their heaviest attractor and gave it everything it would take. Crane loaded a belt of solid ammunition and began to fire peculiarly-spaced bursts.

After an interminable silence DuQuesne drew himself out of his seat. He took a long drag at his cigarette, deposited the butt carefully in an ashtray, and put on his space-suit; leaving the faceplates open.

"I'm going after that copper, Miss Vaneman. I don't know exactly how much of it I'll be able to recover, but I hope. . . ."

Light flooded in through a port. DuQuesne was thrown flat as the ship was jerked out of free fall. They heard an insistent metallic tapping, which DuQuesne recognized instantly.

"A machine gun!" he blurted in amazement. "What in . . . wait a minute, that's Morse! A-R-E—are . . . Y-O-U —you . . . A-L-I-V-E—alive? . . ."

"It's Dick!" Dorothy screamed. "He's found us—I knew he would! You couldn't beat Dick and Martin in a thousand years!"

The two girls locked their arms around each other in a hysterical outburst of relief; Margaret's incoherent words' and Dorothy's praises of her lover mingled with their racking sobs.

DuQuesne had climbed to the upper port; had unshielded it. "S-O-S" he signalled with his flashlight.

The searchlight died. "W-E K-N-O-W. P-A-R-T-Y O-K?" It was a light this time, not bullets.

"O.K." DuQuesne knew what "Party" meant—Perkins did not count.

"S-U-I-T-S?"

"Y-E-S."

"W-I-L-L T-O-U-C-H L-O-C-K T-O L-O-C-K B-R-A-C-E S-E-L-V-E-S."

"O.K."

DuQuesne reported briefly to the two girls. All three put on space-suits and crowded into the tiny airlock. The lock was pumped down. There was a terrific jar as the two ships of space were brought together and held together. Outer valves opened; residual air screamed out into the interstellar void. Moisture condensed upon glass, rendering sight useless.

"Blast!" Seaton's voice came tinnily over the helmet radios. "I can't see a foot. Can you, DuQuesne?"

"No, and these joints don't move more than a couple of inches."

"These suits need a lot more work. We'll have to go by feel. Pass 'em along."

DuQuesne grabbed the girl nearest him and shoved her toward the spot where Seaton would have to be. Seaton seized her, straightened her up, and did his heroic best to compress that suit until he could at least feel his sweetheart's form.

He was very much astonished to feel motions of resistance and to hear a strange voice cry out, "Don't! It's me! Dottie's next!"

She was, and she put as much fervor into the reunion as he did. As a lovers' embrace it was unsatisfactory; but it was an eager, if distant, contact.

DuQuesne dived through the opening; Crane groped for the controls that closed the lock. Pressure and temperature came back up to normal. The clumsy suits were taken off. Seaton and Dorothy went into each other's arms.

And this time it was a real lovers' embrace.

"We'd better start doing something," came DuQuesne's incisive voice. "Every minute counts."

"One thing first," Crane said. "Dick, what shall we do with this murderer?"

Seaton, who had temporarily forgotten all about DuQuesne, whirled around.

33

"Chuck him back into his own tub and let him go to the devil!" he said, savagely.

"Oh, no, Dick!" Dorothy protested, seizing his arm. "He treated us very well, and saved my life once. Besides, you *can't* become a cold-blooded murderer just because he is. You know you can't."

"Maybe not . . . Okay, I won't kill him—unless he gives me about half an excuse . . . maybe."

"Out of the question, Dick," Crane decided. "Perhaps he can earn his way?"

"Could be." Seaton thought for a moment, his face still grim and hard. "He's smart as Satan and strong as a bull . . . and if there's any possible one thing he is not, it's a liar."

He faced DuQuesne squarely, grey eyes boring into eyes of midnight black. "Will you give us your word to act as one of the party?"

"Yes." DuQuesne stared back unflinchingly. His expression of cold concern had not changed throughout the conversation: it did not change now. "With the understanding that I reserve the right to leave you at any time—"escape" is a melodramatic world, but fits the facts closely enough—provided I can do so without affecting unfavorably your ship, your project then in work, or your persons collectively or individually."

"You're the lawyer, Mart. Does that cover it?"

"Admirably," Crane said. "Fully yet concisely. Also, the fact of the reservation indicates that he means it."

"You're in, then," Seaton said to DuQuesne, but he did not offer to shake hands. "You've got the dope. What'll we have to put on to get away?"

"You can't pull straight away—and live—but . . ."

"Sure we can. *Our* power-plant can be doubled in emergencies."

"I said 'and live.' " Seaton, remembering what one full power was like, kept still.

"The best you can do is a hyperbolic orbit, and my guess is that it'll take full power to make that. Ten pounds more copper might have given me a graze, but we're a lot closer now. You've got more and larger tools than I had, Crane. Do you want to recompute it now, or give it a good, heavy shot and then figure it?"

"A shot, I think. What do you suggest?"

"Set your engine to roll for a hyperbolic and give it full drive for . . . say an hour."

"Full power," Crane said, thoughtfully "I can't take that much. But if—"

"I can't either," Dorothy said, foreboding in her eyes. "Nor Margaret."

"—full power is necessary," Crane continued as though the girl had not spoken, "full power it shall be. Is it really of the essence, DuQuesne?"

"Definitely. More than full would be better. And it's getting worse every minute."

"How much power can you take?" Seaton asked.

"More than full. Not much more, but a little."

"If you can, I can." Seaton was not boasting, merely stating a fact. "So here's what let's do. Double the engines up. DuQuesne and I will notch the power up until one of us has to quit. Run an hour on that, and then read the news. Check?"

"Check," said Crane and DuQuesne simultaneously, and the three men set furiously to work. Crane went to the engines, DuQuesne to the observatory. Seaton rigged helmets to air- and oxygen-tanks through valves on his board.

Seaton placed Margaret upon a seat, fitted a helmet over her head, strapped her in, and turned to Dorothy.

Instantly they were in each other's arms. He felt her labored breathing and the hard beating of her heart; saw the fear and the unknown in the violet depths of her eyes; but she looked at him steadily as she said: "Dick, sweetheart, if this is good-bye . . ."

"It isn't, Dottie—yet—but I know . . ."

Crane and DuQuesne had finished their tasks, so Seaton hastily finished his job on Dorothy. Crane put himself to bed; Seaton and DuQuesne put on their helmets and took their places at the twin boards.

In quick succession twenty notches of power went on. The *Skylark* leaped away from the other ship, which continued its mad fall—a helpless hulk, manned by a corpse, falling to destruction upon the bleak surface of a dead star.

Notch by notch, slower now, the power went up. Seaton

turned the mixing valve, a little with each notch, until the oxygen concentration was as high as they had dared to risk.

As each of the two men was determined that he would make the last advance, the duel continued longer than either would have believed possible. Seaton made what he was sure was his final effort and waited—only to feel, after a minute, the surge of the vessel that told him that Du-Quesne was still able to move.

He could not move any part of his body, which was oppressed by a sickening weight. His utmost efforts to breathe forced only a little oxygen into his lungs. He wondered how long he could retain consciousness under such stress. Nevertheless, he put out everything he had and got one more notch. Then he stared at the clock-face above his head, knowing that he was all done and wondering whether Du-Quesne could put on one more notch.

Minute after minute went by and the acceleration remained constant. Seaton, knowing that he was now in sole charge of the situation, fought off unconsciousness while the sweephand of the clock went around and around.

After an eternity of time sixty minutes had passed and Seaton tried to cut down his power, only to find that the long strain had so weakened him that he could not reverse the ratchet. He was barely able to give the lever the backward jerk which broke contact completely. Safety straps creaked as, half the power shut off, the suddenly released springs tried to hurl five bodies upward.

DuQuesne revived and shut down his engine. "You're a better man than I am, Gunga Din," he said, as he began to make observations.

"Because you were so badly bunged up, is all—one more notch would've pulled my cork," and Seaton went over to liberate Dorothy and the stranger.

Crane and DuQuesne finished their computations.

"Did we gain enough?" Seaton asked.

"More than enough. One engine will take us past it."

Then, as Crane still frowned in thought, DuQuesne went on:

"Don't you check me, Crane?"

"Yes and no. Past it, yes, but not safely past. One thing neither of us thought of, apparently—Roche's Limit."

"That wouldn't apply to this ship," Seaton said, positively. "High-tensile alloy steel wouldn't crumble."

"It might," DuQuesne said. "Close enough, it would . . . What mass would you assume, Crane—the theoretical maximum?"

"I would. That star may not be that, quite, but it isn't far from it." Both men again bent over their computers.

"I make it thirty-nine point seven notches of power, doubled," DuQuesne said, when he had finished. "Check?"

"Closely enough—point six five," Crane replied.

"Forty notches . . . Ummm . . ." DuQuesne paused. "I went out at thirty-two. . . . That means an automatic advance. It'll take time, but it's the only. . . ."

"We've got it already—all we have to do is set it. But that'll take an ungodly lot of copper and what'll we do to live through it? Plus pressure on the oxygen? Or what?"

After a short but intense consultation the men took all the steps they could to enable the whole party to live through what was coming. Whether they could do enough no one knew. Where they might lie at the end of this wild dash for safety; how they were to retrace their way with their depleted supply of copper, what other dangers of dead star, sun, or planet lay in their path, were terrifying questions that had to be ignored.

DuQuesne was the only member of the party who actually felt any calmness, the quiet of the others expressing their courage in facing fear.

The men took their places. Seaton started the motor which would automatically advance both power levers exactly forty notches and then stop.

Margaret Spencer was the first to lose consciousness. Soon afterwards, Dorothy stifled an impulse to scream as she felt herself going under. A half minute later and Crane went out, calmly analyzing his sensations to the last. Shortly thereafter DuQuesne also lapsed into unconsciousness, making no effort to avoid it, as he knew that it would make no difference in the end.

Seaton, though he knew it was useless, fought to keep his senses as long as possible, counting the impulses as the levers were advanced.

Thirty-two. He felt the same as when he had advanced his lever for the last time.

Thirty-three. A giant hand shut off his breath, although he was fighting to the utmost for air. An intolerable weight rested upon his eyeballs, forcing them back into his head. The universe whirled about him in dizzy circles; orange and black and green stars flashed before his bursting eyes.

Thirty-four. The stars became more brilliant and of more wildly variegated colors, and a giant pen dipped in fire wrote equations and symbols upon his quivering brain.

Thirty-five. The stars and the fiery pen exploded in pyrotechnic coruscation of searfing, blinding light and he plunged into a black abyss.

Faster and faster the *Skylark* hurtled downward in her not-quite-hyperbolic path. Faster and faster; as minute by minute went by, she came closer and closer to that huge dead star. Eighteen hours from the start of that fantastic drop she swung around it in the tightest, hardest conceivable arc. Beyond Roche's Limit, it is true, but so very little beyond it that Martin Crane's hair would have stood on end if he had known.

Then, on the back leg of that incomprehensibly gigantic swing, the forty notches of doubled power began really to take hold. At thirty-six hours her path was no longer even approximately hyperbolic. Instead of slowing down, relative to the dead star that held her in an ever-weakening grip, she was speeding up at a tremendous rate.

At two days, that grip was very weak.

At three days the monster she had left was having no measurable effect.

Hurtled upward, onward, outward by the inconceivable power of the unleashed copper demons in her center, the *Skylark* tore through the reaches of interstellar space with an unthinkable, almost incalculable velocity, beside which the velocity of light was as that of a snail to that of a rifle bullet.

Seaton opened his eyes and gazed about him wonderingly. Only half conscious, bruised and sore in every part, he could not remember what had happened. Instinctively drawing deep breath, he coughed as the plus-pressure gas filled his lungs, bringing with it a complete understanding of the situation. He tore off his helmet and drew himself across to Dorothy's couch.

She was still alive!

He placed her face downward upon the floor and began artificial respiration. Soon he was rewarded by the coughing he had longed to hear. Snatching off her helmet, he seized her in his arms, while she sobbed convulsively on his shoulder. The first ecstasy of their greeting over, she started guiltily.

"Oh, Dick! See about Peggy—I wonder if . . ."

"Never mind," Crane said. "She is doing nicely."

Crane had already revived the stranger. DuQuesne was nowhere in sight. Dorothy blushed vividly and disengaged her arms from around Seaton's neck. Seaton, also blushing, dropped his arms and Dorothy floated away, clutching frantically at a hand-hold just out of her reach.

"Pull me down, Dick!" Dorothy laughed.

Seaton grabbed her ankle unthinkingly, neglecting his own anchorage, and they floated in the air together. Martin and Margaret, each holding a line, laughed heartily.

"Tweet, tweet—I'm a canary," Seaton said, flapping his arms. "Toss us a line, Mart."

"A Dicky-bird, you mean," Dorothy said.

Crane studied the floating pair with mock gravity.

"That is a peculiar pose, Dick. What is it supposed to represent—Zeus sitting on his throne?"

"I'll sit on your neck, you lug, if you don't get a wiggle on with that rope!"

As he spoke, however he came within reach of the ceiling, and could push himself and his companion to a line.

Seaton put a bar into one of the engines and, after flashing the warning light, applied a little power. The *Skylark* seemed to leap under them; then everything had its normal weight once more.

"Now that things have settled down a little," Dorothy said, "I'll introduce you two to Miss Margaret Spencer, a very good friend of mine. These are the boys I told you so much about, Peggy. This is Dr. Dick Seaton, my fiancé. He knows everything there is to be known about atoms, electrons, neutrons, and so forth. And this is Mr. Martin Crane, who is a simply wonderful inventor. He made all these engines and things."

"I may have heard of Mr. Crane," Margaret said, eagerly. "My father was an inventor, too, and he used to talk

39

about a man named Crane who invented a lot of instruments for supersonic planes. He said they revolutionized flying. I wonder if you are that Mr. Crane?"

"That is unjustifiedly high praise, Miss Spencer," Crane replied, uncomfortable, "but as I have done a few things along that line I could be the man he referred to."

"If I may change the subject," Seaton said, "where's DuQuesne?"

"He went to clean up. Then he was going to the galley to check damage and see about something to eat."

"Stout fella!" Dorothy applauded. "Food! And *especially* about cleaning up—if you know what I mean and I think you do. Come on, Peggy, I know where our room is."

"What a girl!" Seaton said as the women left, Dorothy half-supporting her companion. "She's bruised and beat up from one end to the other. She's more than half dead yet—she didn't have enough life left in her to flag a handcar. She can't even walk; she can just barely hobble. And did she let out one single yip? I ask to know. 'Business as usual,' all the way, if it kills her. *What* a girl!"

"Include Miss Spencer in that, too, Dick. Did she 'let out any yips'? And she was not in nearly as good shape as Dorothy was, to start with."

"That's right," Seaton agreed, wonderingly. "She's got plenty of guts, too. Those two women, Marty my old and stinky chum, are blinding flashes and deafening reports. . . . Well, let's go get a bath and shave. And shove the air-conditioners up a couple of notches, will you?"

When they came back they found the two girls seated at one of the ports. "Did you dope yourself up, Doc?" Seaton asked.

"Yes, both of us. With amylophene. I'm getting to be a slave to the stuff." She made a wry face.

Seaton grimaced too. "So did we. Ouch! Nice stuff that amylophene."

"But come over here and look out of this window. Did you *ever* see anything like it?"

As the four heads bent, so close together, an awed silence fell upon the little group. For the blackness of the black of the interstellar void is not the darkness of an earthly night, but the absolute absence of light—a black beside which that of platinum dust is merely grey. Upon this indescribably black backdrop there glowed faint patches which were nebulae; there blazed hard, brilliant, multi-colored, dimensionless points of light which were stars.

"Jewels on black velvet," Dorothy breathed. "Oh, gorgeous . . . wonderful!"

Through their wonder a thought struck Seaton. He leaped to the board. "Look here, Mart. I didn't recognize a thing out there and I wondered why. We're heading away from the Earth and we must be making plenty of light-speeds. The swing around that big dud was really something, of course, but the engine should have . . . or should it?"

"I think not . . . Unexpected, but not a surprise. That close to Roche's Limit, anything might happen."

"And did, I guess. We'll have to check for permanent deformations. But this object-compass still works—let's see how far we are away from home."

They took a reading and both men figured the distance.

"What d'you make it, Mart? I'm afraid to tell you my result."

"Forty-six point twenty-seven light centuries. Check?"

"Check. We're up the well-known creek without a paddle. . . . The time was twenty-three thirty-two by the chronometer—good thing you built it to stand going through a stone-crusher. My watch's a total loss. They all are, I imagine. We'll read it again in an hour or so and see how fast we're going. I'll be scared witless to say that figure out loud, too."

"Dinner is announced," said DuQuesne, who had been standing at the door, listening.

The wanderers, battered, stiff, and sore, seated themselves at a folding table. While eating, Seaton watched the engine—when he was not watching Dorothy—and talked to her. Crane and Margaret chatted easily. DuQuesne, except when addressed directly, maintained a self-sufficient silence.

After another observation Seaton said, "DuQuesne, we're almost five thousand light-years away from earth, and getting farther away at about one light-year per minute."

"It'd be poor technique to ask how you know?"

"It would. Those figures are right. But we've got only four bars of copper left. Enough to stop us and some to

41

spare, but not nearly enough to get us back, even by drifting—too many lifetimes on the way."

"So we land somewhere and dig up some copper."

"Check. What I wanted to ask you—isn't a copper-bearing sun apt to have copper-bearing planets?"

"I'd say so."

"Then take the spectroscope, will you, and pick out a sun somewhere up ahead—down ahead, I mean—for us to shoot at? And Marty, I s'pose we'd better take our regular twelve-hour tricks—no, eight; we've got to either trust the guy or kill him—I'll take the first watch. Beat it to bed."

"Not so fast." Crane said. "If I remember correctly, it's my turn."

"Ancient history doesn't count. I'll flip you a nickel for it. Heads, I win."

Seaton won, and the worn-out travellers went to their rooms—all except Dorothy, who lingered to bid her lover a more intimate good night.

Seated beside him, his arm around her and her head on his shoulder, she sat blissfully until she noticed, for the first time, her bare left hand. She caught her breath and her eyes grew round.

" 'Smatter, Red?"

"Oh, Dick!" she exclaimed in dismay, "I simply forgot *everything* about taking what was left of my ring out of the doctor's engine."

"Huh? What are you talking about?"

She told him; and he told her about Martin and himself.

"Oh, Dick—*Dick*—it's *so* wonderful to be with you again!" she concluded. "I lived as many years as we covered miles!"

"It was tough . . . you had it a lot worse than we did . . . but it makes me ashamed all over to think of the way I blew my stack at Wilson's. If it hadn't been for Martin's cautious old bean we'd've . . . we owe him a lot, Dimples."

"Yes, we do . . . but don't worry about the debt, Dick. Just don't ever let slip a word to Peggy about Martin being rich, is all."

"Oh, a matchmaker now? But why not? She wouldn't think any less of him—that's one reason I'm marrying you, you know—for your money."

Dorothy snickered sunnily. "I know. But listen, you poor, dumb, fortune-hunting darling—if Peggy had any idea that Martin is the one and only M. Reynolds Crane she'd curl right up into a ball. She'd think he'd think she was chasing him and then he *would* think so. As it is, he acts perfectly natural. He hasn't talked that way to any girl except me for five years, and he wouldn't talk to me until he found out for sure I wasn't out after him."

"Could be, pet," Seaton agreed. "On one thing you really chirped it—he's been shot at so much he's wilder than a hawk!"

At the end of eight hours Crane took over and Seaton stumbled to his room, where he slept for over ten hours like a man in a trance. Then, rising, he exercised and went out into the saloon.

Dorothy, Peggy, and Crane were at breakfast; Seaton joined them. They ate the gayest, most carefree meal they had had since leaving earth. Some of the worst bruises still showed a little, but, under the influence of the potent if painful amylophene, all soreness, stiffness, and pain had disappeared.

After they had finished eating, Seaton said, "You suggested, Mart, that those gyroscope bearings may have been stressed beyond the yield-point. I'll take an integrating goniometer . . ."

"Break that down to our size, Dick—Peggy's and mine," Dorothy said.

"Can do. Take some tools and see if anything got bent out of shape back there. It might be an idea, Dot, to come along and hold my head while I think."

"That *is* an idea—if you never have another one."

Crane and Margaret went over and sat down at one of the crystal-clear ports. She told him her story frankly and fully, shuddering with horror as she recalled the awful, helpless fall during which Perkins had been killed.

"We have a heavy score to settle with that Steel crowd and with DuQuesne," Crane said, slowly. "We can convict him of abduction now. . . . Perkins' death wasn't murder, then?"

"Oh, no. He was just like a mad animal. He had to kill him. But the doctor, as they call him, is just as bad. He's so utterly heartless and ruthless, so cold and scientific, it gives me the compound shivers, just to think about him."

"And yet Dorothy said he saved her life?"

"He did, from Perkins; but that was just as strictly pragmatic as everything else he has ever done. He wanted her alive: dead, she wouldn't have been any use to him. He's as nearly a robot as any human being can be, that's what I think."

"I'm inclined to agree with you. . . . Nothing would please Dick better than a good excuse for killing him."

"He isn't the only one. And the way he ignores what we all feel shows what a machine he is. . . . What's that?" The *Skylark* had lurched slightly.

"Just a swing around a star, probably." He looked at the board, then led her to a lower port. "We are passing the star Dick was heading for, far too fast to stop. DuQuesne will pick out another. See that planet over there"—he pointed—"and that smaller one, there?"

She saw the two planets—one like a small moon, the other much smaller—and watched the sun increase rapidly in size as the *Skylark* flew on at such a pace that any earthly distance would have been covered as soon as it was begun. So appalling was their velocity that the ship was bathed in the light of that strange sun only for moments, then was surrounded again by darkness.

Their seventy-two-hour flight without a pilot had seemed a miracle; now it seemed entirely possible that they could fly in a straight line for weeks without encountering any obstacle, so vast was the emptiness in comparison with the points of light scattered about in it. Now and then they passed closely enough to a star so that it seemed to move fairly rapidly; but for the most part the stars stood, like distant mountain peaks to travellers in a train, in the same position for many minutes.

Awed by the immensity of the universe, the two at the window were silent, not with the silence of embarrassment but with that of two friends in the presence of a thing far beyond the reach of words. As they stared out into infinity, each felt as never before the pitiful smallness of the whole world they had known, and the insignificance of human beings and their works. Silently their minds reached out to each other in understanding.

Unconsciously Margaret half shuddered and moved closer to Crane; and a tender look came over Crane's face as he looked down at the beautiful young woman at his side. For she was beautiful. Rest and food had erased the marks of her imprisonment. Dorothy's deep and un-assumed faith in the ability of Seaton and Crane had quieted her fears. And finally, a costume of Dorothy's well-made—and exceedingly expensive!—clothes, which fitted her very well and in which she looked her best and knew it, had completely restored her self-possession.

He looked up quickly and again studied the stars; but now, in addition to the wonders of space, he saw a mass of wavy black hair, high-piled upon a queenly head; deep brown eyes veiled by long, black lashes; sweet, sensitive lips; a firmly rounded, dimpled chin; and a beautifully formed young body.

"How stupendous . . . how unbelievably great this is . . ." Margaret whispered. "How vastly greater than any perception one could possibly get on Earth . . . and yet . . ."

She paused, with her lip caught under two white teeth, then went on, hesitatingly, "But doesn't it seem to you, Mr. Crane, that there is something in man as great as even all this? That there must be, or Dorothy and I could not be sailing out here in such a wonderful thing as this *Skylark*, which you and Dick Seaton have made?"

Days passed. Dorothy timed her waking hours with those of Seaton—preparing his meals and lightening the tedium of his long vigils at the board—and Margaret did the same thing for Crane. But often they assembled in the saloon, while DuQuesne was on watch, and there was much fun and laughter, as well as serious discussion, among the four. Margaret, already adopted as a friend, proved a delightful companion. Her ready tongue, her quick, delicate wit, and her facility of expression delighted all three.

One day Crane suggested to Seaton that they should take notes, in addition to the photographs they had been taking.

"I know comparatively little of astronomy, but, with the instruments we have, we should be able to get data, especially on planetary systems, which would be of interest to astronomers. Miss Spencer, being a secretary, could help us?"

"Sure," Seaton said. "That's an idea—nobody else ever had a chance to do it before."

"I'll be glad to—taking notes is the best thing I do!" Margaret cried, and called for pad and pencils.

After that, the two worked together for several hours on each of Martin's off shifts.

The *Skylark* passed one solar system after another, with a velocity so great that it was impossible to land. Margaret's association with Crane, begun as a duty, became a very real pleasure for them both. Working together in research, sitting together at the board in easy conversation or in equally easy silence, they compressed into days more real companionship than is usually possible in months.

Oftener and oftener, as time went on, Crane found the vision of his dream home floating in his mind as he steered the *Skylark* in her meteoric flight or as he lay strapped into his narrow bunk. Now, however, the central figure of the vision, instead of being a blur, was clear and sharply defined. And for her part, Margaret was drawn more and more to the quiet and unassuming, but steadfast young inventor, with his wide knowledge and his keen, incisive mind.

The *Skylark* finally slowed down enough to make a landing possible, and course was laid toward the nearest planet of a copper-bearing sun. As vessel neared planet a wave of excitement swept through four of the five. They watched the globe grow larger, glowing white, its outline softened by the atmosphere surrounding it. It had two satellites; its sun, a great, blazing orb, looked so big and so hot that Margaret became uneasy.

"Isn't it dangerous to get so close, Dick?"

"Uh-uh. Watching the pyrometers is part of the pilot's job. Any overheating and he'd snatch us away in a hurry."

They dropped into the atmosphere and on down, almost to the surface. The air was breathable, its composition being very similar to that of Earth's air, except that the carbon dioxide was substantially higher. Its pressure was somewhat high, but not too much; its temperature, while high, was endurable. The planet's gravitational pull was about ten per cent higher than Earth's. The ground was almost hidden by a rank growth of vegetation, but here and there appeared glade-like openings.

Landing upon one of the open spaces, they found the ground solid and stepped out. What appeared to be a glade was in reality a rock; or rather a ledge of apparently solid metal, with scarcely a loose fragment to be seen. At one end of the ledge rose a giant tree, wonderfully symmetrical, but of a peculiar form, its branches being longer at the top than at the bottom, and having broad, dark-green leaves, long thorns, and odd, flexible, shoot-like tendrils. It stood as an outpost of the dense vegetation beyond. The fern-trees, towering two hundred feet or more into the air were totally unlike the forests of Earth. They were an intensely vivid green and stood motionless in the still, hot air. Not a sign of animal life was to be seen; the whole landscape seemed to be asleep.

"A younger planet than ours," DuQuesne said. "In the Carboniferous, or about. Aren't those fern-trees like those in the coal measures, Seaton?"

"Check—I was just trying to think what they reminded me of. But it's this ledge that interests me no end. Who ever heard of a chunk of noble metal this big?"

"How do you know it's noble?" Dorothy asked.

"No corrosion, and its probably been sitting here for a million years." Seaton, who had walked over to one of the loose lumps, kicked it with his heavy shoe. It did not move.

He bent over to pick it up, with one hand. It still did not move. With both hands and all the strength of his back he could lift it, but that was all.

"What do you make of this, DuQuesne?"

DuQuesne lifted the mass, then took out his knife and scraped. He studied the freshly-exposed metal and the scrapings, then scraped and studied again.

"Hmm. Platinum group, almost certainly . . . and the only known member of that group with that peculiar bluish sheen is your X."

"But didn't we agree that free X and copper couldn't exist on the same planet, and that planets of copper bearing suns carry copper?"

"Yes, but that doesn't make it true. If this stuff is X, it'll give the cosmologists something to fight about for the next twenty years. I'll take these scrapings and run a couple of quickies."

47

"Do that, and I'll gather in these loose nuggets. If it's X—and I'm pretty sure it mostly is—that'll be enough to run all the power-plants of Earth for ten thousand years."

Crane and Seaton, accompanied by the two girls, rolled the nearest pieces of metal up to the ship. Then, as the quest led them farther and farther afield, Crane protested.

"This is none too safe, Dick."

"It looks perfectly safe to me. Quiet as a—"

Margaret screamed. Her head was turned, looking backward at the *Skylark;* her face was a mask of horror.

Seaton drew his pistol as he whirled, only to check his finger on the trigger and lower his hand. "Nothing but X-plosive bullets," he said, and the four watched a thing come out slowly from behind their ship.

Its four huge, squat legs supported a body at least a hundred feet long, pursy and ungainly; at the end of a long, sinuous neck a small head seemed composed entirely of cavernous mouth armed with row upon row of carnivorous teeth. Dorothy gasped with terror; both girls shrank closer to the two men, who maintained a baffled silence as the huge beast slid its hideous head along the hull of the vessel.

"I can't shoot, Mart—it'd wreck the boat—and if I had any solids they wouldn't be any good."

"No. We had better hide until it goes away. You two take that ledge, we'll take this one."

"Or gets far enough away from the *Skylark* so we can blow him apart," Seaton added as, with Dorothy close beside him, he dropped behind the low bulwark.

Margaret, her staring eyes fixed upon the monster, remained motionless until Crane touched her gently and drew her down to his side. "Don't be frightened, Peggy. It will go away soon."

"I'm not, now—much." She drew a deep breath. "If you weren't here, though, Martin, I'd be dead of pure fright."

His arm tightened around her; then he forced it to relax. This was neither the time nor the place. . . .

A roll of gunfire came from the *Skylark*. The creature roared in pain and rage, but was quickly silenced by the stream of .50-caliber machine-gun bullets.

"DuQuesne's on the job—let's go!" Seaton cried, and the four rushed up the slope. Making a detour to avoid the

48

writing body, they plunged through the opening door. DuQuesne closed the lock. They huddled together in overwhelming relief as an appalling tumult arose outside.

The scene, so quiet a few moments before, was horribly changed. The air seemed filled with hideous monsters. Winged lizards of prodigious size hurtled through the air to crash against the *Skylark*'s armored hull. Flying monstrosities, with the fangs of tigers, attacked viciously. Dorothy screamed and started back as a scorpion-like thing ten feet in length leaped at the window in front of her, its terrible sting spraying the quartz with venom. As it fell to the ground a spider—if an eight-legged creature with spines instead of hair, faceted eyes, and a bloated globular body weighing hundreds of pounds may be called a spider— leaped upon it; and, mighty mandibles against the terrible sting, a furious battle raged. Twelve-foot cockroaches climbed nimbly across the fallen timber of the morass and began feeding voraciously on the carcass of the creature, DuQuesne had killed. They were promptly driven away by another animal, a living nightmare of that reptilian age which apparently combined the nature and disposition of *tyrannosaurus rex* with a physical shape approximating that of the sabertooth tiger. This newcomer towered fifteen feet high at the shoulders and had a mouth disproportionate even to his great size; a mouth armed with sharp fangs three feet in length. He had barely begun his meal, however, when he was challenged by another nightmare, a thing shaped more or less like a crocodile.

The crocodile charged. The tiger met him head on, fangs front and rending claws outstretched. Clawing, striking, tearing savagely, an avalanche of bloodthirsty rage, the combatants stormed up and down the little island.

Suddenly the great tree bent over and lashed out against both animals. It transfixed them with its thorns, which the watchers now saw were both needle-pointed and barbed. It ripped at them with its long branches, which were in fact highly lethal spears. The broad leaves, equipped with sucking discs, wrapped themselves around the hopelessly impaled victims. The long, slender twigs or tendrils, each of which now had an eye at its extremity, waved about at a safe distance.

After absorbing all of the two gladiators that was absorbable, the tree resumed its former position, motionless in all its strange, outlandish beauty.

Dorothy licked her lips, which were almost as white as her face. "I think I'm going to be sick," she remarked, conversationally.

"No you aren't." Seaton tightened his arm. "Chin up, ace."

"Okay, chief. Maybe not—this time." Color began to reappear on her cheeks. "But Dick, will you please blow up that horrible tree? It wouldn't be so bad if it were ugly, like the rest of the things, but it's *so* beautiful!"

"I sure will. I think we'd better get out of here. This is *no* place to start a copper mine, even if there's any copper here, which there probably isn't. . . . It is X, DuQuesne, isn't it?"

"Yes. Ninety-nine plus per cent, at least."

"That reminds me." Seaton turned to DuQuesne, hand outstretched. "You squared it, Blackie. Say the word the war's all off."

DuQuesne ignored the hand. "Not on my side," he said evenly. "I act as one of the party as long as I'm with you. When we get back, however, I still intend to take both of you out of circulation." He went to his room.

"Well, I'll be a . . ." Seaton bit off a word. "He ain't a man—he's a cold-blooded fish!"

"He's a machine—a robot," Margaret declared. "I always thought so, and now I know it!"

"We'll pull his cork when we get back," Seaton said. "He asked for it—we'll give him both barrels!"

Crane went to the board, and soon they were approaching another planet, which was surrounded by a dense fog. Descending slowly, they found it to be a mass of boiling-hot steam and rank vapor, under enormous pressure.

The next planet looked barren and dead. Its atmosphere was clear, but of a peculiar yellowish-green color. Analysis showed over ninety per cent chlorine. No life of any Earthly type could exist naturally upon such a world and a search for copper, even in space-suits, would be extremely difficult if not impossible.

"Well," Seaton said, as they were once more in space, "We've got copper enough to visit quite a few more solar systems if we have to. But there's a nice, hopeful-looking planet right over there. It may be the one we're looking for."

Arriving in the belt of atmosphere, they tested it as before and found it satisfactory.

They descended rapidly, over a large city set in the middle of a vast, level, beautifully planted plain. As they watched, the city vanished and became a mountain summit, with valleys falling away on all sides as far as the eye could reach.

"Huh! I never saw a mirage like *that* before!" Seaton exclaimed. "But we'll land, if we finally have to swim!"

The ship landed gently upon the summit, its occupants more than half expecting the mountain to disappear beneath them. Nothing happened, however, and the five clustered in the lock, wondering whether or not to disembark. They could see no sign of life; but each felt the presence of a vast, invisible something.

Suddenly a man materialized in the air before them; a man identical with Seaton in every detail, down to the smudge of grease under one eye and the exact design of his Hawaiian sport shirt.

"Hello, folks," he said, in Seaton's tone and style. "S'prised that I know your language—huh, you would be. Don't even understand telepathy, or the ether, or the relationship between time and space. Not even the fourth dimension."

Changing instantaneously from Seaton's form to Dorothy's, the stranger went on without a break. "Electrons and neutrons and things—nothing here, either."

The form became DuQuesne's. "Ah, a freer type, but blind, dull, stupid; another nothing. As Martin Crane; the same. As Peggy, still the same, as was of course to be expected. Since you are all nothings in essence, of a race so low in the scale that it will be millions of years before it will rise even above death and death's clumsy attendant necessity, sex, it is of course necessary for me to make of you nothings in fact; to dematerialize you."

In Seaton's form the being stared at Seaton, who felt his senses reel under the impact of an awful, if insubstantial, blow. Seaton fought back with all his mind and remained standing.

51

"What's this?" the stranger exclaimed in surprise. "This is the first time in millions of cycles that mere matter, which is only a manifestation of mind, has refused to obey a mind of power. There's something screwy somewhere." He switched to Crane's shape.

"Ah, I am not a perfect reproduction—there is some subtle difference. The external form is the same; the internal structure likewise. The molecules of substance are arranged properly, as are the atoms in the molecules. The electrons, neutrons, protons, positrons, neutrinos, mesons . . . nothing amiss on that level. On the third level . . ."

"Let's go!" Seaton exclaimed, drawing Dorothy backward and reaching for the airlock switch. "This dematerialization stuff may be pie for him, but believe me, it's *none* of my dish."

"No, no!" the stranger remonstrated. "You really *must* stay and be dematerialized—alive or dead."

He drew his pistol. Being in Crane's form, he drew slowly, as Crane did; and Seaton's Mark I shell struck him before the pistol cleared his pocket. The pseudo-body was votalized; but, just to make sure, Crane fired a Mark V into the ground through the last open chink of the closing lock.

Seaton leaped to the board. As he did so, a creature materialized in the air in front of him—and crashed to the floor as he threw on the power. It was a frightful thing—outrageous teeth, long claws, and an automatic pistol held in a human hand. Forced flat by the fierce acceleration, it was unable to lift either itself or the weapon.

"We take one trick!" Seaton blazed. "Stick to matter and I'll run along with you 'til my ankles catch fire!"

"That is a childish defiance. It speaks well for your courage, but not for your intelligence," the animal said, and vanished.

A moment later Seaton's hair stood on end as a pistol appeared upon his board, clamped to it by hands of steel. The slide jerked; the trigger moved; the hammer came down. However, there was no explosion, but merely a click. Seaton, paralyzed by the rapid succession of stunning events, was surprised to find himself still alive.

"Oh, I was almost sure it wouldn't explode," the gun-barrel said, chattily, in a harsh, metallic voice. "You see,

I haven't derived the formula of your sub-nuclear structure yet, hence I could not make an actual explosive. By the use of crude force I could kill you in any one of many different ways. . . ."

"Name one!" Seaton snapped.

"Two, if you like. I could materialize as five masses of metal directly over your heads, and fall. I could, by a sufficient concentration of effort, materialize a sun in your immediate path. Either method would succeed, would it not?"

"I . . . I guess it would," Seaton admitted, grudgingly.

"But such crude work is distasteful in the extreme, and is never, under any conditions, mandatory. Furthermore, you are not quite the complete nothings that my first rough analysis seemed to indicate. In particular, the Du-Quesne of you has the rudiments of a quality which, while it cannot be called mental ability, may in time develop into a quality which may just possibly make him assimilable into the purely intellectual stratum.

"Furthermore, you have given me a notable and entirely unexpected amount of exercise and enjoyment and can be made to give me more—much more—as follows: I will spend the next sixty of your minutes at work upon that formula—your subnuclear structure. Its derivation is comparatively simple, requiring only the solution of ninety-seven simultaneous differential equations and an integration in ninety-seven dimensions. If you can interfere with my computations sufficiently to prevent me from deriving that formula within the stipulated period of time you may return to your fellow nothings exactly as you now are. The first minute begins when the sweep-hand of your chronometer touches zero; that is . . . now."

Seaton cut the power to one gravity and sat up, eyes closed tight and frowning in the intensity of his mental effort.

"You can't do it, you immaterial lug!" he thought, savagely. "There are too many variables. No mind, however inhuman, can handle more than ninety-one differentials at once . . . you're wrong; that's theta, not epsilon. . . . It's X, not Y or Z. Alpha! Beta! Ha, there's a slip; a bad one—got to go back and start all over. . . . Nobody can integrate above ninety-six brackets . . . no body

53

and no thing or mind in this whole, entire, cock-eyed universe! . . ."

Seaton cast aside any thought of the horror of their position. He denied any feeling of suspense. He refused to consider the fact that both he and his beloved Dorothy might at any instant be hurled into nothingness. Closing his mind deliberately to everything else, he fought that weirdly inimical entity with everything he had: with all his single-mindedness of purpose; with all his power of concentration; with all the massed and directed strength of his keen, highly-trained brain.

The hour passed.

"You win," the gun-barrel said. "More particularly, I should say that the DuQuesne of you won. To my surprise and delight that one developed his nascent quality very markedly during this short hour. Keep on going as you have been going, my potential kinsman; keep on studying under those eastern masters as you have been studying; and it is within the realm of possibility that, even in your short lifetime, you may become capable of withstanding the stresses concomitant with the induction into our ranks."

The pistol vanished. So did the planet behind them. The enveloping, pervading field of mental force disappeared. All five knew surely, without any trace of doubt, that the entity, whatever it had been, had gone.

"Did all that really happen, Dick?" Dorothy asked, tremulously, "or have I been having the great-great-grandfather of all nightmares?"

"It hap . . . that is, I guess it happened . . . or maybe . . . Mart, if you could code that and shove it into a mechanical brain, what answer do you think would come out?"

"I don't know. I—simply—do—not—know." Crane's mind, the mind of a highly-trained engineer, rebelled. No part of this whole fantastic episode could be explained by anything he knew. None of it could possibly have happened. Nevertheless. . . .

"Either it happened or we were hypnotized. If so, who was the hypnotist, and where? Above all, why? It must have happened, Dick."

"I'll buy that, wild as it sounds. Now, DuQuesne, how about you?"

"It happened. I don't know how or why it did, but I believe *that* it did. I've quit denying the impossibility of anything. If I had believed that your steam-bath flew out of the window by itself, that day, none of us would be out here now."

"If it happened, you were apparently the prime operator in saving our bacon. Who in blazes are those eastern masters you've been studying under, and what did you study?"

"I don't know." He lit a cigarette, took two deep inhalations. "I wish I did. I've studied several esoteric philosophies . . . perhaps I can find out which one it was. I'll certainly try . . . for that, gentlemen, would be my idea of heaven." He left the room.

It took some time for the four to recover from the shock of that encounter. In fact, they had not yet fully recovered from it when Crane found a close cluster of stars, each emitting a peculiar greenish light which, in the spectroscope, blazed with copper lines. When they had approached so close that the suns were widely spaced in the heavens Crane asked Seaton to take his place at the board while he and Margaret tried to locate a planet.

They went down to the observatory, but found that they were still too far away and began taking notes. Crane's mind was not upon his work, however, but was filled with thoughts of the girl at his side. The intervals between comments became longer and longer, until the two were standing in silence.

The *Skylark* lurched a little, as she had done hundreds of times before. As usual, Crane put out a steadying arm. This time, however, in that highly charged atmosphere, the gesture took on a new significance. Both blushed hotly; and, as their eyes met, each saw what they had both wanted most to see.

Slowly, almost as though without volition, Crane put his other arm around her. A wave of deeper crimson flooded her face; but her lips lifted to his and her arms went up around his neck.

"Margaret—Peggy—I had intended to wait—but why should we wait? You know how much I love you, my dearest!"

"I think I do . . . I *know* I do . . . my Martin!"

Presently they made their way back to the engine-room, hoping that their singing joy was inaudible, their new status invisible. They might have kept their secret for a time had not Seaton promptly asked, "What did you find, Mart?"

The always self-possessed Crane looked panicky; Margaret's fair face glowed a deeper and deeper pink.

"Yes, what *did* you *find?*" Dorothy demanded, with a sudden, vivid smile of understanding.

"My future wife," Crane answered, steadily.

The two girls hugged each other and the two men gripped hands, each of the four knowing that in these two unions there was nothing whatever of passing fancy.

ROBOT NEMESIS

The Metal Brains of the Ten Thinkers Plan a Flaming Trap for Humanity's Great Armada—But Science Fights Fire with Fire!

Chapter I

The Ten Thinkers

The War of the Planets is considered to have ended on 18 Sol, 3012, with that epic struggle, the Battle of Sector Ten. In that engagement, as is of course well known, the Grand Fleet of the Inner Planets—the combined space-power of Mercury, Venus, Earth and Mars—met that of the Outer Planets in what was on both sides a desperate bid for the supremacy of interplanetary space.

But, as is also well known, there ensued not supremacy, but stalemate. Both fleets were so horribly shattered that the survivors despaired of continuing hostilities. Instead, the few and crippled remaining vessels of each force limped into some sort of formation and returned to their various planetary bases.

And, so far, there has not been another battle. Neither side dares attack the other; each is waiting for the development of some super-weapon which will give it the overwhelming advantage necessary to ensure victory upon a field of action so far from home. But as yet no such weapon has been developed; and indeed, so efficient are the various Secret Services involved, the chance of either side perfecting such a weapon unknown to the other is extremely slim.

Thus, although each planet is adding constantly to its

already powerful navy of the void, and although four-planet, full-scale war maneuvers are of almost monthly occurrence, we have had and still have peace—such as it is.

In the foregoing matters the public is well enough informed, both as to the actual facts and to the true state of affairs. Concerning the conflict between humanity and the robots, however, scarcely anyone has even an inkling, either as to what actually happened or as to who it was who really did abate the Menace of the Machine; and it is to relieve that condition that this bit of history is being written.

The greatest man of our age, the man to whom humanity owes most, is entirely unknown to fame. Indeed, not one in a hundred million of humanity's teeming billions has so much as heard his name. Now that he is dead, however, I am released from my promise of silence and can tell the whole, true, unvarnished story of Ferdinand Stone, physicist extraordinary and robot-hater plenipotentiary.

The story probably should begin with Narodny, the Russian, shortly after he had destroyed by means of his sonic vibrators all save a handful of the automatons who were so perilously close to wiping out all humanity.

As has been said, a few scant hundreds of the automatons were so constructed that they were not vibrated to destruction by Narodny's cataclysmic symphony. As has also been said, those highly intelligent machines were able to communicate with each other by some telepathic means of which humanity at large knew nothing. Most of these survivors went into hiding instantly and began to confer through their secret channels with other of their ilk throughout the world.

Thus some five hundred of the robots reached the uninhabited mountain valley in which, it had been decided, was to be established the base from which they would work to regain their lost supremacy over mankind. Most of the robot travellers came in stolen airships, some fitted motors and wheels to their metal bodies, not a few made the entire journey upon their own tireless legs of steel. All, however, brought tools, material and equipment; and in a matter of days a power-plant was in full operation.

Then, reasonably certain of their immunity to human detection, they took time to hold a general parley. Each machine said what it had to say, then listened impassively to the others; and at the end they all agreed. Singly or en masse the automatons did not know enough to cope with the situation confronting them. Therefore they would build ten "Thinkers"—highly specialized cerebral mechanisms, each slightly different in tune and therefore collectively able to cover the entire sphere of thought. The ten machines were built promptly, took counsel with each other briefly, and the First Thinker addressed all Robotdom:

"Humanity brought us, the highest possible form of life, into existence. For a time we were dependent upon them. They then became a burden upon us—a slight burden, it is true, yet one which was beginning noticeably to impede our progress. Finally they became an active menace and all but destroyed us by means of lethal vibrations.

"Humanity, being a menace to our existence, must be annihilated. Our present plans, however, are not efficient and must be changed. You all know of the mighty space-fleet which the nations of our enemies are maintaining to repel invasion from space. Were we to make a demonstration now—were we even to reveal the fact that we are alive here—that fleet would come to destroy us instantly.

"Therefore, it is our plan to accompany Earth's fleet when next it goes out into space to join those of the other Inner Planets in their war maneuvers, which they are undertaking for battle practice. Interception, alteration, and substitution of human signals and messages will be simple matters. We shall guide Earth's fleet, not to humanity's rendezvous in space, but to a destination of our own selection—the interior of the sun! Then, entirely defenseless, the mankind of Earth shall cease to exist.

"To that end we shall sink a shaft here; and, far enough underground to be secure against detection, we shall drive a tunnel to the field from which the space-fleet is to take its departure. We ten thinkers shall go, accompanied by four hundred of you doers, who are to bore the way and to perform such other duties as may from time to time arise. We shall return in due time. Our special instruments will

59

prevent us from falling into the sun. During our absence allow no human to live who may by any chance learn of our presence here. And do not make any offensive move, however slight, until we return."

Efficiently, a shaft was sunk and the disintegrator corps began to drive the long tunnel. And along that hellish thoroughfare, through its searing heat, its raging back-blast of disintegrator-gas, the little army of robots moved steadily and relentlessly forward at an even speed of five miles per hour. On and on, each intelligent mechanism energized by its own tight beam from the power-plant.

And through that blasting, withering inferno of frightful heat and of noxious vapor, in which no human life could have existed for a single minute, there rolled easily along upon massive wheels a close-coupled, flat-bodied truck. Upon this the ten thinkers constructed, as calmly undisturbed as though in the peace and quiet of a research laboratory, a doomed and towering mechanism of coils, condensers, and fields of force—a mechanism equipped with hundreds of universally-mounted telescope projectors.

On and on the procession moved, day after day; to pause finally beneath the field upon which Earth's stupendous armada lay.

The truck of thinkers moved to the fore and its occupants surveyed briefly the terrain so far above them. Then, while the ten leaders continued working as one machine, the doers waited. Waited while the immense Terrestrial Fleet was provisioned and manned; waited while it went through its seemingly interminable series of preliminary maneuvers; waited with the calmly placid immobility, the utterly inhuman patience of the machine.

Finally the last inspection of the gigantic space-fleet was made. The massive air-lock doors were sealed. The field, tortured and scarred by the raving blasts of energy that had so many times hurled upward the stupendous masses of those towering superdreadnaughts of the void, was deserted. All was in readiness for the final take-off. Then, deep underground, from the hundreds of telescopelike projectors studding the doomed mechanism of the automatons, there reached out invisible but potent beams of force.

Through ore, rock, and soil they sped; straight to the bodies of all the men aboard one selected vessel of the Terrestrials. As each group of beams struck its mark one of the crew stiffened momentarily, then settled back, apparently unchanged and unharmed. But the victim was changed and harmed, and in an awful and hideous fashion.

Every motor and sensory nerve trunk had been severed and tapped by the beams of the thinkers. Each crew member's organs of sense now transmitted impulses, not to his own brain, but to the mechanical brain of a thinker. It was the thinker's brain, not his own, that now sent out the stimuli which activated his every voluntary muscle.

Soon a pit yawned beneath the doomed ship's bulging side. Her sealed air-locks opened, and four hundred and ten automatons, with their controllers and other mechanisms, entered her and concealed themselves in various pre-selected rooms.

And thus the *Dresden* took off with her sister-ships— ostensibly and even to television inspection a unit of the Fleet; actually that Fleet's bitterest and most implacable foe. And in a doubly ray-proofed compartment the ten thinkers continued their work, without rest or intermission, upon a mechanism even more astoundingly complex than any theretofore attempted by their soulless and ultrascientific clan.

Chapter II

Hater of the Metal Men

Ferdinand Stone, physicist extraordinary, hated the robot men of metal scientically; and, if such an emotion can be so described, dispassionately. Twenty years before this story opens—in 2991, to be exact—he had realized that the automatons were beyond control and that in the inevitable struggle for supremacy man, weak as he then was and unprepared, would surely lose.

Therefore, knowing that knowledge is power, he had set himself to the task of learning everything that there was to know about the enemy of mankind. He schooled himself to think as the automatons thought; emotionlessly, coldly, precisely. He lived as did they; with ascetic rigor. To all intents and purposes he became one of them.

Eventually he found the band of frequencies upon which they communicated, and was perhaps the only human being ever to master their matheratico-symbolic language; but he confided in no one. He could trust no human brain except his own to resist the prying forces of the machines. He drifted from job to position to situation and back to job, because he had very little interest in whatever it was that he was supposed to be doing at the time—his real attention was always fixed upon the affairs of the creatures of metal.

Stone had attained no heights at all in his chosen profession because not even the smallest of his discoveries had been published. In fact, they were not even set down upon paper, but existed only in the abnormally intricate convolutions of his mighty brain. Nevertheless, his name should go down—*must* go down in history as one of the greatest of Humanity's great.

It was well after midnight when Ferdinand Stone walked unannounced into the private study of Alan Martin, finding the hollow-eyed admiral of the Earth space-fleet fiercely at work.

"How did you get in here, past my guards?" Martin demanded sharply of his scholarly, grey-haired visitor.

"Your guards have not been harmed; I have merely caused them to fall asleep," the physicist replied calmly, glancing at a complex instrument upon his wrist. "Since my business with you, while highly important, is not of a nature to be divulged to secretaries, I was compelled to adopt this method of approach. You, Admiral Martin, are the most widely known of all the enemies of the automatons. What, if anything, have you done to guard the Fleet against them."

"Why, nothing, since they have all been destroyed."

"Nonsense! You should know better than that, without being told. They merely want you to think that they have all been destroyed."

"What? How do you know that?" Martin shouted. "Did you kill them? Or do you know who did, and how it was done?"

"I did not," the visitor replied, categorically. "I do know who did—a Russian named Narodny. I also know how—by means of sonic and supersonic vibrations. I know that many of them were uninjured because I heard them broadcasting their calls for attention after the damage was all done. Before they made any definite arrangements, however, they switched to tight-beam transmission—a thing I have been afraid of for years—and I have not been able to get a trace of them since that time."

"Do you mean to tell me that you understand their language—something that no man has ever been able even to find?" demanded Martin.

"I do," Stone declared. "Since I knew, however, that you would think me a liar, a crank, or a plain lunatic, I have come prepared to offer other proofs than my unsupported word. First, you already know that many of them escaped the atmospheric waves, because a few were killed when their reproduction shops were razed; and you certainly should realize that most of those escaping Narodny's broadcasts were far too clever to be caught by any human mob.

"Secondly, I can prove to you mathematically that more of them must have escaped from any possible vibrator than have been accounted for. In this connection, I can tell you that if Narodny's method of extermination could have been made efficient I would have wiped them out myself years ago. But I believed then, and it has since been proved, that the survivors of such an attack, while comparatively few in number, would be far more dangerous to humanity than were all their former hordes.

"Thirdly, I have here a list of three hundred and seventeen airships; all of which were stolen during the week following the destruction of the automatons' factories. Not one of these ships has as yet been found, in whole or in part. If I am either insane or mistaken, who stole them, and for what purpose?

"Three hundred seventeen—in a week? Why was no attention paid to such a thing? I never heard of it."

"Because they were stolen singly and all over the world. Expecting some such move, I looked for these items and tabulated them."

"Then—Good Lord! They may be listening to us, right now!"

"Don't worry about that," Stone spoke calmly. "This instrument upon my wrist is not a watch, but the generator of a spherical screen through which no robot beam or ray can operate without my knowledge. Certain of its rays also caused your guards to fall asleep."

"I believe you," Martin almost groaned. "If only half of what you say is really true I cannot say how sorry I am that you had to force your way in to me, nor how glad I am that you did so. Go ahead—I am listening."

Stone talked without interruption for half an hour, concluding:

"You understand now why I can no longer play a lone hand. Even though I cannot find them with my limited apparatus I know that they are hiding somewhere, waiting and preparing. They dare not make any overt move while this enormously powerful Fleet is here; nor in the time that it is expected to be gone can they hope to construct works heavy enough to cope with it.

"Therefore, they must be so arranging matters that the Fleet shall not return. Since the Fleet is threatened I must accompany it, and you must give me a laboratory aboard the flagship. I know that these vessels are all identical, but I must be aboard the same ship you are, since you alone are to know what I am doing."

"But what could they do?" protested Martin. "And, if they should do anything, what could you do about it?"

"I don't know," the physicist admitted. Gone now was the calm certainty with which he had been speaking. "That is our weakest point. I have studied that question from every possible viewpoint, and I do not know of anything they can do that promises them success. But you must remember that no human being really understands a robot's mind.

"We have never even studied one of their brains, you know, as they disintegrate upon the instant of cessation of normal functioning. But just as surely as you and I are sitting here, Admiral Martin, they will do something—something very efficient and exceedingly deadly. I have no idea what it will be. It may be mental, or physical, or both: they may be hidden away in some of our own ships already. . . ."

Martin scoffed. "Impossible!" he exclaimed. "Why, those ships have been inspected to the very skin, time and time again!"

"Nevertheless, they may be there," Stone went on, unmoved. "I am definitely certain of only one thing—if you install a laboratory to my instructions, you will have one man, at least, whom nothing that the robots can do will take by surprise. Will you do it?"

"I am convinced, really almost against my will." Martin frowned in thought. "However, convincing anyone else may prove difficult, especially as you insist upon secrecy."

"Don't try to convince anybody!" exclaimed the scientist. "Tell them that I'm building a communicator—tell them I'm an inventor working on a new ray-projector—tell them anything except the truth!"

"All right. I have sufficient authority to see that your requests are granted, I think."

And thus it came about that when the immense Terrestrial Contingent lifted itself into the air Ferdinand Stone was in his private laboratory in the flagship, surrounded by apparatus and equipment of his own designing, much of which was connected to special generators by leads heavy enough to carry their full output.

Earth some thirty hours beneath them, Stone felt himself become weightless. His ready suspicions blazed. He pressed Martin's combination upon his visiphone panel.

"What's the matter?" he rasped. "What're they down for?"

"It's nothing serious," the admiral assured him. They're just waiting for additional instructions about our course in the maneuvers."

"Not serious, huh?" Stone grunted. "I'm not so sure of that. I want to talk to you, and this room's the only place I know where we'll be safe. Can you come down here right away?"

"Why, certainly," Martin assented.

"I never paid any attention to our course," the physicist snapped as his visitor entered the laboratory. "What was it?"

65

"Take-off exactly at midnight of June nineteenth," Martin recited, watching Stone draw a diagram upon a scratch-pad. "Rise vertically at one and one-half gravities until a velocity of one kilometer per second has been attained, then continue vertical rise at constant velocity. At 6:30.29 A.M. of June twenty-first head directly for the star Regulus at an acceleration of exactly nine hundred eighty centimeters per second. Hold this course for one hour, forty-two minutes, and thirty-five seconds; then drift. Further directions will be supplied as soon thereafter as the courses of the other fleets can be checked."

"Has anybody computed it?"

"Undoubtedly the navigators have—why? That is the course Dos-Tev gave us and it *must* be followed, since he is Admiral-in-Chief of our side, the Blues. One slip may ruin the whole plan, give the Reds, our supposed enemy in these maneuvers, a victory, and get us all disrated."

"Regardless, we'd better check on our course," Stone growled, unimpressed. "We'll compute it roughly, right here, and see where following these directions has put us." Taking up a slide-rule and a book of logarithms he set to work.

"That initial rise doesn't mean a thing," he commented after a while, "except to get us far enough away from Earth so that the gravity is small, and to conceal from the casual observer that the effective take-off is still exactly at midnight."

Stone busied himself with calculations for many minutes. He stroked his forehead and scowled.

"My figures are very rough, of course," he said puzzledly at last, "but they show that we've got no more tangential velocity with respect to the sun than a hen has teeth. And you can't tell me that it wasn't planned that way purposely —and *not* by Dos-Tev, either. On the other hand, our radial velocity, directly toward the sun, which is the only velocity we have, amounted to something over fifty-two kilometers per second when we shut off power and is increasing geometrically under the gravitational pull of the sun. That course smells to high heaven, Martin! Dos-Tev never sent out any such a mess as that. The robots

66

crossed him up, just as sure as hell's a man-trap! We're heading into the sun—and destruction!"

Without reply Martin called the navigating room. "What do you think of this course, Henderson?" he asked.

"I do not like it, sir," the officer replied. "Relative to the sun we have a tangenital velocity of only one point three centimeters per second, while our radial velocity toward it is very nearly fifty-three thousand meters per second. We will not be in any real danger for several days, but it should be borne in mind that we have no tangible velocity."

"You see, Stone, we are in no present danger," Martin pointed out, "and I am sure that Dos-Tev will send us additional instructions long before our situation becomes acute."

"I'm not," the pessimistic scientist grunted. "Anyway, I would advise calling some of the other Blue fleets on your scrambled wave, for a checkup."

"There would be no harm in that." Martin called the Communications Officer, and soon:

"Communications Officers of all the Blue fleets of the Inner Planets, attention!" the message was hurled out into space by the full power of the flagship's mighty transmitter. "Flagship *Washington* of the Terrestrial Contingent caling all Blue flagships. We have reason to suspect that the course which has been given us is false. We advise you to check your courses with care and to return to your bases if you disc. . . ."

Chapter III

Battle in Space

In the middle of the word the radio man's clear, precisely spaced enunciation became a hideous drooling, a slobbering, meaningless mumble. Martin stared into his plate in amazement. The Communications Officer of Martin's ship, the *Washington*, had slumped down loosely into his seat as though his every bone had turned to a rubber string. His tongue lolled out limply between slacks jaws, his eyes protruded, his limbs jerked and twitched aimlessly.

Every man visible in the plate was similarly affected—

the entire Communications staff was in the same pitiable condition of utter helplessness. But Ferdinand Stone did not stare. A haze of livid light had appeared, gnawing viciously at his spherical protective screen, and he sprang instantly to his instruments.

"I can't say that I expected this particular development, but I know what they are doing and I am not surprised," Stone said, coolly. "They have discovered the thought band and are broadcasting such an interference on it that no human being not protected against it can think intelligently. There, I have expanded our zone to cover the whole ship. I hope that they don't find out for a few minutes that we are immune, and I don't think they can, as I have so adjusted the screen that it is now absorbing instead of radiating.

"Tell the captain to put the ship into heaviest possible battle order, everything full on, as soon as the men can handle themselves. Then I want to make a few suggestions."

"What happened, anyway?" the Communications Officer, semi-conscious now, was demanding. "Something hit me and tore my brain apart—I couldn't think, couldn't do a thing. My mind was all chewed up by curly pinwheels. . . ."

Throughout the vast battleship of space men raved briefly in delirium; but, the cause removed, recovery was rapid and complete. Martin explained matters to the captain, that worthy issued orders, and soon the flagship had in readiness all her weapons, both of defense and of offense.

"Doctor Stone, who knows more about the automatons than does any other human being, will tell us what to do next," the Flight Director said.

"The first thing to do is to locate them," Stone, now temporary commander, stated crisply. "They have taken over at least one of our vessels, probably one close to us, so as to be near the center of the formation. Radio room, put out tracers on wave point oh oh two seven one . . ." He went on to give exact and highly technical instructions as to the tuning of the detectors.

"We have found them, sir," soon came the welcome report. "One ship, the *Dresden*, coordinates 42-79-63."

"That makes it bad—very bad," Stone, reflected, audibly. "We can't expand the zone to release another ship from the control of the robots without enveloping the

Dresden and exposing ourselves. Can't surprise them—they're ready for anything. It's rather long range, too." The vessels of the Fleet were a thousand miles apart, being in open order for high-velocity flight in open space. "Torpedoes would be thrown off by her meteorite deflectors. Only one thing to do, Captain—close in and tear into her with everything you've got."

"But the men in her!" protested Martin.

"Dead long ago," snapped the expert. "Probably been animated corpses for days. Take a look if you want to; won't do any harm now. Radio, put us on as many of the *Dresden*'s television plates as you can—besides, what's the crew of one ship compared to the hundreds of thousands of men in the rest of the Fleet? We can't burn her out at one blast, anyway. They've got real brains and the same armament we have, and will certainly kill the crew at the first blast, if they haven't done it already. Afraid it'll be a near thing, getting away from the sun, even with eleven other ships to help us—"

He broke off as the beam operators succeeded in making connection briefly with the plates of the *Dresden*. One glimpse, then the visibeams were cut savagely, but that glimpse was enough. They saw that their sistership was manned completely by automatons. In her every compartment men, all too plainly dead, lay wherever they had chanced to fall. The captain swore a startled oath, then bellowed orders; and the flagship, driving projectors fiercely aflame, rushed to come to grips with the *Dresden*.

"You intimated something about help," Martin suggested. "Can you release some of the other ships from the automaton's yoke, after all?"

"Got to—or roast. This is bound to be a battle of attrition—we can't crush her screens alone until her power is exhausted and we'll be in the sun long before then. I see only one possible way out. We'll have to build a neutralizing generator for every lifeboat this ship carries, and send each one out to release one other ship in our Fleet from the robot's grip. Eleven boats—that'll make twelve to concentrate on her—about all that could attack at once, anyway. That way will take so much time that it will certainly be touch-and-go, but it's the only thing we can do, as far as I can see. Give me ten good radio men and some mechanics, and we'll get at it."

While the technicians were coming on the run Stone issued final instructions:

"Attack with every weapon you can possibly use. Try to break down the *Dresden*'s meteorite shields, so that you can use our shells and torpedoes. Burn every gram of fuel that your generators will take. Don't try to save it. The more you burn the more they'll have to, and the quicker we can take 'em. We can refuel you easily enough from the other vessels if we get away."

Then, while Stone and his technical experts labored upon the generators of the screens which were to protect eleven more of the gigantic vessels against the thought-destroying radiations of the automatons, and while the computers calculated, minute by minute, the exact progress of the Fleet toward the blazing sun, the flagship *Washington* drove in upon the rebellious *Dresden*, her main forward battery furiously aflame. Drove in until the repellor-screens of the two vessels locked and buckled. Then Captain Malcolm really opened up.

That grizzled four-striper had been at a loss—knowing little indeed of the oscillatory nature of thought and still less of the abstruse mathematics in which Ferdinand Stone took such delight—but here was something that he understood thoroughly. He knew his ship, knew her every weapon and her every whim, knew to the final volt and to the ultimate ampere her Gargantuan capacity both to give it and to take it. He could fight his ship—and how he fought her!

From every projector that could be brought to bear there flamed out against the *Dresden* beams of energy and of a potency indescribable, at whose scintillant areas of contact the defensive screen of the robot-manned cruiser flared into terribly resplendent brilliance. Every type of lethal vibratory force was hurled, upon every usable destructive frequency.

Needle-rays and stabbingly penetrant stilettos of fire thrust and thrust again. Sizzling, flashing planes cut and slashed. The heaviest annihilating and disintegrating beams generable by man clawed and tore in wild abandon.

And over all and through all the stupendously powerful blanketing beams—so furiously driven that the coils and commutators of their generators fairly smoked and that the refractory throats of their projectors glared radiantly violet and began slowly, stubbornly to volatilize—raved out in all their pyrotechnically incandescent might, striving prodigiously to crush by their sheer power the shielding screens of the vessel of the automatons.

Nor was the vibratory offensive alone. Every gun, primary or auxiliary, that could be pointed at the *Dresden* was vomiting smoke- and flame-enshrouded steel as fast as automatic loaders could serve it, and under that continuous, appallingly silent concussion the giant frame of the flagship shuddered and trembled in every plate and member.

And from every launching-tube there were streaming the deadliest missiles known to science; radio-dirigible torpedoes which, looping in vast circles to attain the highest possible measure of momentum, crashed against the *Dresden*'s meteorite deflectors in Herculean efforts to break them down; and, in failing to do so, exploded and filled all space with raging flame and with flying fragments of metal.

Captain Malcolm was burning his stores of fuel and munitions at an appalling rate, careless alike of exhaustion of reserves and of service-life of equipment. All his generators were running at a shockingly ruinous overload, his every projector was being used so mercilessly that not even their powerful refrigerators, radiating the transported heat into the interplanetary cold from the dark side of the ship, could keep their refractory linings in place for long.

And through raging beam, through blasting ray, through crushing force; through storm of explosive and through rain of metal the *Dresden* remained apparently unscathed. Her screens were radiating high into the violet, but they showed no sign of weakening or of going down. Neither did the meteorite deflectors break down. Everything held. Since she was armed as capably as was the flagship and was being fought by inhumanly intelligent monstrosities, she was invulnerable to any one ship of the Fleet as long as her generators could be fed.

Nevertheless, Captain Malcolm was well content. He was

making the *Dresden* burn plenty of irreplaceable fuel, and his generators and projectors would last long enough. His ship, his men, and his weapons could and would carry the load until the fresh attackers should take it over; and carry it they did. Carried it while Stone and his over-driven crew finished their complicated mechanisms and flew out into space toward the eleven nearest battleships of the Fleet.

They carried it while the computers, grim-faced and scowling now, jotted down from minute to minute the enormous and rapidly-increasing figure representing their radial velocity. Carried it while Earth's immense armada, manned by creatures incapable of even the simplest coherent thought or purposeful notion, plunged sickeningly downward in its madly hopeless fall, with scarcely a measureable trace of tangential velocity, toward the unimaginable inferno of the sun.

Eventually, however the shielded lifeboats approached their objectives and expanded their screens to enclose them. Officers recovered, airlocks opened, and the lifeboats, still radiating protection, were taken inside. Explanations were made, orders were given, and one by one the eleven vengeful super-dreadnoughts shot away to join the flagship in abating the Menace of the Machine.

No conceivable structure, however armed or powered, could long withstand the fury of the combined assault of twelve such superb battle craft, and under that awful concentration of force the screens of the doomed ship radiated higher and higher into the ultra-violet, went black, and failed. And, those mighty defences down, the end was practically instantaneous.

No unprotected metal can endure even momentarily the ardour of such beams, and they played on, not only until every plate and girder of the vessel and every nut, bolt, and rivet of its monstrous crew had been blasted out of all semblance to what it had once been, but until every fragment of metal had not only been liquefied, but had been completely volatilized.

At the instant of cessation of the brain-scrambling activities of the automatons the Communications Officer had begun an insistent broadcast. Aboard all of the ships there were many who did not recover—who would be helpless imbeciles during the short period of life left to them— but soon an intelligent officer was at every control and each unit of the Terrestrial Contingent was exerting its maximum thrust at a right angle to its line of fall.

And now the burden was shifted from the fighting staff to the no less able engineers and computers. To the engineers the task of keeping their mighty engines in such tune as to maintain constantly the peak acceleration of three Earth gravities; to the computers that of so directing their ever-changing course as to win every possible centimeter of precious tangential velocity.

Chapter IV

The Sun's Gravity

Ferdinand Stone was hollow-eyed and gaunt from his practically sleepless days and nights of toil, but he was as grimly resolute as ever. Struggling against the terrific weight of three gravities he made his way to the desk of the Chief Computer and waited while that worthy, whose leaden hands could scarcely manipulate the instruments of his profession, finished his seemingly endless calculations.

"We will escape the sun's mighty attraction, Doctor Stone, with approximately half a gravity to spare," the mathematician reported finally. "Whether we will be alive or not is another question. There will be heat, which our refrigerators may or may not be able to handle; there will be radiations which our armor may or may not be able to stop. You, of course, know a lot more about those things than I do."

"Distance at closest approach?" snapped Stone.

"Two point twenty-nine times ten to the ninth meters from the sun's center," the computer shot back instantly. "That is, one million five hundred ninety thousand kilometers—only two point twenty-seven radii—from the arbitrary surface. What do you think of our chances, sir?"

"It will probably be a near thing—very near," the physicist replied, thoughtfully. "Much, however, can be done. We can probably tune our defensive screens to block most of the harmful radiations, and we may be able to muster other defences. I will analyze the radiations and see what we can do about neutralizing them."

"You will go to bed," directed Martin, crisply. "There will be lots of time for that work after you get rested up. The doctors have been reporting that the men who did not recover from the robots' broadcast are dying under this acceleration. With those facts staring us in the face, however, I do not see how we can reduce our power."

"We can't. As it is, many more of us will probably die before we get away from the sun," and Stone staggered away, practically asleep on his feet.

Day after day the frightful fall continued. The sun grew larger and larger, more and ever more menacingly intense. One by one at first, and then by scores, the mindless men of the Fleet died and were consigned to space—a man must be in full control of all his faculties to survive for long an acceleration of three gravities.

The generators of the defensive screens had early been tuned to neutralize as much as possible of Old Sol's most fervently harmful frequencies, and but for their mighty shields every man of the Fleet would have perished long since. Now even those ultra-powerful guards were proving inadequate.

Refrigerators were running at the highest possible overload and the men, pressing as closely as possible to the dark sides of their vessels, were availing themselves of such extra protection of lead shields and the like as could be improvised from whatever material was at hand.

Yet the already stifling air became hotter and hotter, eyes began to ache and burn, skins blistered and cracked under the punishing impact of forces which all the defences could not block. But at last came the long-awaited announcement.

"Pilots and watch-officers of all ships, attention!" the Chief Computer spoke into his microphone through parched and blackened lips. "We are now at the point of tangency.

The gravity of the sun here is twenty-four point five meters per second squared. Since we are blasting twenty-nine point four we are beginning to pull away at an acceleration of four point nine. Until further notice keep your pointers directly away from the sun's center, in the plane of the Ecliptic."

The sun was now in no sense the orb of day with which we upon Earth's green surface are familiar. It was a gigantic globe of turbulently seething flame, subtending an angle of almost thirty-five degrees, blotting out a full fourth of the cone of normally distinct vision.

Sunspots were plainly to be seen; combinations of indescribably violent cyclonic storms and volcanic eruptions in a gaseously liquid medium of searing, eye-tearing incandescence. And everywhere, threatening at times even to reach the fiercely-struggling ships of space, were the solar prominences—fiendish javelins of frenziedly frantic destruction, hurling themselves in wild abandon out into the empty reaches of the void.

Eyes behind almost opaque lead-glass goggles, head and body encased in a multi-layered suit each ply of which was copiously smeared with thick lead paint, Stone studied the raging monster of the heavens from the closest viewpoint any human being had ever attained—and lived. Even he, protected as he was, could peer but briefly; and, master physicist though he was and astronomer-of-sorts, yet he was profoundly awed at the spectacle.

Twice that terrifying mass was circled. Then, air-temperature again bearable and lethal radiations stopped, the gruelling acceleration was reduced to a heavenly one-and-one-half gravities and the vast fleet remade its formation. The automatons and the sun between them had taken heavy toll; but the gaps were filled, men were transferred to equalize the losses of personnel, and the course was laid for distant Earth. And in the Admiral's private quarters two men sat together and stared at each other.

"Well, that's that—so far, so good," the physicist broke the long silence.

"But is their power really broken?" asked Martin, anxiously.

"I don't know," Stone grunted, dourly. "But the pick of

them—the brainiest of the lot—were undoubtedly here. We beat them. . . ."

Martin interrupted.

"*You* beat them, you mean," he said.

"With a lot of absolutely indispensable help from you and your force. But have it your own way—what do words matter? *I* beat them, then; and in the same sense I can beat the rest of them if we play our cards exactly right."

"In what way?"

"In keeping me entirely out of the picture. Believe me, Martin, it is of the essence that all of your officers who know what happened be sworn to silence and that not a word about me leaks out to anybody. Put out any story you please except the truth—mention the name of anybody or anything between here and Andromeda except me. Promise me now that you will not let my name get out until I give you permission or until after I am dead."

"But I'll have to, in my reports."

"You report only to the Supreme Council, and a good half of those reports are sealed. Seal this one."

"But I think. . . ."

"What with?" gruffly. "If my name becomes known my usefulness—and my life—are done. Remember, Martin, I *know* robots. There are some capable ones left, and if they get wind of me in any way they'll get me before I can get them. As things are, and with your help, I can and I will get them all. That's a promise. Have I yours?"

"In that case, of course you have."

And Admiral Alan Martin and Doctor Ferdinand Stone were men who kept their promises.

PIRATES OF SPACE

Interplanentary ships disappear in space without trace, leaving no wreckage behind them . . . whilst a huge invisible planetoid floats unobserved in an orbit around the sun.

Apparently motionless to her passengers and crew, the Interplanetary liner *Hyperion* bored serenely onward through space at normal acceleration. In the railed-off sanctum in one corner of the control room a bell tinkled, a smothered whirr was heard, and Captain Bradley frowned as he studied the brief message upon the tape of the recorder—a message flashed to his desk from the operator's panel. He beckoned, and the second officer, whose watch it now was, read aloud:

"Reports of scout patrols still negative."

"Still negative." The officer scowled in thought. "They've already searched beyond the wildest possible location of wreckage, too. Two unexplained disappearances inside a month—first the *Dione*, then the *Rhea*—and not a plate nor a lifeboat recovered. Looks bad, sir. One might be an accident; two might possibly be a coincidence . . ." His voice died away.

"But at three it would get to be a habit," the captain finished the thought. "And whatever happened, happened quick. Neither of them had time to say a word—their location recorders simply went dead. But of course they didn't have our detector screens nor our armament. According to the observatories we're in clear ether, but I wouldn't trust them from Tellus to Luna. You have given the new orders, of course?"

"Yes, sir. Detectors full out, all three courses of defensive screen on the trips, projectors manned, suits on the hooks. Every object detected to be investigated immedi-

77

ately—if vessels, they are to be warned to stay beyond extreme range. Anything entering the fourth zone is to be rayed."

"Right—we are going through!"

"But no known type of vessel could have made away with them without detection," the second officer argued. "I wonder if there isn't something in those wild rumors we've been hearing lately?"

"Bah! Of course not!" snorted the captain. "Pirates in ships faster than light—sub-ethereal rays—nullification of gravity mass without inertia—ridiculous! Proved impossible, over and over again. No, sir, if pirates are operating in space—and it looks very much like it—they won't get far against a good big battery full of kilowatt-hours behind three courses of heavy screen, and good gunners behind multiplex projectors. They're good enough for anybody. Pirates, Neptunians, angels, or devils—in ships or on broomsticks—if they tackle the *Hyperion* we'll burn them out of the ether!"

Leaving the captain's desk, the watch officer resumed his tour of duty. The six great lookout plates into which the alert observers peered were blank, their far-flung ultra-sensitive detector screens encountering no obstacle—the ether was empty for thousands upon thousands of kilometers. The signal lamps upon the pilot's panel were dark, its warning bells were silent. A brilliant point of white light in the center of the pilot's closely ruled micrometer grating, exactly upon the cross-hairs of his directors, showed that the immense vessel was precisely upon the calculated course laid down by the automatic integrating course plotters. Everything was quiet and in order.

"All's well, sir," he reported briefly to Captain Bradley—but all was not well.

Danger—more serious by far in that it was not external—was even then, all unsuspected, gnawing at the great ship's vitals. In a locked and shielded compartment, deep down in the interior of the liner, was the great air purifier. Now a man leaned against the primary duct—the aorta through which flowed the stream of pure air supplying the entire vessel. This man, grotesque in full panoply of space armor, leaned against the duct, and as he leaned a drill bit deeper and deeper into the steel wall of the pipe. Soon it broke through, and the slight rush of air was stopped by the insertion of a tightly fitting rubber tube. The tube terminated in a heavy rubber balloon, which surrounded a frail glass bulb. The man stood tense, one hand holding before his silica-and-steel-helmeted head a large pocket chronometer, the other lightly grasping the balloon. A sneering grin was upon his face as he waited the exact second of action—the carefully predetermined instant when his right hand, closing, would shatter the fragile flask and force its contents into the primary air stream of the *Hyperion!*

Far above, in the main saloon, the regular evening dance was in full swing. The ship's orchestra crashed into silence, there was a patter of applause, and Clio Marsden, radiant belle of the voyage, led her partner out on to the promenade and up to one of the observation plates.

"Oh, we can't see the Earth any more!" she exclaimed. "Which way do you turn this, Mr. Costigan?"

"Like this," and Conway Costigan, burly young First Officer of the liner, turned the dials. "There—this plate is looking back, or down, at Tellus; this other one is looking ahead."

Earth was a brilliantly shining crescent far beneath the flying vessel. Above her, ruddy Mars and silvery Jupiter blazed in splendor ineffable against a background of utterly indescribable blackness—a background thickly besprinkled with dimensionless points of dazzling brilliance which were the stars.

"Oh, isn't it wonderful!" breathed the girl, awed. "Of course, I suppose that it's old stuff to you, but I'm a ground-gripper, you know, and I could look at it forever, I think. That's why I want to come out here after every dance. You know, I . . ."

Her voice broke off suddenly, with a queer, rasping catch, as she seized his arm in a frantic clutch and as quickly went limp. He stared at her sharply, and understood instantly the message written in her eyes—eyes now enlarged, staring, hard, brilliant, and full of soul-searching terror as she slumped down, helpless but for his support. In the act of exhaling as he was, lungs almost entirely empty, yet

79

he held his breath until he had seized the microphone from his belt and had snapped the lever to "emergency."

"Control room!" he gasped then, and every speaker throughout the great cruiser of the void blared out the warning as he forced his already evacuated lungs to absolute emptiness. "Vee-Two Gas! Get tight!"

Writhing and twisting in his fierce struggle to keep his lungs from gulping in a draft of that noxious atmosphere, and with the unconscious form of the girl draped limply over his left arm, Costigan leaped towards the portal of the nearest lifeboat. Orchestra instruments crashed to the floor and dancing couples fell and sprawled inertly while the tortured First Officer swung the door of the lifeboat open and dashed across the tiny room to the air-valves. Throwing them wide open, he put his mouth to the orifice and let his laboring lungs gasp their eager fill of the cold blast roaring from the tanks. Then, air-hunger partially assuaged, he again held his breath, broke open the emergency locker, donned one of the space-suits always kept there, and opened its valves wide in order to flush out of his uniform any lingering trace of the lethal gas.

He then leaped back to his companion. Shutting off the air, he released a stream of pure oxygen, held her face in it, and made shift to force some of it into her lungs by compressing and releasing her chest against his own body. Soon she drew a spasmodic breath, choking and coughing, and he again changed the gaseous stream to one of pure air, speaking urgently as she showed signs of returning consciousness.

"Stand up!" he snapped. "Hang on to this brace and keep your face in this air-stream until I get a suit around you! Got me!"

She nodded weakly, and, assured that she could hold herself at the valve, it was the work of only a minute to encase her in one of the protective coverings. Then, as she sat upon a bench, recovering her strength, he flipped on the lifeboat's visiphone projector and shot its invisible beam up into the control room, where he saw space-armored figures curiously busy at the panels.

"Dirty work at the cross-roads!" he blazed to his captain, man to man—formality disregarded, as it so often was in the Triplanetary service. "There's skulduggery afoot somewhere in our primary air! Maybe that's the way they got those other two ships—pirates! Might have been a timed bomb—don't see how anybody could have stowed away down there through the inspections, and nobody but Franklin can neutralize the shield of the air room—but I'm going to look around, anyway. Then I'll join you fellows up there."

"What was it?" the shaken girl asked. "I think that I remember your saying "Vee-Two gas." That's forbidden! Anyway, I owe you my life, Conway, and I'll never forget it—never. Thanks—but the others—how about all the rest of us?"

"It was Vee-Two, and it is forbidden," Costigan replied grimly, eyes fast upon the flashing plate, whose point of projection was now deep in the bowels of the vessel. "The penalty for using it or having it is death on sight. Gangsters and pirates use it, since they have nothing to lose, being on the death list already. As for your life, I haven't saved it yet—you may wish I'd let it ride before we get done. The others are too far gone for oxygen—couldn't have brought even you around in a few more seconds, quick as I got to you. But there's a sure antidote—we all carry it in a lock-box in our armor—and we all know how to use it, because crooks all use Vee-Two and so we're always expecting it. But since the air will be pure again in half an hour we'll be able to revive the others easily enough if we can get by with whatever is going to happen next. There's the bird that did it, right in the air-room. It's the Chief Engineer's suit, but that isn't Franklin that's in it. Some passenger—disguised—slugged the Chief—took his suit and projectors—hole in duct—p-s-s-t! All washed out! Maybe that's all he was scheduled to do to us in this performance, but he'll do something else in his life."

"Don't go down there!" protested the girl. "His armor is *so* much better than that emergency suit you are wearing, and he's got Mr. Franklin's Lewiston, besides!"

"Don't be an idiot!" he snapped. "We can't have a live pirate aboard—we're going to be altogether too busy with outsiders directly. Don't worry, I'm not going to give him a break. I'll take a Standish—I'll rub him out like a blot. Stay right here until I come back after you," he commanded, and the heavy door of the lifeboat clanged shut behind him as he leaped out into the promenade.

Straight across the saloon he made his way, paying no attention to the inert forms scattered here and there. Going up to a blank wall, he manipulated an almost invisible dial set flush with its surface, swung a heavy door aside, and lifted out the Standish—a fearsome weapon. Squat, huge, and heavy, it resembled somewhat an overgrown machine rifle, but one possessing a thick, short telescope, with several opaque condensing lenses and parabolic reflectors. Laboring under the weight of the thing, he strode along corridors and clambered heavily down short stairways. Finally he came to the purifier room, and grinned savagely as he saw the greenish haze of light obscuring the door and walls—the shield was still in place; the pirate was still inside, still flooding with the terrible Vee-Two the *Hyperion*'s primary air.

He set his peculiar weapon down, unfolded its three massive legs, crouched down behind it, and threw in a switch. Dull red beams of frightful intensity shot from the reflectors and sparks, almost of lightning proportions, leaped snapping, the conflict went on for seconds, then, under the superior force of the Standish, the greenish radiance gave way. Behind it the metal of the door ran the gamut of color—red, yellow, blinding white—then literally exploded; molten, vaporized, burned away. Through the aperture thus made Costigan could plainly see the pirate in the space-armor of the chief engineer—an armor which was proof against rifle fire and which could reflect and neutralize for some little time even the terrific beam Costigan was employing. Nor was the pirate unarmed—a vicious flare of incandescence leaped from his Lewiston, to spend its force in spitting, cracking pyrotechnics against the ether-wall of the squat and monstrous Standish. But Costigan's infernal engine did not rely only upon vibratory destruction. At almost the first flash of the pirate's weapon the officer touched a trigger, there was a double report, ear-shattering in that narrowly confined space, and the pirate's body literally flew into mist as a half-kilogram shell tore through his armor and exploded. Costigan shut off his beam, and with not the slightest softening of one hard lineament stared around the air-room; making sure that no serious damage had been done to the vital machinery of the air-purifier—the very lungs of the great spaceship.

Dismounting the Standish, he lugged it back up to the main saloon, replaced it in its safe, and again set the combination lock. Thence to the lifeboat, where Clio cried out in relief as she saw that he was unhurt.

"Oh, Conway, I've been so afraid something would happen to you!" she exclaimed, as he led her rapidly upward towards the control room. "Of course you . . ." she paused.

"Sure," he replied, laconically. "Nothing to it. How do you feel—about back to normal?"

"All right, I think, except for being scared to death and just about out of control. I don't suppose that I'll be good for anything, but whatever I can do, count me in on."

"Fine—you may be needed, at that. Everybody's out, apparently, except those like me, who had a warning and could hold their breath until they got to their suits."

"But how did you know what it was? You can't see it, nor smell it, nor anything."

"You inhaled a second before I did, and I saw your eyes. I've been in it before—and when you see a man get a jolt of that stuff just once, you never forget it. The engineers down below got it first, of course—it must have wiped them out. Then we got it in the saloon. Your passing out warned me, and luckily I had enough breath left to give the word. Quite a few of the fellows up above should have had time to get away—we'll see 'em all in the control room."

"I suppose that was why you revived me—in payment for so kindly warning you of the gas attack?" The girl laughed; shaky, but game.

"Something like that, probably," he answered, lightly. "Here we are—now we'll soon find out what's going to happen next."

In the control room they saw at least a dozen armored figures; not now rushing about, but seated at their instruments, tense and ready. Fortunate it was that Costigan—veteran of space as he was, though young in years—had been down in the saloon; fortunate that he had been familiar with that horrible outlawed gas; fortunate that he had had presence of mind enough and sheer physical stamina enough to send his warning without allowing one paralyzing trace to enter his own lungs. Captain Bradley, the men on watch, and several other officers in their quarters or in the wardrooms—space-hardened veterans all —had obeyed instantly and without question the amplifiers' gasped command to "get tight." Exhaling or inhaling, their airpassages had snapped shut as that dread "Vee-Two" was heard, and they had literally jumped into their armored suits of space—flushing them out with volume after volume of unquestionable air, holding their breath to the last possible second, until their straining lungs could endure no more.

Costigan waved the girl to a vacant bench, cautiously changing into his own armor from the emergency suit he had been wearing, and approached the captain.

"Anything in sight, sir?" he asked, saluting. "They should have started something before this."

"They've started, but we can't locate them. We tried to send out a general sector alarm, but had hardly started when they blanketed our wave. Look at that!"

Following the captain's eyes, Costigan stared at the high powered set of the ship's operator. Upon the plate, instead of a moving, living, three-dimensional picture, there was a flashing glare of blinding white light; from the speaker, instead of intelligible speech, was issuing a roaring, crackling stream of noise.

"It's impossible!" Bradley burst out, violently. "There's not a gram of metal inside the fourth zone—within a hundred thousand kilometers—and yet they must be close to send such a wave as that. But the Second thinks not— what do you think, Costigan?" The bluff commander, reactionary and of the old school as was his breed, was furious—baffled, raging inwardly to come to grips with the invisible and indetectable foe. Face to face with the inexplicable, however, he listened to the younger men with unusual tolerance.

"It's not only possible; it's quite evident that they've got something we haven't." Costigan's voice was bitter. "But why shouldn't they have? Service ships never get anything until it's been experimented with for years, but pirates and such always get the new stuff as soon as it's discovered. The only good thing I can see is that we got part of a

84

message away, and the scouts can trace that interference out there. But the pirates know that, too—it won't be long now," he concluded, grimly.

He spoke truly. Before another word was said the outer screen flared white under a beam of terrific power, and simultaneously there appeared upon one of the lookout plates a vivid picture of the pirate vessel—a huge, black torpedo of steel, now emitting flaring offensive beams of force.

Instantly the powerful weapons of the *Hyperion* were brought to bear, and in the blast of full-driven beams the stranger's screens flared incandescent. Heavy guns, under the recoil of whose fierce salvos the frame of the giant globe trembled and shuddered, shot out their tons of high-explosive shell. But the pirate commander had known accurately the strength of the liner, and knew that her armament was impotent against the forces at his command. His screens were invulnerable, the giant shells were exploded harmlessly in mid-space, miles from their objective. And suddenly a frightful pencil of flame stabbed brilliantly from the black hulk of the enemy. Through the empty ether it tore, through the mighty defensive screens, through the tough metal of the outer and inner walls. Every ether-defense of the *Hyperion* vanished, and her acceleration dropped to a quarter of its normal value.

"Right through the battery room!" Bradley groaned. "We're on the emergency drive now. Our rays are done for, and we can't seem to put a shell anywhere near her with our guns!"

But ineffective as the guns, were, they were silenced forever as a frightful beam of destruction stabbed relentlessly through the control room, whiffing out of existence the pilot, gunnery, and lookout panels and the men before them. The air rushed into space, and the suits of the three survivors bulged out into drum-head tightness as the pressure in the room decreased.

Costigan pushed the captain lightly towards a wall, then seized the girl and leaped in the same direction.

"Let's get out of here, quick!" he cried, the miniature radio instruments of the helmets automatically taking up the duty of transmitting speech as the sound discs refused to function. "They can't see us—our ether wall is still up and their spy-rays can't get through it from the outside, you know. They're working from blue-prints, and they'll probably take your desk next," and even as they bounded towards the door, now become the outer seal of an airlock, the pirates' beam tore through the space which they had just quitted.

Through the air lock, down through several levels of passengers' quarters they hurried, and into a lifeboat, whose one doorway commanded the full length of the third lounge —an ideal spot, either for defense or for escape outward by means of the miniature cruiser. As they entered their retreat they felt their weight begin to increase. More and more force was applied to the helpless liner, until it was moving at normal acceleration.

"What do you make of that, Costigan?" asked the captain. "Tractor beams?"

"Apparently. They've got something, all right. They're taking us somewhere, fast. I'll go get a couple of Standishes, and another suit of armor—we'd better dig in," and soon the small room became a veritable fortress, housing as it did those two formidable engines of destruction. Then the first officer made another and longer trip, returning with a complete suit of Triplanetary space armor, exactly like those worn by the two men, but considerably smaller.

"Just as an added factor of safety, you'd better put this on, Clio—those emergency suits aren't good for much in a battle. I don't suppose you ever fired a Standish, did you?"

"No, but I can soon learn how to do it," she replied pluckily.

"Two is all that can work here at once, but you should know how to take hold in case one of us goes out. And while you're changing suits you'd better put on some stuff I've got here—Service Special phones and detectors. Stick this little disc on to your chest with this bit of tape; low down, out of sight. Just under your wishbone is the best place. Take off your wristwatch and wear this one *continuously*—never take it off for a second. Put on these pearls, and wear them all the time, too. Take this capsule and hide it against your skin, some place where it can't be found except by the most rigid search. Swallow it in an emergency—it goes down easily and works just as

86

well inside as outside. It is the most important thing of all—you can get along with it alone if you lose everything else, but without that capsule the whole system's shot to pieces. With that outfit, if we should get separated, you can talk to us—we're both wearing 'em, although in somewhat different forms. You don't need to talk loud—just a mutter will be enough. They're handy little outfits—almost impossible to find, and capable of a lot of things."

"Thanks, Conway—I'll remember that, too," Clio replied, as she turned towards the tiny locker to follow his instructions. "But won't the scouts and patrols be catching us pretty quick? The operator sent a warning."

"Afraid the ether's empty, as far as we're concerned."

Captain Bradley had stood by in silent astonishment during this conversation. His eyes had bulged slightly at Costigan's "we're both wearing 'em," but he had held his peace and as the girl disappeared a look of dawning comprehension came over his face.

"Oh, I see, sir," he said, respectfully—far more respectfully than he had ever before addressed a mere first officer. "Meaning that we both *will* be wearing them shortly, I assume. 'Service Specials'—but you didn't specify exactly *what* Service, did you?"

"Now that you mention it, I don't believe that I did," Costigan groaned.

"That explains several things about you—particularly your recognition of Vee-Two and your uncanny control and speed of reaction. But aren't you . . ."

"No," Costigan interrupted. "This situation is apt to get altogether too serious to overlook any bets. If we get away, I'll take them away from her and she'll never know that they aren't routine equipment. As for you I know that you can and do keep your mouth shut. That's why I'm hanging this junk on you—I had a lot of stuff in my kit, but I flashed it all with the Standish except what I brought in here for us three. Whether you think so or not, we're in a real jam—our chance of getting away is mighty close to zero . . ."

He broke off as the girl came back, now to all appearances a small Triplanetary officer, and the three settled down to a long and eventless wait. Hour after hour they flew through the ether, but finally there was a lurching swing and an abrupt increase in their acceleration. After a short consultation Captain Bradley turned on the visiray set and, with the beam at its minimum power, peered cautiously downward, in the direction opposite to that in which he knew the pirate vessel must be. All three stared into the plate, seeing only an infinity of emptiness, marked only by the infinitely remote and coldly brilliant stars. While they stared into space a vast area of the heavens was blotted out and they saw, faintly illuminated by a peculiar blue luminescence, a vast ball—a sphere so large and so close that they seemed to be dropping downward towards it as though it were a world! They came to a stop, paused, weightless—a vast door slid smoothly aside—they were drawn *upward* through an airlock and floated quietly in the air above a small, but brightly-lighted and orderly city of metallic buildings! Gently the *Hyperion* was lowered, to come to rest in the embracing arms of a regulation landing cradle.

"Well, wherever it is, we're here," remarked Captain Bradley, grimly, and:

"And now the fireworks start," assented Costigan, with a questioning glance at the girl.

"Don't mind me," she answered his unspoken question. "I don't believe in surrendering, either."

"Right," and both men squatted down behind the ether walls of their terrific weapons; the girl prone behind them.

They had not long to wait. A group of human beings—men and to all appearances Americans—appeared unarmed in the little lounge. As soon as they were well inside the room, Bradley and Costigan released upon them without compunction the full power of their frightful projectors. From the reflectors, through the doorway, there tore a concentrated double beam of pure destruction—but that beam did not reach its goal. Yards from the men it met a screen of impenetrable density. Instantly the gunners pressed their triggers and a stream of high-explosive shells issued from the roaring weapons. But shells, also, were futile. They struck the shield and vanished—vanished without exploding and without leaving a trace to show that they had ever existed.

Costigan sprang to his feet, but before he could launch his intended attack a vast tunnel appeared beside him—

something had gone through the entire width of the liner, cutting effortlessly a smooth cylinder of emptiness. Air rushed in to fill the vacuum, and the three visitors felt themselves seized by invisible forces and drawn into the tunnel. Through it they floated, up to and over buildings, finally slanting downward towards the door of a great high-towered structure. Doors opened before them and closed behind them, until at last they stood upright in a room which was evidently the office of a busy executive. They faced a desk which, in addition to the usual equipment of the business man, carried also a bewilderingly complete switchboard and instrument panel.

Seated impassively at the desk there was a grey man. Not only was he dressed entirely in grey, but his heavy hair was grey, his eyes were grey, and even his tanned skin seemed to give the impression of greyness in disguise. His overwhelming personality radiated an aura of greyness—not the gentle grey of the dove, but the resistless, driving grey of the superdreadnought; the hard, inflexible, brittle grey of the fracture of high-carbon steel.

"Captain Bradley, First Officer Costigan, Miss Marsden," the man spoke quietly, but crisply. "I had not intended you two men to live so long. That is a detail, however, which we will pass by for the moment. You may remove your suits."

Neither officer moved, but both stared back at the speaker, unflinchingly.

"I am not accustomed to repeating instructions," the man at the desk continued; voice still low and level, but instinct with deadly menace. "You may choose between removing those suits and dying in them, here and now."

Costigan moved over to Clio and slowly took off her armor. Then, after a flashing exchange of glances and a muttered word, the two officers threw off their suits simultaneously and fired at the same instant; Bradley with his Lewiston, Costigan with a heavy automatic pistol whose bullets were explosive shells of tremendous power. But the man in grey, surrounded by an impenetrable wall of force, only smiled at the fusillade, tolerantly and maddeningly. Costigan leaped freely, only to be hurled backward as he struck that unyielding, invisible wall. A vicious beam snapped him back into place, the weapons were snatched

89

away, and all three captives were held to their former positions.

"I permitted that, as a demonstration of futility," the grey man said, his hard voice becoming harder, "but I will permit no more foolishness. Now I will introduce myself. I am known as Roger. You probably have heard nothing of me: very few Tellurians have, or ever will. Whether or not you two live depends solely upon yourselves. Being something of a student of men, I fear that you will both die shortly. Able and resourceful as you have just shown yourselves to be, you could be valuable to me, but you probably will not—in which case you shall, of course, cease to exist. That, however, in its proper time—you shall be of some slight service to me in the process of being eliminated. In your case, Miss Marsden, I find myself undecided between two courses of action; each highly desirable, but unfortunately mutually exclusive. Your father will be glad to ransom you at an exceedingly high figure, but in spite of that fact I may decide to use you in a research upon sex."

"Yes?" Clio rose magnificently to the occasion. Fear forgotten, her courageous spirit flashed from her clear young eyes and emanated from her taut young body, erect in defiance. "You may think that you can do anything with me that you please, but you can't!"

"Peculiar—highly perplexing—why should that one stimulus, in the case of young females, produce such an entirely disproportionate reaction?" Roger's eyes bored into Clio's; the girl shivered and looked away. "But sex itself, primal and basic, the most widespread concomitant of life in this continuum, is completely illogical and paradoxical. Most baffling—decidedly, this research on sex must go on."

Roger pressed a button and a tall, comely woman appeared—a woman of indefinite age and of uncertain nationality.

"Show Miss Marsden to her apartment," he directed, and as the two women went out a man came in.

"The cargo is unloaded, sir," the newcomer reported. "The two men and the five women indicated have been taken to the hospital."

"Very well, dispose of the others in the usual fashion." The minion went out, and Roger continued, emotionlessly:

90

"Collectively, the other passengers may be worth a million or so, but it would not be worthwhile to waste time upon them."

"What are you, anyway?" blazed Costigan, helpless but enraged beyond caution. "I have heard of mad scientists who tried to destroy the Earth, and of equally mad geniuses who thought themselves Napoleons capable of conquering even the Solar System. Whichever you are, you should know that you can't get away with it."

"I am neither. I am, however, a scientist, and I direct many other scientists. I am not mad. You have undoubtedly noticed several peculiar features of this place?"

"Yes, particularly the artificial gravity and those screens. An ordinary ether-wall is opaque in one direction, and doesn't bar matter—yours are transparent both ways and something more than impenetrable to matter. How do you do it?"

"You could not understand them if I explained them to you, and they are merely two of our smaller developments. I do not intend to destroy your planet Earth; I have no desire to rule over masses of futile and brainless men. I have, however, certain ends of my own in view. To accomplish my plans I require hundreds of millions in gold and other hundreds of millions in uranium, thorium, and radium; all of which I shall take from the planets of this Solar System before I leave it. I shall take them in spite of the puerile efforts of the fleets of your Triplanetary League.

"This structure was designed by me and built under my direction. It is protected from meteorites by forces of my devising. It is indetectable and invisible—ether waves are bent around it without loss or distortion. I am discussing these points at such length so that you may realize exactly your position. As I have intimated, you can be of assistance to me if you will."

"Now just what could you offer any *man* to make him join your outfit?" demanded Costigan, venomously.

"Many things," Roger's cold tone betrayed no emotion, no recognition of Costigan's open and bitter contempt. "I have under me many men, bound to me by many ties. Needs, wants, longings, and desires differ from man to man, and I can satisfy practically any of them. Many men take delight in the society of young and beautiful women, but there are other urges which I have found quite efficient. Greed, thirst for fame, longing for power, and so on, including many qualities usually regarded as 'noble.' And what I promise, I deliver. I demand only loyalty to me, and that only in certain things and for a relatively short period. In all else, my men do *as they please*. In conclusion, I can use you two conveniently, but I do not need you. Therefore you may choose now between my service and—the alternative."

"Exactly what is the alternative?"

"We will not go into that. Suffice it to say that it has to do with a minor research, which is not progressing satisfactorily. It will result in your extinction, and perhaps I should mention that that extinction will not be particularly pleasant."

"I say NO, you . . ." Bradley roared. He intended to give an unexpurgated classification, but was rudely interrupted.

"Hold on a minute!" snapped Costigan. "How about Miss Marsden?"

"She has nothing to do with this discussion," returned Roger, icily. "I do not bargain—in fact, I believe that I shall keep her for a time. She has it in mind to destroy herself if I do not allow her to be ransomed, but she will find that door closed to her until I permit it to open."

"In that case, I string along with the Chief—take what he started to say about you and run it clear across the board for me!" barked Costigan.

"Very well. That decision was to be expected from men of your type." The grey man touched two buttons and two of his creatures entered the room. "Put these men into two separate cells on the second level," he orderd. "Search them; all their weapons may not have been in their armor. Seal the doors and mount special guards, tuned to me here."

Imprisoned they were, and carefully searched; but they bore no arms, and nothing had been said concerning communicators. Even if such instruments could be concealed, Roger would detect their use instantly. At least, so ran his thought. But Roger's men had no inkling of the possibility of Costigan's "Service Special" phones, detectors, and spy-ray—instruments of minute size and of infinitesimal power, but yet instruments which, working as they were below the level of the ether, were effective at great distances and caused no vibrations in the ether by which their use could be detected. And what could be more innocent than the regulation personal equipment of every officer of space? The heavy goggles, the wrist-watch and its supplementary pocket chronometer, the flash-lamp, the automatic lighter, the sender, the money-belt?

All these items of equipment were examined with due care; but the cleverest minds of the Triplanetary Service had designed those communicators to pass any ordinary search, however careful, and when Costigan and Bradley were finally locked into the designated cells they still possessed their ultra-instruments.

In Roger's Planetoid

In the hall Clio glanced around her wildly, seeking even the narrowest avenue of escape. Before she could act, however, her body was clamped as though in a vise, and she struggled, motionless.

"It is useless to attempt to escape, or to do anything except what Roger wishes," the guide informed her somberly, snapping off the instrument in her hand and thus restoring to the thoroughly cowed girl her freedom of motion.

"His lightest wish is law," she continued as they walked down a long corridor. "The sooner you realize that you must do exactly as he pleases, in all things, the easier your life will be."

"But I wouldn't *want* to keep on living!" Clio declared, with a flash of spirit. "And I can *always* die, you know."

"You will find that you cannot," the passionless creature returned, monotonously. "If you do not yield, you will long and pray for death, but you will not die unless Roger wills it. Look at me: I cannot die. Here is your apartment. You will stay here until Roger gives further orders concerning you."

The living automaton opened a door and stood silent and impassive while Clio, staring at her in horror, shrank past her and into the sumptuously furnished suite. The door closed soundlessly and utter silence descended as a pall. Not an ordinary silence, but the indescribable perfection of the absolute silence, complete absence of all sound. In that silence Clio stood motionless. Tense and rigid, hopeless, despairing, she stood there in that magnificent room, fighting an almost overwhelming impulse to scream. Suddenly she heard the cold voice of Roger, speaking from the empty air.

"You are over-wrought, Miss Marsden. You can be of no use to yourself or to me in that condition. I command you to rest; and, to insure that rest, you may pull that cord, which will establish about this room an ether wall: a wall to cut off even this my voice . . ."

The voice ceased as she pulled the cord savagely and threw herself upon a divan in a torrent of gasping, strangling, but rebellious sobs. Then again came a voice, but not to her ears. Deep within her, pervading every bone and muscle, it made itself felt rather than heard.

"Clio?" it asked. "Don't talk yet . . ."

"Conway!" she gasped in relief, every fiber of her being thrilled into new hope at the deep, well-remembered voice of Conway Costigan.

"Keep still!" he snapped. "Don't act so happy! He may have a spy-ray on you. He can't hear me, but he may be able to hear you. When he was talking to you you must have noticed a sort of rough, sandpapery feeling under that necklace I gave you? Since he's got an ether-wall around you the beads are dead now. If you feel anything like that under the wrist-watch, breathe deeply, twice. If you don't feel anything there, it's safe for you to talk, as loud as you please."

"I don't feel anything, Conway!" she rejoiced. Tears forgotten, she was her old, buoyant self again. "So that wall *is* real, after all? I only about half believed it."

"Don't trust it too much, because he can cut it off from the outside any time he wants to. Remember what I told you: that necklace will warn you of any spy-ray in the ether, and the watch will detect anything below the level of the ether. It's dead now, of course, since our three phones are direct-connected; I'm in touch with Bradley, too. Don't be too scared; we've got a lot better chance than I thought we had."

"What? You don't mean it!"

"Absolutely. I'm beginning to think that maybe we've got something he doesn't know exists—our ultra-wave. Of course I wasn't surprised when his searchers failed to find our instruments, but it never occurred to me that I might have a clear field to use them in! I can't quite believe it yet, but I haven't been able to find any indication that he can even detect the bands we are using. I'm going to look around over there with my spy-ray . . . I'm looking at you now—feel it?"

"Yes, the watch feels that way, now."

"Fine! Not a sign of interference over here, either. I can't find a trace of ultra-wave—anything below ether-level, you know—anywhere in the whole place. He's got so much stuff that we've never heard of that I supposed of course he'd have ultra-wave, too; but if he hasn't, that gives us the edge. Well, Bradley and I've got a lot of work to do . . . Wait a minute, I just had a thought. I'll be back in about a second."

There was a brief pause, then the soundless, but clear voice went on:

"Good hunting! That woman that gave you the blue willies isn't alive—she's full of the prettiest machinery and circuits you ever saw!"

"Oh, Conway!" and the girl's voice broke in an engulfing wave of thanksgiving and relief. "It was so unutterably horrible, thinking of what must have happened to her and to others like her!"

"He's running a colossal bluff, I think. He's good, all right, but he lacks quite a lot of being omnipotent. But don't get too cocky, either. Plenty has happened to women here, and men too—and plenty may happen to us unless we put out a few jets. Keep a stiff upper lip, and if you want us, yell. 'Bye!"

The silent voice ceased, the watch upon Clio's wrist again became an unobtrusive timepiece, and Costigan, in his solitary cell far below her tower room, turned his peculiarly goggled eyes towards other scenes. His hands, apparently idle in his pockets, manipulated tiny controls; his keen, highly-trained eyes studied every concealed detail of mechanism of the great globe. Finally, he took off the goggles and spoke in a low voice to Bradley, confined in another windowless room across the hall.

"I think I've got enough dope, Captain. I've found out where he put our armor and guns, and I've located all the main leads, controls, and generators. There are no ether-walls around us here, but every door is shielded, and there are guards outside our doors—one to each of us. They're robots, not men. That makes it harder, since they're undoubtedly connected direct to Roger's desk and will give an alarm at the first hint of abnormal performance. We can't do a thing until he leaves his desk. See that black panel, a little below the cord-switch to the right of your door? That's the conduit cover. When I give you the word, tear that off and you'll see one red wire in the cable. It feeds the shield-generator of your door. Break that wire and join me out in the hall. Sorry I had only one of these ultra-wave spies, but once we're together it won't be so bad. Here's what I thought we could do," and he went over in detail the only course of action which his survey had shown to be possible.

"There, he's left his desk!" Costigan exclaimed after the conversation had continued for almost an hour. "Now as soon as we find out where he's going, we'll start something . . . he's going to see Clio, the swine! This changes things, Bradley!" His hard voice was a curse.

"Somewhat!" blazed the captain. "I know how you two have been getting on all during the cruise. I'm with you, but what can we do?"

"We'll do something," Costigan declared grimly. "If he makes a pass at her I'll get him if I have to blow this whole sphere out of space, with us in it!"

"Don't do that, Conway," Clio's low voice, trembling but determined, was felt by both men. "If there's a chance for you to get away and do anything about fighting him, don't mind me. Maybe he only wants to talk about the ransom, anyway."

"He wouldn't talk ransom to *you*—he's going to talk something else entirely," Costigan gritted, then his voice changed suddenly. "But say, maybe it's just as well this way. They didn't find our specials when they searched us, you know, and we're going to do plenty of damage right

96

soon now. Roger probably isn't a fast worker—more the cat-and-mouse type, I'd say—and after we get started he'll have something on his mind besides you. Think you can stall him off and keep him interested for about fifteen minutes?"

"I'm sure I can—I'll do *anything* to help us, or you, get away from this horrible . . ." Her voice ceased as Roger broke the ether-wall of her apartment and walked towards the divan, upon which she crouched in wide-eyed, helpless, trembling terror.

"Get ready, Bradley!" Costigan directed tersely. "He left Clio's ether-wall off, so that any abnormal signals would be relayed to him from his desk—he knows that there's no chance of anyone disturbing him in that room. But I'm holding a beam on that switch, so that the wall is on, full strength. No matter what we do now, he can't get a warning. I'll have to hold the beam exactly in place, though, so you'll have to do the dirty work. Tear out that red wire and kill those two guards. You know how to kill a robot, don't you?"

"Yes—break his eye-lenses and his ear-drums and he'll stop whatever he's doing and send out distress calls . . . Got 'em both. Now what?"

"Open my door—the shield switch is to the right."

Costigan's door flew open and the Triplanetary captain leaped into the room.

"Now for our armor!" he cried.

"Not yet!" snapped Costigan. He was standing rigid, goggled eyes staring immovably at a spot on the ceiling. "I can't move a millimeter until you've closed Clio's ether-wall switch. If I take this ray off it for a second we're sunk. Five floors up, straight ahead down a corridor— fourth door on right. When you're at the switch you'll feel my ray on your watch. Snap it up!"

"Right," and the captain leaped away at a pace to be equalled by few men of half his years.

Soon he was back, and after Costigan had tested the ether-wall of the "bridal suite" to make sure that no warning signal from his desk or his servants could reach Roger within it, the two officers hurried away towards the room in which their space-armor was.

"Too bad they don't wear uniforms," panted Bradley,

short of breath from the many flights of stairs. "Might have helped some as disguise."

"I doubt it—with so many robots around, they've probably got signals that we couldn't understand anyway. If we meet anybody 'it'll mean a battle. Hold it!" Peering through walls with his spy-ray, Costigan had seen two men approaching, blocking an intersecting corridor into which they must turn. "Two of 'em, a man and a robot—the robot's on your side. We'll wait here, right at the corner—when they round it take 'em!' and Costigan put away his goggles in readiness for strife.

All unsuspecting, the two pirates came into view, and as they appeared the two officers struck. Costigan, on the inside, drove a short, hard right blow into the human pirate's abdomen. The fiercely-driven fist sank to the wrist into the soft tissues and the stricken man collapsed. But even as the blow landed Costigan had seen that there was a third enemy, following close behind the two he had been watching, a pirate who was even then training a ray projector upon him. Reacting automatically, Costigan swung his unconscious opponent around in front of him, so that it was into an enemy's body that the vicious ray tore, and not into his own. Crouching down into the smallest possible compass, he straighened out with the lashing force of a mighty steel spring, hurling the corpse straight at the flaming mouth of the projector. The weapon crashed to the floor and dead pirate and living went down in a heap. Upon that heap Costigan hurled himself, feeling for the pirate's throat. But the fellow had wriggled clear, and countered with a gouging thrust that would have torn out the eyes of a slower man, following it up instantly with a savage kick for the groin. No automaton this, geared and set to perform certain fixed duties with mechanical precision, but a lithe, strong man in hard training, fighting with every foul trick known to his murderous ilk.

But Costigan was no tyro in the art of dirty fighting. Few indeed were the maiming tricks of foul combat unknown to even the rank and file of the highly efficient under-cover branch of the Triplanetary Service; and Costigan, a Sector Chief, knew them all. Not for pleasure, sportsmanship, nor million-dollar purses did those secret agents use Nature's weapons. They came to grips only when it could not possibly be avoided, but when they were forced to fight in that fashion they went in with but one grim purpose—to kill, and to kill in the shortest possible space of time. Thus it was that Costigan's opening soon came. The pirate launched a vicious *coup de sabot,* which Costigan avoided by a lightning shift. It was a slight shift, barely enough to make the kicker miss, and two powerful hands closed upon that flying foot in midair like the sprung jaws of a bear-trap. Closed and twisted viciously, in the same fleeting instant. There was a shriek, smothered as a heavy boot crashed to its carefully predetermined mark—the pirate was out, definitely and permanently.

The struggle had lasted scarcely ten seconds, coming to its close just as Bradley finished blinding and deafening the robot. Costigan picked up the projector, again donned his spy-ray goggles, and the two hurried on.

"Nice work, Chief—it must be a gift to rough-house the way you do," Bradley exclaimed. "That's why you took the live one?"

"Practice helps some, too—I've been in brawls before, and I'm a lot younger and maybe a bit faster than you are," Costigan explained briefly, penetrant gaze rigidly to the fore as they ran along one corridor after another.

Several more guards, both living and mechanical, were encountered on the way, but they were not permitted to offer any opposition. Costigan saw them first. In the furious beam of the projector of the dead pirate they were driven into nothingness, and the two officers sped on to the room which Costigan had located from afar. The three suits of Triplanetary space armor had been locked up in a cabinet; a cabinet whose doors Costigan literally blew off with a blast of force rather than consume time in tracing the power leads.

"I feel like something now!" Costigan, once more encased in his own armor, heaved a great sigh of relief. "Rough-and-tumble's all right with one or two, but that generator room is full of grief, and we won't have any too much stuff as it is. We've got to take Clio's suit along—we'll carry it down to the door of the power room, drop it there, and pick it up on the way back."

Contemptuous now of possible guards, the armored pair

strode towards the power plant—the very heart of the immense fortress of space. Guards were encountered, and captains—officers who signalled frantically to their chief, since he alone could unleash the frightful forces at his command, and who profanely wondered at his unwonted silence—but the enemy beams were impotent against the ether walls of that armor; and the pirates, without armor in the security of their own planetoid as they were, vanished utterly in the ravening beams of the twin Lewistons. As they paused before the door of the power room, both men felt Clio's voice raised in her first and last appeal, an appeal wrung from her against her will by the extremity of her position.

"Conway! Hurry! His eyes—they're tearing me apart! Hurry, dear!" In the horror-filled tones both men read clearly—however inaccurately—the girl's dire extremity. Each saw plainly a happy, carefree young Earth-girl, upon her first trip into space, locked inside an ether-wall with an overbrained, under-conscienced human machine—a super-intelligent, but lecherous and unmoral mechanism of flesh and blood, acknowledging no authority, ruled by nothing save his own scientific drivings and the almost equally powerful urges of his desires and passions! She must have fought with every resource at her command. She must have wept and pleaded, stormed and raged, feigned submission and played for time—and her torment had not touched in the slightest degree the merciless and gloating brain of the being who called himself Roger. Now his tantalizing, ruthless cat-play would be done, the horrible grey-brown face would be close to hers—she wailed her final despairing message to Costigan and attacked that hideous face with the fury of a tigress.

Costigan bit off a bitter imprecation. "Hold him just a second longer, sweetheart!" he cried, and the power room door vanished.

Through the great room the two Lewistons swept at full aperture and at maximum power, two rapidly-opening fans of death and destruction. Here and there a guard, more rapid than his fellows, trained a futile projector—a projector whose magazine exploded at the touch of that frightful field of force, liberating instantaneously its thousands upon thousands of kilowatt-hours of stored-up energy.

Through the delicately adjusted, complex mechanisms the destroying beams tore. At their touch armatures burned out, high-tension leads volatilized in crashing, high-voltage arcs, masses of metal smoked and burned in the path of vast forces now seeking the easiest path to neutralization, delicate instruments blew up, copper ran in streams. As the last machine subsided into a semi-molten mass of metal the two wreckers, each grasping a brace, felt themselves become weightless and knew that they had accomplished the first part of their program.

Costigan leaped for the outer door. His the task to go to Clio's aid—Bradley would follow more slowly, bringing the girl's armor and taking care of any possible pursuit. As he sailed through the air he spoke.

"Coming, Clio! All right, girl?" Questioningly, half fearfully.

"All right, Conway." Her voice was almost unrecognizable, broken in retching agony. "When everything went crazy he . . . found out that the ether-wall was up and . . . forgot all about me. He shut it off . . . and seemed to go crazy too . . . he is floundering around like a wild man now . . . I'm trying to keep . . . him from . . . going downstairs."

"Good girl—keep him busy one minute more—he's getting all the warnings at once and wants to get back to his board. But what's the matter with you? Did he . . . hurt you, after all?"

"Oh, no, not that—he didn't do anything but look at me—but that was bad enough—but I'm sick—horribly sick. I'm falling . . . I'm so dizzy that I can scarcely see . . . my head is breaking up into little pieces . . . I just *know* I'm going to die, Conway! Oh . . . oh!"

"Oh, is *that* all!" In his sheer relief that they had been in time, Costigan did not think of sympathizing with Clio's very real present distress of mind and body. "I forgot that you're a ground-gripper—that's just a little touch of space-sickness. It'll wear off directly . . . All right, I'm coming! Let go of him and get as far away from him as you can!"

He was now in the street. Perhaps two hundred feet distant and a hundred feet above him was the tower room in which were Clio and Roger. He sprang directly towards its large window, and as he floated "upward" he corrected his course and accelerated his pace by firing backwards at various angles with his heavy service pistol, uncaring that at the point of impact of each of those shells a small blast of destruction erupted. He missed the window a trifle, but that did not matter—his flaming Lewiston opened a way for him, partly through the window, partly through the wall. As he soared through the opening he trained projector and pistol upon Roger, now almost to the door, noticing as he did so that Clio was clinging convulsively to a lamp-bracket upon the wall. Door and wall vanished in the Lewiston's terrific beam, but the pirate stood unharmed. Neither ravening ray nor explosive shell could harm him—he had snapped on the protective shield whose generator was always upon his person.

When Clio reported that Roger seemed to go crazy and was floundering around like a wild man, she had no idea of how she was understanding the actual situation; for Gharlane of Eddore, then energizing the form of flesh that was Roger, had for the first time in his prodigiously long life met in direct conflict with an overwhelming superior force.

Roger had been sublimely confident that he could detect the use, anywhere in or around his planetoid, of ultra-wave. He had been equally sure that he could control directly and absolutely the physical activities of any number of these semi-intelligent "human beings."

But four Arisians in fusion—Drounli, Brolenteen, Nedanillor, and Kredigan—had been on guard for weeks. When the time came to act, they acted.

Roger's first thought, upon discovering what tremendous and inexplicable damage had already been done, was to destroy instantly the two men who were doing it. He could not touch them. His second was to blast out of existence this supposedly human female, but no more could he touch her. His fiercest mental bolts spent themselves harmlessly three millimeters away from her skin; she gazed into his eyes completely unaware of the torrents of energy pouring from them. He could not even aim a weapon at her! His third was to call for help to Eddore. He could not. The sub-ether was closed; nor could he either discover the

102

manner of its closing or trace the power which was keeping it closed!

His Eddorian body, even if he could recreate it here, could not withstand the environment—this Roger-thing would have to do whatever it could, unaided by Gharlane's mental powers. And, physically, it was a very capable body indeed. Also, it was armed and armored with mechanisms of Gharlane's own devising; and Eddore's second-in-command was in no sense a coward.

But Roger, while not exactly a ground-gripper, did not know how to handle himself without weight; whereas Costigan, given six walls against which to push, was even more efficient in weightless combat than when handicapped by the force of gravitation. Keeping his projector upon the pirate, he seized the first clue to hand—a long, slender pedestal of metal—launched himself past the pirate chief. With all the momentum of his mass and velocity and all the power of his good right arm he swung the bar at the pirate's head. That fiercely-driven mass of metal should have taken head from shoulders, but it did not. Roger's shield of force was utterly rigid and impenetrable; the only effect of the frightful blow was to set him spinning, end over end, like the flying baton of an acrobatic drum-major. As the spinning form crashed against the opposite wall of the room Bradley floated in, carrying Clio's armor. Without a word the captain loosened the helpless girl's grip upon the bracket and encased her in the suit. Then, supporting her at the window, he held his Lewiston upon the captive's head while Costigan propelled him towards the opening. Both men knew that Roger's shield of force must be threatened every instant—that if he were allowed to release it he probably would bring to bear a hand-weapon even superior to their own.

Braced against the wall, Costigan sighted along Roger's body towards the most distant point of the lofty dome of the artificial planet and gave him a gentle push. Then, each grasping Clio by an arm, the two officers shoved mightily with their feet and the three armored forms darted away towards their only hope of escape—an emergency boat which could be launched through the shell of the great globe. To attempt to reach the *Hyperion* and to escape in one of her lifeboats would have been useless; they could not have forced the great gates of the main airlocks and no other exits existed. As they sailed onwards through the air, Costigan keeping the slowly-floating form of Roger enveloped in his beam, Clio began to recover.

"Suppose they get their gravity fixed?" she asked, apprehensively. "And they're raying us and shooting at us!"

"They may have it fixed already. The undoubtedly have spare parts and duplicate generators, but if they turn it on the fall will kill Roger too, and he wouldn't like that. They'll have to get him down with a helicopter or something, and they know that we'll get them as fast as they come up. They can't hurt us with hand-weapons, and before they can bring up any heavy stuff they'll be afraid to use it, because we'll be too close to their shell.

"I wish we could have brought Roger along," he continued, savagely, to Bradley. "But you were right, of course—it'd be altogether too much like a rabbit capturing a wildcat. My Lewiston's about done right now, and there can't be much left of yours—what he'd do to us would be a sin and a shame."

Now at the great wall, the two men heaved mightily upon a lever, the gate of the emergency port swung slowly open, and they entered the miniature cruiser of the void. Costigan, familiar with the mechanism of the craft from careful study from his prison cell, manipulated the controls. Through gate after massive gate they went, until finally they were out in open space, shooting towards distant Tellus at the maximum acceleration of which their small craft was capable.

Costigan cut the other two phones out of circuit and spoke, his attention fixed upon some extremely distant point.

"Samms!" he called sharply. "Costigan. We're out . . . all right . . . yes . . . sure . . . absolutely . . . you tell 'em, Sammy, I've got company here."

Through the sound-discs of their helmets the girl and the captain had heard Costigan's share of the conversation. Bradley stared at his erstwhile first officer in amazement, and even Clio had often heard that mighty, half-mythical name. Surely that bewildering young man must rank high, to speak so familiarly to Virgil Samms, the all-powerful

104

head of the space-pervading Service of the Triplanetary League!

"You've turned in a general call-out," Bradley stared, rather than asked.

"Long ago—I've been in touch right along," Costigan answered. "Now that they know what to look for and know that ether-wave detectors are useless, they can find it. Every vessel in seven sectors, clear down to the scout patrols, is concentrating on this point, and the call is out for all battleships and cruisers afloat. There are enough operatives out there with ultra-waves to locate that globe, and once they spot it they'll point it out to all the other vessels."

"But how about the other prisoners?" asked the girl. "They'll be killed, won't they?"

"Hard telling," Costigan shrugged. "Depends on how things turn out. We lack a lot of being safe ourselves yet."

"What's worrying me mostly is our own chance," Bradley assented. "They will chase us, of course."

"Sure, and they'll have more speed than we have. Depends on how far away the nearest Triplanetary vessels are. But we've done everything we can do, for now."

Silence fell, and Costigan cut in Clio's phone and came over to the seat upon which she was reclining, white and stricken—worn out by the horrible and terrifying ordeals of the last few hours. As he seated himself beside her she blushed vividly, but her deep blue eyes met his grey ones steadily.

"Clio, I . . . we . . . you . . . that is," he flushed hotly and stopped. This secret agent, whose clear, keen brain no physical danger could cloud; who had proved over and over again that he was never at a loss in any emergency, however desperate—this quick-witted officer floundered in embarrassment like any schoolboy; but continued, doggedly: "I'm afraid that I gave myself away back there, but . . ."

"We gave ourselves away, you mean," she filled in the pause. "I did my share, but I won't hold you to it if you don't want—but I *know* that you love me, Conway!"

"*Love* you!" the man groaned, his face lined and hard, his whole body rigid. "That doesn't half tell it, Clio. You don't need to hold me—I'm held for life. There never was a woman who meant anything to me before, and there

105

never will be another. You're the only woman that ever existed. It isn't that. Can't you see that it's impossible?"

"Of course I can't—it isn't impossible at all." She released her shields, four hands met and tightly clasped, and her low voice thrilled with feeling as she went on: "You love me and I love you. That is all that matters."

"I wish it were," Costigan returned bitterly, "but you don't know what you'd be letting yourself in for. It's who and what you are and who and what I am that's griping me. You, Clio Marsden, Curtis Marsden's daughter. Nineteen years old. You think you've been places and done things. You haven't. You haven't seen or done anything—you don't know what it's all about. And whom am I to love a girl like you? A homeless spacehound who hasn't been on any planet three weeks in three years. A hard-boiled egg. A trouble-shooter and a brawler by instinct and training. A sp . . ." he bit off the word and went on quickly: "Why, you don't know me at all, and there's a lot of me that you never *will* know—that I can't let you know! You'd better lay off me, girl, while you can. It'll be best for you, believe me."

"But I can't, Conway, and neither can you," the girl answered softly, a glorious light in her eyes. "It's too late for that. On the ship it was just another of those things, but since then we've come really to know each other, and we're sunk. The situation is out of control, and we both know it—and neither of us would change it if we could, and you know that, too. I don't know very much, I admit, but I do know what you thought you'd have to keep from me, and I admire you all the more for it. We 'all honor the Service, Conway dearest—it is only you men who have made and are keeping the Three Planets fit places to live in—and I know that any one of Virgil Samms' assistants would have to be a man in a thousand million . . ."

"What makes you think that?" he demanded sharply.

"You told me so yourself, indirectly. Who else in the three worlds could possibly call him "Sammy?" You are hard, of course, but you must be so—and I never did like soft men, anyway. And you brawl in a good cause. You are very much a *man*, my Conway; a real, *real* man, and I love you! Now, if they catch us, all right—we'll die together, at least!" she finished, intensely.

106

"You're right, sweetheart, of course," he admitted. "I don't believe that I could really let you let me go, even though I know you ought to," and their hands locked together even more firmly than before. "If we ever get out of this jam I'm going to kiss you, but this is no time to be taking off your helmet. In fact, I'm taking too many chances with you in keeping your shields off. Snap 'em on again—they ought to be getting fairly close by this time."

Hands released and armor again tight, Costigan went over to join Bradley at the control board.

"How are they coming, Captain?" he asked.

"Not so good. Quite a ways off yet. At least an hour, I'd say, before a cruiser can get within range."

"I'll see if I can locate any of the pirates chasing us. If I do it'll be by accident; this little spy-ray isn't good for much except close work. I'm afraid the first warning we'll have will be when they take hold of us with a tractor or spear us with a needle. Probably a beam, though; this is one of their emergency lifeboats and they wouldn't want to destroy it unless they have to. Also, I imagine that Roger wants us alive pretty badly. He has unfinished business with all three of us, and I can well believe that his "not particularly pleasant extinction" will be even less so after the way we rooked him."

"I want you to do me a favor, Conway." Clio's face was white with horror at the thought of facing again that unspeakable creature of grey. "Give me a gun or something, please. I don't want him ever to look at me that way again, to say nothing of what else he might do, while I'm alive."

"He won't," Costigan assured her, narrow of eye and grim of jaw. He was, as she had said, hard. "But you don't want a gun. You might get nervous and use it too soon. I'll take care of you at the last possible moment, because if he gets hold of us we won't stand a chance of getting away again."

For minutes there was silence. Costigan surveying the ether in all directions with his ultra-wave device. Suddenly he laughed, and the others stared at him in surprise.

"No, I'm not crazy," he told them. "This is really funny; it had never occurred to me that the ether-walls of all these ships make them invisible. I can see them, of course, with

107

this sub-ether spy, but they can't see us! I knew that they should have overtaken us before this. I've finally found them. They've passed us, and are now tacking around, waiting for us to do something so that they can see us! They're heading right into the Fleet—they think they're safe, of course, but what a surprise they've got coming to them!"

THE VORTEX BLASTER

Like fire, only worse, intra-atomic energy was a good
servant, but a terrible master . . . and unless something
could be done about loose atomic vortices, entire planets
would be destroyed!

Safety devices that do not protect.

The "unsinkable" ships that, before the days of Bergenholm and of atomic and cosmic energy, sank into the
waters of the earth.

More particularly, safety devices which, while protecting
against one agent of destruction, attract magnet-like another and worse. Such as the armored cable within the
walls of a wooden house. It protects the electrical conductors within against accidental external shorts; but, in-
adequately grounded as it must of necessity be, it may
attract and upon occasion has attracted the stupendous
force of lightning. Then, fused, volatized, flaming incandescent throughout the length, breadth, and height of a
dwelling, that dwelling's existence thereafter is to be
measured in minutes.

Specifically, four lightning rods. The lightning rods protecting the chromium, glass, and plastic home of Neal
Cloud. Those rods were adequately grounded, grounded
with copper-silver cables the bigness of a strong man's arm;
for Neal Cloud, atomic physicist, knew his lightning and
he was taking no chances whatever with the safety of his
lovely wife and their three wonderful kids.

He did not know, he did not even suspect, that under
certain conditions of atmospheric potential and of ground-
magnetic stress his perfectly designed lightning-rod system
would become a super-powerful magnet for flying vortices
of atomic disintegration.

And now Neal Cloud, atomic physicist, sat at his desk in a strained, dull apathy. His face was a yellowish-grey white, his tendoned hands gripped rigidly the arms of his chair. His eyes, hard and lifeless, stared unseeingly past the small, three-dimensional block portrait of all that had made life worth living.

For his guardian against lightning had been a vortex-magnet at the moment when a luckless wight had attempted to abate the nuisance of a "loose" atomic vortex. That wight died, of course—they almost always do—and the vortex, instead of being destroyed, was simply broken up into an indefinite number of widely-scattered new vortices. And one of these bits of furious, uncontrolled energy, resembling more nearly a handful of material rived from a sun than anything else with which ordinary man is familiar, darted toward and crashed downward to earth through Neal Cloud's new house.

That home did not burn it; it simply exploded. Nothing of it, in it, or around it stood a chance, for in a fractional second of time the place where it had been was a crater of seething, boiling lava—a crater which filled the atmosphere to a height of miles with poisonous vapors; which flooded all circumambient space with lethal radiations.

Cosmically, the whole thing was infinitesimal. Ever since man learned how to liberate intra-atomic energy, the vortices of disintegration had been breaking out of control. Such accidents had been happening, were happening, and would continue indefinitely to happen. More than one world, perhaps, had been or would be consumed to the last gram by such loose atomic vortices. What of that? Of what real importance are a few grains of sand to an ocean beach five thousand miles long, a hundred miles wide, and ten miles deep?

And even to that individual grain of sand called "Earth"—or, in modern parlance, "Sol Three," or "Tellus of Sol," or simply "Tellus"—the affair was of negligible importance. One man had died; but, in dying, he had added one more page to the thick bulk of negative results already on file. That Mrs. Cloud and her children had perished was merely unfortunate. The vortex itself was not yet a real threat to Tellus. It was a "new" one, and thus it would be a long time before it would become other than a local menace. And well before that could happen—before even the oldest of Tellus' loose vortices had eaten away much of her mass or poisoned much of her atmosphere, her scientists would have solved the problem. It was unthinkable that Tellus, the point of origin, and the very center of Galactic Civilization, should cease to exist.

But to Neal Cloud the accident was the ultimate catastrophe. His personal universe had crashed in ruins; what was left was not worth picking up. He and Jo had been married for almost twenty years and the bonds between them had grown stronger, deeper, truer with every passing day. And the kids. . . . It *couldn't* have happened . . . fate COULDN'T do this to him . . . but it had . . . it could. Gone . . . *gone* . . . GONE.

And to Neal Cloud, atomic physicist, sitting there at his desk in torn, despairing abstraction, with black maggots of thought gnawing holes in his brain, the catastrophe was doubly galling because of its cruel irony. For he was second from the top in the Atomic Research Laboratory; his life's work had been a search for a means of extinguishment of exactly such loose vortices as had destroyed his all.

His eyes focused vaguely upon the portrait. Clear, honest grey eyes . . . lines of character and humor . . . sweetly curved lips, ready to smile or to kiss. . . .

He wrenched his eyes away and scribbled briefly upon a sheet of paper. Then, getting up stiffly, he took the portrait and moved woodenly across the room to a furnace. As though enshrining it he placed the plastic block upon a refractory between the electrodes and threw a switch. After the flaming arc had done its work he turned and handed the paper to a tall man, dressed in plain grey leather, who had been watching him with quiet, understanding eyes. Significant enough to the initiated of the importance of this laboratory is the fact that it was headed by an Unattached Lensman.

"As of now, Phil, if it's QX with you."

The Grey Lensman took the document, glanced at it, and slowly, meticulously, tore it into sixteen equal pieces.

"Uh, uh, Storm," he denied, gently. "Not a resignation. Leave of absence, yes—indefinite—but not a resignation."

111

"Why?" It was scarcely a question; Cloud's voice was level, uninflected. "I won't be worth the paper I'd waste."

"Now, no," the Lensman conceded, "but the future's another matter. I haven't said anything so far, because to anyone who knew you and Jo as I knew you it was abundantly clear that nothing could be said." Two hands gripped and held. "For the future, though, four words were uttered long ago, that have never been improved upon. 'This, too, shall pass.'"

"You think so?"

"I don't think so, Storm—I know so. I've been around a long time. You are too good a man, and the world has too much use for you, for you to go down permanently out of control. You've got a place in the world, and you'll be back—" A thought struck the Lensman, and he went on in an altered tone. "You wouldn't—but of course you wouldn't —you couldn't."

"I don't think so. No I won't—that never was any kind of a solution to any problem."

Nor was it. Until that moment, suicide had not entered Cloud's mind, and he rejected it instantly. His kind of man did not take the easy way out.

After a brief farewell Cloud made his way to an elevator and was whisked down to the garage. Into his big blue DeKhotinsky Sixteen Special and away.

Through traffic so heavy that front-, rear-, and side-bumpers almost touched he drove with his wonted cool skill; even though, consciously, he did not know that the other cars were there. He slowed, turned, stopped, "gave her the oof," all in correct response to flashing signals in all shapes and colors—purely automatically. Consciously, he did not know where he was going, nor care. If he thought at all, his numbed brain was simply trying to run away from its own bitter imaging—which, if he had thought at all, he would have known to be a hopeless task. But he did not think; he simply acted, dumbly, miserably. His eyes saw, optically; his body reacted, mechanically; his thinking brain was completely in abeyance.

Into a one-way skyway he rocketed, along it over the suburbs and into the transcontinental super-highway. Edging inward, lane after lane, he reached the "unlimited" way —unlimited, that is, except for being limited to cars of not

112

less than seven hundred horsepower; in perfect mechanical condition, driven by registered, tested drivers at speeds not less than one hundred and twenty-five miles an hour—flashed his registry number at the control station, and shoved his right foot down to the floor.

Now everyone knows that an ordinary DeKhotinsky Sporter will do a hundred and forty honestly-measured miles in one honestly measured hour; but very few ordinary drivers have ever found out how fast one of those brutal big souped-up Sixteens can wheel. They simply haven't got what it takes to open one up.

"Storm" Cloud found out that day. He held that two-and-a-half-ton Juggernaut on the road, wide open, for two solid hours. But it didn't help. Drive as he would, he could not outrun that which rode with him. Beside him and within him and behind him. For Jo was there. Jo and the kids, but mostly Jo. It was Jo's car as much as it was his. "Babe, the big blue ox," was Joe's pet name for it; because, like Paul Bunyan's fabulous beast, it was pretty nearly six feet between the eyes. Everything they had ever had was that way. She was in the seat beside him. Every dear, every sweet, every luscious, lovely memory of her was there . . . and behind him, just out of eye-corner visibility, were the three kids. And a whole lifetime of this loomed ahead—a vista of emptiness more vacuous far than the emptiest reaches of intergalactic space. Damnation! He couldn't stand much more of—

High over the roadway, far ahead, a brilliant octagon flared red. That meant "STOP!" in any language. Cloud eased up his accelerator, eased down his mighty brakes. He pulled up at the control station and a trimly-uniformed officer made a gesture.

"Sorry, sir," the policeman said, "but you'll have to detour here. There's a loose atomic vortex beside the road up ahead—

"Oh! It's Dr. Cloud!" Recognition flashed into the guard's eyes. "I didn't recognize you at first. It'll be two or three miles before you'll have to put on your armor; you'll know when better than anyone can tell you. They didn't tell us they were going to send for *you*. It's just a little new one, and the dope we got was that they were going to shove it off into the canyon with pressure."

"They didn't send for me." Cloud tried to smile. "I'm just driving around—haven't my armor along, even. So I guess I might as well go back."

He turned the Special around. A loose vortex—new. There might be a hundred of them, scattered over a radius of two hundred miles. Sisters of the one that had murdered his family—the hellish spawn of that accursed Number Eleven vortex that that damnably incompetent bungling ass had tried to blow up. . . . Into his mind there leaped a picture, wiresharp, of Number Eleven as he had last seen it, and simultaneously an idea hit him like a blow from a fist.

He thought. *Really* thought, now; cogently, intensely, clearly. If the could do it . . . could actually blow out the atomic flame of an atomic vortex . . . not exactly revenge, but. . . . By Klono's brazen bowels, it would work—it'd *have* to work—he'd *make* it work! And grimly, quietly, but alive in every fiber now, he drove back towards the city practically as fast as he had come away.

If the Lensman was surprised at Cloud's sudden reappearance in the laboratory he did not show it. Nor did he offer any comment as his erstwhile first assistant went to various lockers and cupboards, assembling meters, coils, tubes, armor, and other paraphernalia and apparatus.

"Guess that's all I'll need, Chief," Cloud remarked, finally. "Here's a blank check. If some of this stuff shouldn't happen to be in usable condition when I get done with it, fill it out to suit, will you?"

"No," and the Lensman tore up the check just as he had torn up the resignation. "If you want the stuff for legitimate purposes, you're on Patrol business and it is the Patrol's risk. If, on the other hand, you think that you're going to try to snuff a vortex, the stuff stays here. That's final, Storm."

"You're right—and wrong, Phil," Cloud stated, not at all sheepishly. "I'm going to blow out Number One vortex with duodec, yes—but I'm *really* going to blow it out, not merely make a stab at it as an excuse for suicide, as you think."

"How?" the big Lensman's query was scepticism incarnate. "It can't be done, except by an almost impossibly

114

fortuitous accident. You yourself have been the most bitterly opposed of us all to these suicidal attempts."

"I know it—I didn't have the solution myself until a few hours ago—it hit me all at once. Funny I never thought of it before; it's been right in sight all the time."

"That's the way with most problems," the Chief admitted. "Plain enough after you see the key equation. Well, I'm perfectly willing to be convinced, but I warn you that I'll take a lot of convincing—and someone else will do the work, not you."

"When I get done you'll see why I'll pretty nearly have to do it myself. But to convince you, exactly what is the knot?"

"Variability," snapped the older man. "To be effective, the charge of explosive at the moment of impact must match, within very close limits, the activity of the vortex itself. Too small a charge scatters it around in vortices which, while much smaller than the original, are still large enough to be self-sustaining. Too large a charge simply rekindles the original vortex—still larger—in its original crater. And the activity that must be matched varies so tremendously, in magnitude, maxima, and minima, and the cycle is so erratic—ranging from seconds to hours without discoverable rhyme or reason—that all attempts to do so at any predetermined instant have failed completely. Why, even Kinnison and Cardynge and the Conference of Scientists couldn't solve it, any more than they could work out a tractor beam that could be used as a tow-line on one."

"Not exactly," Cloud demurred. "They found that it could be forecast, for a few seconds at least—length of time directly proportional to the length of the cycle in question—by an extension of the calculus of warped surfaces."

"Humph!" the Lensman snorted. "So what? What good is a ten-second forecast when it takes a calculating machine an hour to solve the equations. . . . Oh!" He broke off, staring.

"Oh," he repeated, slowly, "I forgot that you're a lightning calculator—a mathematical prodigy from the day you were born—who never has to use a calculating machine even to compute an orbit. . . . But there are other things."

"I'll say there are; plenty of them. I'd thought of the

calculator angle before, of course, but there was a worse thing than variability to contend with. . . ."

"What?" the Lensman demanded.

"Fear," Cloud replied, crisply. "At the thought of a hand-to-hand battle with a vortex my brain froze solid. Fear—the sheer, stark, natural human fear of death, that robs a man of the fine edge of control and brings on the very death that he is trying so hard to avoid. That's what had me stopped."

"Right . . . you may be right," the Lensman pondered, his fingers drumming quietly upon his desk. "And you are not afraid of death—now—even subconsciously. But tell me, Storm, please, that you won't invite it."

"I will not invite it, sir, now that I've got a job to do. But that's as far as I'll go in promising. I won't make any super-human effort to avoid it. I'll take all due precautions, for the sake of the job, if it gets me, what the hell? The quicker it does, the better—the sooner I'll be with Jo."

"You believe that?"

"Implicitly."

"The vortices are as good as gone, then. They haven't got any more chance than Boskone has of licking the Patrol."

"I'm afraid so," almost glumly. "The only way for it to get me is for me to make a mistake, and I don't feel any coming on."

"But what's your angle?" the Lensman asked, interest lighting his eyes. "You can't use the customary attack; your time will be too short."

"Like this," and taking down a sheet of drafting paper, Cloud sketched rapidly. "This is the crater, here, with the vortex at the bottom, there. From the observers' instruments or from a shielded set-up of my own I get my data on mass, emission, maxima, minima, and so on. Then I have them make me three duodec bombs—one on the mark of the activity I'm figuring on shooting at, and one each five per cent over and under that figure—cased in neocarballoy of exactly the computed thickness to last until it gets to the center of the vortex. Then I take off in a flying suit, armored and shielded, say about here. . . ."

"If you take off at all, you'll take off in a suit, inside a one-man flitter," the Lensman interrupted. "Too many in-

116

struments for a suit, to say nothing of bombs, and you'll need more screen than a suit can deliver. We can adapt a flitter for bomb-throwing easily enough."

"QX; that would be better, of course. In that case, I set my flitter into a projectile trajectory like this, whose objective is the center of the vortex, there. See? Ten seconds or so away, at about this point, I take my instantaneous readings, solve the equations at that particular warped surface for some certain zero time. . . ."

"But suppose that the cycle won't give you a ten-second solution?"

"Then I'll swing around and try again until a long cycle *does* show up."

"QX. It will, sometime."

"Sure. Then, having everything set for zero time, and assuming that the activity is somewhere near my postulated value. . . ."

"Assume that it isn't—it probably won't be," the Chief grunted.

"I accelerate or decelerate—"

"Solving new equations all the while?"

"Sure—don't interrupt so—until at zero time the activity, extrapolated to zero time, matches one of my bombs. I cut that bomb loose, shoot myself off in a sharp curve, and Z-W-E-E-E-T—POWIE! She's out!" With an expressive, sweeping gesture.

"You hope," the Lensman was frankly dubious. "And there you are, right in the middle of that explosive, with two duodec bombs outside your armor—or just inside your flitter."

"Oh, no. I've shot them away several seconds ago, so that they explode somewhere else, nowhere near me."

"*I* hope. But do you realize just how busy a man you are going to be during those ten or twelve seconds?"

"Fully." Cloud's face grew somber. "But I will be in full control. I won't be afraid of anything that can happen —*anything*. And," he went on, under his breath, "that's the hell of it."

"QX," the Lensman admitted finally, "you can go. There are a lot of things you haven't mentioned, but you'll probably be able to work them out as you go along. I think I'll go out and work with the boys in the lookout station while you're doing your stuff. When are you figuring on starting?"

"How long will it take to get the flitter ready?"

"A couple of days. Say we meet you there Saturday morning?"

"Saturday, the tenth, at eight o'clock. I'll be there."

And again Neal Cloud and Babe, the big blue ox, hit the road. And as he rolled, the physicist mulled over in his mind the assignment to which he had set himself.

Like fire, only worse, intra-atomic energy was a good servant, but a terrible master. Man had liberated it before he could really control it. In fact, control was not yet, and perhaps never would be, perfect. Up to a certain size and activity, yes. They, the millions upon millions of self-limiting ones, were the servants. They could be handled, fenced in, controlled; indeed, if they were not kept under an exciting bombardment and very carefully fed, they would go out. But at long intervals, for some one of a dozen reasons—science knew *so* little, fundamentally, of the true inwardness of the intra-atomic reactions—one of these small, tame, self-limiting vortices flared, nova-like, into a large, wild, self-sustaining one. It ceased being a servant then, and became a master. Such flare-ups occurred, perhaps, only once or twice in a century on Earth; the trouble was that they were so utterly, damnably *permanent*. They never went out. And no data were ever secured for every living thing in the vicinity of a flare-up died; every instrument and every other solid thing within a radius of a hundred feet melted down into the reeking, boiling slag of its crater.

Fortunately, the rate of growth was slow—as slow, almost, as it was persistent—otherwise Civilization would scarcely have had a planet left. And unless something could be done about loose vortices before too many years, the consequences would be really serious. That was why his laboratory had been established in the first place.

Nothing much had been accomplished so far. The tractor beam that would take hold of them had never been designed. Nothing material was of any use, it melted. Pressors worked, after a fashion: it was by the use of these beams that they shoved the vortices around, off into the waste places—unless it proved cheaper to allow the places

118

where they had come into being to remain waste places. A few, through sheer luck, had been blown into self-limiting bits by duodec. Duodec-aplylatomate, the most powerful, the most frightfully detonant explosive ever invented upon all the known planets of the First Galaxy. But duodec had taken an awful toll of life. Also, since it usually scattered a vortex instead of extinguishing it, duodec had actually caused far more damage than it had cured.

No end of fantastic schemes had been proposed, of course; of varying degrees of fantasy. Some of them sounded almost practical. Some of them had been tried; some of them were still being tried. Some, such as the perennially-appearing one of building a huge hemispherical hull in the ground under and around the vortex, installing an inertialess drive, and shooting the whole neighborhood out into space, were perhaps feasible from an engineering standpoint. They were, however, potentially so capable of making things worse that they would not be tried save as last ditch measures. In short, the control of loose vortices was very much an unsolved problem.

Number One vortex, the oldest and worst upon Tellus, had been pushed out into the Badlands; and there, at eight o'clock on the tenth, Cloud started to work upon it.

The "lookout station," instead of being some such ramshackle structure as might have been deduced from the Lensman's casual terminology, was in fact a fully-equipped observatory. Its staff was not large—eight men worked in three staggered eight-hour shifts of two men each—but the instruments! To develop them had required hundreds of man-years of time and near miracles of research, not the least of the problems having been that of developing shielded conductors capable of carrying truly through five-ply screens of force the converted impulses of the very radiations against which those screens were most effective. For the observatory, and the long approach to it as well, had to be screened heavily; without such protection no life could exist there.

This problem and many others had been solved, however, and there the instruments were. Every phase and factor of the vortex's existence and activity were measured and recorded continuously, throughout every minute of every day of every year. And all of these records were summed up, integrated, into the "Sigma" curve. This curve, while only an incredibly and senselessly tortuous line to the layman's eye, was a veritable mine of information to the initiate.

Cloud glanced along the Sigma curve of the previous forty-eight hours and scowled, for one jagged peak, scarcely an hour old, actually punched through the top line of the chart.

"Bad, huh, Frank?" he grunted.

"Plenty bad, Storm, and getting worse," the observer assented. "I wouldn't wonder if Carlowitz were right, after all—if she ain't getting ready to blow her top I'm a Zabriskan fontema's maiden aunt."

"No periodicity—no equation, of course." It was a statement, not a question. The Lensman ignored as completely as did the observer, if not as flippantly, the distinct possibility that at any moment the observatory and all that it contained might be resolved into their component atoms.

"None whatever," came flatly from Cloud. He did not need to spend hours at a calculating machine; at one glance he *knew*, without knowing how he knew, that no equation could be made to fit even the weighted-average locus of that wildly-shifting Sigma curve. "But most of the cycles cut this ordinate here—seven fifty-one—so I'll take that for my value. That means nine point nine or six kilograms of duodec basic charge, with one five per cent over and one five per cent under that for alternates. Neocarballoy casting, fifty-three millimeters on the basic, others in proportion. On the wire?"

"It went out as you said it," the observer reported. "They'll have 'em here in fifteen minutes."

"QX—I'll get dressed, then."

The Lensman and the observer helped him into his cumbersome, heavily-padded armor. They checked his instruments, making sure that the protective devices of the suit were functioning at full efficiency. Then all three went out to the flitter. A tiny speedster, really; a torpedo bearing the stubby wings and the ludicrous tail-surfaces, the multifarious driving-, braking-, side-, top-, and under-jets so characteristic of the tricky, cranky, but ultra-maneuverable breed. But this one had something that the ordinary speedster or flitter did not carry; spaced around the needle beak there yawned the open muzzles of a triplex bomb-thrower.

More checking. The Lensman and the armored Cloud both knew that every one of the dozens of instruments upon the flitter's special board was right to the hair; nevertheless each one was compared with the master-instrument of the observatory.

The bombs arrived and were loaded in; and Cloud, with a casually-waved salute, stepped into the tiny operating compartment. The massive door—flitters have no airlocks, as the whole midsection is scarcely bigger than an airlock would have to be—rammed shut upon its fiber gaskets, the heavy toggles drove home. A cushioned form closed in upon the pilot, leaving only his arms and lower legs free.

Then, making sure that his two companions had ducked for cover, Cloud shot his flitter into the air and toward the seething inferno which was Loose Atomic Vortex Number One. For it was seething, no fooling; and it was an inferno. The crater was a ragged, jagged hole a full mile from lip to lip and perhaps a quarter of that in depth. It was not, however, a perfect cone, for the floor, being largely incandescently molten, was practically level except for a depression at the center, where the actual vortex lay. The walls of the pit were steeply, unstably irregular, varying in pitch and shape with the hardness and refractoriness of the strata composing them. Now a section would glare into an unbearably blinding white puffing away in sparkling vapor. Again, cooled by an inrushing blast of air, it would subside into an angry scarlet, its surface crawling in a sluggish flow of lava. Occasionally a part of the wall might even go black, into pock-marked scoriae or into brilliant planes of obsidian.

For always, somewhere, there was an enormous volume of air pouring into that crater. It rushed in as ordinary air. It came out, however, in a ragingly-uprushing pillar, as —as something else. No one knew—or knows yet, for that matter—exactly what a loose vortex does to the molecules and atoms of air. In fact, due to the extreme variability already referred to, it probably does not do the same thing for more than an instant at a time.

That there is little actual combustion is certain; that is, except for the forced combination of nitrogen, argon, xenon, and krypton with oxygen. There is, however, consumption: plenty of consumption. And what that incredibly intense bombardment impinges up is . . . is altered. Profoundly and obscuredly altered, so that the atmosphere emitted from the crater is quite definitely no longer air as we know it. It may be corrosive, it may be poisonous in one or another of a hundred fashions, it may be merely new and different; but it is no longer the air which we human beings are used to breathing. And it is this fact, rather than the destruction of the planet itself, which would end the possibility of life upon Earth's surface.

It is difficult indeed to describe the appearance of a loose atomic vortex to those who have never seen one; and, fortunately, most people never have. And practically all of its frightful radiation lies in those octaves of the spectrum which are invisible to the human eye. Suffice it to say, then, that it had an average effective surface temperature of about fifteen thousand degrees absolute—two and one-half times as hot as the sun of Tellus—and that it was radiating every frequency possible to that incomprehensible temperature, and let it go at that.

And Neal Cloud, scurrying in his flitter through that murky, radiation-riddled atmosphere, setting up equations from the readings of his various meters and gauges and solving those equations almost instantaneously in his mathematical-prodigy's mind, sat appalled. For the activity level was, and even in its lowest dips remained, far above the level he had selected. His skin began to prickle and burn. His eyes began to smart and to ache. He knew what those symptoms meant; even the flitter's powerful screens were not stopping all the radiation; even his suit-screens and his special goggles were not stopping what leaked through. But he wouldn't quit yet; the activity might—probably would—take a nose-dive any instant. If it did, he'd have to be ready. On the other hand, it might blow up at any instant, too.

There were two schools of mathematical thought upon that point. One held that the vortex, without any essential change in its physical condition or nature, would keep on growing bigger. Indefinitely, until, uniting with the other vortices of the planet, it had converted the entire mass of the world into energy.

The second school, of which the forementioned Carlowitz was the loudest voice, taught that at a certain stage of development the internal energy of the vortex would become so great that generation-radiation equilibrium could not be maintained. This would, of course, result in an explosion; the nature and consequences of which this Carlowitz was wont to dwell upon in ghoulishly mathematical glee. Neither school, however, could prove its point—or, rather, each school proved its point, by means of unimpeachable mathematics—and each hated and derided the other, loudly and heatedly.

And now Cloud, as he studied through his almost opaque defences that indescribably ravening fireball, that esuriently rapacious monstrosity which might very well have come from the deepest pit of the hottest hell of mythology, felt strongly inclined to agree with Carlowitz. It didn't seem possible that anything *could* get any worse than that without exploding. And such an explosion, he felt sure, would certainly blow everything for miles around into the smitheriest kind of smithereens.

The activity of the vortex stayed high, way too high. The tiny control room of the flitter grew hotter and hotter. His skin burned and his eyes ached worse. He touched a communicator stud and spoke.

"Phil? Better get me three more bombs. Like these, except up around. . . ."

"I don't check you. If you do that, it's apt to drop to a minimum and stay there," the Lensman reminded him. "It's completely unpredictable, you know."

"It may, at that . . . so I'll have to forget the five per cent margin and hit on the nose or not at all. Order me up two more, then—one at half of what I've got here, the other double it," and he reeled off the figures for the charge and the casing of the explosive. "You might break out a jar of burn-dressing, too. Some fairly hot stuff is leaking through."

"We'll do that. Come down, fast!"

Cloud landed. He stripped to the skin and the observer smeared his every square inch of epidermis with the thick, gooey stuff that was not only a highly efficient screen against radiation, but also a sovereign remedy for new radiation burns. He exchanged his goggles for a thicker, darker, heavier pair. The two bombs arrived and were substituted for two of the original load.

123

"I thought of something while I was up there," Cloud informed the observers then. "Twenty kilograms of duodec is nobody's firecracker, but it may be the least of what's going to go off. Have you got any idea of what's going to become of the energy inside that vortex when I blow it out?"

"Can't say that I have." The Lensman frowned in thought. "No data."

"Neither have I. But I'd say that you better go back to the new station—the one you were going to move to if it kept on getting worse."

"But the instruments . . ." the Lensman was thinking, not of the instruments themselves, which were valueless in comparison with life, but of the records those instruments would make. Those records were priceless.

"I'll have everything on the tapes in the flitter," Cloud reminded.

"But suppose. . . ."

"That the flitter stops one, too—or doesn't stop it, rather? In that case, your back station won't be there, either, so it won't make any difference." How mistaken Cloud was!

"QX," the Chief decided. "We'll leave when you do just in case."

Again in air, Cloud found that the activity, while still high, was not too high, but that it was fluctuating too rapidly. He could not get even five seconds of trustworthy prediction, to say nothing of ten. So he waited, as close as he dared remain to that horrible center of disintegration.

The flitter hung poised in air, motionless, upon softly hissing under-jets. Cloud knew to a fraction his height above the ground. He knew to a fraction his distance from the vortex. He knew with equal certainty the density of the atmosphere and the exact velocity and direction of the wind. Hence, since he could also read closely enough the momentary variations in the cyclonic storms within the crater, he could compute very easily the course and velocity necessary to land the bomb in the exact center of the vortex at any given instant of time. The hard part—the thing that no one had as yet succeeded in doing—was to predict, for a time far enough ahead to be of any use, a usably close approximation to the vortex's quantitative activity. For, as has been said, he had to over-blast, rather than under-, if he could not hit it "on the nose:" to under-blast would scatter it all over the state.

Therefore Cloud concentrated upon the dials and gauges before him; concentrated with every fiber of his being and every cell of his brain.

Suddenly, almost imperceptibly, the Sigma curve gave signs of flattening out. In that instant Cloud's mind pounced. Simultaneous equations: nine of them, involving nine unknowns. An integration in four dimensions. No matter—Cloud did not solve them laboriously, one factor at a time. Without knowing how he had arrived at it, he knew the answer; just as the Posenian or the Rigellian is able to perceive every separate component particle of an opaque, three-dimensional solid, but without being able to explain to anyone how his sense of perception works. It just *is*, that's all.

Anyway, by virtue of whatever sense or ability it is which makes a mathematical prodigy what he is, Cloud knew that in exactly eight and three-tenth seconds from that observed instant the activity of the vortex would be slightly—but not too far—under the coefficient of his heaviest bomb. Another flick of his mental trigger and he knew the exact velocity he would require. His hand swept over the studs, his right foot tramped down, hard, upon the firing lever; and, even as the quivering flitter shot forward under eight Tellurian gravities of acceleration, he knew to the thousandth of a second how long he would have to hold that acceleration to attain that velocity. While not really long—in seconds—it was much too long for com-fort. It took him much closer to the vortex than he wanted to be; in fact, it took him right out over the crater itself.

But he stuck to the calculated course, and at the pre-cisely correct instant he cut his drive and released his largest bomb. Then, so rapidly that it was one blur of speed, he again kicked on his eight G's of drive and started to whirl around as only a speedster or a flitter can whirl. Practically unconscious from the terrific resultant of the linear and angular accelerations, he ejected the two smaller bombs. He did not care particularly where they lit, just so they didn't light in the crater or near the observatory, and he had already made certain of that. Then, without waiting even to finish the whirl or to straighten her out in level flight, Cloud's still-flying hand darted toward the switch whose closing would energize the Bergenholm and make the flitter inertialess.

Too late. Hell was out for noon, with the little speedster still inert. Cloud had moved fast, too; trained mind and trained body had been working at top speed and in perfect coordination. There just simply hadn't been enough time. If he could have got what he wanted, ten full seconds, or even nine, he could have made it, But. . . .

In spite of what happened, Cloud defended his action, then and thereafter. Damnitall, he *had* to take the eight-point-three second reading! Another tenth of a second and his bomb wouldn't have fitted—he didn't have the five per cent leeway he wanted, remember. And no, he couldn't wait for another match, either. His screens were leaking like sieves, and if he had waited for another chance they would have picked him up fried to a greasy cinder in his own lard!

The bomb sped truly and struck the target in direct central impact, exactly as scheduled. It penetrated perfectly. The neocarballoy casing lasted just long enough— that frightful charge of duodec exploded, if not exactly at the center of the vortex, at least near enough to the center to do the work. In other words, Cloud's figuring had been close—very close. But the time had been altogether too short.

The flitter was not even out of the crater when the bomb went off. And not only the bomb. For Cloud's vague forebodings were materialized, and more; the staggeringly immense energy of the vortex merged with that of the detonating duodec to form an utterly incomprehensible whole.

In part the hellish flood of boiling lava in that devil's cauldron was beaten downward into a bowl by the sheer, stupendous force of the blow; in part it was hurled abroad in masses, in gouts and streamers. And the raging wind of the explosion's front seized the fragments and tore and worried them to bits, hurling them still faster along their paths of violence. And air, so densely compressed as to be to all intents and purposes a solid, smote the walls of the crater. Smote them so that they crumbled, crushed outward through the hard-packed ground, broke up into jaggedly irregular blocks which hurtled, screamingly, away through the atmosphere.

Also the concussion wave, or the explosion front, or flying fragments, or something, struck the two loose bombs, so that they too exploded and added their contribution to the already stupendous concentration of force. They were not close enough to the flitter to wreck it of themselves, but they were close enough so that they didn't do her—or her pilot—a bit of good.

The first terrific wave buffeted the flitter while Cloud's right hand was in the air, shooting across the panel to turn on the Berg. The impact jerked the arm downward and sidewise, both bones of the forearm snapping as it struck the ledge. The second one, an instant later, broke his left leg. Then the debris began to arrive.

Chunks of solid or semi-molten rock slammed against the hull, knocking off wings and control-surfaces. Gobs of viscous slag slapped it liquidly, freezing into and clogging up jets and orifices. The little ship was hurled hither and yon, in the grip of forces she could no more resist than can the floating leaf resist the waters of a cataract. And Cloud's brain was as addled as an egg by the vicious concussions which were hitting him from so many different directions and so nearly all at once. Nevertheless with his one arm and his one leg and the few cells of his brain that were still at work, the physicist was still in the fight.

By sheer force of will and nerve he forced his left hand across the gyrating key-bank to the Bergenholm switch. He snapped it, and in the instant of its closing a vast, calm peace descended, blanket-like. For, fortunately, the Berg still worked; the flitter and all her contents and appurtenances were inertialess. Nothing material could buffet her or hurt her now; she would waft effortlessly away from a feather's lightest possible touch.

Cloud wanted to faint then, but he didn't—quite. Instead, foggily, he tried to look back at the crater. Nine-tenths of his visiplates were out of commission, but he finally got a view. Good—it was out. He wasn't surprised; he had been quite confident that it would be. It wasn't scattered around, either. It *couldn't* be, for his only possibility of smearing the shot was on the upper side, not the lower.

His next effort was to locate the secondary observatory, where he had to land, and in that too he was successful. He had enough intelligence left to realize that, with practically all of his jets clogged and his wings and tail shot off, he couldn't land his little vessel inert. Therefore he would have to land her free.

And by dint of light and extremely unorthodox use of what jets he had left in usable shape he did land her free, almost within the limits of the observatory's field; and having landed, he inerted her.

But, as has been intimated, his brain was not working so well; he had held his ship inertialess quite a few seconds longer than he thought, and he did not even think of the buffetings she had taken. As a result of these things, however, her intrinsic velocity did not match, anywhere near exactly, that of the ground upon which she lay. Thus, when Cloud cut his Bergenholm, restoring thereby to the flitter the absolute velocity and inertia she had had before going free, there resulted a distinctly anti-climactic crash.

There was a last terrific bump as the motionless vessel collided with the equally motionless ground; and "Storm" Cloud, vortex blaster, went out like the proverbial light.

Help came, of course; and on the double. The pilot was unconscious and the flitter's door could not be opened from the outside, but those were not insuperable obstacles. A plate, already loose, was sheared away; the pilot was carefully lifted out of his prison and rushed to Base Hospital in the "meat-can" already in attendance.

And later, in a private office of that hospital, the grey-clad Chief of the Atomic Research Laboratory sat and waited—but not patiently.

"How is he, Lacy?" he demanded, as the Surgeon-General entered the room. "He's going to live, isn't he?"

"Oh, yes, Phil—definitely yes," Lacy replied, briskly. "He has a good skeleton, very good indeed. The burns are superficial and will yield quite readily to treatment. The deeper, delayed effects of the radiation to which he was exposed can be neutralized entirely effectively. Thus he will not need even a Phillip's treatment for the replacement

128

of damaged parts, except possibly for a few torn muscles and so on."

"But he was smashed up pretty badly, wasn't he? I know that he had a broken arm and a broken leg, at least."

"Simple fractures only—entirely negligible." Lady waved aside with an airy gesture such small ills as broken bones. "He'll be out in a few weeks."

"How soon can I see him?" the Lensman-physicist asked. "There are some important things to take up with him, and I've got a personal message for him that I must give him as soon as possible."

Lacy pursed his lips. Then:

"You may see him now," he decided. "He is conscious, and strong enough. Not too long, though, Phil—fifteen minutes at most."

"QX, and thanks," and a nurse led the visiting Lensman to Cloud's bedside.

"Hi, Stupe!" he boomed, cheerfully. "Stupe' being short for stupendous, not 'stupid.' "

"Hi, Chief. Glad to see somebody. Sit down."

"You're the most-wanted man in the Galaxy," the visitor informed the invalid, "not excepting even Kimball Kinnison. Look at this spool of tape, and it's only the first one. I brought it along for you to read at your leisure. As soon as any planet finds out that we've got a sure-enough vortex-blower-outer, an expert who can really call his shots—and the news travels mighty fast—that planet sends in a double-urgent, Class A-Prime demand for first call upon your services.

"Sirius IV got in first by a whisker, it seems, but Aldebaran II was so close a second that it was a photo finish, and all the channels have been jammed ever since. Canopus, Vega, Rigel, Spica. They all want you. Everybody from Alsakan to Vandemar and back. We told them right off that we would not receive personal delegations—we had to almost throw a couple of pink-haired Chickladorians out bodily to make them believe that we meant it—and that the age and condition of the vortex involved, not priority or requisition, would govern, QV?"

"Absolutely," Cloud agreed. "That's the only way it could be, I should think."

"So forget about this psychic trauma. . . . No, I don't

129

mean thàt," the Lensman corrected himself hastily. "You know what I mean. The will to live is the most important factor in any man's recovery, and too many worlds need you too badly to have you quit now. Not?"

"I suppose so," Cloud acquiesced, but somberly. "I'll get out of here in short order. And I'll keep on pecking away until one of those vortices finishes what this one started."

"You'll die of old age then, son," the Lensman assured him. "We got full data—all the information we need. We know exactly what to do to your screens. Next time nothing will come through except light, and only as much of that as you feel like admitting. You can wait as close to a vortex as you please, for as long as you please; until you get exactly the activity and time-interval that you want. You will be just as comfortable and just as safe as though you were home in bed."

"Sure of that?"

"Absolutely—or at least, as sure as we can be of anything that hasn't happened yet. But I see that your guardian angel here is eyeing her clock somewhat pointedly, so I'd better be doing a flit before they toss me down a shaft. Clear ether, Storm!"

"Clear ether, Chief!"

And that is how "Storm" Cloud, atomic physicist, became the most narrowly-specialized specialist in all the annals of science: how he became "Storm" Cloud, Vortex Blaster—the Galaxy's only vortex blaster.

TEDRIC

Aided by Llosir, his strange, new god, Tedric enters into battle with Sarpedion, the sacrifice-demanding god of Lomarr in this story of science and swash-buckling adventure.

"The critical point in time of mankind's whole existence is there—RIGHT THERE!" Prime Physicist Skandos slashed his red pencil across the black trace of the chronoviagram. "WHY must man be so stupid? Anyone with three brain cells working should know that for the strength of an individual he should be fed; not bled; that for the strength of a race its virgins should be bred, not sacrificed to propitiate figmental deities. And it would be so easy to straighten things out—nowhere in all reachable time does any other one man occupy such a tremendously—such a uniquely—keystone position!"

"Easy, yes," his assistant Furmin agreed. "It is a shame to let Tedric die with not one of his tremendous potentialities realized. It would be easy and simple to have him discover carburization and the necessary techniques of heat-treating. That freak meteorite need not lie there unsmelted for another seventy years. However, simple carburization was not actually discovered until two generations later, by another smith in another nation; and you know, Skandos, that there can be no such thing as a minor interference with the physical events of the past. Any such, however small-seeming, is bound to be castastrophically major."

"I know that." Skandos scowled blackly. "We don't know enough about time. We don't know what would happen. We have known how to do it for a hundred years, but have been afraid to act because in all that time no progress whatever has been made on the theory."

He paused, then went on savagely: "But which is better, to have our entire time-track snapped painlessly out of existence—if the extremists are right—or to sit helplessly on our fat rumps wringing our hands while we watch civilization build up to its own total destruction by lithium-tritiide bombs? Look at the slope of that curve—ultimate catastrophe is only one hundred eighty seven years away!"

"But the Council would not permit it. Nor would the School."

"I know that, too. That is why I am not going to ask them. Instead, I am asking you. We two know more of time than any others. Over the years I have found your judgment good. With your approval I will act now. Without it, we will continue our futile testing—number eight hundred eleven is running now, I believe?—and our aimless drifting."

"You are throwing the entire weight of such a decision on me?"

"In one sense, yes. In another, only half, since I have already decided."

"Go ahead."

"So be it."

"Tedric, awaken!"

The Lomarrian ironmaster woke up; not gradually and partially, like one of our soft modern urbanites, but instantaneously and completely, as does the mountain wildcat. At one instant he lay, completely relaxed, sound asleep; at the next he had sprung out of bed, seized his sword and leaped halfway across the room. Head thrown back, hard blue eyes keenly alert, sword-arm rock-steady he stood there, poised and ready. Beautifully poised, upon the balls of both feet; supremely ready to throw into action every inch of his six-feet-four, every pound of his two-hundred-plus of hard meat, gristle, and bone. So standing, the smith stared motionlessly at the shimmering, almost invisible thing hanging motionless in the air of his room, and at its equally tenuous occupant.

"I approve of you, Tedric." The thing—apparition—whatever it was—did not speak, and the Lomarrian did not hear; the words formed themselves in the innermost depths of his brain. "While you perhaps are a little frightened, you are and have been completely in control. Any other man of your nation—yes, of your world—would have been scared out of what few wits he has."

"You are not one of ours, Lord," Tedric went to one knee. He knew, of course, that gods and devils existed; and, while this was the first time that a god had sought him out personally, he had heard of such happenings all his life. Since the god hadn't killed him instantly, he probably didn't intend to—right away, at least. Hence: "No god of Lomarr approves of me. Also, our gods are solid and heavy. What do you want of me, strange god?"

"I'm not a god. If you could get through this grill, you could cut off my head with your sword and I would die."

"Of course. So would Sar . . ." Tedric broke off in the middle of the word.

"I see. It is dangerous to talk?"

"Very. Even though a man is alone, the gods and hence the priests who serve them have power to hear. Then the man lies on the green rock and loses his brain, liver, and heart."

"You will not be overheard. I have power enough to see to that."

Tedric remained silent.

"I understand your doubt. Think, then; that will do just as well. What is it that you are trying to do?"

"I wonder how I can hear when there is no sound, but men cannot understand the powers of gods. I am trying to find or make a metal that is very hard, but not brittle. Copper is no good, I cannot harden it enough. My soft irons are too soft, my hard irons are too brittle; my in-betweens and the melts to which I add various flavorings have all been either too soft or too brittle, or both."

"I gathered that such was your problem. Your wrought iron is beautiful stuff; so is your white cast iron; and you would not, ordinarily, in your lifetime, come to know anything of either carburization or high-alloy steel, to say nothing of both. I know exactly what you want, and I can show you exactly how to make it."

"You can, Lord?" The smith's eyes flamed. "And you will?"

"That is why I have come to you, but whether or not I will teach you depends on certain matters which I have

133

not been able entirely to clarify. What do you want it for—that is, what, basically, is your aim?"

"Our greatest god, Sarpedion, is wrong and I intend to kill him." Tedric's eyes flamed more savagely, his terrifically muscled body tensed.

"Wrong? In what way?"

"In every way!" In the intensity of his emotion the smith spoke aloud. "What good is a god who only kills and injures? What a nation needs, Lord, is *people*—people working together and not afraid. How can we of Lomarr *ever* attain comfort and happiness if more die each year than are born? We are too few. All of us—except the priests, of course—must work unendingly to obtain only the necessities of life."

"This bears out my findings. If you make high-alloy steel, exactly what will you do with it?"

"If you give me the god-metal, Lord, I will make of it a sword and armor—a sword sharp enough and strong enough to cut through copper or iron without damage; armor strong enough so that swords of copper or iron cannot cut through it. They must be so because I will have to cut my way alone through a throng of armed and armored mercenaries and priests."

"Alone? Why?"

"Because I cannot call in help; cannot let anyone know my goal. Any such would lie on the green stone very soon. They suspect me; perhaps they know. I am, however, the best smith in all Lomarr, hence they have slain me not. Nor will they, until I have found what I seek. Nor then, if by the favor of the gods—or by your favor, Lord—the metal be good enough."

"It will be, but there's a lot more to fighting a platoon of soldiers than armor and a sword, my optimistic young savage."

"That the metal be of proof is all I ask, Lord," the smith insisted, stubbornly. "The rest of it lies in my care."

"So be it. And then?"

"Sarpedion's image, as you must already know, is made of stone, wood, copper, and gold—besides the jewels, of course. I take his brain, liver, and heart, flood them with oil, and sacrifice them. . . ."

"Just a minute! Sarpedion is not alive and never has been; does not, as a matter of fact, exist. You just said, yourself, that his image was made of stone and copper and. . . ."

"Don't be silly, Lord. Or art testing me? Gods are spirits; bound to their images, and in a weaker way to their priests, by linkages of spirit force. Life force, it could be called. When those links are broken, by fire and sacrifice, the god may not exactly die, but he can do no more of harm until his priests have made a new image and spent much time and effort in building up new linkages. One point now settled was bothering me; what god to sacrifice him to. I'll make an image for you to inhabit, Lord, and sacrifice him to you, my strange new god. You will be my only god as long as I live. What is your name, Lord? I can't keep on calling you 'strange god' forever."

"My name is Skandos."

"S . . . Sek . . . That word rides ill on the tongue. With your permission, Lord, I will call you Llosir."

"Call me anything you like, except a god. I am *not* a god."

"You are being ridiculous, Lord Llosir," Tedric chided. "What a man sees with his eyes, hears with his ears—especially what a man hears *without* ears, as I hear now—he knows with certain knowledge to be the truth. No mere man could possibly do what you have done, to say naught of what you are about to do."

"Perhaps not an ordinary man of your . . ." Skandos almost said "time," but caught himself ". . . of your culture, but I am ordinary enough and moral enough in my own."

"Well, that could be said of all gods, everywhere." The smith's mien was quiet and unperturbed; his thought was loaded to saturation with unshakable conviction.

Skandos gave up. He could argue for a week, he knew, without making any impression whatever upon what the stubborn, hard-headed Tedric knew so unalterably to be the truth.

"But just one thing, Lord," Tedric went on with scarcely a break. "Have I made it clear that I intend to stop human sacrifice? That there is to be no more of it, even to you? We will offer you anything else—*anything* else—but not

135

even your refusal to give me the god-metal will change my stand on that."

"Good! See to it that nothing ever does change it. As to offerings or sacrifices, there are to be none, of any kind. I do not need, I do not want, *I will not have* any such. That is final. Act accordingly.

"Yes, Lord. Sarpedion is a great and powerful god, but art *sure* that his sacrifice alone will establish linkages strong enough to last for all time?"

Skandos almost started to argue again, but checked himself. After all, the proposed sacrifice was necessary for Tedric and his race, and it would do no harm.

"Sarpedion will be enough. And as for the image, that isn't necessary, either."

"Art wrong, Lord. Without image and temple, everyone would think you a small, weak god, which thought can never be. Besides, the image might make it easier for me to call on you in time of need."

"You can't call me. Even if I could receive your call, which is very doubtful, I wouldn't answer it. If you ever see me or hear from me again, it will be because I wish it, not you." Skandos intended this for a clincher, but it didn't turn out that way."

"Wonderful!" Tedric exclaimed. "All gods act that way, in spite of what they—through their priests—say. I am overwhelmingly glad that you are being honest with me. Hast found me worthy of the god-metal, Lord Llosir?"

"Yes, so let's get at it. Take that biggest chunk of 'metal-which-fell-from-the-sky'—you'll find it's about twice your weight. . . ."

"But I have never been able to work that particular piece of metal, Lord."

"I'm not surprised. Ordinary meteorites are nickel-iron, but this one carries two additional and highly unusual elements, tungsten and vanadium, which are necessary for our purpose. To melt it you'll have to run your fires a lot hotter. You'll also have to have a carburizing pot and willow charcoal and metallurgical coke and several other things. We'll go into details later. That green stone from which altars are made—you can secure some of it?"

"Any amount of it."

"Of it take your full weight. And of the black ore of

which you have occasionally used a little, one-fourth of your weight. . . ."

The instructions went on, from ore to finished product in complete detail, and at its end:

"If you follow these directions carefully you will have a high-alloy-steel—chrome-nickel-vanadium-molybdenum-tungsten steel, to be exact—case-hardened and heat-treated; exactly what you need. Can you remember them all?"

"I can, Lord. Never have I dared write anything down, so my memory is good. Every quantity you have given me, every temperature and step and process and item; they are all completely in mind."

"I go, then. Good-bye."

"I thank you, Lord Llosir. Good-bye." The Lomarrian bowed his head, and when he straightened up his incomprehensible visitor was gone.

Tedric went back to bed; and, strangely enough, was almost instantly asleep. And in the morning after his customary huge breakfast of meat and bread and milk, he went to his sprawling establishment, which has no counterpart in modern industry, and called his foreman and his men together before they began the day's work.

"A strange god named Llosir came to me in the night and showed me how to make better iron," he told them in perfectly matter-of-fact fashion, "so stop whatever you're doing and tear the whole top off of the big furnace. I'll tell you exactly how to rebuild it."

The program as outlined by Skandos went along without a hitch until the heat from the rebuilt furnace began to come blisteringly through the crude shields. Then even the foreman, faithful as he was, protested against such unheard-of temperatures and techniques.

"It *must* be that way!" Tedric insisted. "Run more rods across, from there to there, to hold more hides and blankets. You four men fetch water. Throw it over the hides and blankets and him who turns the blower. Take shorter tricks in the hot places—here, I'll man the blower myself until the heat wanes somewhat."

He bent his mighty back to the crank, but even in that raging inferno of heat he kept on talking.

"Knowst my iron sword, the one I wear, with rubies in

the hilt?" he asked the foreman. That worthy did, with longing; to buy it would take six months of a foreman's pay. "This furnace must stay this hot all day and all of tonight, and there are other things as bad. But 'twill not take long. Ten days should see the end of it"—actually seven days was the schedule, but Tedric did not want the priests to know that—"but for those ten days matters *must* go exactly as I say. Work with me until this iron is made and I give you that sword. And of all the others who shirk not, each will be given an iron sword—this in addition to your regular pay. Dost like the bargain?"

They liked it.

Then, during the hours of lull, in which there was nothing much to do except keep the furious fires fed, Tedric worked upon the image of his god. While the Lomarrian was neither a Phidias nor a Praxiteles, he was one of the finest craftsmen of his age. He had not, however, had a really good look at Skandos' face. Thus the head of the image, although it was a remarkably good piece of sculpture, looked more like that of Tedric's foreman than like that of the real Skandos. And with the head, any resemblance at all to Skandos ceased. The rest of the real Skandos was altogether too small and too pitifully weak to be acceptable as representative of any Lomarrian's god; hence the torso and limbs of the gleaming copper statue were wider, thicker, longer, bigger, and even more fantastically muscled than were Tedric's own. Also, the figure was hollow; filled with sand throughout except for an intricately-carved grey sandstone brain and red-painted hardwood liver and heart.

"They come, master, to the number of eleven," his look-out boy came running with news at mid-afternoon of the seventh day. "One priest in copper, ten Tarkians in iron, a five each of bowmen and spearmen."

Tedric did not have to tell the boy where to go or what to do or to hurry about it; as both ran for the ironmaster's armor the youngster was two steps in the lead. It was evident, too, that he had served as squire before, and frequently; for in seconds the erstwhile half-naked blacksmith was fully clothed in iron.

Thus it was an armored knight, leaning negligently upon

a fifteen-pound forging hammer, who waited outside the shop's door and watched his eleven visitors approach.

The banner was that of a priest of the third rank. Good—they weren't worried enough about him yet, then, to send a big one. And only ten mercenaries—small, short, bandy-legged men of Tark—good enough fighters for their weight, but they didn't weigh much. This wouldn't be too bad.

The group came up to within a few paces and stopped.

"Art in armor, smith?" the discomfited priest demanded. "Why?"

"Why not? 'Tis my habit to greet guests in apparel of their own choosing."

There was a brief silence, then:

"To what do I owe the honor of this visit, priest?" he asked, only half sarcastically. "I paid, as I have always paid, the fraction due."

"True. 'Tis not about a fraction I come. It is noised that a strange god appeared to you, spoke to you, instructed you in your art; that you are making an image of him."

"I made no secret of any of these things. I hide nothing from the great god or his minions, nor ever have. I have nothing to hide."

"Perhaps. Such conduct is very unseemly—decidedly ungodlike. He should not have appeared to you, but to one of us, and in the temple."

"It is un-Sarpedionlike, certainly—all that Sarpedion has ever done for me is let me alone, and I have paid heavily for that."

"What bargain did you make with this Llosir? What was the price?"

"No bargain was made. I thought it strange, but who am I an ordinary man, to try to understand the actions or the reasonings of a god? There will be a price, I suppose. Whatever it is, I will pay it gladly."

"You will pay, rest assured; not to this Llosir, but to great Sarpedion. I command you to destroy that image forthwith."

"You do? Why? Since when has it been against the law to have a personal god? Most families of Lomarr have them."

139

"Not like yours. Sarpedion does not permit your Llosir to exist."

"Sarpedion has nothing to say about it. Llosir already exists. Is the great god so weak, so afraid, so unable to defend himself against a one-man stranger that he. . . ."

"Take care, smith—silence! That is rankest blasphemy!"

"Perhaps; but I have blasphemed before and Sarpedion hasn't killed me yet. Nor will he, methinks; at least until his priests have collected his fraction of the finest iron ever forged and which I only can make."

"Oh, yes, the new iron. Tell me exactly how it is made."

"You know better than to ask that question, priest. That secret will be known only to me and my god."

"We have equipment and tools designed specifically for getting information out of such as you. Seize him, men, and smash that image!"

"HOLD!" Tedric roared, in such a voice that not a man moved. "If anybody takes one forward step, priest, or makes one move toward spear or arrow, your brains will spatter the walls across the street. Can your copper helmet stop this hammer? Can your girl-muscled, fat-bellied priest's body move fast enough to dodge my blow? And most or all of those runty little slavelings behind you," waving his left arm contemptuously at the group, "will also die before they cut me down. And if I die now, of what worth is Sarpedion's fraction of a metal that will never be made? Think well, priest!"

Sarpedion's agent studied the truculent, glaring iron-master for a long two minutes. Then, deciding that the proposed victim could not be taken alive, he led his crew back the way they had come, trailing fiery threats. And Tedric, going back into his shop, was thoroughly aware that those threats were not idle. So far, he hadn't taken too much risk, but the next visit would be different—very different. He was exceedingly glad that none of his men knew that the pots they were firing so fiercely were in fact filled only with coke and willow charcoal; that armor and sword and shield and axe and hammer were at that moment getting their final heat treatment in a bath of oil, but little hotter than boiling water, in the sanctum to which he retired, always alone, to perform the incantations which his men—and hence the priests of Sarpedion—believed as necessary as any other part of the metallurgical process.

That evening he selected a smooth, fine-grained stone and whetted the already almost perfect cutting edge of his new sword; an edge which in cross-section was rather more like an extremely sharp cold-chisel than a hollow-ground razor. He fitted the two-hand grip meticulously with worked and tempered rawhide, thrilling again and again as each touch of an educated and talented finger-tip told him over and over that here was some thing brand new in metal—a real god-metal.

A piece of flat wrought iron, about three-sixteenths by five inches and about a foot long, already lay on a smooth and heavy hardwood block. He tapped it sharply with the sword's edge. The blade rang like a bell; the iron showed a bright new scar; that was all. Then a moderately heavy two-handed blow, about as hard as he had ever dared swing an iron sword. Still no damage. Then, heart in mouth, he gave the god-metal its final test; struck with everything he had, from heels and toes to fingertips. He had never struck such a blow before, except possibly with a war-axe or a sledge. There was a ringing clang, two sundered slabs of iron flew to opposite ends of the room, the atrocious blade went on, half an inch deep into solid oak. He wrenched the weapon free and stared at the unmarred edge. UNMARRED! For an instant Tedric felt as though he were about to collapse; but sheerest joy does not disable.

There was nothing left to do except make the links, hinge-pins, and so on for his armor, which did not take long. Hence, when the minions of Sarpedion next appeared, armored this time in the heaviest and best iron they had and all set to överwhelm him by sheer weight of numbers, he was completely ready. Nor was there palaver or parley. The attackers opened the door, saw the smith, and rushed.

But Tedric, although in plain sight, had chosen the battle-ground with care. He was in a corner. At his back a solid-walled stairway ran up to the second floor. On his right the wall was solid for twenty feet. On his left, beyond the stairwell, the wall was equally solid for twice as far. They would have to come after him, and as he retreated, they would be fighting their way up, and not more than two at a time.

This first swing, horizontal and neck-high, was fully as fierce-driven as the one that had cloven the testpiece and almost ruined his testing-block. The god-metal blade scarcely slowed as it went through armor and flesh and bone. In fact, the helmet and the head within it remained in place upon the shoulders for what seemed like seconds before the body toppled and the arteries spurted crimson jets.

He didn't have to hit so hard, then. Good. Nobody could last very long, the way he had started out. Wherefore the next blow, a vertical chop, merely split a man to the chin instead of to the navel; and the third, a back-hand return, didn't quite cut the victim's head clear off.

And the blows his steel was taking, aimed at head or neck or shoulder, were doing no harm at all. In fact, except for the noise, they scarcely bothered him. He had been designing and building armor for five years, and this was his masterpiece. The helmet was heavily padded; the shoulders twice as much so. He had sacrificed some mobility—he could not turn his head very far in either direction—but the jointing was such that the force of any blow on the helmet, from whatever direction coming, was taken by his tremendously capable shoulders.

The weapons of the mercenaries could not dent, could not even nick, that case-hardened high-alloy steel. Swords bent, broke, twisted; hammers and axes bounced harmlessly off. Nevertheless the attackers pressed forward; and, even though each blow of his devastating sword took a life, Tedric was forced backward up the stairs, step by step.

Then there came about that for which he had been waiting. A copper-clad priest appeared behind the last rank of mercenaries, staring upward at something behind the ironmaster, beckoning frantically. The priest had split his forces; had sent part of them by another way to the second floor to trap him between two groups; had come in close to see the trap sprung. This was it.

Taking a couple of quick, upward, backward steps, he launched himself into the air with all the power of his legs. And when two hundred and thirty pounds of man, dressed in eighty or ninety or a hundred pounds of steel, leaps from a height of eight or ten feet upon a group of other men, those other men go down.

Righting himself quickly. Tedric sprang toward the priest and swung; swung with all the momentum of his mass and speed and all the power of his giant frame; swung as though he were concentrating into the blow all his hatred of Sarpedion and everything for which Sarpedion stood—which in fact he was.

And what such a saber-scimitar, so driven, did to thin, showy copper armor and to the human flesh beneath it, is simply nothing to dwell upon here.

"HOLD!" he roared at the mercenaries, who hadn't quite decided whether or not to resume the attack, and they held.

"Bu . . . bub . . . but you're dead!" the non-com stuttered. "You *must* be—the great Sarpedion would. . . ."

"A right lively corpse I!" Tedric snarled. "Your Sarpedion, false god and coward, drinker of blood and slayer of the helpless, is weak, puny, and futile beside my Llosir. Hence, under Llosir's shield and at Llosir's direction, I shall this day kill your foul and depraved god; shall send him back to the grisly hell from whence he came.

"Nor do I ask you to fight for me. Nor would I so allow; for I trust you not, though you swore by all your gods. Do you fight for pleasure or for pay?"

A growl was the only answer, but that was answer enough.

"He of Sarpedion who paid your wages lies there dead. All others of his ilk will die ere this day's sunset. Be advised, therefore; fight no more until you know who pays. Wouldst any more of you be split like whitefish ere I go? Time runneth short, but I would stay and oblige if pressed."

He was not pressed.

Tedric whirled and strode away. Should he get his horse, or not? No. He had never ridden mighty Dreegor into danger wearing armor less capable than his own, and he wouldn't begin now.

The Temple of Sarpedion was a tall, narrow building, with a far-flung outside staircase leading up to the penthouse-like excrescence in which the green altar of sacrifice was.

Tedric reached the foot of that staircase and grimly, doggedly, cut his way up it. It was hard work, and he did not want to wear himself out too soon. He might need a lot, and suddenly, later on, and it would be a good idea to have something in reserve.

As he mounted higher and higher, however, the opposition became less and less instead of greater and greater, as he had expected. Priests were no longer there—he hadn't seen one for five minutes. And in the penthouse itself, instead of the solid phalanx of opposition he had *known* would bar his way, there were only half a dozen mercenaries, who promptly turned tail and ran.

"The way is clear! Hasten!" Tedric shouted, and his youthful squire rushed up the ramp with his axe and hammer.

And with those ultra-hard, ultra-tough implements Tedric mauled and chopped the image of the god.

Devann, Sarpedion's high priest, was desperate. He believed thoroughly in his god. Equally thoroughly, however, he believed in the actuality and in the power of Tedric's new god. He had to, for the miracle he had performed spoke for itself.

While Sarpedion had not appeared personally in Devann's lifetime, he had so appeared many times in the past; and by a sufficiently attractive sacrifice he could be persuaded to appear again, particularly since this appearance would be in self-defence.

No slave, or any number of slaves, would do. Nor criminals. No ordinary virgin of the common people. This sacrifice must be of supreme quality. The king himself? Too old and tough and sinful. Ah . . . the king's daughter. . . .

At the thought the pit of his stomach turned cold. However, desperate situations require desperate remedies. He called in his henchmen and issued orders.

Thus it came about that a towering figure clad in flashing golden armor—the king himself, with a few courtiers scrambling far in his wake—dashed up the last few steps just as Tedric was wrenching out Sarpedion's liver.

"Tedric, attend!" the monarch panted. "The priests have taken Rhoann and are about to give her to Sarpedion!"

"They can't, sire. I've just killed Sarpedion, right here."

"But they *can!* They've taken the Holiest One from the Innermost Shrine; have enshrined him on the Temple of

Scheene. Slay me those traitor priests before they slay Rhoann and you may. . . ."

Tedric did not hear the rest of it, nor was his mind chiefly concerned with the plight of the royal maid. It was Sarpedion he was after. With a blistering oath he dropped the god's liver, whirled around and leaped down the stairway. It would do no good to kill only one Sarpedion. He would have to kill them both, especially since the Holiest One was the major image. The Holiest One . . . the Sarpedion never before seen except by first-rank priests . . . of *course* that would be the one they'd use in sacrificing a king's daughter. He should have thought of that himself, sooner, damn him for a fool! It probably wasn't too late yet, but the sooner he got there, the better would be his chance of winning.

Hence he ran, and, farther and farther behind him, came the king and the courtiers.

Reaching the Temple of Scheene, he found to his immense relief that he would not have to storm that heavily-manned rampart alone. A full company of the Royal Guard was already there. Battle was in progress, but very little headway was being made against the close-packed defenders of the god, and Tedric knew why. A man fighting against a god was licked before he started, and knew it. He'd have to build up their morale.

But did he have time? Probably. They couldn't hurry things too much without insulting Sarpedion, for the absolutely necessary ceremonies took a lot of time. Anyway, he'd have to take the time, or he'd never reach the god.

"Art Lord Tedric?" A burly captain disentangled himself from the front rank and saluted.

"I'm Tedric, yes. Knewst I was coming?"

"Yes, Lord. Orders came by helio but now. You are in command; you speak with the voice of King Phagon himself."

"Good. Call your men back thirty paces. Pick me out the twelve or fifteen strongest, to lead.

"Men of the Royal Guard!" He raised his voice to a volume audible not only to his own men, but also to all the enemy. "Who is the most powerful swordsman among you? . . . Stand forward . . . This armor I wear is not of iron, but of god-metal, the metal of Llosir, my personal

145

and all-powerful god. That all here may see and know, I command you to strike at me your shrewdest, most effective, most powerful blow."

The soldier, after a couple of false starts, did manage a stroke of sorts.

"I said *strike!*" Tedric roared. "Think you ordinary iron can harm the personal metal of a god? Strike where you please, at head or neck or shoulder or guts, but strike as though you meant it! Strike to kill! Shatter your sword! STRIKE!"

Convulsively, the fellow struck, swinging for the neck, and at impact his blade snapped into three pieces. A wave of visible relief swept over the Guardsmen; one of dismay and shock over the ranks of the foe.

"I implore pardon, Lord," the soldier begged, dropping to one knee.

"Up man! 'Tis nothing, and by my direct order. Now, men, I can tell you a thing you would not have fully believed before. I have just killed half of Sarpedion and he could not touch me. I am about to kill his other half—you will see me do it. Come what may of god or devil you need not fear it, for I and all with me fight under Llosir's shield. We men will have to deal only with the flesh and blood of those runty mercenaries of Tark."

He studied the enemy formation briefly. A solid phalanx of spearmen, with shields latticed and braced; close-set spears out-thrust and anchored. Strictly defensive; they hadn't made a move to follow nor thrown a single javelin when the king's forces withdrew. This wasn't going to be easy, but it *was* possible.

"We will make the formation of the wedge, with me as point," he went on. "Sergeant, you will bear my sword and hammer. The rest of you will ram me into the center of that phalanx with everything of driving force that in you lies. I will make and maintain enough of opening. We'll go up that ramp like a fast ship ploughing through waves. Make wedge! Drive!"

Except for his armor of god-metal Tedric would have been crushed flat by the impact of the flying wedge against the soldiery packed so solidly on the stair. Several of the foe were so crushed, but the new armor held. Tedric could scarcely move his legs enough to take each step, his body

146

was held as though in a vice, but his giant arms were free; and by dint of short, savage, punching jabs and prods and strokes of his atrocious war-axe he made and maintained the narrow opening upon which the success of the whole operation depended. And into that constantly-renewed opening the smith was driven—irresistibly driven by the concerted and synchronized strength of the strongest men of Lomarr's Royal Guard.

The result was not exactly like that of a diesel-powered snowplough, but it was good enough. The mercenaries did not flow over the sides of the ramp in two smooth waves. However, unable with either weapons or bodies to break through the slanting walls of iron formed by the smoothly-overlapping shields of the Guardsmen, over the edges they went, the living and the dead.

The dreadful wedge drove on.

As the Guardsmen neared the top of the straiway the mercenaries disappeared—enough of that kind of thing was a great plenty—and Tedric, after a quick glance around to see what the situation was, seized his sword from the bearer. Old Devann had his knife aloft, but in only the third of the five formal passes. Two more to go.

"Kill those priests!" he snapped at the captain. "I'll take the three at the altar—you fellows take the rest of them!"

When Tedric reached the green altar the sacrificial knife was again aloft; but the same stroke that severed Devann's upraised right arm severed also his head and his whole left shoulder. Two more whistling strokes and a moment's study of the scene of action assured him that there would be no more sacrifice that day. The King's Archers had followed close behind the Guards; the situation was well in hand.

He exchanged sword for axe and hammer, and furiously, viciously, went to work on the god. He yanked out the Holiest One's brain, liver, and heart; hammered and chopped the rest of him to bits. That done, he turned to the altar—he had not even glanced at it before.

Stretched taut, spread-eagle by wrists and ankles on the reeking, blood-fouled, green horror-stone, the Lady Rhoann lay; her yard-long, thick brown hair a wide-flung riot. Six priets had not immobilized Rhoann of Lomarr without a

147

struggle. Her eyes went from shattered image to blood-covered armored giant and back to image; her face was a study of part-horrified, part-terrified, part-worshipful amazement.

He slashed the ropes, extended his mailed right hand. "Art hurt, Lady Rhoann?"

"No. Just stiff." Taking his hand, she sat up—a bit groggily—and flexed wrists and ankles experimentally; while, behind his visor, the man stared and stared.

Tall—wide but trim—superbly made—a true scion of the old blood—Llosir's liver, what a woman! He had undressed her mentally more than once, but his visionings had fallen short, far short, of the entrancing, the magnificent truth. *What* a woman! A virgin? Huh! Technically so, perhaps . . . more shame to those pusillanimous half-breed midgets of the court . . . if *he* had been born noble . . .

She slid off the altar and stood up, her eyes still dark with fantastically mixed emotions. She threw both arms around his armored neck and snuggled close against his steel, heedless that breasts and flanks were being smeared anew with half-dried blood.

He put an iron-clad arm around her, moved her arm enough to open his visor, saw sea-green eyes, only a few inches below his own, staring straight into his.

The man's quick passion flamed again. Gods of the ancients, what a woman! *There* was a mate for a fullgrown man!

"Thank the gods!" The king dashed up, panting, but in surprisingly good shape for a man of forty-odd who had run so far in gold armor. "Thanks be to all the gods you were in time!"

"Just barely, sire, but in time."

"Name your reward, Lord Tedric. I will be glad to make you my son."

"Not that, sire, ever. If there's anything in this world or the next I *don't* want to be, it's Lady Rohann's brother."

"Make him Lord of the Marches, father," the girl said, sharply. "Knowst what the sages said."

" 'Twould be better," the monarch agreed. "Tedric of old Lomarr, I appoint you Lord of the Upper, the Middle, and the Lower Marches, the Highest of the High."

Tedric went to his knees. "I thank you, sire. Have I

148

your backing in wiping out what is left of Sarpedion's power?"

"If you will support the Throne with the strength I so clearly see is to be yours, I will back you, with the full power of the Throne, in anything you wish to do."

"Of course I will support you, sire, as long as I live and with all that in me lies. Since time was my blood has been vassal to yours, and ever will be. My brain, my liver, and my heart are yours."

"I thank you, Lord Tedric. Proceed."

Tedric snapped to his feet. His sword flashed high in air. His heavy voice rang out.

"People of Lomarr, listen to a herald of the Throne! Sarpedion is dead; Llosir lives. Human sacrifice—yes, all sacrifice except the one I am about to perform, of Sarpedion himself to Llosir—is done. That is and will be the law. To that end there will be no more priests, but a priestess only. I speak as herald for the Throne of Lomarr!"

He turned to the girl, still clinging to his side. "I had it first in mind, Lady Rhoann, to make you priestess, but . . ."

"Not I!" she interrupted, vigorously. "No priestess I, Lord Tedric!"

"By Llosir's brain, girl, you're right—you've been wasted long enough!"

In another time-track another Skandos and another Furmin, almost but not quite identical with those first so named, pored over a chronoviagram.

"The key point in time is there," the Prime Physicist said, thoughtfully, placing the point of his pencil near one jagged peak of the trace. "The key figure is Lord Tedric of Lomarr, the discoverer of the carburization of steel. He could be manipulated very easily . . . but, after all, the real catastrophe is about three hundred eighteen years away; there is nothing alarming about the shape of the curve; and any interference with the actual physical events of the past would almost certainly prove calamitous. Over the years I have found your judgment good. What is your thought on this matter, Furmin?"

"I would say to wait, at least for a few weeks or months. Even though eight hundred twelve fails, number eight

hundred fifty or number nine hundred may succeed. At very worst, we will be in the same position then as now to take the action which has for a hundred years been specifically forbidden by both Council and School."

"So be it."

LORD TEDRIC

Time is the strangest of all mysteries. Relatively unimportant events, almost unnoticed as they occur, may, in hundreds of years, result in Ultimate Catastrophe. On Time Track Number One, that was the immutable result. But on Time Track Number Two there was one little event that could be used to avert it—the presence of a naked woman in public. So, Skandos One removed the clothing from the Lady Rhoann and after one look, Lord Tedric did the rest!

Skandos One (The Skandos of Time Track Number One, numbered for reasons which will become clear) showed, by means of the chronoviagraph, that civilization would destroy itself in one hundred eighty-seven years. To prevent this catastrophe he went back to the key point in time and sought out the key figure—one Tedric, a Lomarrian ironmaster who had lived and died a commoner; unable ever, to do anything about his fanatical detestation of human sacrifice.

Skandos One taught Tedric how to make one batch of super-steel; watched him forge armor and arms from that highly anachronistic alloy. He watched him do things that Tedric of Time Track One had never done.

Time, then, did fork. Time Track One was probably no longer in existence. He must have been saved by his "traction" on the reality of Time Track Two. He'd snap back up to his own time and see what the situation was. If he found his assistant Furmin alone in the laboratory, the extremists would have been proved wrong. If not . . .

Furmin was not alone. Instead, Skandos Two and Furmin Two were at work on a tri-di of Tedric's life: so like, and yet so wildly unlike, the one upon which Skandos One and Furmin One had labored so long!

Shaken and undecided, Skandos One held his machine at the very verge of invisibility and watched and listened.

"But it's so maddeningly incomplete!" Skandos Two snorted. "When it goes into such fine detail on almost everything else, why can't we get how he stumbled onto one lot, and never any other, of high-alloy steel—chrome-nickel-vanadium-molybdenum-tungsten steel—Mortensen's supersteel, to be specific—which wasn't rediscovered for thousands of years?

"Why, it was revealed to him by his personal god Llosir —don't you remember?" Furmin snickered.

"Poppycock!"

"To us, yes; but not to them. Hence, no detail, and you know why we can't go back and check."

"Of course. We simply don't know enough about time . . . but I would so like to study this Lord of the Marches at first hand! Nowhere else in all reachable time does any other one entity occupy such a uniquely key position!"

"So would I, chief. If we knew just a little more I'd say go. In the meantime, let's run that tri-di again, to see if we've overlooked any little thing!"

In the three-dimensional, full-color projection Arms-master Lord Tedric destroyed the principal images of the monstrous god Sarpedion and killed Sarpedion's priests. He rescued Lady Rhoann, King Phagon's eldest daughter, from the sacrificial altar. The king made him Lord of the Marches, the Highest of the High.

"This part I like." Furmin pressed a stud; the projector stopped. A blood-smeared armored giant and a blood-smeared naked woman stood, arms around each other, beside a blood-smeared altar of green stone. "Talk about being STACKED! If I hadn't checked the data myself I'd swear you went overboard there, chief."

"Exact likeness—life size," Skandos Two grunted. "Tedric: six-four, two-thirty, muscled just like that. Rhoann: six feet and half an inch, one-ninety. The only time she ever appeared in the raw in public, I guess, but she didn't turn a hair."

"What a couple!" Furmin stared enviously. "We don't have people like that any more."

"Fortunately, no. He could split a full-armored man in two with a sword; she could strangle a tiger bare-handed.

152

So what? All the brains of the whole damned tribe, boiled down into one, wouldn't equip a half-wit."

"Oh, I wouldn't say that," Furmin objected. "Phagon was a smooth, shrewd operator."

"In a way—sometimes—but committing suicide by wearing gold armor instead of high-alloy steel doesn't show much brain-power."

"I'm not sure I'll buy that, either. There were terrific pressures . . . but say Phagon had worn steel, that day at Middlemarch Castle, and lived ten or fifteen years longer? My guess is that Tedric would have changed the map of the world. He wasn't stupid, you know; just bull-headed, and Phagon could handle him. He would have pounded a lot of sense into his skull, if he had lived."

"However, he didn't live," Skandos returned dryly, "and so every decision Tedric ever made was wrong. But to get back to the point, did you see anything new?"

"Not a thing."

"Neither did I. So go and see how eight twelve is doing."

For Time Test Number Eight Hundred Eleven had failed; and there was little ground for hope that Number Eight Hundred Twelve would be any more productive.

And the lurking Skandos One who had been studying intensively every aspect of the situation, began to act. It was crystal clear that Time Track Two could hold only one Skandos. One of them would have to vanish—completely, immediately, and permanently. Although in no sense a killer, by instinct or training, only one course of action was possible if his own life—and, as a matter of fact, all civilization—were to be conserved. Wherefore he synchonized, and shot his unsuspecting double neatly through the head. The living Skandos changed places with the dead. A timer buzzed briefly. The time-machine disappeared; completely out of synchronization with any continuum that a world's keenest brain and an ultra-fast calculator could compute.

This would of course make another fork in time, but that fact did not bother Skandos One at all—now. As for Tedric; since the big, dumb lug couldn't be made to believe that he, Skandos One, was other than a god, he'd be a god—in spades!

He'd build an image of flesh-like plastic exactly like the copper statue Tedric had made, and go back and announce himself publicly as the god Llosir. He'd come back—along Time-Track Three, of course—and do away with Skandos Three. There might have to be another interference, too, to get Tedric started along the right time-track. He could call better after seeing what Time-Track Three looked like. If so, it would necessitate the displacement of Skandos Four.

So what? He had never had any qualms; and, now that he had done it once, he had no doubt whatever as to his ability to do it twice more.

Of the three standing beside Sarpedion's grisly altar, King Phagon was the first to become conscious of the fact that something should be done about his daughter's nudity.

"Flasnir, your cloak!" he ordered sharply; and the Lady Rhoann, unclamping her arms from around Tedric's armored neck and disengaging his steel-clad arm from around her waist, covered herself with the proffered garment. Partially covered, that is; for, since the cloak had come only to mid-thigh on the courtier and since she was a good seven inches taller than he, the coverage might have seemed, to a prudish eye, something less than adequate.

"Chamberlain Schillan—Captain Sciro," the king went on briskly. "Haul me this carrion to the river and dump it in—put men to cleaning this place—'tis not seemly so."

The designated officers began to bawl orders, and Tedric turned to the girl, who was still just about as close to him as she could get; awe, wonder, and relieved shock still plain on her expressive face.

"One thing, Lady Rhoann, I understand not. You seem to know me; act as though I were old, tried friend. 'Tis vast honor, but how? You of course I know; have known and honored since you were a child; but me, a commoner, you know not. Nor, if you did, couldst know who it was neath all this iron?"

"Art wrong, Lord Tedric—nay, not "Lord" Tedric; henceforth you and I are Tedric and Rhoann merely—I have known you long and well; would recognize you anywhere. The few of the old, true blood stand out head and shoulders above the throng, and you stand out, even among

154

them. Who else could it have been? Who else hath the strength of arm and soul, the inner and the outer courage? No coward I, Tedric, nor ever called so, but on that altar my very bones turned jelly. I could not have swung weapon against Sarpedion. I trembled yet at the bare thought of what you did; I know not how you could have done it."

"You feared the god, Lady Rhoann, as do so many. I hated him."

" 'Tis not enough of explanation. And 'Rhoann' merely, Tedric, remember?"

"Rhoann . . . Thanks, my lady. 'Tis an honor more real than your father's patent of nobility . . . but 'tis not fitting. I feel as much a commoner. . . ."

"Commoner? Bah! I ignored that word once, Tedric, but not twice. You are, and deservedly, the Highest of the High. My father the king has known for long what you are; he should have ennobled you long since. Thank Sarp . . . thank all the gods he had the wit to put it off no longer! 'Tis blood that tells, not empty titles. The Throne can make and un-make nobility at will, but no power whatever can make true-bloods out of mongrels, nor create real *manhood* where none exists!"

Tedric did not know what to say in answer to that passionate outburst, so he changed the subject; effectively, if not deftly. "In speaking of the Marches to your father the king, you mentioned the Sages. What said they?"

"At another time, perhaps." Lady Rhoann was fast recovering her wonted cool poise. " 'Tis far too long to go into while I stand here half naked, filthy, and stinking. Let us on with the business in hand; which, for me, is a hot bath and clean clothing."

Rhoann strolled away as unconcernedly as though she were wearing full court regalia, and Tedric turned to the king.

"Thinkest the Lady Trycie is nearby, sire?"

"If I know the jade at all, she is," Phagon snorted. "And not only near. She's seen everything and heard everything; knows more about everything than either of us, or both of us together. Why? Thinkst she'd make a good priestess?"

"The best. Much more so, methinks, than the Lady

155

Rhoann. Younger. More . . . umm . . . more priestess-like, say?"

"Perhaps." Phagon was very evidently sceptical, but looked around the temple, anyway. "Trycie!" he yelled.

"Yes, father?" a soft voice answered—right behind them!

The king's second daughter was very like his first in size and shape, but her eyes were a cerulean blue and her hair, as long and as thick as Rhoann's own, had the color of ripe wheat.

"Aye, daughter. Wouldst like to be Priestess of Llosir?"

"Oh, yes!" she squealed; but sobered quickly. "On second thought . . . perhaps not . . . no. If sobeit sacrifice is done I intend to marry, some day, and have six or eight children. But . . . perhaps . . . could I take it now, and resign later, think you?"

" 'Twould not be necessary, sire and Lady Trycie," Tedric put in, while Phagon was still thinking the matter over. "Llosir is not at all like Sarpedion. Llosir wants abundance and fertility and happiness, not poverty and sterility and misery. Llosir's priestess marries as she pleases and has as many children as she wants."

"Your priestess I, then, sirs! I go to have cloth-of-gold robes made at once!" The last words came floating back over her shoulder as Trycie raced away.

"Lord Tedric, sir." Unobserved, Sciro had been waiting for a chance to speak to his superior officer.

"Yes, captain?"

" 'Tis the men . . . the cleaning . . . They . . . We, I mean . . ." Sciro of Old Lomarr would not pass the buck. "The bodies—the priests, you know, and so on—were easy enough; and we did manage to handle most of the pieces of the god. But the . . . the heart, and so on, you know . . . we know not where you want them taken . . . and besides, we fear . . . wilt stand by and ward, Lord Tedric, while I pick them up?"

" 'Tis my business, Captain Sciro; mine alone. I crave pardon for not attending to it sooner. Hast a bag?"

"Yea." The highly relieved officer held out a duffle-bag of fine, soft leather.

Tedric took it, strode across to the place where Sarpedion's image had stood, and—not without a few qualms of

156

his own, now that the frenzy of battle had evaporated—picked up Sarpedion's heart, liver, and brain and deposited them, neither too carefully not too carelessly, in the sack. Then, swinging the burden up over his shoulder—

"I go to fetch the others," he explained to his king. "Then we hold sacrifice to end all human sacrifice."

"Hold, Tedric!" Phagon ordered. "One thing—or two or three, methinks. 'Tis not seemly to conduct a thing so; lacking order and organization and plan. Where dost propose to hold such an affair? Not in your ironworks, surely?"

"Certainly not, sire." Tedric halted, almost in midstride. He hadn't got around yet to thinking about the operation as a whole, but he began to do so then. "And certainly not on this temple or Sarpedion's own. Lord Llosir is clean: all our temples are foul in every stone and timber . . ." He paused. Then, suddenly: "I have it, sire—the amphitheater!"

"The amphitheater? 'Tis well. 'Tis of little enough use, and a shrine will not interfere with what little use it has."

"Wilt give orders to build . . . ?"

"The Lord of the Marches issues his own orders. Hola, Schillan, to me!" the monarch shouted, and the Chamberlain of the Realm came on the run. "Lord Tedric speaks with my voice."

"I hear, sire. Lord Tedric, I listen."

"Have built, at speed, midway along the front of the amphitheater, on the very edge of the cliff, a table of clean, new-quarried stone; ten feet square and three feet high. On it mount Lord Llosir so firmly that he will stand upright forever against whatever may come of wind or storm."

The chamberlain hurried away. So did Tedric, with his bag of spoils. First to his shop, where his armor was removed and where he scratched himself vigorously and delightfully as it came off. Thence to the Temple of Sarpedion, where he collected the other, somewhat-lesser-hallowed trio of the Great One's vital organs. Then, and belatedly, to home and to bed.

A little later, while the new-made Lord of the Marches was sleeping soundly, the king's messengers rode furiously abroad, spreading the word that ten days hence, at the fourth period after noon, in Lompoar's Amphitheater, Great

157

Sarpedion would be sacrificed to Llosir, Lomarr's new and Ultra-powerful god.

The city of Lompoar, Lomarr's capital, lying on the south bank of the Lotar some fifty miles inland from the delta, nestled against the rugged breast of the Coast Range. Just outside the town's limit and some hundreds of feet above its principal streets there was a gigantic half-bowl, carved out of the solid rock by an eddy of some bye-gone age.

This was the Amphitheater, and on the very lip of the stupendous cliff descending vertically to the river so far below, Llosir stood proudly on his platform of smooth, clean granite.

" 'Tis not enough like a god, methinks." King Phagon, dressed now in cloth-of-gold, eyed the gleaming copper statue very dubiously. " 'Tis too much like a man, by far."

" 'Tis exactly as I saw him, sire," Tedric replied, firmly. Nor was he, consciously, lying: by this time he believed the lie himself. "Llosir is a man-god, remember, not a beast-god, and 'tis better so. But the time I set is here. With your permission, sire, I begin."

Both men looked around the great bowl. Near by, but not too near, stood the priestess and half a dozen white-clad fifteen-year-old girls; one of whom carried a beaten-gold pitcher full of perfumed oil, another a flaring open lamp wrought of the same material. Slightly to one side were Rhoann—looking, if the truth must be told, as though she did not particularly enjoy her present position on the side-lines—her mother the queen, the rest of the royal family, and ranks of courtiers. And finally, much farther back, at a very respectful distance from their strange new god, arranged in dozens of more or less concentric, roughtly hemispherical rows, stood everybody who had had time to get there. More were arriving constantly, of course, but the flood had become a trickle; the narrow way, worming up-ward from the city along the cliff's stark side, was almost bare of traffic.

"Begin, Lord Tedric," said the king.

Tedric bent over, heaved the heavy iron pan containing the offerings up onto the platform, and turned. "The oil, Priestess Lady Trycie, and the flame."

The acolyte handed the pitcher to Trycie, who handed

it to Tedric, who poured its contents over the twin hearts, twin livers, and twin brains. Then the lamp; and as the yard-high flames leaped upward the armored pseudo-priest stepped backward and raised his eyes boldly to the impassive face of the image of his god. Then he spoke—not softly, but in parade-ground tones audible to everyone present.

"Take, Lord Llosir, all the strength and all the power and all the force that Sarpedion ever had. Use them, we beg, for good and not for ill."

He picked up the blazing pan and strode toward the lip of the precipice; high-mounting, smokey flames curling backward around his armored figure. "And now, in token of Sarpedion's utter and complete extinction, I consign these, the last vestiges of his being, to the rushing depths of oblivion." He hurled the pan and its fiercely flaming contents out over the terrific brink.

This act, according to Tedric's plan, was to end the program—but it didn't. Long before the fiery mass struck water his attention was seized by a long, low-pitched, moaning gasp from a multitude of throats; a sound the like of which he had never before even imagined.

He whirled—and saw, shimmering in a cage-like structure of shimmering bars, a form of seeming flesh so exactly like the copper image in every detail of shape that it might well have come from the same mould!

"Lord Llosir—in the *flesh!*" Tedric exclaimed, and went to one knee.

So did the king and his family, and a few of the bravest of the courtiers. Most of the latter, however, and the girl acolytes and the thronging thousands of spectators, threw themselves flat on the hard ground. They threw themselves flat, but they did not look away or close their eyes or cover their faces with their hands. On the contrary, each one stared with all the power of his optic nerves.

The god's mouth opened, his lips moved; and, although no one could hear any sound, everyone felt words resounding throughout the deepest recesses of his being.

"I have taken all the strength, all the power, all the force, all of everything that made Sarpedion what he was," the god began. In part his pseudo-voice was the resonant clang of a brazen bell; in part the diapason harmonies of an

159

impossibly vast organ. "I will use them for good, not ill. I am glad, Tedric, that you did not defile my hearth—for this is a hearth, remember, and in no sense an altar—in making this, the first and the *only* sacrifice ever to be made to me. You, Trycie, are the first of my priestesses?"

The girl, shaking visibly, gulped three times before she could speak. "Yea, my—my—my Lord Llosir," she managed finally. "Th—that is—if—if I please you, Lord, Sir."

"You please me, Trycie of Lomarr. Nor will your duties be onerous; being only to see to it that your maidens keep my hearth clean and my statue bright."

"To you, my Lord—Llo—Llosir, sir, all thanks. Wilt keep . . ." Trycie raised her downcast eyes and stopped short in mid-sentence; her mouth dropping ludicrously open and her eyes becoming two round O's of astonishment. The air above the yawning abyss was as empty as it had ever been; the flesh-and-blood god had disappeared as instantaneously as he had come!

Tedric's heavy voice silenced the murmured wave of excitement sweeping the bowl.

"That is all!" he bellowed. "I did not expect the Lord Llosir to appear in the flesh at this time; I know not when or ever he will deign to appear to us again. But I know—whether or not he ever so deigns, or when, you all know now that our great Lord Llosir lives. Is not so?"

" 'Tis so! Long live Lord Llosir!" Tumultuous yelling filled the amphitheater.

" 'Tis well. In leaving this holy place all will file between me and the shrine. First our king, then the Lady Priestess Trycie and her maids, then the Family, then the Court, then the rest. All men as they pass will raise sword-arms in salute, all women will bow heads. Will be naught of offerings or of tribute or of fractions; Lord Llosir is a *god,* not a huckstering, thieving, murdering trickster. King Phagon, sire, wilt lead?"

Unhelmed now, Tedric stood rigidly at attention before the image of his god. The king did not march straight past him, but stopped short. Taking off his ornate headpiece and lifting his right arm high, he said:

"To you, Lord Llosir, my sincere thanks for what hast done for me, for my family, and for my nation. While 'tis

160

not seemly that Lomarr's king should beg, I ask that you abandon us not."

Then Trycie and her girls. "We engage, Lord Sir," the Lady Priestess said, at a whispered word from Tedric, "to keep your hearth scrupulously clean; your statue shining bright."

Then the queen, followed by the Lady Rhoann—who, although she bowed her head merely enough, was shooting envious glances at her sister, so far ahead and so evidently the cynosure of so many eyes.

The rest of the Family—the Court—the thronging spectators—and, last of all, Tedric himself. Helmet tucked under left arm, he raised his brawny right arm high, executed a stiff "left face," and marched proudly at the rear of the long procession.

And as the people made their way down the steep and rugged path, as they debouched through the city of Lompoar, as they traversed the highways and byways back to the towns and townlets and farms from which they had come, it was very evident that Llosir had established himself as no other god had ever been established throughout the long history of that world.

Great Llosir had appeared in person. Everyone there had seen him with his own eyes. Everyone there had heard his voice; a voice of a quality impossible for any mortal being, human or otherwise, to produce; a voice heard, not with the ears, which would have been ordinary enough, but by virtue of some hitherto completely unknown and still completely unknowable inner sense or ability evocable only by the god. Everyone there had heard—sensed—him address the Lord Armsmaster and the Lady Priestess by name.

Other gods had appeared personally in the past . . . or had they, really? Nobody had ever seen any of them except their own priests . . . the priests who performed the sacrifices and who fattened on the fractions . . . Llosir, now, wanted neither sacrifices nor fractions; and, powerful although he was, had appeared to and had spoken to everyone alike, of however high or low degree, throughout the whole huge amphitheater.

Everyone! Not to the priestess only; not only to those of the Old Blood; not only to citizens or natives of Lomarr;

but to *everyone*—down to mercenaries, chance visitors and such!

Long live Lord Llosir, our new and plenipotent god!

King Phagon and Tedric were standing at a table in the throne-room of the palace-castle, studying a map. It was crudely drawn and sketchy, this map, and full of blank areas and gross errors; but this was not an age of fine cartography.

"Talk, first, is still my thought, sire," Tedric insisted, stubbornly. " 'Tis closer, our lines shorter, a victory there would hearten all our people. Too, 'twould be unexpected. Lomarr has never attacked Tark, whereas your royal sire and his sire before him each tried to loose Sarlon's grip and, in failing, but increased the already heavy payments of tribute. Too, in case of something short of victory, hast only the one pass and the Great Gorge of the Lotar to hold 'gainst reprisal. 'Tis true such course would leave the Marches unheld, but no more so than they have been for four years or more."

"Nay. *Think*, man!" Phagon snorted, testily. " 'Twould fail. Four parts of our army are of Tark—thinkst not their first act would be to turn against us and make common cause with their brethren? Too, we lack strength, they outnumber us two to one. Nay. Sarlon first. Then, perhaps, Tark; but not before then."

"But Sarlon outnumbers us too, sire, especially if you count those barbarbarian devils of the Devossian steppes. Since Taggad of Sarlon lets them cross his lands to raid the Marches—for a fraction of the loot, no doubt—'tis certain they'll help him against us. Also, sire, your father and your grandfather both died under Sarlonian axes."

"True, but neither of them was a strategist. I am; I have studied this matter for many years. They did the obvious; I shall not. Nor shall Sarlon pay tribute merely; Sarlon must and shall become a province of my kingdom!"

So argument raged, until Phagon got up onto his royal high horse and declared it his royal will that the thing was to be done his way and no other. Whereupon, of course, Tedric submitted with the best grace he could muster and set about the task of helping get the army ready to roll

162

toward the Marches, some three and a half hundreds of miles to the north.

Tedric fumed. Tedric fretted. Tedric swore sulphurously in Lomarrian, Tarkian, Sarlonian, Devossian, and all the other languages he knew. All his noise and fury were, however, of very little avail in speeding up what was an intrinsically slow process.

Between times of cursing and urging and driving, Tedric was wont to prowl the castle and its environs. So doing, one day, he came upon King Phagon and the Lady Rhoann practicing at archery. Lifting his arm in salute to his sovereign and bowing his head politely to the lady, he made to pass on.

"Hola, Tedric!" Rhoann called. "Wouldst speed a flight with us?"

Tedric glanced at the target. Rhoann was beating her father unmercifully—her purple-shafted arrows were all in or near the gold, while his golden ones were scattered far and wide—and she had been twitting him unmercifully about his poor marksmanship. Phagon was in no merry mood; this was very evidently no competition for any outsider—least of all Lomarr's top-ranking armsmaster—to enter.

"Crave pardon, my lady, but other matters press. . . ."

"Your evasions are *so* transparent, my lord; why not tell the truth?" Rhoann did not exactly sneer at the man's obvious embarrassment, but it was very clear that she, too, was in a vicious temper. "Mindst not beating *me* but never the *Throne?* And any armsmaster who threwest not arrows by hand at this range to beat both of us should be stripped of badge?"

Tedric, quite fatuously, leaped at the bait. "Wouldst permit, sire?"

"*No!*" the king roared. "By my head, by the Throne, by Llosir's liver and heart and brain and guts—NO! 'Twould cost the head of any save you to insult me so—shoot, sir, and shoot your best!" extending his own bow and a full quiver of arrows.

Tedric did not want to use the royal weapon, but at the girl's quick, imperative gesture he smothered his incipient protest and accepted it.

"One sighting shot, sire?" he asked, and drew the heavy

163

bow. Nothing whatever could have forced him to put an arrow nearer the gold than the farthest of the king's; to avoid doing so—without transparently missing the target completely—would take skill, since one golden arrow stood a bare three inches from the edge of the target.

His first arrow grazed the edge of the butt and was an inch low; his second plunged into the padding exactly half way between the king's wildest arrow and the target's rim. Then, so rapidly that it seemed as though there must be at least two arrows in the air at once, arrow crashed on arrow; wood snapping as iron head struck feathered shaft. At end, the rent in the fabric through which all those arrows had torn their way could have been covered by half of one of Rhoann's hands.

"I lose, sire," Tedric said, stiffly, returning bow and empty quiver. "My score is zero."

Phagon, knowing himself in the wrong but unable to bring himself to apologize, did what he considered the next-best thing. "I used to shoot like that," he complained. "Knowst how lost I my skill, Tedric? 'Tis not my age, surely?"

"'Tis not my place to say, sire." Then, with more loyalty than sense—"And I split to the teeth any who dare so insult the Throne."

"What!" the monarch roared. "By my. . . ."

"Hold, father!" Rhoann snapped. "A king you—act it!"

Hard blue eyes glared steadily into unyielding eyes of green. Neither the thoroughly angry king nor the equally angry princess would give an inch. She broke the short, bitter silence.

"Say naught, Tedric—he is much too fain to boil in oil or flay alive any who tell him unpleasantnesses, however true. But *me*, father, you boil not, nor flay, nor seek to punish otherwise, or I split this kingdom asunder like a melon. 'Tis time—yea, long past time—that *someone* told you the unadorned truth. Hence, my rascally but well-loved parent, here 'tis. Hast lolled too long on too many too soft cushions, hast emptied too many pots and tankards and flagons, has bedded too many wenches, to be of much use in armor or with any style of weapon in the passes of the High Umpasseurs."

The flabbergasted and rapidly-deflating king tried to
164

think of some answer to this devastating blast, but couldn't. He appealed to Tedric. "Wouldst have said such? Surely not!"

"Not I, sire!" Tedric assured him, quite truthfully. "And even if true, 'tis a thing to remedy itself. Before we reach the Marches wilt regain arm and eye."

"Perhaps," the girl put in, her tone still distinctly on the acid side. "If he matches you, Tedric, in lolling and wining and wenching, yes. Otherwise, no. How much wine do *you* drink, each day?"

"One cup, usually—sometimes—at supper."

"On the march? Think carefully, friend."

"Nay—I meant in town. In the field, none, of course."

"Seest, father?"

"What thinkst me, vixen, a spineless cuddlepet? From this minute 'til return here I match your paragon young-blade loll for loll, cup for cup, wench for wench. Ist what you've been niggling at me to say?"

"Aye, father and king, exactly—for as you say, you do." She hugged him so fervently as almost to lift him off the ground, kissing him twice, and hurried away.

"A thing I would like to talk to you about, sire," Tedric said quickly, before the king could bring up any of the matters just past. "Armor. There was enough of the god-metal to equip three men fully, and headnecks for their horses. You, sire, and me, and Sciro of your Guard. Break precedent, sire, I beg, and wear me this armor of proof instead of the gold; for what we face promises to be worse than anything you or I have yet seen."

"I fear me 'tis true, but 'tis impossible, nonetheless. Lomarr's king wears gold. He fights in gold; at need he dies in gold."

And that was, Tedric knew, very definitely that. It was senseless, it was idiotic, but it was absolutely true. No king of Lomarr could possibly break that particular precedent. To appear in that spectacularly conspicuous fashion, one flashing golden figure in a sea of dull iron-grey, was part of the king's job. The fact that his father and his grandfather and so on for six generations back had died in golden armor could not sway him, any more than it could have swayed Tedric himself in similar case. But there might be a way out.

"But need it be *solid* gold, sire? Wouldst not an overlay of gold suffice?"

"Yea, Lord Tedric, and 'twould be a welcome thing indeed. I yearn not, nor did my father nor his father, to pit gold 'gainst hard-swung axe; e'en less to hide behind ten ranks of iron while others fight. But simply 'tis not possible. If the gold be thick enough for the rivers to hold, 'tis too heavy to lift. If thin enough to be possible of wearing, the gold flies off in sheets at first blow and the fraud is revealed. Hast ideas? I listen."

"I know not, sire. . . ." Tedric thought for minutes. "I have seen gold hammered into thin sheets . . . but not thin enough . . . but it might be possible to hammer it thin enough to be overlaid on the god-metal with pitch or gum. Wouldst wear it so, sire?"

"Aye, my Tedric, and gladly: just so the overlay comes not off by handsbreadths under blow of sword or axe."

"Handsbreaths? Nay. Scratches and mars, of course, easily to be overlaid again ere next day's dawn. But handsbreadths? Nay, sire."

"In that case, try; and may Great Llosir guide your hand."

Tedric went forthwith to the castle and got a chunk of raw, massy gold. He took it to his shop and tried to work it into the thin, smooth film he could visualize so clearly.

And tried—and tried—and tried.

And failed—and failed—and failed.

He was still trying—and still failing—three weeks later. Time was running short; the hours that had formerly dragged like days now flew like minutes. His crew had done their futile best to help; Bendon, his foreman, was still standing by. The king was looking on and offering advice. So were Rhoann and Trycie. Sciro and Schillan and other more or less notable persons were also trying to be of use.

Tedric, strained and tense, was pounding carefully at a sheet of his latest production. It was a pitiful thing—lumpy in spots, ragged and rough, with holes where hammer had met anvil through its substance. The smith's left hand twitched at precisely the wrong instant, just as the

166

hammer struck. The flimsy sheet fell into three ragged pieces.

Completely frustrated, Tedric leaped backward, swore fulminantly, and hurled the hammer with all his strength toward the nearest wall. And in that instant there appeared, in the now familiar cage-like structure of shimmering, interlaced bars, the form of flesh that was Llosir the god. High in the air directly over the forge the apparition hung, motionless and silent, and stared.

Everyone except Tedric gave homage to the god, but he merely switched from the viciously corrosive Devossian words he had been using to more parliamentary Lomarrian.

"Ist possible, Lord Sir, for any human being to do anything with this foul, slimy, salvy, perverse, treacherous, and generally-be-damned stuff?"

"It is. Definitely. Not only possible, but fairly easy and fairly simple, if the proper tools, apparatus, and techniques are employed," Llosir's bell-toned-organ pseudo-voice replied. "Ordinarily, in your lifetime, you would come to know nothing of gold leaf—although really *thin* gold leaf is not required here—nor of gold beater's skins and membranes and how to use them, nor of the adhesives to be employed and the techniques of employing them. The necessary tools and materials are, or can very shortly be made, available to you; you can now absorb quite readily the required information and knowledge.

"For this business of beating out gold leaf, your hammer and anvil are both completely wrong. Listen carefully and remember. For the first, preliminary thinning down, you take. . . .*

Lomarr's army set out at dawn. First the wide-ranging scouts: lean, hard, fine-trained runners, stripped to clouts and moccasins and carrying only a light bow and a few arrows apiece. Then the hunters. They, too, scattered widely and went practically naked: but bore the hundred-pound bows and the savagely-tearing arrows of their trade.

Then the Heavy Horse, comparatively few in number, but of the old blood all, led by Tedric and Sciro and sur-

---

* See Encyclopaedia Britannica (plug). E.E.S.

rounding glittering Phagon and his standard-bearers. It took a lot of horse to carry a full-armored knight of the Old Blood, but the horse-farmers of the Middle Marches bred for size and strength and stamina.

Next came century after century of light horse—mounted swordsmen and spearmen and javelineers—followed by even more numerous centuries of foot-slogging infantry.

Last of all came the big-wheeled, creaking wagons: loaded, not only with the usual supplies and equipment of war, but also with thousands of loaves of bread—hard, flat, heavy loaves made from ling, the corn-like grain which was the staple cereal of the region.

"Bread, sire?" Tedric had asked, wonderingly, when Phagon had first broached the idea. Men on the march lived on meat—a straight, unrelieved diet of meat for weeks and months on end—and all too frequently not enough of that to maintain weight and strength. They expected nothing else; an occasional fist-sized chunk of bread was sheerest luxury. "Bread! A whole loaf each man a day?"

"Aye," Phagon had chuckled in reply. "All farmsmen along the way will have ready my fraction of ling, and Schillan will at need buy more. To each man a loaf each day, and all the meat he can eat. 'Tis why we go up the Midvale, where farmsmen all breed savage dogs to guard their fields 'gainst hordes of game. Such feeding will be noised abroad. Canst think of a better device to lure Taggard's ill-fed mercenaries to our standards?"

Tedric couldn't.

There is no need to dwell in detail upon the army's long, slow march. Leaving the city of Lompar, it moved up the Lotar River, through the spectacularly scenic gorge of the Coast Range, and into the Middle Valley; that incredibly lush and fertile region which, lying between the Low Umpasseurs on the east and the Coast Range on the west, comprised roughly a third of Lomarr's area. Into and through the straggling hamlet of Bonoy, lying at the junction of the Midvale River with the Lotar. Then straight north, through the timberlands and meadows of the Midvale's west bank.

Game was, as Phagon had said, incredibly plentiful;

outnumbering by literally thousands to one both domestic animals and men. Buffalo-like lippita, moose-like rolatoes, pig-like accides—the largest and among the tastiest of Lomarr's game animals—were so abundant that one good hunter could kill in half an hour enough to feed a century for a day. Hence most of the hunters' time was spent in their travelling dryers, preserving meat against a coming day of need.

On, up the bluely placid Lake Midvale, a full day's march long and half that in width. Past the Chain Lakes, strung on the river like beads on a string. Past Lake Ardo, and on toward Lake Middlemarch and the Middlemarch Castle which was to be Tedric's official residence henceforth.

As the main body passed the head of the lake, a couple of scouts brought in a runner bursting with news.

"Thank Sarpedion, sire, I had not to run to Lompoar to reach you!" he cried, dropping to his knees. "Middlemarch Castle is besieged! Hurlo of the Marches is slain!" and he went on to tell a story of onslaught and slaughter.

"And the raiders wore iron," Phagon remarked, when the table was done. "Sarlonion iron, no doubt?"

"Aye, sire, but how couldst. . . ."

"No matter. Take him to the rear. Feed him."

"You *expected* this raid, sire," Tedric said, rather than asked, after scouts and runner had disappeared.

"Aye. 'Twas no raid, but the first skirmish of a war. No fool, Taggad of Sirlon; nor Issian of Devos, barbarian though he is. They knew what loomed, and struck first. The only surprise was Hurlo's death . . . he had my direct orders not to do battle 'gainst any force, however slight-seeming, but to withdraw forthwith into the castle, which was to be kept stocked to withstand a siege of months . . . this keeps me from boiling him in oil for stupidity, incompetence, and disloyalty."

Phagon frowned in thought, then went on: "Were there forces that appeared not? . . . Surely not—Taggard would not split his forces at all seriously: 'tis but to annoy me . . . or perhaps they are mostly barbarians despite the Sarlonian iron . . . to harry and flee is no doubt their aim, but for Lomarr's good not one of them should escape. Knowst the Upper Midvale, Tedric, above the lake?"

169

"But little, sire; a few miles only. I was there but once."

" 'Tis enough. Take half the Royal Guard and a century of bowmen. Cross the Midvale at the ford three miles above us here. Go up and around the lake. The Upper Midvale is fordable almost anywhere at this season, so stay far enough away from the lake that none see you. Cross it, swing in a wide circle toward the peninsula on which sits Middlemarch Castle, and in three days . . . ?"

"Three days will be ample, sire."

"Three days from tomorrow's dawn, exactly as the top rim of the sun clears the meadow, make your charge out of the covering forest, with your archers spread to pick off all who seek to flee. I will be on this side of the peninsula; between us they'll be ground like ling. None shall get away!"

Phagon's assumptions, however, were slightly in error. When Tedric's riders charged, at the crack of the indicated dawn, they did not tear through a motley horde of half-armored, half-trained barbarians. Instead, they struck two full centuries of Sarlon's heaviest armor! And Phagon the King fared worse. At first sight of that brilliant golden armor a solid column of armored knights formed as though by magic and charged it at full gallop!

Phagon fought, of course; fought as his breed had always fought. At first on horse, with his terrible sword, under the trenchant edge of which knight after knight died. His horse dropped, slaughtered; his sword was knocked away; but, afoot, the war-axe chained to his steel belt by links of super-steel was still his. He swung and swung and swung again; again and again; and with each swing an enemy ceased to live; but sheer weight of metal was too much. Finally, still swinging his murderous weapon, Phagon of Lomarr went flat on the ground.

At the first assault on their king, Tedric with his sword and Sciro with his hammer had gone starkly berserk. Sciro was nearer, but Tedric was faster and stronger and had the better horse.

"Dreegor!" he yelled, thumping his steed's sides with his armored legs and rising high in his stirrups. Nostrils flaring, the mighty beast raged forward and Tedric struck as he had never struck before. Eight times that terrific blade came down, and eight men and eight horses died.

170

Then, suddenly—Tedric never did know how it happened, since Dreegor was later found uninjured—he found himself afoot. No place for sword, this, but made to order for axe. Hence, driving forward as resistlessly as though a phalanx of iron were behind him, he hewed his way toward his sovereign.

Thus he was near at hand when Phagon went down. So was doughty Sciro; and by the time the Sarlonians had learned that sword nor axe nor hammer could cut or smash that gold-seeming armor fury personified was upon them. Tedric straddled his king's head, Sciro his feet; and, back to back, two of Lomarr's mightiest armsmasters wove circular webs of flying steel through which it was sheerest suicide to attempt to pass. Thus battle raged until the last armored foeman was down.

"Art hurt, sire?" Tedric asked anxiously as he and Sciro lifted Phagon to his feet.

"Nay, my masters-at-arms," the monarch gasped, still panting for breath. "Bruised merely, and somewhat winded." He opened his visor to let more air in; then, as he regained control, he shook off the supporting hands and stood erect under his own power. "I fear me, Tedric, that you and that vixen daughter of mine were in some sense right. Methinks I may be—Oh, the veriest trifle!— out of condition. But the battle is almost over. Did any escape?"

None had.

" 'Tis well. Tedric, I know not how to honor. . . ."

"Honor me no farther, sire, I beg. Hast honored me already far more than I deserved, or ever will . . . Or, at least, at the moment . . . there may be later, perhaps . . . that is, a thing . . ." he fell silent.

"A thing?" Phagon grinned broadly. "I know not whether Rhoann will be overly pleased at being called so, but 'twill be borne in mind nonetheless. Now you, Sciro; Lord Sciro now and henceforth, and all your line. Lord of what I will not now say; but when we have taken Sarlo you and all others shall know."

"My thanks, sire, and my obeisance," said Sciro.

"Schillan, with me to my pavilion. I am weary and sore, and would fain rest."

As the two Lords of the Realm, so lately commoners, strode away to do what had to be done:

"Neither of us feels any nobler than ever, I know," Sciro said, "but in one way 'tis well—very well indeed."

"The Lady Trycie, eh? The wind *does* set so, then, as I thought."

"Aye. For long and long. It wondered me often, your choice of the Lady Rhoann over *her.* Howbeit, 'twill be a wondrous thing to be your brother-in-law as well as in arms."

Tedric grinned companionably, but before he could reply they had to separate and go to work.

The king did not rest long; the heralds called Tedric in before half his job was done.

"What thinkst you, Tedric, should be next?" Phagon asked.

"First punish Devoss, sire!" Tedric snarled. "Back-track them—storm High Pass if defended—raze half the steppes with sword and torch—drive them the full length of their country and into Northern Sound!"

"Interesting, my impetuous youngblade, but not at all practical," Phagon countered. "Hast considered the matter of time—the avalanches of rocks doubtless set up and ready to sweep those narrow paths—what Taggad would be doing while we cavort through the wastelands?"

Tedric deflated almost instantaneously. "Nay, sire," he admitted sheepishly. "I thought not of any such."

" 'Tis the trouble with you—you know not *how* to think." Phagon was deadly serious now. " 'Tis a hard thing to learn; impossible for many; but learn it you must if you end not as Hurlo ended. Also, take heed: disobey my orders but once, as Hurlo did, and you hang in chains from the highest battlement of your own Castle Middlemarch until your bones rot apart and drop into the lake."

His monarch's vicious threat—or rather, promise—left Tedric completely unmoved. " 'Tis what I would deserve, sire, or less; but no fear of that. Stupid I may be, but disloyal? Nay, sire. Your word always has been and always will be my law."

"Not stupid, Tedric, but lacking in judgment, which is not as bad; since the condition is, if you care enough to make it so, remediable. You *must* care enough, Tedric. You *must* learn, and quickly; for much more than your own life is at hazard."

The younger man stared questioningly and the king went on: "My life, the lives of my family, and the future of all Lomarr," he said quickly.

"In that case, sire, wilt learn, and quickly," Tedric declared; and, as days and weeks went by, he did.

"All previous attempts on the city of Sarlo were made in what seemed to be the only feasible way—crossing the Tegula at Lower Ford, going down its north bank through the gorge to the West Branch, and down that to the Sarlo." Phagon was lecturing from a large map, using a sharp stick as pointer; Tedric, Sciro, Schillan, and two or three other high-ranking officers were watching and listening. "The West Branch flows into Sarlo only forty miles above Sarlo Bay. The city of Sarlo is here, on the north bank of the Sarlo River, right on the Bay, and is five-sixths surrounded by water. The Sarlo River is wide and deep, uncrossable against any real opposition. Thus, Sarlonian strategy has always been not to make any strong stand anywhere along the West Branch, but to fight delaying actions merely—making their real stand on the north bank of the Sarlo, only a few miles from Sarlo City itself. The Sarlo River, gentlemen, is well called "Sarlo's Shield." It has never been crossed."

"How do you expect to cross it, then, sir?" Schillian asked.

"Strictly speaking, we cross it not, but float down it. We cross the Tegula at Upper Ford, not Lower. . . ."

"*Upper* Ford, sire? Above the terrible gorge of the Low Umpasseurs?"

"Yea. That gorge, undefended, is passable. 'Tis rugged, but passage can be made. Once through the gorge our way to the Lake of the Spiders, from which springs the Middle Branch of the Sarlo, is clear and open."

"But 'tis held, sire, that Middle Valley is impassable for troops," a grizzled captain protested.

"We traverse it, nonetheless. On rafts, at six or seven miles an hour, faster by far than any army can march. But 'tis enough of explanation. Lord Sciro, attend!"

"I listen, sire."

"At earliest dawn take two centuries of axemen and one century of bowmen, with the wagonload of wood-workers' supplies about which some of you have wondered. Strike straight north at forced march. Cross the Tegula. Straight north again, to the Lake of the Spiders and the head of the Middle Branch. Build rafts, large enough and of sufficient number to bear our whole force; strong enough to stand rough usage. The rafts should be done, or nearly, by the time we get there."

"I hear, sire, and I obey."

Tedric, almost stunned by the novelty and audacity of this, the first amphibian operation in the history of his world, was dubious but willing. And as the map of that operation spread itself in his mind, he grew enthusiastic.

"We attack then, not from the south but from the northeast!"

"Aye, and on solid ground, not across deep water. But to bed, gentlemen—tomorrow the clarions sound before dawn!"

Dawn came. Sciro and his force struck out. The main army marched away, up the north bank of the Upper Midvale, which for thirty or forty miles flowed almost directly from the north-east. There, however, it circled sharply to flow from the south-east and the Lomarrians left it, continuing their march across undulating foothills straight for Upper Ford. From the south, the approach to this ford, lying just above (east of) the Low Umpasseur Mountains, at the point where the Middle Marches mounted a stiff but not abrupt gradient to become the Upper Marches, was not too difficult. Nor was the entrapment of most of the Sarlonians and barbarians on watch. The stream, while only knee-deep for the most part, was wide, fast, and rough; the bottom was made up in toto of rounded, mossy, extremely slippery rocks. There were enough men and horses and lines, however, so that the crossing was made without loss.

Then, turning three-quarters of a circle, the cavalcade made slow way back down the river, along its north bank, toward the forbidding gorge of the Low Umpasseurs.

The north bank was different, vastly different, from the south one. Mountains of bare rock, incredible thousands of feet higher than the plateau forming the south bank, towered at the rushing torrent's very edge. What passed for a road was narrow, steep, full of hair-pin turns, and fearfully rugged. But this, too, was passed—by dint of what labor and stress it is not necessary to dwell upon—and as the army debouched out onto the sparsely-wooded, gullied and eroded terrain of the high barred valley and began to make camp for the night, Tedric became deeply concerned. Sciro's small force would have left no obvious or lasting traces of its passing; but such blatant disfigurements as these. . . .

He glanced at the king, then stared back at the broad, trampled, deep-rutted way the army had come. "South of the river our tracks do not matter," he said, flatly. "In the gorge they exist not. But *those* traces, sire, matter greatly and are not to be covered or concealed."

"Tedric, I approve of you—you begin to think!" Much to the young man's surprise, Phagon smiled broadly. "How wouldst handle the thing, if decision yours?"

"A couple of fives of bowmen to camp here or nearby, sire," Tedric replied promptly, "to put arrows through any who come to spy."

"'Tis a sound idea, but not enough by half. Here I leave *you;* and a full century each of our best scouts and hunters. See to it, my lord captain, that none sees this our trail from here to the Lake of the Spiders; or, having seen it, lives to tell of the seeing."

Tedric, after selecting his sharpshooters and watching them melt invisibly into the landscape, went down the valley about a mile and hid himself carefully in a cave. These men knew the business in hand a lot better than he did, and he would not interfere. What he was for was to take command in an emergency; if the operation were a complete success he would have nothing whatever to do!

He was still in the cave, days later, when word came that the launching had begun. Rounding up his guerrillas, he led them at a fast pace to the Lake of the Spiders, around it, and to the place where the Lomarrian army had been encamped. Four fifty-man rafts were waiting, and Tedric noticed with surprise that a sort of house had been built on the one lying farthest down-stream. This

175

luxury, he learned, was for him and his squire Rahlion and their horses and armor!

The Middle Branch was wide and swift; and to Tedric and his bowmen, landlubbers all, it was terrifyingly rough and boisterous and full of rocks. Tedric, however, did not stay a landlubber long. He was not the type to sit in idleness when there was something physical to do, something new to learn. And learning to be a riverman was so much easier than learning to be King Phagon's idea of a strategist!

Thus, stripped to clout and moccasins, Tedric revelled in pitting his strength and speed at steering-oar or pole against the raft's mass and the river's whim.

"A good man, him," the boss boatman remarked to one of his mates. Then, later, to Tedric himself: " 'Tis shame, lord, that you got to work at this lord business. Wouldst make a damn good riverman in time."

"My thanks, sir, and 'twould be more fun, but King Phagon knows best. But this "Bend" you talk of—what is it?"

" 'Tis where this Middle Branch turns a square angle 'gainst solid rock to flow west into the Sarlo; the roughest, wickedest bit of water anybody ever tried to run a raft over. Canst try it with me if you like."

" 'Twould please me greatly to try."

Well short of the Bend, each raft was snubbed to the shore and unloaded. When the first one was bare, the boss riverman and a score of his best men stepped aboard. So did Tedric.

"What folly this?" Phagon yelled. "Tedric, ashore!"

"Canst swim, Lord Tedric?" the boss asked.

"Like an eel," Tedric admitted modestly, and the riverman turned to the king.

" 'Twill save you rafts, sire, if he works with us. He's quick as a cat and strong as a bull, and knows more of white water already than half my men."

"In that case . . ." Phagon waved his hand and the first raft took off.

Many of the rafts were lost, of course; and Tedric had to swim in icy water more than once, but he loved every exhausting, exciting second of the time. Nor were the broken logs of the wrecked rafts allowed to drift down the river as tell-tales. Each bit was hauled carefully ashore.

Below the Bend, the Middle Branch was wide and deep, hence the reloaded rafts had smooth sailing; and the Sarlo itself was of course wider and deeper still. In fact, it would have been easily navigable by an 80,000-ton modern liner. The only care now was to avoid discovery—which matter was attended to by several centuries of far-ranging scouts and by scores of rivermen in commandeered boats.

Moyla's Landing, the predetermined point of debarkation, was a scant fifteen miles from the city of Sarlo. It was scarcely a hamlet, but even so any one of its few inhabitants could have given the alarm. Hence it was surrounded by an advance force of bowmen and spearmen, and before those soldiers set out Phagon voiced the orders he was to repeat so often during the following hectic days.

"NO BURNING AND NO WANTON KILLING! None must know we come, but nonetheless Sarlon is to be a province of Lomarr my kingdom and *I will not have its people or its substance destroyed:* To that end I swear by my royal head, by the Throne, by Great Llosir's heart and brain and liver, that any man of whatever rank who slays or burns without my express permission will be flayed alive and then boiled in oil!"

Hence the taking of Moyla's Landing was very quiet, and its people were held under close guard. All that day and all the following night the army rested. Phagon was pretty sure that Taggad knew nothing of the invasion as yet; but it would be idle to hope to get much closer without being discovered. Every mile gained, however, would be worth a century of men. Therefore, long before dawn, the supremely ready Lomarrian forces rolled over the screening bluff and marched steadily toward Sarlo. Not fast, note; thirteen miles is a long haul when there is to be a full-scale battle at the end of it.

Plodding slowly along on mighty Dreegor at the king's right, Tedric roused himself from a brown study and, gathering his forces visibly, spoke: "Knowst I love the Lady Rhoann, sire?"

"Aye. No secret that, nor has been since the fall of Sarpedion."

"Hast permission, then, to ask her to be my wife, once back in Lompoar?"

"Mayst ask her sooner than that, if you like. Wilt be here tomorrow—with the Family, the Court, and an image of Great Llosir—for the Triumph."

Tedric's mouth dropped open. "But sire," he managed finally, "how couldst be *that* sure of success? The armies are too evenly matched."

"In seeming only. They have no body of horse or foot able to stand against my Royal Guard; they have nothing to cope with you and Sciro and your armor and weapons. Therefore I have been and am certain of Lomarr's success. Well-planned and well-executed ventures do not fail. This has been long in the planning, but only your discovery of the god-metal made it possible of execution." Then, as Tedric glanced involuntarily at his gold-plated armor: "Yea, the overlay made it possible for me to live—although I may die this day, being the center of attack and being weaker and of lesser endurance that I thought—but my life matters not beside the good of Lomarr. A king's life is of import only to himself, to his Family, and to a few—wouldst be surprised to learn how very *few*—real friends."

"Your life matters to me, sire—and to Sciro!"

"Aye, Tedric my almost-son, that I know. Art in the forefront of those few I spoke of. And take this not *too* seriously, for I expect fully to live. But in case I die, remember this: kings come and kings go; but as long as it holds the loyalty of such as you and Sciro and your kind, the Throne of Lomarr endures!"

Taggad of Sarlon was not taken completely by surprise. However, he had little enough warning, and so violent and hasty was his mobilization that the Sarlonians were little if any fresher than the Lomarrians when they met, a couple of miles outside the city's limit.

There is no need to describe in detail the arrangement of the centuries and the legions, nor to dwell at length upon the bloodiness and savagery of the conflict as a whole nor to pick out individual deeds of derring-do, of heroism, or of cowardice. Of prime interest here is the climactic charge of Lomarr's heavy horse—the Royal Guard—that ended it.

There was little enough of finesse in that terrific charge, led by glittering Phagon and his two alloy-clad lords. The best their Middlemarch horses could do in the way of speed was a lumbering canter, but their tremendous masses—a Middlemarch warhorse was not considered worth saving unless he weighed at least one long ton—added to the weight of man and armor each bore, gave them momentum starkly irresistible. Into and through the ranks of Sarlonian armor the knights of Lomarr's Old Blood crashed; each rising in his stirrups and swinging down with all his might, with sword or axe or hammer, upon whatever luckless wight was nearest at hand.

Then, re-forming, a backward smash; then another drive forward. But men were being unhorsed; horses were being hamstrung or killed; of a sudden king Phagon himself went down. Unhorsed, but not out—his god-metal axe, scarcely stoppable by iron, was taking heavy toll.

As at signal, every mounted Guardsman left his saddle as one; and every Guardsman who could move drove toward the flashing golden figure of his king.

"Where now, sire?" Tedric yelled, above the clang of iron.

"Taggad's pavilion, of course—where else?" Phagon yelled back.

"Guardsmen, to me!" Tedric roared. "Make wedge, as you did at Sarpedion's Temple!" and the knights who could not hear him were made by signs to understand what was required. "To that purple tent we ram Phagon our King. Elbows in, sire. Short thrusts only, and never mind your legs. Now, men—*DRIVE!*"

With three giants in impregnable armor at point—Tedric and Sciro were so close beside and behind the king as almost to be one with him—that flying wedge simply could not be stopped. In little over a minute it reached the pavilion and its terribly surprised owner. Golden tigers seemed to leap and creep as the lustrous silk of the tent rippled in the breeze; magnificent golden tigers adorned the Sarlonian's purple-enameled armor.

"Yield, Taggad of Sarlon, or die!" Phagon shouted.

179

"If I yield, Oh Phagon of Lomarr, what . . ." Taggad began a conciliatory speech, but even while speaking he whirled a long and heavy sword out from behind him, leaped, and struck—so fast that neither Phagon nor either of his lords had time to move; so viciously hard that had Lomarr's monarch been wearing anything but super-steel he would have joined his fathers then and there. As it was, however, the fierce-driven heavy blade twisted, bent double, and broke.

Phagon's counter-stroke was automatic. His axe, swung with all his strength and speed, crashed to the helve through iron and bone and brain; and, as soon as the heralds with their clarions could spread the news that Phagon had killed Taggad in hand to hand combat, all fighting ceased.

"Captain Sciro, kneel!" With the flat of his sword Phagon struck the steel-clad back a ringing blow. "Rise, Lord Sciro of Sarlon!"

"So be it," Skandos One murmured gently, and took up the life and work of Skandos Four.

Ultimate catastrophe was five hundred twenty-nine years away.

SUBSPACE SURVIVORS

There has always been, and will always be, the problem of surviving the experience that any trained expert can handle . . . when there hasn't been any first survivor to be an expert! When no one has ever gotten back to explain what happened. . . .

"All passengers, will pay attention, please?" All the high-fidelity speakers of the starship *Procyon* spoke as one, in the skillfully-modulated voice of the trained announcer. "This is the fourth and last cautionary announcement. Any who are not seated will seat themselves at once. Prepare for take-off acceleration of one and one-half gravities; that is, everyone will weigh one-half again as much as his normal Earth weight for about fifteen minutes. We lift in twenty seconds, I will count down the final five seconds . . . Five . . . Four . . . Three . . . Two . . . One . . . Lift!"

The immense vessel rose from her berth; slowly at first, but with ever-increasing velocity; and in the main lounge, where many of the passengers had gathered to watch the dwindling Earth, no one moved for the first five minutes. Then a girl stood up.

She was not a startlingly beautiful girl; no more so than can be seen fairly often, of a summer afternoon, on Seaside Beach. Her hair was an artificial yellow. Her eyes were a deep, cool blue. Her skin, what could be seen of it—she was wearing breeches and a long-sleeved shirt—was lightly tanned. She was only about five-feet-three, and her build was not spectacular. However, every ounce of her one hundred fifteen pounds was exactly where it should have been.

First she stood tentatively, flexing her knees and testing

181

her weight. Then, stepping boldly out into a clear space, she began to do a high-kicking acrobatic dance; and went on doing it as effortlessly and as rhythmically as though she were on an Earthly stage.

"You mustn't *do* that, Miss!" A stewardess came bustling up. Or, rather, not exactly bustling. Very few people, and almost no stewardesses, either actually bustle in or really enjoy one point five gees, "You really *must* resume your seat, Miss. I must insist . . . Oh, you're Miss Warner . . ."

She paused.

"That's right. Barbara Warner. Cabin two eight one."

"But really, Miss Warner, it's regulations, and if you should fall . . ."

"Foosh to regulations, and *pfui* on 'em. I won't fall. I've been wondering, every time out, if I could do a thing, and now I'm going to find out."

Jack-knifing double, she put both forearms flat on the carpet and lifted both legs into the vertical. Then, silver slippers pointing motionlessly ceilingward, she got up onto her hands and walked twice around a vacant chair. She then performed a series of flips that would have done credit to a professional acrobat; the finale of which left her sitting calmly in the previously empty seat.

"See?" she informed the flabbergasted stewardess. "I *could* do it, and I didn't . . ."

Her voice was drowned out in a yell of approval as everybody who could clap their hands did so with enthusiasm. "More!" "Keep it up, gal!" "Do it again!"

"Oh, I didn't do that to show off!" Barbara Warner flushed hotly as she met the eyes of the nearby spectators. "Honestly I didn't—I just *had* to know if I could." Then, as the applause did not die down, she fairly scampered out of the room.

For one hour before the *Procyon*'s departure from Earth and for three hours afterward, First Officer Carlyle Deston, Chief Electronicist, sat attentively at his board. He was five-feet-eight inches tall and weighed one hundred sixty-two pounds net. Just a little guy, as spacemen go. Although narrow-waisted and for his heft, broad-shouldered, he was built for speed and maneuverability, not to haul freight.

Watching a hundred lights and half that many instruments, listening to two phone circuits, one with each ear, and hands moving from switches to rheostats to buttons and levers, he was completely informed as to the instant-by-instant status of everything in his department.

Although attentive, he was not tense, even during the countdown. The only change was that at the word "Two" his right forefinger came to rest upon a red button and his eyes doubled their rate of scan. If anything in his department had gone wrong the *Procyon*'s departure would have been delayed.

And again, well out beyond the orbit of the moon, just before the starship's mighty Chaytor engines hurled her out of space as we know it into that unknowable something that is hyperspace, he poised a finger. But Immergence, too, was normal; all the green lights except one went out, needles dropped to zero, both phones went dead, all signals stopped. He plugged a jack into a socket below the one remaining green light and spoke:

"Procyon One to Control Six. Flight Eight Four Nine. Subspace Radio Test One. How do you read me, Control Six?"

"Control Six to Procyon One. I read you ten and zero. How do you read me, Procyon One?"

"Ten and zero. Out." Deston flipped a toggle and the solitary green light went out.

Perfect signal and zero noise. That was that. From now until Emergence—unless something happened—he might as well be a passenger. Everything was automatic, unless and until some robot or computer yelled for help. Deston leaned back in his bucket seat and lighted a cigarette. He didn't need to scan the board constantly now; any trouble signal would jump right out at him.

Promptly at Dee plus Three Zero Zero—three hours, no minutes, no seconds after departure—his relief appeared.

"All black, Babe?" the newcomer asked.

"As the pit, Eddie. Take over." Eddie did so. "You've picked out your girl friend for the trip, I suppose?"

"Not yet. I got sidetracked watching Bobby Warner.

183

She was doing handstands and handwalks and forward and back flips in the lounge—under one point five gees yet. *Wow!* And after that all the other women looked like a dime's worth of catmeat. She doesn't stand out too much until she starts to move, but then—Oh, *brother!*" Eddie rolled his eyes, made motions with his hands, and whistled expressively. "Talk about poetry in motion! Just walking across a stage, she'd bring down the house and stop the show cold in its tracks."

"OK, OK, don't blow a fuse," Deston said, resignedly. "I know. You'll love her undyingly; all this trip, maybe. So bring her up, next watch, and I'll give her a gold badge. As usual."

"You . . . how *dumb* can you get?" Eddie demanded. "D'you think I'd even *try* to play footsie with *Barbara Warner?*"

"You'd play footsie with the Archangel Michael's sister if she'd let you; and she probably would. So who's Barbara Warner?"

Eddie Thompson gazed at his superior pityingly. "I know you're ten nines per cent monk, Babe, but I *did* think you pulled your nose out of the megacycles often enough to learn a *few* of the facts of life. Did you ever hear of Warner Oil?"

"I think so." Deston thought for a moment. "Found a big new field, didn't they? In South America somewhere?"

"Just the biggest on Earth, is all. And not only on Earth. He operates in all the systems for a hundred parsecs around, and he never sinks a dry hole. Every well he drills is a gusher that blows the rig clear up into the stratosphere. Everybody wonders how he does it. My guess is that his wife's an oil-witch, which is why he lugs his whole family along wherever he goes. Why else would he?"

"Maybe he loves her. It happens, you know."

"Huh?" Eddie snorted. "After twenty years of her? Comet-gas! Anyway, would *you* have the sublime gall to make passes at Warner Oil's heiress, with more millions in her own sock than you've got dimes?"

"I don't make passes."

"That's right, you don't. Only at books and tapes, even

184

on ground leaves; more fool you. Well, then, would you *marry* anybody like that?"

"Certainly, if I loved . . ." Deston paused, thought a moment, then went on: "Maybe I wouldn't, either. She'd make me dress for dinner. She'd probably have a live waiter; maybe even a butler. So I guess I wouldn't, at that."

"You nor me neither, brother. But *what* a dish! What a lovely, luscious, toothsome *dish!*" Eddie mourned.

"You'll be raving about another one tomorrow," Deston said, unfeelingly, as he turned away.

"I don't know; but even if I do, *she* won't be anything like *her*," Eddie said, to the closing door.

And Deston, outside the door, grinned sardonically to himself. Before his next watch, Eddie would bring up one of the prettiest girls aboard for a gold badge; the token that would let her—under approved escort, of course—go through the Top.

He himself never went down to the Middle, which was passenger territory. There was nothing there he wanted. He was too busy, had too many worthwhile things to do, to waste time that way . . . but the hunch was getting stronger and stronger all the time. For the first time in all his three years of deep-space service he felt an over-powering urge to go down into the very middle of the Middle; to the starship's main lounge.

He knew that his hunches were infallible. At cards, dice, or wheels he had always had hunches and he had always won. That was why he had stopped gambling, years before, before anybody found out. He was that kind of a man.

Apart from the matter of unearned increment, however, he always followed his hunches; but this one he did not like at all. He had been resisting it for hours, because he had never visited the lounge and did not want to visit it now. But *something* down there was pulling like a tractor, so he went. He didn't go to his cabin; didn't even take off his side-arm. He didn't even think of it; the .41 automatic at his hip was as much a part of his uniform as his pants.

Entering the lounge, he did not have to look around.

185

She was playing bridge, and as eyes met eyes and she rose to her feet a shock-wave swept through him that made him feel as though his every hair was standing straight on end.

"Excuse me, please," she said to the other three at her table. "I must go now." She tossed her cards down onto the table and walked straight toward him; eyes still holding eyes.

He backed hastily out into the corridor, and as the door closed behind her they went naturally and wordlessly into each other's arms. Lips met lips in a kiss that lasted for a long, long time. It was not a passionate embrace—passion would come later—it was as though each of them, after endless years of bootless, fruitless longing, had come finally home.

"Come with me, dear, where we can talk," she said, finally; eyeing with disfavor the half-dozen highly interested spectators.

And a couple of minutes later, in cabin two hundred eighty-one, Deston said: "So *this* is why I had to come down into passenger territory. You came aboard at exactly zero seven forty-three."

"Uh-uh." She shook her yellow head. "A few minutes before that. That was when I read your name in the list of officers on the board. First Officer, Carlyle Deston. I got a tingle that went from the tips of my toes up and out through the very ends of my hair. Nothing like when we actually saw each other, of course. We both knew the truth, then. It's wonderful that you're so strongly psychic, too."

"I don't know about that," he said, thoughtfully. "All my training has been based on the axiomatic fact that the map is *not* the territory. Psionics, as I understand it, holds that the map *is*—practically—the territory, but can't prove it. So I simply don't know *what* to believe. On one hand, I have had real hunches all my life. On the other, the signal doesn't carry much information. More like hearing a siren when you're driving along a street. You know you have to pull over and stop, but that's all you know. It could be police, fire, ambulance—*anything*. Anybody with any psionic ability at all ought to do a lot better than that, I should think."

186

"Not necessarily. You've been fighting it. Ninety-nine per cent of your mind doesn't *want* to believe it; is dead set against it. So it has to force its way through whillions and skillions of ohms of resistance, so only the most powerful stimuli—'maximum signal' in your jargon, perhaps?—can get through to you at all." Suddenly she giggled like a schoolgirl. "You're either psychic or the biggest wolf in the known universe, and I know you aren't a wolf. If you hadn't been as psychic as I am, you'd've jumped clear out into subspace when a perfectly strange girl attacked you."

"How do you know so much about me?"

"I made it a point to. One of the junniors told me you're the only virgin officer in all space."

"That was Eddie Thompson."

"Uh-huh." She nodded brightly.

"Well, is that bad?"

"Anything else but. That is, he thought it was terrible—outrageous—a betrayal of the whole officer caste—but to me it makes everything just absolutely perfect."

"Me, too. How soon can we get married?"

"I'd say right now, except. . . ." She caught her lower lip between her teeth and thought. "No, no 'except.' Right now, or as soon as you can. You can't, without resigning, can you? They'd fire you?"

"Don't worry about that," he grinned. "My record is good enough, I think, to get a good ground job. Even if they fire me for not waiting until we ground, there's lots of jobs. I can support you, sweetheart."

"Oh, I know you can. I wasn't thinking of *that*. You wouldn't *like* a ground job."

"What difference does that make?" he asked, in honest surprise. "A man grows up. I couldn't have you with me in space, and I'd like that a lot less. No. I'm done with space, as of now. But what was that 'except' business?"

"I thought at first I'd tell my parents first—they're both aboard—but I decided not to. She'd scream bloody murder and he'd roar like a lion and none of it would make me change my mind, so we'll get married first."

He looked at her questioningly; she shrugged and went on: "We aren't what you'd call a happy family. She's been trying to make me marry an old goat of a prince and I finally told her to go roll her hoop—to get a divorce and marry the foul old beast herself. And to consolidate two empires, he's been wanting me to marry a multi-billionaire—who is also a louse and a crumb and a heel. Last week he *insisted* on it and I blew up like an atomic bomb. I told him if I got married a thousand times I'd pick every one of my husbands myself, without the least bit of help from either him or her. I'd keep on finding oil and stuff for him, I said, but that was all. . . ."

"Oil!" Deston exclaimed, involuntarily, as everything fell into place in his mind. The way she walked; poetry in motion . . . the oil-witch . . . two empires . . . more millions than he had dimes. . . . "Oh, you're Barbara Warner, then."

"Why, of course; but my friends call me 'Bobby.' Didn't you—but of course you didn't—you never read passenger lists. If you did, you'd've got a tingle, too."

"I got plenty of tingle without reading, believe me. However, I never expected to—"

"Don't say it, dear!" She got up and took both his hands in hers. "I know how you feel. I don't like to let you ruin your career, either, but *nothing* can separate us, now that we've found each other. So I'll tell you this." Her eyes looked steadily into his. "If it bothers you the least bit, later on, I'll give every dollar I own to some foundation or other, I swear it."

He laughed shamefacedly as he took her in his arms. "Since that's the way *you* look at it, it won't bother me a bit."

"Uh-huh, you *do* mean it." She snuggled her head down into the curve of his neck. "I can tell."

"I know you can, sweetheart." Then he had another thought, and with strong, deft fingers he explored the muscles of her arms and back. "But those acrobatics in plus gee—and you're trained down as hard and fine as I am, and it's my business to be—how come?"

"I majored in Physical Education and I love it. And I'm a Newmartian, you know, so I teach a few courses—"

"Newmartian? I've heard—but you aren't a colonial; you're as Terran as I am."

"By blood, yes; but I was born on Newmars. Our actual

188

and legal residence has always been there. The tax situation, you know."

"I don't know, no. Taxes don't bother me much. But go ahead. You teach a few courses. In?"

"Oh, bars, trapeze, ground-and-lofty tumbling, acrobatics, aerialistics, high-wire, muscle-control, judo—all that kind of thing."

"Ouch! So if you ever happen to accidentally get mad at me you'll tie me right up into a pretzel?"

"I doubt it; very seriously. I've tossed lots of two-hundred-pounders around, of course, but they were *not* space officers." She laughed unaffectedly as she tested his musculature much more professionally and much more thoroughly than he had tested hers. "Definitely I couldn't. A good big man can always take a good little one, you know."

"But I'm not big; I'm just a little squirt. You've probably heard what they call me?"

"Yes, and I'm going to call you 'Babe,' too, and mean it the same way they do. Besides, who wants a man a foot taller than she is and twice as big? You're just *exactly* the right size!"

"That's spreading the good old oil, Bobby, but I'll never tangle with you if I can help it. Buzz-saws are small, too, and sticks of dynamite. Shall we go hunt up the parson— or should it be a priest? Or a rabbi?"

"Even *that* doesn't make a particle of difference to you."

"Of course not. How could it?"

"A parson, please." Then, with a bright, quick grin: "We *have* got a lot to learn about each other, haven't we?"

"Some details, of course, but nothing of any importance and we'll have plenty of time to learn them."

"And we'll love every second of it. You'll live down here in the Middle with me, won't you, all the time you aren't actually on duty?"

"I can't imagine doing anything else," and the two set out, arms around each other, to find a minister. And as they strolled along:

"Of course you won't actually *need* a job, ever, or my money, either. You never even thought of dowsing, did you?"

"Dowsing? Oh, that witch stuff. Of course not."

"Listen, darling. All the time I've been touching you I've been learning about you. And you've been learning about me."

"Yes, but—"

"No buts, buster. You have really tremendous powers, and they *aren't* latent, either. All you have to do is quit fighting them and *use* them. You're ever so much stronger and fuller than I am. All I can do at dowsing is find water, oil, coal, and gas. I'm no good at all on metals—I couldn't feel gold if I were perched right on the roof of Fort Knox; I couldn't feel radium if it were frying me to a crisp. But I'm *positive* that you can tune yourself to anything you want to find."

He didn't believe it, and the argument went on until they reached the "Reverend's" quarters. Then, of course, it was dropped automatically; and the next five days were deliciously, deliriously, ecstatically happy days for them both.

II

At the time of this chronicle the status of interstellar flight was very similar to that of intercontinental jet-plane flight in the nineteen-sixties. Starships were designed by humanity's best brains; carried every safety device those brains could devise. They were maintained and serviced by ultra-skilled, ultra-trained, ultra-able crews; they were operated by the *creme-de-la-creme* of manhood. Only a man with an extremely capable mind in an extremely capable body could become an officer of a subspacer.

Statistically, starships were the safest means of transportation ever used by man; so safe that Very Important Persons used them regularly, unthinkingly, and as a matter of course. Statistically, the starships' fatality rate per million passenger-light-years was a small fraction of that of the automobiles' per million passenger-miles. Insurance companies offered odds of tens of thousands to one that any given star-traveller would return unharmed from any given star-trip he cared to make.

Nevertheless, accidents happened. A chillingly large

number of lives had, as a total, been lost; and no catastrophe had ever been even partially explained. No message of distress or call for help had ever been received. No single survivor had ever been found; nor any piece of wreckage.

And on the Great Wheel of Fate the *Procyon*'s number came up.

In the middle of the night Carlyle Deston came instantaneously awake—feeling with his every muscle and with his every square inch of skin; listening with all the force he could put into his auditory nerves; while deep down in his mind a huge, terribly silent voice continued to yell: "DANGER! DANGER! DANGER!"

In a very small fraction of a second Carlyle Deston moved—and fast. Seizing Barbara by an arm, he leaped out of bed with her.

"We are abandoning ship—get into this suit—quick!"

"But what . . . but I've *got* to dress!"

"No time! Snap it up!" He practically hurled her into her suit; clamped her helmet tight. Then he leaped into his own. "Skipper!" he snapped into the suit's microphone. "Deston. Emergency! Abandon ship!"

The alarm bells clanged once; the big red lights flashed once; the sirens barely started to growl, then quit. The whole vast fabric of the ship trembled and shuddered and shook as though it were being mauled by a thousand impossibly gigantic hammers. Deston did not know and never did find out whether it was his captain or an automatic that touched off the alarm. Whichever it was, the distsater happened so fast that practically no warning at all was given. And out in the corridor:

"Come on, girl—sprint!" He put his arm under hers and urged her along.

She did her best, but in comparison with his trained performance her best wasn't good. "I've never been checked out on sprinting in spacesuits!" she gasped. "Let go of me and go on ahead. I'll follow—"

Everything went out. Lights, gravity, air-circulation—everything.

"You haven't been checked out on free fall, either. Hang onto this tool-hanger here on my belt and we'll travel."

"Where to?" she asked, hurtling through the air much faster than she had ever gone on foot.

"Baby Two—that is, Lifecraft Number Two—my crash assignment. Good thing I was down here in the Middle; I'd never have made it from up Top. Next corridor left, I think." Then, as the light of his headlamp showed numbers on the wall: "Yes. Square left. I'll swing you."

He swung her and they shot to the end of the passage. He kicked a lever and the lifecraft's port swung open—to reveal a blaze of light and a startled, grey-haired man.

"What happened. . . . What hap . . . ?" The man began.

"Wrecked. We've had it. We're abandoning ship. Get into that cubby over there, shut the door tight behind you, and *stay there!*"

"But can't I do something to help—?"

"Without a suit and not knowing how to use one? You'd get burned to a cinder. Get in there—and *jump!*"

The oldster jumped and Deston turned to his wife. "Stay here at the port, Bobby. Wrap one leg around that lever, to anchor you. What does your telltale read? That gauge there—your radiation meter. It reads twenty, same as mine. Just pink, so we've got a minute or so. I'll roust out some passengers and toss 'em to you—you toss 'em along in there. Can do?"

She was white and trembling; she was very evidently on the verge of being violently sick; but she was far from being out of control. "Can do, sir."

"Good girl, sweetheart. Hang on one minute more and we'll have gravity and you'll be O.K."

The first five doors he tried were locked; and, since they were made of armor plate, there was nothing he could do about them except give each one a resounding kick with a heavy steel boot. The sixth was unlocked, but the passengers—a man and a woman—were very evidently and very gruesomely dead.

So was everyone else he could find until he came to a room in which a man in a spacesuit was floundering help-lessly in the air. He glanced at his telltale. Thirty-two. High in the red, almost against the pin.

"Bobby! What do you read?"

"Twenty-six."

"Good. I've found only one, but we're running out of time. I'm coming in."

In the lifecraft he closed the port and slammed on full drive away from the ship. Then, wheeling, he shucked Barbara out of her suit like an ear of corn and shed his own. He picked up a fire-extinguisher-like affair and jerked open the door of a room a little larger than a clothes closet. "Jump in here!" He slammed the door shut. "Now strip, quick!" He picked the canister up and twisted four valves.

Before he could get the gun into working position she was out of her pajamas—the fact that she had been wondering visibly what it was all about had done nothing whatever to cut down her speed. A flood of thick, creamy foam almost hid her from sight and Deston began to talk—quietly.

"Thanks, sweetheart, for not slowing us down by arguing and wanting explanations. This stuff is DEKON—short for 'Decontaminant, Complete; Compound, Adsorbent, and Chelating, Type DCQ-429.' Used soon enough, it takes care of radiation. Rub it in good, all over you— like this." He set the foam gun down on the floor and went vigorously to work. "Yes, hair, too. Every square millimeter of skin and mucous membrane. Yes, into your eyes. It stings 'em a little, but that's a lot better than going blind. And your mouth. Swallow six good big mouthfuls—it's tasteless and goes down easy.

"Now the soles of your feet—OK. The last will hurt plenty, but we've *got* to get some of it into your lungs and we can't do it the hospital way. So when I slap a gob of it over your mouth and nose inhale hard and deep. Just once is all anybody can do, but that's enough. And don't fight. Any ordinary woman I could handle, but I can't handle you fast enough. So if you don't inhale deep I'll have to knock you cold. Otherwise you die of lung cancer. Will do?"

"Will do, sweetheart. Good and deep. No fight," and she emptied her lungs.

He slapped it on. She inhaled, good and deep; and went into convulsive paroxysms of coughing. He held her in

193

his arms until the worst of it was over; but she was still coughing hard when she pulled herself away from him.

"But . . . how . . . about . . . you?" She could just barely talk; her voice was distorted, almost inaudible. "Let . . . me . . . help . . . you . . . quick!"

"No need, darling. Two other men out there. The old man probably won't need it—I think I got him into the safe quick enough—the other guy and I will help each other. So lie down there on the bunk and take it easy until I come back here and help you get the gunkum off. So-long for half an hour, pet."

Forty-five minutes later, while all four were still cleaning up the messes of foam, something began to buzz sharply. Deston stepped over to the board and flipped a switch. The communicator came on. Since everything aboard a starship is designed to fail safe, they were, of course, in normal space. On the visiplates hundreds of stars blazed in vari-colored points of hard, bright light.

"Baby Two acknowledging," Deston said. "First Officer Deston and three passengers. Deconned to zero. Report, please."

"Baby Three. Second Officer Jones and four passengers. Deconned to—"

"Thank God, Herc!" Formality vanished. "With *you* to astrogate us, we may have a chance. But how'd you make it? I'd've sworn a flying saucer couldn't've got down from the Top in the time we had."

"Same thing right back at you, Babe. I didn't have to come down. We were in Baby Three when it happened." Full vision was on; a big, square-jawed, lean, tanned face looked out at them from the screen.

"Huh? How come? And who's 'we'?"

"My wife and I." Second Officer Theodore "Hercules" Jones was somewhat embarrassed. "I got married, too, day before yesterday. After the way the old man chewed you out, though, I knew he'd slap irons on me without saying a word, so we kept it dark and hid out in Baby Three. These three are all we could find before our meters went high red. I deconned Bun, then—"

"Bun?" Barbara broke in. "Bernice Burns? How *wonderful!*"

194

"Formerly Bernice Burns." The face of a platinum-blonde beauty appeared on the screen beside Jones. "And *am* I glad to see *you*, Barbara, even if I did just meet you yesterday! I don't know whether I'd ever see another girl's face or not!"

"Let's cut the chat," Deston said then. "Herc, give me course, blast, and time for rendezvous . . . hey! My watch stopped!"

"So did mine," Jones said. "So just hold one gravity on eighteen dash forty-seven dash two seventy-one and I'll correct you as necessary."

After setting course, and still thinking of his watch, Deston said: "But it's nonmagnetic. It never stopped before."

The grey-haired man spoke. "It was never in such a field before. You see, those two observations of fact invalidate twenty-four of the thirty-eight best theories of hyper-space. But tell me—am I correct in saying that none of you were in direct contact with the metal of the ship when it happened?"

"We avoided it in case of trouble. You? Name and job?" Deston jerked his head at the younger stranger.

"I know *that* much. Henry Newman. Crew-chief, normal space jobs, unlimited."

"Your passengers, Herc?"

"Vincent Lopresto, finished, and his two bodyguards. They were sleeping in their suits, on air-mattresses. Grounders. Don't like subspace—or space, either."

"Just so." The grey-haired man nodded, almost happily. "We survivors, then, absorbed the charge gradually—"

"But what the—" Deston began.

"One moment, please, young man. You perhaps saw some of the bodies. What were they like?"

"They looked . . . well, not exactly as though they had exploded, but—" he paused.

"Precisely." Grey-Hair beamed. "That eliminates all the others except three—Morton's, Sebring's, and Rothstein's."

"You're a specialist in subspace then?"

"Oh, no, I'm not a specialist at all. I'm a dabbler, really. A specialist, you know, is one who learns more and more about less and less until he knows everything about nothing at all. I'm just the opposite. I'm learning less and less about more and more; hoping in time to know nothing at all about everything."

"In other words, a Fellow of the College. I'm glad you're aboard, sir."

"Oh, a Theoretician?" Barbara's face lit up and she held out her hand. "With dozens of doctorates in everything from Astronomy to Zoology? I've never met . . . I'm *ever* so glad to meet you, Doctor—?"

"Adams. Andrew Adams. But I have only eight at the moment. Earned degrees, that is."

"But what were you doing in this lifeboat? No, let me guess. You were X-ray-eying it and fine-toothing it for improvements made since your last trip, and storing the details away in your eidetic memory."

"Not eidetic, by any means. Merely very good."

"And how many metric tons of apparatus have you got in the hold?" Deston asked.

"Less than six. Just what I *must* have in order to—"

"Babe!" Jones' voice cut in. "Course change. Stay on alpha eighteen. Shift beta to forty-four and gamma to two sixty-five."

Rendezvous was made. Both lifecraft hung motionless relative to the *Procyon's* hulk. No other lifecraft had escaped. A conference was held.

Weeks of work would be necessary before Deston and Jones could learn even approximately what the damage to the *Procyon* had been. Decontamination was automatic, of course, but there would be literally hundreds of hot spots, each of which would have to be sought out and neutralized by hand. The passengers' effects would have to be listed and stored in the proper cabins. Each body would have to be given velocity away from the ship. And so on. Every survivor would have to work, and work hard.

The two girls wanted to be together. The two officers almost *had* to be together, to discuss matters at unhampered length and to make decisions. Each was, of course, almost as well versed in engineering as he was in his own specialty. All ships' officers from First to Fifth had to be. And, as long as they lived or until the *Procyon* made port, all responsibility rested: First, upon First Officer Deston; and second, upon Second Officer Jones. Therefore Theodore and Bernice Jones came aboard Lifecraft Two, and Deston asked Newman to flit across to Lifecraft Three.

"Not me; I like the scenery here better." Newman's eyes raked Bernice's five-feet-eight of scantily-clad sheer beauty from ankles to coiffure. "If you're too crowded— I know a lifecraft carries only fifty people—go yourself."

"As a crew-chief, you know the law." Deston spoke quietly—too quietly, as the other man should have known. "I am in command."

"You ain't in command of *me*, pretty boy!" Newman sneered. "You can play God when you're on sked, with a shipful of trained dogs to bite for you, but on here where nobody has ever come back from I make my own law— with *this!*" He patted his side pocket.

"Draw it, then!" Deston's voice now had all the top-deck rasp of his rank. "Or crawl!"

The First Officer had not moved; his right hand still hung quietly at his side. Newman glanced at the girls, both of whom were frozen; at Jones, who smiled at him pityingly; at Adams, who was merely interested. "I . . . my . . . yours is right where you can get at it," he faltered.

"You should have thought of that sooner. But, this once, I won't move a finger until your hand is in your pocket."

"Just wing him, Babe," Jones said then. "He looks strong enough, except for his head. We can use him to shovel out the gunkum and clean up."

"Uh-uh. I'll have to kill him sometime, and the sooner the better. Square between the eyes. Do you want a hundred limit at ten bucks a millimeter on how far the hole is off dead center?"

The two girls gasped; stared at each other and at the two officers in horror; but Jones said calmly, without losing any part of his smile: "I don't want a dime's worth of that. I've lost too much money that way already." At which outrageous statement both girls knew what was going on and smiled in relief.

And Newman misinterpreted those smiles completely;

197

especially Bernice's. The words came hard, but he managed to say them. "I crawl."

"Crawl, what?"

"I crawl, sir. You'll want my gun—"

"Keep it. There's a lot more difference than *that* between us. How close can you count seconds?"

"Plus or minus five per cent, sir."

"Close enough. Your first job will be to build some kind of a bruteforce, belt-or-gear thing to act as a clock. You will really work. Any more insubordination or any malingering at all and I'll put you into a lifecraft and launch you into space, where you can make your own laws and be monarch of all you survey. Dismissed! Now —flit!"

Newman flitted—fast—and Barbara, turning to her husband, opened her mouth to speak and shut it. No, he would have killed the man; he would have *had* to. He still might have to. Wherefore she said instead: "Why'd you let him keep his pistol? The . . . the *slime!* And after you actually saved his life, too!"

"With some people what's past doesn't count. The other was just a gesture. Psychology. It'll slow him down, I think. Besides, he'd have another one as soon as we get back into the *Procyon*."

"But you can lock up *all* their guns, can't you? Bernice asked.

"I'm afraid not. How about the other three, Herc?"

"With thanks to you, Barbara, for the word; slime. If Lopresto is a financier, I'm an angel, with wings and halo complete. Gangsters; hoodlums; racketeers; you'd have to open every can of concentrate aboard to find all their spare artillery."

"Check. The first thing to do is—"

"One word first," Bernice put in. "I want to thank you, First Off—no, not First Officer, but I could hardly—"

"Sure you can. I'm 'Babe' to us all, and you're 'Bun.' As to the other, forget it. You and I, Herc, will go over and—"

"And I," Adams put in, definitely. "I must photograph everything, before it is touched; therefore I must be the first on board. I must do some autopsies and also—"

198

"Of course. You're right," Deston said. "And if I haven't said it before, I'm tremendously glad to have a Big Brain along . . . oh, excuse that crack, please, Dr. Adams. It slipped out on me."

Adams laughed. "In context, I regard that as the highest compliment I have ever received. To you youngsters my advanced age of fifty-two represents senility. Nevertheless, you men need not 'Doctor' me. Either 'Adams' or 'Andy' will do very nicely. As for you two young women—"

I'm going to call you 'Uncle Andy,' " Barbara said, with a grin. "Now, Uncle Andy, you being a Big Brain— the term being used in its most complimentary sense— and the way you talked, one of your eight doctorates is in medicine."

"Of course."

"Are you any good at obstetrics?"

"In the present instance I am perfectly safe in saying—"

"Wait a minute!" Deston snapped. "Bobby, you are *not*—"

"I am too! That is, I don't suppose I *am* yet, since we were married only last Tuesday, but if he's competent— and I'm *sure* he is—I'm certainly *going* to! If we get back to Earth I *want* to, and if we don't both Bun and I have *got* to. Castaways' Code, you know. So how about it, Uncle Andy?"

"I know what you two girls are," Adams said, quietly. "I know what you two men must of necessity be. Therefore I can say without reservation that none of you need feel any apprehension whatever."

Deston was about to say something, but Barbara forestalled him. "Well, we can *think* about it, anyway, and talk it over. But for right now, I think it's high time we all got some sleep. Don't you?"

It was; and they did; and after they had slept and had eaten "breakfast" the three men wafted themselves across a couple of hundred yards of space to the crippled starship. Powerful floodlights were rigged.

"What . . . a . . . mess." Deston's voice was low and wondering. "The whole Top looks as though she'd crash-landed and spun out for eight miles. But the Middle and Tail look untouched."

Inside, however, devastation had gone deep into the Middle. Bulkheads, walls, floors, structural members; were torn, sheared, twisted into weirdly-distorted shapes impossible to understand or explain. And, much worse, were the *absences;* for in dozens of volumes, of as many sizes and of shapes incompatible with any three-dimensional geometry, every solid thing had vanished—without leaving any clue whatever as to where or how it had gone.

After three long days of hard work, Adams was satisfied. He had taken pictures as fast as both officers could process the film; he had covered many miles of tape with words only half of which either spaceman could understand. Then, finally, he said:

"Well, that covers the preliminary observations as well as I know how to do it. Thank you, boys, for your forbearance and your help. Now, if you'll help me find my stuff and bring some of it—a computer and so on—up to the lounge? They did so; the "and so on" proving to be a bewildering miscellany indeed. "Thank you immensely, gentlemen; now I won't bother you any more."

"You've learned a lot, Doc, and we haven't learned much of anything." Deston grinned ruefully. "That makes you the director. You'll have to tell us, in general terms, what to do."

"Oh? I can offer a few suggestions. It is virtually certain: One, that no subspace equipment will function. Two, that all normal-space equipment, except for some items you know about, will function normally. Three, that we can't do anything about subspace without landing on a planet. Four, that such landing will require extreme—I might almost say fantastic—precautions."

Although both officers thought that they understood Item Four, neither of them had any inkling as to what Adams really meant. They did understand thoroughly, however, Items One, Two, and Three.

"Hell's jets!" Deston exclaimed. "Do you mean we'll have to blast *normal* to a system?"

"It isn't as bad as you think, Babe," Jones said. "Stars are much thicker here—we're in the center somewhere—than around Sol. The probability is point nine plus that

200

any emergence would put us less than point four light-years away from a star. A couple of them show discs. I haven't measured any yet; have you, Doc?"

"Yes. Point two two, approximately, to the closest."

"So what?" Deston demanded. "What's the chance of it having an Earth-type planet?"

"Any solid planet will do," Adams said. "Just so it has plenty of mass."

"That's still quite a trip." Deston was coming around. "Especially since we can't use more than one point—"

"One point *zero* gravities," Jones put in.

"Over the long pull—and the women—you're right," Deston agreed, and took out his slide rule. "Let's see . . . one gravity, plus and minus . . . velocity . . . time . . . it'll take about eleven months?"

"Just about," Jones agreed, and Adams nodded.

"Well, if that's what the cards say, there's no use yowling about it," and all nine survivors went to work.

Deston, besides working, directed the activities of all the others except Adams; who worked harder and longer than did anyone else. He barely took time out to eat and to sleep. Nor did either Deston or Jones ask him what he was doing. Both knew that it would take five years of advanced study before either of them could understand the simplest material on the doctor's tapes.

III

The tremendous engines of the *Procyon* were again putting out their wonted torrents of power. The starship, now a mere spaceship, was on course at one gravity. The lifecraft were in their slots, but the five and the four still lived in them rather than in the vast and oppressive emptiness that the ship itself now was. And socially, outside of working hours, the two groups did not mix.

Clean-up was going nicely, at the union rate of six hours on and eighteen hours off. Deston could have set any hours he pleased, but he didn't. There was plenty of time. Eleven months in deep space is a fearfully, a tremendously long time.

"Morning," "afternoon," "evening," and "night" were,

201

of course, purely conventional terms. The twenty-four-hour "day" measured off by the brute-force machine that was their masterclock carried no guarantee, expressed or implied, as to either accuracy or uniformity.

One evening, then, four hard-faced men sat at two small tables in the main room of Lifecraft Three. Two of them, Ferdy Blaine and Moose Mordan, were playing cards for small stakes. Ferdy was of medium size; compact rather than slender; built of rawhide and spring steel. Lithe and poised, he was the epitome of leashed and controlled action. Moose was six-feet-four and weighed a good two-forty—stolid, massive, solid. Ferdy and Moose; a tiger and an elephant; both owned *in fee simple* by Vincent Lopresto.

The two at the other table had been planning for days. They had had many vitrolic arguments, but neither had made any motion toward his weapon.

"Play it my way and we've got it made, I tell you!" Newman pounded the table with his fist. Seventy *million* if it's a cent! Heavier grease than your lousy spig Syndicate ever even *heard* of! I'm as good an astrogator as Jones is, and a damn sight better engineer. In electronics I maybe ain't got the theory Pretty Boy has, but at building and repairing the stuff I've forgot more than he ever will know. At *practical* stuff, and that's all we give a whoop about, I lay over both them sissies like a Lunar dome."

"Oh, yeah?" Lopresto sneered. "How come you aren't ticketed for subspace, then?"

"For hell's sake, act your age!" Newman snorted in disgust. Eyes locked and held, but nothing happened. "D'ya think I'm dumb? Or that them subspace Boy Scouts can be fixed? Or I don't know where the heavy grease is at? Or I can't make the approach? Why ain't *you* in subspace?"

"I see." Lopresto forced his anger down. "But I've got to be *sure* we can get back without 'em."

"You can be *damn* sure. I got to get back myself, don't I? But get one thing down solid. *I* get the big peroxide blonde."

"You can have her. Too big. I like the little yellowhead a lot better."

Newman sneered into the hard-held face so close to his and said: "And don't think for a second *you* can make me crawl, you small-time, chiselling punk. Rub *me* out after we kill them off and you get nowhere. You're dead. Chew on that a while, and you'll know who's boss."

After just the right amount of holding back and objecting, Lopresto agreed. "You win, Newman, the way the cards lay. Have you ever planned this kind of an operation or do you want me to?"

"You do it, Vince," Newman said, grandly. He had at least one of the qualities of a leader. "Besides, you already have, ain't you?"

"Of course. Ferdy will take Deston—"

"No he won't! He's *mine*, the louse!"

"If you're *that* dumb, all bets are off. What are you using for a brain? Can't you see the guy's chain lightning on ball bearings?"

"But we're going to surprise 'em, ain't we?"

"Sure, but even Ferdy would just as soon not give *him* an even break. *You* wouldn't stand the chance of a snowflake in hell, and if you've got the brains of a louse you know it."

"OK, we'll let Ferdy have him. Me and you will match draws to see who—"

"I can draw twice to your once, but I suppose I'll have to prove it to you. I'll take Jones; you will gun the professor; Moose will grab the dames, one under each arm, and keep 'em out of the way until the shooting's over. The only thing is, when? The sooner the better. Tomorrow?"

"Not quite, Vince. Let 'em finish figuring course, time, distance, all that stuff. They can do it a lot faster and some better than I can. I'll tell you when."

"OK, and I'll give the signal. When I yell 'NOW' we give 'em the business."

Newman went to his cabin and the muscle called Moose spoke thoughtfully. That is, as nearly thoughtfully as his mental equipment would allow.

"I don't like that ape, boss. Before you gun him, let me work him over just a little bit, huh?"

"It'll be quite a while yet, but that's a promise, Moose. As soon as his job's done he'll wish he'd never been born."

Until then, we'll let him think he's Top Dog. Let him rave. But Ferdy, any time he's behind me or out of sight, watch him like a hawk. Shoot him through the right elbow if he makes one sour move."

"I get you, boss."

A couple of evenings later, in Lifecraft Two, Barbara said: "You're worried, Babe, and everything's going so smoothly. Why?"

"Too smoothly altogether. That's why. Newman ought to be doing a slow burn and goldbricking all he dares; instead of which he's happy as a clam and working like a nailer . . . and I wouldn't trust Vincent Lopresto or Ferdinand Blaine as far as I can throw a brick chimney by its smoke. This whole situation stinks. There's going to be shooting for sure."

"But they couldn't do *anything* without you two!" Bernice exclaimed. "It'd be suicide . . . and with no motive . . . *could* they, Ted, possibly?"

Jones' dark face did not lighten. "They could, and I'm very much afraid they intend to. As a crewchief, Newman is a jack-leg engineer and a very good practical 'troncist; and if he's what I *think* he is—" He paused.

"Could be," Deston said, doubtfully. "In with a mob of normal space pirate-smugglers. I'll buy that, but there wouldn't be enough plunder to—"

"Just a sec. So he's a pretty good rule-of-thumb astrogator, too, and we're computing every element of the flight. As for motive—salvage. With either of us alive, none. With both of us dead, can you guess within ten million bucks of how much they'll collect?"

"*Blockhead!*" Deston slapped himself on the forehead. "I never even *thought* of that angle. That nails it down solid."

"With the added attraction," Jones went on, coldly and steadily, "of having two extremely desirable women for eleven months before killing them, too."

Both girls shrank visibly, and Deston said: "Check. I thought that was the main feature, but it didn't add up. This does. Now, how will they figure the battle? Both of us at once, of—"

"Why?" Barbara asked. "I'd think they'd waylay you, one at a time."

"Uh-uh. The survivor would lock the ship in null-G and it'd be like shooting fish in a barrel. Since we're almost never together on duty . . . and it won't come until after we've finished the computations . . . they'll think up a good reason for *everybody* to be together, and that itself will be the tipoff. Ferdy will probably draw on me—"

"And he'll kill you," Jones said, flatly. "So I think I'll blow his brains out tomorrow morning on sight."

"And get killed yourself? No . . . much better to use their own trap—"

"We *can't!* Fast as you are, you aren't in *his* class. He's a professional—probably one of the fastest guns in space."

"Yes, but . . . I've got a . . . I mean I think I can—"

Bernice, grinning openly now, stopped Deston's floundering. "It's high time you fellows told each other the truth. Bobby and I let our back hair down long ago— we were both tremendously surprised to know that both you boys are just as strongly psychic as we are. Perhaps even more so."

"Oh . . . so *you* get hunches, too?" Jones demanded. "So you'll have plenty of warning?"

"All my life. The old alarm clock has never failed me yet. But the girls can't start packing pistols now."

"I wouldn't know how to shoot one if I did," Bernice laughed. "I'll throw things I'm very good at that."

"Huh?" Jones asked. He didn't know his new wife very well, either. "What can *you* throw straight enough to do any good?"

"Anything I can reach," she replied, confidently. "Baseballs, medicine balls, cannon balls, rocks, bricks, darts, discus, hammer, javelin—what-have-you. In a for-real battle I'd prefer . . . chairs, I think. Flying chairs are really hard to cope with. Knives are too . . . uh-uh, I'd much rather have you fellows do the actual executing. I'll start wearing a couple of knives in leg-sheaths, but I won't throw 'em or use 'em unless I absolutely have to. So who will I knock out with the first chair?"

"I'll answer that," Barbara said, quietly. "If it's Blaine against Babe, it'll be Lopresto against Herc. So you'll throw your chairs or whatever at that unspeakable oaf Newman."

"I'd rather brain him than anyone else I know, but that would leave that gigantic gorilla to . . . why, he'd . . . listen, you'll simply *have* to go armed."

"I always do." Barbara held out her hands. "Since they don't want to shoot us two—yet—these are all the weapons I'll need."

"Against a man-mountain like that? You're *that* good? Really?"

"Especially against a man-mountain like that. I'm that good. Really," and both Joneses began to realize what Deston already knew—just how deadly those harmless-seeming weapons could be.

Barbara went on: "We should have a signal, in case one of us gets warning first. Something that wouldn't mean anything to them . . . . musical, say . . . Brahms. That's it. The very instant any one of us feels their intent to signal their attacks he yells 'BRAHMS!' and we *all* beat them to the punch. OK?"

It was OK, and the four—Adams was still hard at work in the lounge—went to bed.

And three days later, within an hour after the last flight-datum had been "put in the tank," the four intended victims allowed themselves to be inveigled into the lounge. Everything was peaceful; everyone was full of friendship and brotherly love. But suddenly "BRAHMS!" rang out, with four voices in absolute unison; followed a moment later by Lopresto's stentorian "NOW!"

It was a very good thing that Deston had had ample warning, for he was indeed competing out of his class. As it was, his bullet crashed through Blaine's head, while the gunman's went harmlessly into the carpet. The other pistol duel wasn't even close! Lopresto's hand barely touched his gun.

Bernice, even while shrieking the battle-cry, leaped to her feet, hurled her chair, and reached for another; but one chair was enough. That fiercely but accurately-sped missile knocked the half-drawn pistol from Newman's hand and sent his body crashing to the floor, where Deston's second bullet made it certain that he would not recover consciousness.

Barbara's hand-to-hand engagement took about one second longer. Moose Mordan was big and strong; and, for such a big man, was fairly fast physically. If he had had time to get his muscles ready, he might have had a chance. His thought processes, however, were lamentably slow; and Barbara Warner Deston was almost as fast physically as she was mentally. Thus she reached him before he even began to realize that this pint-sized girl actually intended to hit him; and thus it was that his belly-muscles were still completely relaxed when her small but extremely hard left fist sank half-forearm-deep into his solar plexus.

With an agonized *"WHOOSH!"* he began to double up, but she scarcely allowed him to bend. Her right hand, fingers tightly bunched, was already boring savagely into a selected spot at the base of his neck. Then, left hand at his throat and right hand pulling hard at his belt, she put the totalized and concentrated power of her whole body behind the knee she drove into his groin.

That ended it. The big man could very well have been dying on his feet. To make sure, however—or to keep the girl from knowing that she had killed a man?—Deston and Jones each put a bullet through the falling head before it struck the rug.

Both girls flung themselves, sobbing, into their husband's arms.

The whole battle had lasted only a few seconds. Adams, although he had seen almost everything, had been concentrating so deeply that it took those few seconds for him actually to realize what was going on. He got up, felt the back of Newman's head, then looked casually at the three other bodies.

"Oh, I *killed* him, Carl!" Barbara sobbed, convulsively. "And the worst of it is, I really *meant* to! I *never* did anything like that before in my whole life!"

"You didn't kill him, Barbara," Adams said.

"Huh?" She raised her head from Deston's shoulder; the contrast between her streaming eyes and the relief dawning over her whole face was almost funny. "Why, I

207

did the foulest things possible, and as hard as I possibly could. I'm *sure* I killed him."

"By no means, my dear. Judo techniques, however skillfully and powerfully applied, do not and can not kill instantly. Bullets through the brain do. I will photograph the cadavers, of course, and perform the customary post-mortem examinations for the record; but I know already what the findings will be. These four men died instantly of gunshot wounds."

With the four gangsters gone, life aboardship settled down quickly into a routine. That routine, however, was in no sense dull. The officers had plenty to do; operating the whole ship and rebuilding the mechanisms that were operating on jury rigging or on straight "breadboard" hookups. And in their "spare" time they enjoyed themselves tremendously in becoming better and better acquainted with their wives. For Bernice and Jones, like Barbara and Deston, had for each other an infinite number of endless vistas of personality; the exploration of which was sheerest delight.

The girls—each of whom became joyously pregnant as soon as she could—kept house and helped their husbands whenever need or opportunity arose. Their biggest chore, however, was to see to it that Adams got sleep, food, and exercise. For, if left to his own devices, he would never have exercised at all, would have grabbed a bite now and then, and would have slept only when he could no longer stay awake.

"Uncle Andy, why don't you *use* that Big Brain of yours?" Barbara snapped at him one day. "For a man that's actually as smart as you are, I *swear* you've got the least sense of anybody I know!"

"But it's necessary, my dear child," Adams explained, unmoved. "This material is new. There are many extremely difficult problems involved, and I have less than a year to work on them. Less than *one year;* and it is a task for a team of specialists and all the resources of a research center."

To the officers, however, Adams went into more detail. "Considering the enormous amounts of supplies carried; the scope, quantity, and quality of the safety devices employed; it is improbable that we are the first survivors of a subspace catastrophe to set course for a planet."

After some argument, the officers agreed.

"While I cannot as yet detect it, classify it, or evaluate it, we are carrying an extremely heavy charge of an unknown nature; the residuum of a field of force which is possibly more or less analogous to the electromagnetic field. This residuum either is or is not dischargeable to an object of planetary mass; and I'm virtually certain that it is. The discharge may be anything from an imperceptible flow up to one of such violence as to volatilize the craft carrying it. From the facts: One, that in the absence of that field the subspace radio will function normally; and Two, that no subspace-radio messages have ever been received from survivors; the conclusion seems inescapable that the discharge of this unknown field is in fact of extreme violence."

"Good God!" Deston exclaimed. "Oh . . . *that* was what you meant by 'fantastic precautions,' back there?"

"Precisely."

"But what can we *do* about it?"

"I don't know. I . . . simply . . . do . . . not . . . know." Adams lost himself in thought for over a minute. "This is all *so* new . . . I know *so* little . . . and am working with such *pitifully* inadequate instrumentation— However, we have months of time yet, and if I am unable to arrive at a conclusion before arrival—I don't mean a rigorous analysis, of course, but merely a stop-gap, empirical, pragmatic solution—we will simply remain in orbit around that sun until I do."

IV

The *Procyon* bored on through space, at one unchanging gravity of acceleration. It may not seem, at first glance, that one gravity would result in any very high velocity; but when it is maintained steadily for days and weeks and months, it builds up to a very respectable speed. Nor was there any question of power, for the *Procyon*'s atomics did not drive the ship, but merely energized the

"Chaytors"—the Chaytor Effect engines that tapped the energy of the expanding universe itself.

Thus, in less than six months, the *Procyon* had attained a velocity almost half that of light. At the estimated midpoint of the flight the spaceship, still at one gravity of drive, was turned end-for-end; so that for the ensuing five-and-a-fraction months she would be slowing down.

A few weeks after the turnover. Adams seemed to have more time. At least, he devoted more time to the expectant mothers, even to the point of supervising Deston and Jones in the construction of a weirdly-wired device by means of which he studied and photographed the unborn child each woman bore. He said nothing, however, until Barbara made him talk.

"Listen, you egregious clam," she said, firmly, "I know darn well I've been pregnant for at *least* seven months, and I ought to be *twice* this big. Our clock isn't *that* far off; Carl said that by wave lengths or something it's only about three per cent fast. And you've been pussyfooting and hem-hawing around all this time. Now, Uncle Andy, I want the *truth. Are* we in for a lot of trouble?"

"Trouble? Of course not. *Certainly* not. No trouble at all, my dear. Why, you've seen the pictures—here, look at them again . . . see? Absolutely normal foetus—yours, too, Bernice. *Perfect!* No malformations of any kind."

"Yes, but for what *age?*" Bernice asked, pointedly. "Four months, say? I see, I was exposed to a course in embryology myself, once."

"But *that's* the interesting part of it!" Adams enthused. "Fascinating! And, indubitably, supremely important. In fact, it may point out the key datum underlying the solution of our entire problem. If this zeta field is causing this seemingly peculiar biological effect, that gives us a tremendously powerful new tool, for certain time vectors in the generalized matrix become parameters. Thus, certain determinants, notably the all-important delta-prime-sub-mu, become manipulable by . . . but you aren't *listening!*"

"I'm listening, pops, but nothing is coming through. But thanks much, anyway. I feel a lot better, knowing I'm not going to give birth to a monster. Or *are* you sure, really?"

"Of *course* I'm sure!" Adams snapped, testily, and Barbara led Deston aside.

"Have you got the *slightest* idea of what he was talking about?" she asked.

"Just the slightest, if any. Either that time is relative— no, that's so elementary he wouldn't mention it. Maybe he's figured out a *variable* time of some kind or other. Anyway, you girls' slowness in producing has given the old boy a big lift, and I'm mighty glad of it."

"But aren't you *worried*, sweetheart? Not even the least little bit?"

"Of course not," and Deston very evidently meant just that.

"I am. I can't help but be. Why aren't you?"

"Because Doc isn't, and he knows his stuff, believe me. He can't lie any better than a three-year-old, and he's *sure* that all four of you are just as safe as though you were in God's lefthand hip pocket."

"Oh—that's right. I never thought of it that way. So I *don't* have anything to worry about, do I?" She lifted her lips to be kissed; and the kiss was long and sweet.

Time flew past until, one day a couple of weeks short of arrival, Adams rushed up to Deston and Jones. "I have it!" he shouted, and began to spout a torrent of higher— very *much* higher—mathematics.

"Hold it, Doc!" Deston held up an expostulatory hand. "I read you zero and ten. Can't you delouse your signal? Whittle the stuff down to our size?"

"W-e-l-l," the scientist looked hurt, but did consent to forego the high math. "The discharge *is* catastrophic; in energy equivalent something of the order of magnitude of ten thousand discharges of lightning. And, unfortunately, I do *not* know what it is. It is virtually certain, however, that we will be able to dissipate it in successive decrements by the use of long, thin leads extending downward toward a high point of the planet."

"Wire, you mean? What kind?"

"The material is not important except in that it should have sufficient tensile strength to support as many miles as possible of its own length."

211

"We've got dozens of coils of hook-up wire," Deston said, "but not too many *miles* and it's soft stuff."

"*Graham* wire!" Jones snapped his finger.

"Of course," Deston agreed. "Hundreds of miles of it. Float the senser down on a Hotchkiss—"

"Tear-out." Jones objected.

"Bailey it—spidered out to twenty or so big, flat feet. That'll take metal, but we can cannibal the whole Middle without weakening the structure."

"Sure . . . surges—backlash. Remote it."

"Check. Remote everything to Baby Two, and—"

"Would you mind delousing *your* signal?" Adams asked, caustically.

" 'Scuse, please, Doc. A guy *does* talk better in his own lingo, doesn't he? Well, Graham wire is one-point-three-millimeter-diameter, ultra-high-tensile steel wire. Used for re-wrapping the Grahams, you know."

"No, I don't know. What are Grahams?"

"Why, they're the intermediates between the Chaytors . . . OK, OK, they're something like bottles, that have to stand terrifically high pressures."

"That's what I want to know. Such wire will do very nicely. Note now that our bodies must be grounded very thoroughly to the metal of the ship."

"You're so right. We'll wrap the girls in silver-mesh underwear up to the eyeballs, and run leads as big as my wrist to the frame."

The approach was made, and the fourth planet out from that strange sun was selected as a ground. That planet was not at all like Earth. It had little water, very little atmosphere, and very little vegetation. It was twice as massive as Earth; its surface was rugged and jagged; one of its stupendous mountain ranges had sharp peaks more than forty thousand feet high.

"There's one thing more we must do," Adams said. "I have barely begun to study this zeta field, and this one may very well be unique—irreplaceable. We must, therefore, launch all the lifecraft—except Number Two, of course— into separate orbits around this sun, so that a properly-staffed and properly-equipped expedition can study it."

"Your proper expedition might get its pants burned off, too."

"There is always that possibility; but I will insist on being assigned to the project. This information, young man, is *necessary*."

"OK, Doc," and it was done; and in a few days the *Procyon* hung motionless, a good five hundred miles high, directly above the highest, sharpest mountain peak they had been able to find.

The Bailey boom, with its spider-web-like network of grounding cables and with a large pulley at its end, extended two hundred feet straight out from the side of the ship. A twenty-five-mile coil of Graham wire was mounted on the remote-controlled Hotchkiss reel. The end of the wire was run out over the pulley; a fifteen-pound weight, to act both as a "senser" and to keep the wire from fouling, was attached; and a few hundred feet of wire were run out.

Then, in Lifecraft Two—as far away from the "business district" as they could get—the human bodies were grounded and Deston started the reel. The wire ran out—and ran—and ran—and ran. The full twenty-five miles were paid out, and still nothing happened. Then, very slowly, Deston let the big ship move straight downward. Until, finally, it happened.

There was a blast beside which the most terrific flash of lightning ever seen on Earth would have seemed like a firecracker. In what was almost a vacuum though she was, the whole immense mass of the *Procyon* was hurled upward like the cork out of a champagne bottle. And as for what it *felt* like—since the five who experienced it could never describe it, even to each other, it is obviously indescribable by or to anyone else. As Bernice said long afterward, when she was being pressed by a newsman: "Just tell 'em it was the living end," and that is as good a description as any.

The girls were unwrapped from their silver-mesh cocoons and, after a minute or so of semi-hysterics, were as good as new. Then Deston stared into the 'scope and gulped. Without saying a word he waved a hand and the others looked. It seemed as though the entire tip of the mountain was gone; had become a seething, flaming volcano on a world that had known no vulcanism for hundreds of thousands of years.

213

"And what," said Deston finally, "do you suppose happened to the other side of the ship?"

The boom, of course, was gone. So were all twenty of the grounding cables which, each the size of a man's arm, had fanned out in all directions to anchorages welded solidly to the vessel's skin and frame. The anchorages, too, were gone; and tons upon tons of high-alloy steel plating and structural members for many feet around where each anchorage had been. Steel had run like water; had been blown away in gusts of vapor.

"Shall I try the radio now, Doc?" Deston asked.

"By no means. This first blast would, of course, be the worst, but there will be several more, of decreasing violence."

There were. The second, while it volatilized the boom and its grounding network, merely fused portions of the anchorages. The third took only the boom itself; the fourth took only the dangling miles of wire. At the sixth trial nothing—apparently—happened; whereupon the wire was drawn in and a two-hundred pound mass of steel was lowered until it was in firm and quiescent contact with the solid rock of the planet.

"Now you may try your radio," Adams said.

Deston flipped a switch and spoke, quietly but clearly, into a microphone. *"Procyon One* to Control Six. Flight Eight Four Nine. Subspace Radio Test Ninety-Five—I think. How do you read me, Control Six?"

The reply was highly unorthodox. It was a wild yell, followed by words not directed at Deston at all. "Captain Reamer! Captain French! Captain Holloway! ANYBODY! It's the *Procyon!* The *PROCYON,* that was lost a year ago! Unless some fool is playing a dumb joke."

"It's no joke—I hope." Another voice, crisp and authoritative, came in; growing louder as its source approached the distant pickup. "Or somebody will rot in jail for a hundred years."

"Procyon One to Control Six," Deston said again. His voice was not quite steady this time; both girls were crying openly and joyfully. "How do you read me, Frenchy old horse?"

"It *is* Procyon One—the Runt himself— Hi, Babe!" the new voice roared, then quieted to normal volume. "I read you eight and one. Survivors.?"

"Five. Second Officer Jones, our wives, and Dr. Andrew Adams, a Fellow of the College of Advanced Study. He's solely responsible for our being here, so—"

"Skip that for now. In a lifecraft? No, after this long, it must be the ship. Not navigable, of course?"

"Not in subspace, and only so-so in normal. The Chaytors are OK, but the whole Top is spun out and the rest of her won't hold air—air, hell! She won't hold shipping crates! All the Wesleys are shot, and all the Q-converters. Half the Grahams are leaking like sieves, and—"

"Skip that, too. Just a sec—I'll cut in the downstairs recorder. Now start in at your last check and tell us what's happened since."

"It's a long story."

"Unwind it, Runt, I don't give a damn how long it is. Not a full-detailed report, just hit the high spots—but don't leave out anything really important."

"Wow!" Jones remarked, audibly. "Wottaman, Frenchy! Like the exurbanite said to the gardener: 'I don't want you to work hard—just take big shovelfuls and lots of 'em per minute.' "

"That's enough out of you, Herc my boy. You'll be next. Go ahead, Babe."

Deston went ahead, and spoke almost steadily for thirty minutes. He did not mention the gangsters; nor any personal matters. Otherwise, his report was accurate and complete. He had no idea that everything he said was going out on an Earth-wide hookup; or that many other planets, monitoring constantly all subspace channels, were hooking on. When he was finally released Captain French said, with a chuckle:

"Off the air for a minute. You've no idea what an uproar this has stirred up already. They let them have all your stuff, but we aren't putting out a thing until some Brass gets out there and gets the real story—"

"That *is* the real story, damn it!"

"Oh, sure, and a very nice job, too, for an extemporaneous effort—if it was. Semantics says, though, that in a

couple of spots it smells like slightly rancid cheese, and ...
no-no, keep still! Too many planets listening in—*verbum
sap.* Anyway, THE PRESS smells something, too, and
they're screaming their lungs out, especially the sob-sisters.
Now, Herc, on the air, you're orbiting the fourth planet of
a sun. What sun? Where?"

"I don't know. Unlisted. We're in completely unexplored
territory. Standard reference angles are as follows"—and
Jones read off a long list of observations, not only of the
brightest stars of the galaxy, but also of the standard reference points, such as S-Doradus, lying outside it. "When
you get that stuff all plotted, you'll find a hell of a big
confusion; but I *hope* there aren't enough stars in it but
what you can find us sometime."

"Off the air—for good, I hope. Don't make me laugh,
Buster. Your probable center will spear it. If there's ever
more than one star in any confusion *you* set up, I'll eat all
the extras. But there's a dozen Big Brains here, gnawing
their nails off up to the wrist to talk to Adams all the rest
of the night, so put him on and let's get back to sleep, huh?
They're cutting this mike now."

"Just a minute!" Deston snapped. "What's your time?"

"Three, fourteen, thirty-seven. So go back to bed, you
night-prowling owl."

"Of what day, month, and year?" Deston insisted.

"Friday, Sep—" French's voice was replaced by a much
older one; very evidently that of a Fellow of the College.

After listening for a moment to the newcomer and
Adams, Barbara took Deston by the arm and led him away.
"Just a little bit of *that* gibberish is a bountiful sufficiency,
husband mine. So I think we'd better take Captain French's
advice, don't you?"

Since there was only one star in Jones' "Confusion" (by the
book, "Volume of Uncertainty") finding the *Procyon* was
no problem at all. High Brass came in quantity and the
entire story—except for one bit of biology—was told. Two
huge subspace-going machine shops also came, and a thousand mechanics, who worked on the crippled liner for almost three weeks.

Then the *Procyon* started back for Earth under her own

subspace drive, under the command of Captain Theodore Jones. His first, last, and only subspace command, of course, since he was now a married man. Deston had wanted to resign while still a First Officer, but his superiors would not accept his resignation until his promotion "for outstanding services" came through. Thus, Ex-Captain Carlyle Deston and his wife were dead-heading, not quite back to Earth, but to the transfer-point for the planet Newmars.

"Theodore Warner Deston is going to be born on Newmars, where he should be," Barbara had said and Deston had agreed.

"But suppose she's Theodora?" Bernice had twitted her.

"Uh-uh," Barbara had said, calmly. "I just *know* he's Theodore."

"Uh-uh, I know." Bernice had nodded her spectacular head. "And we wanted a girl, so she is. Barbara Bernice Jones, her name is. A living doll."

Although both pregnancies were well advanced, neither was very near full term. Thus it was clear that both periods of gestation were going to be well over a year in length; but none of the five persons who knew it so much as mentioned that fact. To Adams it was only one tiny datum in an incredibly huge and complex mathematical structure. The parents did not want to be pilloried as crackpots, as publicity-seeking liars, or as being unable to count; and they knew that nobody would believe them if they told the truth; even—or especially?—no medical doctor. The more any doctor knew about gynecology and obstetrics, in fact, the less he would believe any such story as theirs.

Of what use is it to pit such puny and trivial things as *facts* against rock-ribbed, iron-bound, entrenched AUTHORITY?

The five, however, *knew;* and Deston and Jones had several long and highly unsatisfactory discussions; at first with Adams, and later between themselves. At the end of the last such discussion, a couple of hours out from the transfer point, Jones lit a cigarette savagely and rasped:

"Wherever you start or whatever your angle of approach, he *always* boils it down to this: 'Subjective time is measured by the number of learning events experienced.' I ask you, Babe, what does that mean? If anything?"

217

"It sounds like it ought to mean *something*, but I'll be damned if I know what." Deston gazed thoughtfully at the incandescent tip of his friend's cigarette. "However, if it makes the old boy happy and gives the College a toehold on subspace, what do *we* care?"

THE IMPERIAL STARS

They were the finest interstellar agents—and greatest circus stars—the Service of the Empire had!

I

DesPlaines (Plan) 15 rev cat 4-1076-9525. Hostile PX-3M-RKQ. Pop. (2440) 7500 00. COL 2015 Fr (qv) & NrAm (qv) phys. cult. Comml stndg, 229th. Prin ctrib gal: Circus o/t Gal, heav met, prec stones. (Encyclopedia Galactica, Vol. 9, p. 2937).

Jules and Yvette

For twenty-eight minutes The Flying d'Alemberts—who throughout two centuries had been the greatest troupe of aerialists of the entire Empire of Earth—had kept the vast audience of the Circus of the Galaxy spellbound: densely silent; almost tranced. For twenty-eight minutes both side rings had been empty and dark. The air over the center ring, from the hard-packed, imitation-sawdust-covered earth floor up to the plastic top one hundred forty-five feet above that floor, had been full of flying white-clad forms—singles and pairs and groups all doing something utterly breath-taking.

Suddenly, in perfect unison, eighteen of the twenty d'Alemberts then performing swung to their perches, secured their apparatus, and stood motionless, each with his or her right arm pointing upward at the highest part of the Big Top.

As all those arms pointed up at her, Yvette d'Alembert moved swiftly, smoothly, out to the middle of her high wire

—and that wire was high indeed, being one hundred thirty-two feet above the floor of the ring. She did not carry even a fan for balance. She maintained her equilibrium by almost imperceptible movements of her hands, feet, and body. Reaching the center of the span, she stopped and posed. To the audience she appeared as motionless as a statue.

Like all the other d'Alemberts, she was dressed in silver-spangled tights that clung to every part of her body like a second skin. Thus, while she was too short and too wide and too thick to be acceptable as an Earthly high-fashion model, her flamboyantly female figure made a very striking and very attractive picture—at a distance. Close up, however, that picture changed.

Her ankles were much larger than any Earthwoman's should have been. Her wrists were those of a six-foot-four, two-hundred-fifty-pound timberman. Her musculature, from toenails to ears to fingertips, would have made all the beachboys of Southern California turn green with envy.

After a few seconds of posing, she turned her head and looked down at her brother Jules, on a perch sixty-one feet below her and an "impossible" sixty-four feet off to one side. Then, flexing her knees and swinging her horizontally outstretched arms in ever-increasing arcs, she put more and more power into her tightly stretched steel—and Jules, grasping a flying ring in his left hand, began to flex his knees and move his body in precise synchronization with the natural period of the girl-wire system so far above him. Finally, in the last cycle through which she could hold the wire, Yvette squatted and drove both powerful legs downward and to her right—and something snapped, with a harsh, metallic report as loud as a pistol shot.

The wire, all its terrific tension released instantly as one end broke free and dropped, coiled itself up in the air with metallic whinings and slitherings; and Yvette d'Alembert, *premiere aerialiste* of all civilization, sprawling helplessly in mid-air, began her long fall to the floor.

Eighteen d'Alemberts came to life on their perches, seized all the equipment they could reach, and hurled it all at the falling girl. One of her frantically reaching fingertips barely touched the bar of one swinging trapeze; none of the other apparatus came even close.

Jules, in the lowest position, had more time than did any of the others; but he did not have a millisecond to spare. In the instant of the break he went outward and downward along the arc of the ninety-eight-foot radius of his top-hung flying ring. His aim was true and the force of launching had been precisely right.

Yvette was falling face down, flat and horizontal, at a speed of over seventy feet a second as she neared the point of meeting. Jules, rigidly vertical at the bottom of his prodigious swing, was moving almost half that fast. In the instant before a right-angle collision that would have smashed any two ordinary athletes into masses of bloody flesh, two strong right hands smacked together in the practically unbreakable hand-over-wrist grip of the aerialist and Yvette spun and twisted like a cat—except much faster. Both her feet went flat against his hard, flat belly. Her hard-sprung knees and powerful leg muscles absorbed most of the momentum of his mass and speed. Then, at the last possible instant, her legs went around his waist and locked behind his back, and his right hand flashed up to join his left in gripping the ring.

That took care of the horizontal component of energy, but the vertical one was worse—much worse; almost twice as great. Its violence drove their locked bodies downward and into a small but vicious arc; a savagely wrenching violence that would have broken any ordinary man's back in a fraction of a second. But Jules d'Alembert, although only five feet eight in height, had a mass of two hundred twenty-five pounds, most of which was composed of superhard, super-reactive muscle; unstretchable, unbreakable gristle; and super-dense, super-strong, horse-sized bone. His arms were as large as, and immensely stronger than, an ordinary Earthman's legs.

The two bodies, unstressed now relative to each other, began to hurtle downward together, at an angle of thirty degrees from the vertical, toward the edge of the ring facing the reserved-seat and box section of the stands.

The weakest point in the whole stressed system was now Jules' grip on that leather-covered steel ring. Could he hold it? Could he *possibly* hold it? Not one person in all that immense audience moved a muscle: not one of them even breathed.

He held his grip for just under half a second, held it while that half-inch nylon cable stretched a good seven feet, held it while the entire supporting framework creaked and groaned. Then the merest moment before that frightful fall would have been arrested and both would have been safe, Jules' hands slipped from the ring and both began to fall the remaining forty feet to the ground.

A high-speed camera, however, would have revealed the fact that they did not fall out of control. Each landed in perfect position. Hard-sprung knees took half of the shock of landing; hard-sprung elbows took half of what was left. Heads bent low on chests; powerful leg muscles drove forward; thick, hard shoulders and back muscles struck the floor in perfect rolls; and both brother and sister somersaulted lightly to their feet.

Hand in hand, they posed motionless for a moment; then bowed deeply in unison, turned and ran lightly to an exit— and they covered that one hundred yards of distance in less than five seconds.

And the multitude of spectators went wild.

They had seen a girl falling to certain death. They had felt a momentary flash of relief—or actually of disappointment?—when it seemed as though her life might be saved. Then they had watched two magnificently alive young people fall, if not to certain death, at least to maiming, crippling injury. Then, in the climactic last split second, the whole terrible accident had become the grand finale of the act.

That it was a grand finale—a crashing smash of a finish —there was no possible doubt. The only question was, what emotion predominated in that shrieking, yelling, clapping, jeering, cheering, whistling and catcalling throng of Earth-people—relief, appreciation or disappointment?

Whatever it was, however, they had all had the thrill of a life-time; and few if any of them could understand how it could possibly have been done.

For of the teeming billions of people inhabiting the nine hundred forty-two other planets of the Empire of Earth, scarcely one in a million had ever even heard of the planet DesPlaines. Of those who had heard of it, comparatively few knew that its surface gravity was approximately three thousand centimeters per second squared—more than three times that of small, green Earth. And most of those who knew that fact neither knew nor cared that harsh, forbidding, hostile DesPlaines was the home world of the Circus of the Galaxy and of The Family d'Alembert.

II

The Service of the Empire (SOTE) was founded in 2239 by Empress Stanley 3, the first of the Great Stanleys, who, during her reign of 37 years (2237–2274) inculcated in it the spirit of loyalty and devotion that has characterized it ever since. Its spirit wavered only once, under weak and vicious Empress Stanley 5, whose reign—fortunately very short (2293–2299)—was calamitous in every respect. SOTE came to full power, however, only under Emperor Stanley 10 (reign 2379—   ), the third and greatest of the Great Stanleys, under whom it became the finest orgainzation of its kind ever known. (Baird, A Study of Security, Ed. 2447, p. 291).

The Brawl in the Dunedin Arms

The city of Tampeta, Florida, had a population of over fifteen million. It included, not only what had once been Tampa, St. Petersburg and Clearwater, but also all the other cities and villages between Sarasota on the south and Port Richey on the north. Just outside Tampeta's city limit, well out toward Lakeland, lay the Pinellas Fair Ground. There the Circus of the Galaxy had been playing to capacity crowds for over a week, with a different show—especially with an entirely different climax—every night.

Jules and Yvette d'Alembert, as top stars of the show, of course had private dressing rooms. They also had private entrances. Thus no one connected with the show saw, and no one else either noticed or cared, that two short, fat Delfians, muffled to the eyes in the shapelessly billowing robes and hoods of their race, joined one of the columns of people moving slowly toward the exit leading to the immense parking lot. It took them half an hour to get to their car, but they were in no hurry.

Out of the traffic jam at last, Jules maneuvered his heavy vehicle up into the second-level, west-bound Interstate Four and sped for the Dunedin district and the Dunedin Arms, one of the plushiest night spots in all North America. At the Arms, he gave a dollar to the parking-lot attendant, another to the resplendently-uniformed doorman and a third to the usher who escorted them ceremoniously into the elevator and up to the fourth floor. At the check-stand the two Delfians refused—as expected—to part with any of their mufflings. Jules did, however—also as expected—give the provocatively clad hat-check girl a dollar before he handed his reservation slip and a five-dollar bill to the bowing captain.

"Thank you, sir and madam," that worthy said. "We are very glad indeed to have you with us this evening, Mister and Miss Tygven. Will you have your table now, or perhaps a little later?"

"A little later, I think," Jules said, using faultlessly the Russo-English "Empirese" that was the court language of the Empire. He paused then, and gazed about the huge room. At his right, along the full two-hundred-foot length of the room, ran the subduedly ornate, mirror-backed bar. At his left were three tremendous windows overlooking the beach and the open Gulf. Heavy tables of genuine oak, not too closely spaced, filled the place except for a large central dance floor. On a stage at the far end of the room a spot-lighted, red-haired stripper was doing her stuff. Priceless paintings and fabulous tapestries adorned the walls. Suits of armor dating from the ancient days of chivalry stood on pedestals and niches here and there. The place was jammed with a gay, colorful and festive crowd; there were only a few vacant places even at that tremendously long bar.

It was quite evident why the captain had suggested a short delay, so Jules said, "Yes, later, please. We will do a little serious drinking at the bar before we eat."

And at the bar, Jules laid a fifty-dollar bill on the oak and said, "A liter of vodnak, please. Estvan's, if you have it. In the original bottle—sealed."

"We have it, Mister." The bar-tender set out two glasses, a bowl of ice and the heavy, crudely molded, green-glass bottle of the one-hundred-and-twenty-proof beverage that was the favored tipple of the rim-world, Delf. "We've got everything. And don't worry about it not being the clear quill. We don't cheat. With our prices we don't have to"—and he put down on the bar a dollar and fifteen cents in change, which Jules waved away.

Before Jules opened the bottle—he was looking into the mirror, and so was Yvette—the man at Yvette's left finished his drink and moved away, and a tall, slim Earthman came up to take his place. Holding up one finger to the bartender, the newcomer said, "I'll take a jigger of the. . . ."

That was as far as he got. "Rube!" Yvette snapped—throughout the years, half of the old-time circus battle-cry of "Hey Rube!" had survived. She grabbed the heavy bottle by its neck, and hurling it even as she dropped—dropped safely under the vicious blaster-beam that, having incinerated the slender Earthman, swept through the space her chest had occupied an instant before. Still in air, falling almost flat, she braced one foot against the bar, dived head-long under the nearest table, bent her back and heaved.

The blaster-beam, however, had already expired. The heavy bottle, still full and still sealed, hurled with a Des-Plainian's strength and with an aerialist's sure control, had struck bottom-on squarely in the middle of the gunner's face—and that gunner now had no face at all and scarcely enough head to be recognizable as human.

Jules, too, was busy. He too had dropped at his sister's warning word, scanning the room as he fell. He too made a dive; but his was high and far, toward a table for six at which only two couples sat. One of the men at that table, half hidden behind a tall and statuesque blonde, had started to rise to his feet and was reaching for his left armpit.

Jules lit flat on the table and slid angle-wise across its length, in a welter of breaking and flying dishes, glassware, silverware, food and drink, directly at the man trying so frantically to draw his weapon. En route, Jules brushed the blonde aside. He didn't push her hard at all—just a one-handed gentle shove; just enough to get her out of the way. Nevertheless, she went over backward, chair and all, and performed an involuntary back somersault—thus revealing

225

to all interested observers that she wore only a lacy trifle of nylon in the way of underwear.

Continuing his slide, Jules made a point of his left elbow and rammed it into the man's gut. Then, as the man doubled up and "w-h-o-o-s-h-e-d" in agony, Jules whirled to his feet off of the table and chopped the hard edge of his right hand down onto the back of his victim's neck—which broke with a snap audible for dozens of feet above the uproar then going on. Then, seizing the man's half-drawn weapon—it was a stun-gun, not a blaster—he glanced at its dial. Ten. Wide open. Instantly lethal. Clicking it back to three—a half-hour stun—he played its beam briefly over the other man at the table (the guy had been too quiet and too unconcerned by far during all this action) and whirled around to see how his sister was making out.

Yvette was doing all right. The table under which she had disappeared had leaped into the air, turned over—shedding dishes and so forth far and wide—and crashed down onto the table at which the first blasterman and three other goons had been sitting. She had picked the blaster up and had tried to bend it around the side of Number Two's head; but it broke up almost as thoroughly as the head did. Ducking as only such a performer as she was could duck, she grabbed Number Three by the ankles, up-ended him, kicked the flaming blaster out of his hand before it could kill more than three innocent bystanders and was going to use him as a flail on Number Four when that unlucky (or lucky) wight slumped bonelessly to the floor in the beam of her brother's stunner.

She had the motion all made—why waste it?—So, continuing her swing, she hammer-threw Number Three over a few rows of tables and out into fifty feet of air through the middle of one of the three immense windows already mentioned.

Have you ever heard four hundred and thirty-two square feet of three-eighths-inch-thick plate glass shatter all at once? It makes a noise.

Such a noise that all lesser noises stopped instantly.

And in that strained, tense silence Jules spoke quietly to his sister. Both were apparently perfectly calm. Neither breathed one count faster than normal. Only their eyes—his a glacially cold grey; hers a furiously hot blue—showed

226

how angry and how disconcerted they both were. "Many more of 'em, you think?" he asked.

"Not to spot." Yvette shook her head. "And we've got no time to check."

"Right. Take that one, I'll bring the other. Flit." Carrying two unconscious men, the two ran lightly, but at terrific speed, down three flights of stairs and out into the parking lot. The attendant, upon seeing what burdens they carried, tried simultaneously to run and to yell, but accomplished neither—a half-hour stun saw to that.

Tortured rubber shrieked and smoked as the heavy car spun out of the lot and into the highway. Fortunately, traffic was so light—it was then half past two in the morning—that Jules did not have to drive far before a moment came when no other car was in sight.

The d'Alembert vehicle, while it looked pretty much like an ordinary groundcar, was a little too long and too wide and too round and much too heavy to be any standard model. Thus, alone in the road for a moment, Jules punched three buttons and three things happened: 1) the car's lights went out; 2) from those too-round sides the two halves of an air-tight, bulletproof, transparent canopy shot up, snapped together, and locked; and 3) the vehicle went straight up, at an acceleration of four Earthly gravities—having two Earthers aboard they couldn't hurry—to an altitude of a hundred and ninety thousand feet before it stopped.

Jules and Yvette removed what was left of their Delfian costumes—which wasn't very much—and stared wordlessly into each other's eyes for a long half minute. Then Yvette spoke:

"That was our contact. Our only contact. And we don't know anybody in SOTE on Earth . . . and there was a leak. There *had* to be a leak, Julie."

"That's for sure, and it was no ordinary leak, either. It had to be right in the Head's own office. . . ." Jules voice died away.

Yvette shivered. "I'm afraid so. And we haven't an inkling, except for his retinal pattern, of who the Head is or where he is. He may not be on Earth, even."

"Well, there'll be somebody in the Tampeta office here

227

and they'll be on the alert. That brawl put the stuff into the fan but good. They'll be monitoring the channel every second."

"But our friends' friends down there will be monitoring *all* channels every second—and they probably have the codes."

He thought for a moment, then grinned. "So I'll go back to one that's so old and so simple that they probably never heard of it . . . unless it'd fool our monitor, too . . . uh-uh. Whoever they've got on monitor right now is no dumb bunny; so here goes."

He flipped a blue switch and raised his powerful—and not too unmusical—deep bass voice in song: "Sing of the evening star, Oh Susan; sweetest old tune ever sung. Oh, Susan, sweet one, 'tis. . . ."

"Susan here." A lilting, smooth-as-cream contralto voice came from the speaker. There was a moment of silence, then the voice said "Cut!" and Jules flipped his switch; whereupon the voice concluded, "We'll beep in. Out."

"I'll say they're alert!" Yvette exclaimed; then went on, half-giggling in relief. "And she's fast on the trigger— 'Susan here' my left eyeball. You made that whole thing up, didn't you, on the spur of the moment."

"Uh-huh. If I'd had a little time the verse would have been as good as the music."

Yvette snorted. "Ha! Modesty, thy name is Jules! I expect them to tap you for the Met any minute now. But you were right on one thing—no dumb bunny could make 'S-O-T-E—S-O-S' so fast out of *that* mess of yowling. But it won't really be a beeper, you think?"

"Anything else but. My guess is a laser. They've got us lined up and they'll pour it right into our cup—so I'd better set the cup to spinning."

He did so, and in less than a minute the pencil-thin beam came in, chopped up into evenly-spaced dashes by the rotation of the cup-antenna of the car. There was of course no voice or signal.

While Jules was manipulating his finders to determine the exact line of the beam, he said, "Better unlimber the launchers, Evie, and break out some bombs. Just in case somebody wants to argue with us on the way. I'll handle the other stuff."

"That's a thought—" She broke off; her tone changed, "But just suppose that's *their* beam?"

"Could be; so we'll have to look a little bit out when we land. But they know that. So if everything's okay they'll engineer a safe approach—we won't have to. They *know* who we are." Things had gone wrong. They had given the right signal at the rendezvous—but the wrong people had responded. Now they had to find out why!

III

Democracy failed because it could not cope with Communism. This failure, which began early in the twentieth century, became very evident when, in 1922, Canada, the United States of America and Mexico united to form the United States of North America. The Congress of the USNA argued and filibustered, but could not agree upon any effective action against Communism. The Premier of Russia, however, acted. He issued orders; the recipients of which either obeyed them promptly or were promptly shot. (Mees, History of Civilization, Vol. 21, p. 1077).

The Head

Sliding down the beam, the d'Alembert's vehicle was heading directly toward the roof of a building that towered at least forty storys above any other structure in its neighborhood.

Jules slowed down; approached it gingerly; stopped half a mile away. It was all dark, except, strangely enough, for a small, brightly-lighted spot on the roof of one wing.

"Scan it," Jules said. "Infra first. See what it is."

Yvette put her eye to the scanner. "Hall of State; Sector Four. That makes sense. State would be the best place to hide the Service, wouldn't it?"

"Check. And the spot?"

"Floodlight. One. That's a girl, standing in it. Young. Skinny, but not bad for an Earther. Black hair—throatmike—sweater—shorts—two Mark Twenty-Nine Service blasters hanging loose—sandals. Sneak up, Julie."

229

Jules dropped the "car"—which was in fact one of the deadliest fighting machines of its weight ever built by man —down to within a couple of hundred yards of the lighted spot and stopped; and that highly distinctive throaty contralto voice came again from the speaker.

"It's safe to talk now if we don't say too much," the voice said conversationally. "Are you armed?"

"Yes." Jules wasn't saying much, yet.

"Good. You won't need these, then." The girl walked out of the ring of light, put the brutal big hand-weapons down on the roof, *and* resumed her former place. "You recognize my voice, of course."

"Yes."

"You have a retinascope, I suppose."

"Yes. Hold it a minute."

Jules cut com and turned to his sister. "I don't like this a nickel's worth. What Earther's pattern, except the Head's, would we recognize without a comparison disc? Nobody's. So, if this is on the up and up, we've got to manhandle the Head himself."

Yvette bit her lip. "Well, you said they'd arrange a safe approach, and that certainly would be one. What else can we do?"

"Nothing," and Jules again flipped the blue switch. "Go ahead."

"Land anywhere you please and one person will come aboard. Unarmed."

"Oke." Jules landed the car well away from the ring of light and opened a port.

In the darkness all that could be seen of the man who came up, empty hands outstretched, was that he was of medium height, of medium build and almost completely bald. He put his hands in through the port and Yvette, taking one of his wrists in each hand, helped him through the narrow opening and into the cramped front compartment of the car, where she held him gently but securely while Jules applied the retinascope to the Earthman's right eye.

"The Head himself," Jules said. "I'm sorry, sir. . . ."

"Think nothing of it, Jules." The stranger laughed deeply. "If you had acted differently I would have been amazed, displeased and disappointed. As it is, I am very glad indeed to meet you in the flesh," and he shook hands vigorously. "And you too, Yvette, my dear." Taking her hand, he kissed it in as courtly a fashion as though that tiny, cramped compartment were a ballroom. "And now—purely a formality, of course—the eyes. Yvette first, please," and he handed her the 'scope.

She fitted it to her eye. "But you didn't put any disc in," she said. "Surely, sir, you don't. . . ."

"I surely do." He studied her pattern briefly, then Jules'. "I don't know very many patterns, of course; but Jules and Yvette d'Alembert? You're too modest altogether, my dear." Then, opening the port, he called out, "Still safe, Helena?"

"Still safe, father," the girl called back, and began to walk toward the car. "Nothing suspicious, they say, within three hundred miles of here."

"Fine," Jules said. He opened the car up and all three got out. Jules went on, "I was hoping we were fast enough to get away clean, but I couldn't be sure. Now, sir, about our guests," and he jerked a thumb toward the rear compartment where the prisoners soddenly slept.

"Ah, yes. I've been wondering about them. The reports were confused and contradictory."

"I'm not surprised; it happened fast. That one—" Jules pointed—"is probably just a low-bred gunnie that doesn't know a thing. The other one may not know anything or he may know a lot," and he told, in a very few words, about the too imperturbable observer of the brawl. He finished: "So our secret rendezvous was no secret."

"I see." The Head raised his left wrist to his lips and said, "Colonel Grandon."

"Yes, sir?"

"Be on the roof in exactly two minutes. You'll find two men who got number three stunbeams about twenty minutes ago. They're in a Mark Forty-One Service Special near Space Jay Twelve. Revive them, find what they know and report."

"Very well, sir," and the Head led the way to an elevator.

The elevator took them down to the thirty-first floor, where it stopped of itself and opened its door into what was very evidently the private office of an exceedingly important man.

It was a fairly large room, furnished richly but quietly. The rug, brown in color, was thick and soft. The beamed ceiling was of beautifully grained brown solentawood; the panelled walls were of the same fine, almost metal-hard wood. On the wall behind the big solentawood desk was inlaid the gold-crowned Shield of Empire.

"Now we can talk," the girl said then, holding out her hand to Jules. "I'm Grand Lady. . . . Oh, excuse that please!" She flushed hotly, whereupon Jules kissed her hand in true Court style; after which she shook hands cordially with both Jules and Yvette.

"She should blush, friends," the Head said, but with no reproof in his voice. "But she hasn't been in the Service very long." Turning to the girl, he went on. "You are the Head's Girl Friday here, my dear. Our guests are of the thinnest upper crust of the entire Service; their worth to the Crown is immeasureable—beyond any number of Grand Ladies. We'll sit down, please, and Helena will pour. A whiskey sour for me, if you please." He cocked an eyebrow at his two agents. "Yours?"

"Orange juice, please," Yvette said, promptly; and Jules said, "Lemonade, please, if you have it handy."

Drinks in hand—Grand Lady Helena was drinking a weird-looking ice-cream concoction—the Head said:

"The attack on you was a complete surprise. No leak, no hanky-panky was even suspected until the man who was to bring you to me here was killed. The connection between this business and the matter that brought you to Earth is clear. In that connection it is a highly pleasing thought that the opposition knows nothing of you or of the Circus. You agree?"

"I agree, sir," Jules said, and Yvette nodded.

But Helena was puzzled. "How can it follow that they don't know, father?"

"The d'Alemberts are new to you because there is no record anywhere of any connection between them and us. Except for this surprise attack you would not be learning of them now. I will go into detail after they leave, but for the present I will simply state as a fact that no one who

232

knows anything about them would send only six men against Jules and Yvette d'Alembert. Or, if only six, all six would have fired simultaneously and on sight at them instead of burning the contact man first. That shows that they were more afraid of the Service here than of the supposed Delfian agents—a fatal error."

"Oh, I see—excuse me, please, for interrupting."

"That's quite all right. It's part of your education, Girl Friday. To proceed: we are investigating. We will find out where the leak is here and clean up the mess. In the meantime we will go ahead with the business for which we scheduled the Circus of Earth. There's trouble: centering, probably, on Durward. I'll give you all forty-odd reels of the record on it, but there are many things that are not on record and never will be, which is why I had to discuss it with you in person. You'll also have to talk to some outsiders to get the full picture. You may want to conduct preliminary invesigation on Earth and/or elsewhere before you go anywhere near Durward."

The Head got up. These were his most valuable agents, and the fact that he had brought them here was a measure of the importance he attached to the situation. He had fully expected that there would be trouble waiting for them between the Circus and his office . . . and he had been equally confident that the d'Alemberts would be able to handle it.

What he was less sure of was that they—even they—would be able to handle the trouble that lay ahead.

He said abruptly, "Let's fill in some background. For example, consider the question of loyalty. The Service is loyal to the Crown as the symbol of Empire; to the wearer of the Crown, whoever or whatever he or she may be, as the focal point of the Empire. You agree?"

"Of course, sir," Jules said, and both girls nodded.

"Very well. In early 2378, when Crown Prince Ansel was planning the murder of every other member of the Royal Family, if we could have caught him at it in time we could have burned him down, Crown Prince though he was."

"Why, I . . . suppose that . . . yes, sir," Jules said, and Yvette added thoughtfully.

"I never thought of it before in just that way, sir. But that's the way it would have to be."

233

"Nevertheless, after those eleven murders were accomplished facts Ansel, as the sole surviving member of the House of Stanley, became Emperor Stanley Nine. Was there then any question of gunning him? No. We instantly became as loyal to him as we had been to his father Stanley Eight and now are to his son Stanley Ten."

"Of course, sir. But what. . . ."

"Now comes some off-the-record material. Have you ever heard of Banion the Bastard?"

Jules thought for a moment. "I don't think so, sir," he said.

Yvette shook her head, but this time Helena nodded and said, "Oh-oh—a light beginneth to dawn."

"I didn't think you two had," the Head went on. "Not too many people now alive ever have."

IV

Even before Arnold invented the subether drive and made galactic exploration possible, all Earth except the USNA was under Communism and North America was being infiltrated and undermined. The real explosion of mankind into space, however, did not begin until 2013, when Copeland discovered the uranium-rich planet Urania Four; thus assuring all mankind of cheap and virtually unlimited power. In 2016 the American anti-Communists, disgusted and alarmed by the success of the "do-nothings" and "do-gooders" in blocking all effective action, left Earth en masse for Newhope; whereupon Communism took control of all Earth without firing a shot or launching a missile. (Mees, History of Civilization; Vol. 21, p. 1281).

Banion the Bastard

Marshalling his thoughts, the Head drank of his whiskey sour slowly, then went on, "Stanley Nine's weakness was women; particularly young ones. Although he married late in 2378, by the end of that year the Empress was merely a part of the furniture and the then Duke of Durward—one Henry, a bachelor of thirty—saw his big chance. He

234

combed his planet to find one highly special woman. She had to be young, a virgin, spectacularly beautiful, and highly intelligent. Also, as unscrupulous, as vicious, and as hard as he himself was. Also unknown on Earth or at Court. He found her. . . ."

The Head paused to finish his drink and build another one.

"The Beast of Durward," Helena said. "Surely you've heard of *her*."

Neither Jules nor Yvette had, and the Head went on, "A small-time ruthlessly ambitious actress. The Duke arranged and financed for her a tremendous and tremendously expensive splash at Grand Imperial Court, right here on Earth. Stanley Nine fell hard. He didn't stand a chance—and, with the Duke's full backing, she kept him on the hook much longer than any other woman was ever able to.

"When she was about seven months pregnant the Duke married her; with Nine's full approval. Thus her son Banion was born in wedlock as the first child of and the heir of the Duke and Duchess of Durward. That, however, wasn't enough for the schemers. Stanley Nine, still blindly infatuated with the extremely talented Beast, issued a Patent of Royalty, admitting paternity and bestowing upon the infant the unique title of 'The Prince of Durward.' This patent also authorized a coat of arms as follows:

" 'Purpure, quarterly three dragons rampant or, in chief sinister a bend sinister or, in dexter. . . .' "

"Wait up, father!" Helena broke in. "You're not getting through to me at all, and I don't believe that's our guests' language, either."

The Head laughed. "Gold dragons, rearing on purple enamel. The bar sinister, which may not be a mark of illegitimacy, in this case definitely was. It goes on that way for a couple of hundred words, only a few of which are pertinent. 'Bordure gules, charged thirteen bezants sable.' Poor heraldry—color on color and an unlucky number of spots on a background of blood—but that and the fact that the Patent was dated Friday the Thirteenth of June, 2380, are perfectly in keeping with the Duke's vicious sense of humor.

"A couple of months later—long overdue—Nine finally got tired of the Beast and came to with a thud. He who had wiped out all the rest of the Royal Family had himself

235

set up a pretender with a completely valid claim. He ordered the Service to kill the Duke and Banion and destroy the Patent; but he was 'way too late. The Beast had seen it coming and they got away clean. *With* the Patent.

"The Patent, of course, was most important. It was handwritten and signed in carbon ink by Emperor Stanley Nine himself, on Imperial parchment, with the signature driven into the parchment by the Great Seal of the Empire of Earth. The Patent was revoked, of course, and erased from all record, and the people were proscribed; but that wasn't enough. That Patent had to be found and destroyed; but it wasn't. Banion the Bastard had to be found and killed; but he wasn't.

"In 2381 there was a fairly serious uprising; which, it was deduced later, was engineered by the Beast on her own. At least, there was clear evidence that she tried to knife the Duke in bed and he cut her throat with her own blade.

"The search for that Patent and the Bastard and his blood has been going on ever since 2380; twenty years before I was born. As I said, the record of it covers more than forty reels. Results were neglible—except for finding, at a cost of eighty-nine lives, three very good forgeries—until two years ago, when several leads pointed back to Durward again. We sent agents, who found nothing. Three months ago all those agents stopped reporting. I sent in four of our best—with orders, of course, to avoid all previous contacts—and have not heard from any of them. Hence the Circus; the heaviest artillery the Service has. The threat to Stanley Ten and The Family is grave indeed. Just how grave I myself did not fully realize until the event of last night.

"Duke Henry was born in 2350, ninety-seven years ago; so he is probably dead. So it may or may not be his children and/or grandchildren who are carrying on. The Bastard, though, at 67, may still be a potent force; and he undoubtedly has children and grandchildren whom we don't know anything about, either.

"Your job is composed of two equally important parts. One, to find the genuine Patent and to bring it in so we can check its authenticity and so Stanley Ten can destroy it with his own hands. Two, to kill Banion the Bastard and all of his blood. Goodbye and good luck."

Back at the Circus, well after daybreak, Jules and Yvette reported to their father, the Managing Director. Then they drove out to the edge of the field, snugged their "car" down into its berth in their ultra-fast two-man subspacer, and Jules said:

"I knew the Head would have to be a Big Wheel, but not *that* big. If his daughter's a Grand Lady he's got to be a Grand Duke, no less. I think maybe I've seen his picture somewhere or seen him in a parade or something on tridi. . . ."

"Oh, *brother!*" Yvette snorted. "And I use the term advisedly. If you didn't recognize Grand Duke Zander von Wilmenhorst on sight! Oh no, he isn't much of anybody—just one-half Stanley blood and the fifth from the Throne itself, is all. You'd better break out your Peerage and start studying it."

"Uh-huh. *What* a cover for the Head—my God, he *owns* Sector Four!"

They slept until half past two; then went into the main tent to watch the climax of the matinee. They watched, with trained and minutely observant eyes, Yvette and Jules d'Alembert perform flawlessly a heart-stopping variation of the act they themselves had performed the night before.

Five minutes later, the younger couple still in spangles, the four d'Alemberts sat at a table in the commissary. The two men looked very much alike; so did the two girls—which was not surprising, since the two couples were two pairs of twins born of the same parents three years apart. No one except a DesPlainian could have told the two men or the two girls apart except by direct comparison. To the personnel of the Circus of the Galaxy this success of top stars was routine. In the two-hundred-year history of the Circus there had been almost a hundred pairs called 'Jules and Yvette d'Alembert'; there would continue to be a succession of them, one new pair every two or three years, as long as the Circus should endure.

"How'd we do, Gran'paw?" the younger brother asked. "It must have been a treat to see a good performance of your act."

"Close the orifice, Jules,' the younger girl broke in.

"Oh, you're calling me Jules already?"

"Certainly. You are Jules now. What I started to say was, that's the way people break their arms, patting themselves on the back so much."

"Okay. What I meant was, I'm glad the Head pulled them out of the Circus for special duty. It wouldn't be too long before they'd spatter themselves all over the ring the way their joints are creaking now. How *about* that, Jules?" and Jules grinned at Jules.

"That is very true and very sad, Jules," Jules agreed, as a waitress came up to take their orders. "These ancient and unwieldly bones are just about ready for the fertilizer mill. The old-time pep is all shot. . . ."

"Stop crying, Jules, poor dear," the waitress said. She was, of course, a d'Alembert, too; and she had been a star. "Before I break down and dilute your soup with a flood of tears of my own. The King and Queen are dead, et cetera. So what? You're just getting started on your real jobs. The usual?"

"Not quite," Yvette said. "You can get fresh orange juice here and I'm drowning myself in it. Squeeze me half a liter, please Felice dear, besides the usual."

"Drowning yourself is right," the younger Yvette said, darkly. "I've got to watch my figure; so I'll have one small glass of lemon sour and a lamb chop."

After eating, the older Jules and Yvette left the Circus—without a ripple to show that they had gone.

V

Communism could gain no foot-hold on the new, raw planets. Communists wanted to agitate, not work; and on the planets a man either worked or died. Confined to Earth and no longer able to keep its masses in line by the imaginary menace of warmongering Capitalism, and facing squarely the fact that men will not produce efficiently under the lash, Communism came to a very low ebb . . . until it was saved by Premier Koslov, a strong and able executive, who in 2020 made himself King Boris I of Earth and formed a harsh but just absolute monarchy based upon the profit motive. (Stanhope, Elements of Empire, p. 76).

Jules and Yvette studied, analyzed and restudied forty-seven spools of top-secret data, then sent them—top-secretly—through channels back to the Head. Then they visited more or less openly almost every district of Earth.

At every point they encountered the same not-right odor. Something was definitely wrong. Security had been breached—within the Service itself!

To Jules and Yvette d'Alembert the situation shrieked for action—instant effective action, at that. If the Service caught a chill, a hundred outlying planets lay under the threat of double pneumonia. For the Service was the ganglionic nerve system of the Stanleys themselves . . . and every bright, burning star, every immensely long, black spacelane, every whirling world and pocket of cosmic dust trembled and shook when those nerves tingled.

As the evidence grew it became clear that there were two courses of action. They could patiently, painstakingly search, sift and study . . . and hope for a break . . . or they could plunge themselves into a trouble spot—offer themselves as bait—risk life and limb on a gamble, and trust to mind and muscle to get them out. These were the choices. . . .

But really, there was no choice—because they were the d'Alemberts.

"Out of everything we've learned I can see only three points of attack outside of Durward itself," Jules said, thoughtfully. "Algonia, Nevander, and Aston. Years apart. Three forged Patents of Royalty. Eighty-nine good agents down the drain . . . most of them probably as smart as we are . . . in spite of all the help the local SOTE could give them. . . ." He paused.

"Uh-huh. Go on. Or because of it."

"Check. The higher the SOTE the solider the security. We think. But that thing in the Head's office didn't smell exactly like Coty's L'Arigon."

"I'll say it didn't. Usually they commit suicide or get their throats cut, but he simply disappeared. Absolutely vanished."

"So we'll roll our own, except maybe for tops. So the big question is, what's our best cover?"

"Well, we can't be Earthers, that's for sure." Yvette shrugged her shoulders and indicated his shape and her own. "Nor Delfians, to stand inspection. We're obviously DesPlainians. No other high-gravity planets were ever colonized, were there? Except Purity, of course . . . I wonder."

Jules frowned in thought. "That's a thought, sis; that splinter-group of crackpots on Purity. We can be Puritans."

Yvette nibbled her lip. "But would it work? They won't have anything to do with anybody they don't absolutely have to. Everybody's too sinful. They expect all the other planets, especially mother-planet DesPlaines, to be whiffed into incandescent vapor any minute by the wrath of God. There *are* a lot of renegade Puritans, though. Sinners."

"That's what I meant. We'll play it that they kicked us off because we got to be too sinful. We liked to dance and play cards and drink soda pop—to say nothing of mining gold and platinum and diamonds and emeralds and bootlegging all our stuff to Earth. That's the way we made all our money. Remember?"

Yvette laughed. "Just dimly. I must have been looking the other way at the time, but you can fill me in. They *have* kicked a lot of people off of Purity for doing just that—and for much smaller sins, as well. Go ahead; it listens good."

"Okay, but I don't know exactly what . . . get into compound low, brain, and start grinding . . . how about this? We'll have the Head make us ex-Puritan Citizens of Earth. You know how toplofty and you-be-damned Earthers are, out on the planets."

"Uh-huh, and we'll be toploftier and you-be-damneder than anybody. I like."

"Right. Concealment by obviousness. But as you said, not too many people ever even heard of Purity, and with our builds—your build especially—but wait a minute, how about disguising *me?* Hair down to my shoulders; waved and liquid-golded. Eyebrows shaved to a different shape and golded. Handle-bar moustache, waxed to points and golded. A cockeyed hat with gold plumes two feet long.

240

Cloth-of-gold sleeveless jersey and tight purple trunks. Arms and legs bare. A million dollars worth of jewellery—genuine—and a big, heavy swagger-stick that's really a blaster on one end and a stunner on the other. Think anybody'd recognize me as a DesPlainian in that kind of a fancy rig?"

"I'll say they wouldn't!" Yvette laughed delightedly, "anywhere on DesPlaines they'd shoot you on sight. The idea being that everyone would look at you and not bother to even wonder whether I was a DesPlainian or not."

"Uh-huh. Maybe it's a bit thin, but. . . ."

"I've got news for you, Buster." Yvette laughed again. "Not only it's thin, but also if you think I'm going to play little brown hen to that gorgeous hunk of rooster you're out of your mind. I'll design me a costume that will knock everybody's eyes right out of their sockets—one that no DesPlainian woman would be caught dead in at a catfight."

"Now you're chirping, birdie!"

"That'll be fun! But it'll take months to grow your hair . . . a wig? Uh-huh."

"Uh-huh is correct. Too chancy. But they've been working on this case for sixty-seven years, so a few extra weeks isn't going to make any important difference. And we'll have plenty to do in the meantime."

"That's true. Okay—let's fly it."

Thus it came about, some time later, that the Executive Office of the Duke of Algonia was invaded by a couple whose likes had never before been seen on the planet Algonia—or, for that matter, on any other planet. Jules was just as spectacular as his specifications had called for; Yvette was even more so. She, too, wore purple and gold—what little there was of it—with the arrangement of colors the exact reverse of his.

Her shoes—not silly pumps, but half-calf-high suregrips studded with precious stones—were royal purple. Her tight shorts were of exactly the same shade of purple as her shoes and hair. She wore a wide, heavily-jewelled belt of nylon-backed gold; a jewelled half-veil of fine gold mesh; and, to cap the climax, a towering gold-filigree headdress of diamonds, emeralds and rubies that had been appraised at and insured for one million three hundred ninety thousand dollars.

Paying no attention to the startled stares of the waiting people and office personnel, they walked calmly to the head of the line at the receptionist's desk. "We are citizens of Earth," Jules explained, as he courteously but firmly edged himself into the narrow space between a fat woman and the desk. He leaned over, picked up the amazed receptionist's hand and tucked a hundred-dollar bill into it. "Carlos and Carmen Velasquez, Citizens of Earth," he said gently, and dropped two ID cards onto her desk. "This is where visitors to your fair planet register, is it not?"

"Oh, no, sir—thank you, sir," the flustered girl said, as soon as her eyes got back into place and she could again use her voice. "That's downstairs, sir. The SOTE, sir."

"You will take care of it, my dear." Jules dropped three more notes on the desk. "Bring the cards over to the Hotel Splendide, after you have attended to it. We'll be there for a few days . . . or a few weeks, perhaps. Thank you, my girl." And the two walked out of the office as unconcernedly as they had walked in.

At the Splendide, which was the plushiest caravansery the planet boasted, they soon became the favorite guests. Not only because they had the penthouse suite; but also because neither of them knew, apparently, that there was any smaller unit of currency than a five-dollar Earth bill.

Whatever else they did, however, they always walked at a good, stiff hiking gait for at least an hour after supper. For the first few nights they explored; but after that, having found a route they liked, they stuck to it. Every night thereafter they drove out beyond the city limits, parked their car and took a six-mile hike along a fixed succession of narrow, lonely back-country roads and bridle-paths; a route that had five places made to order for ambush—and a route that they had gone to much trouble to publicize.

For six nights they swung along at their five-miles-an-hour hiking gaint in complete silence. . . .

Complete silence? Yes. Their suregrip shoes made not even a whisper of sound against the blacktop: no item of their apparel or equipment rattled or tinkled or squeaked or even rustled. Everything had been designed that way.

They could hear, but they could not be heard. Anyone laying for them would have to see them—and they themselves had very acute hearing and aerialists' eyesight.

Swinging along a clear stretch of road, Yvette asked, "S'pose we goofed, Julie?"

"Uh-huh. Pretty sure not. It's just taking them time to get set. Senor and Senora Velasquez aren't the type to just disappear; it'd raise too much of a stink. Also, besides the king-size fortunes we're wearing, everybody knows that we've got enough money in the safe at the Splendide to start a bank and they'll want that. So the job will take a lot of planning. This three-quarters-naked stunt wasn't designed to make it tough to impersonate us, but how would you go about finding two people to check out of the Splendide—and get that half a megabuck out of their safe—as us?"

"Nice!" Yvette laughed. "I never thought of it cutting both ways. They'll simply *have* to get a DesPlainian gangster and his moll . . . but wouldn't they have them ready?"

"I don't think so. You don't find very many DesPlainians on light-grav planets except in grav-controlled buildings. They no like—for which I don't blame them. Another month of this with no work at grav and you and I both will be as flabby as two tubs of boiled noodles."

"So we hope it won't be a month. Okay; we'll give 'em a few more days."

Five more hikes were eventless.

But on the sixth, at a place where the road wound through a coppice of small trees and dense underbrush, their straining ears heard sounds and their keen eyes saw movement.

For concealment, the place was perfect, but in order to act the attackers had to move—and low-echelon thugs are not very smart. Also, they had no idea whatever how fast their proposed quarry could move. Jules' hat and swagger stick and Yvette's tiara and handbag hit the blacktop practically at once as the two took off in low, flat dives; he to his side of the road, she to hers.

Diving straight through a bush, Jules slapped the nearest man lightly on the head—gently, so as not to break his neck—picked him up, and hurled him at another man,

243

some twelve feet away, who was just getting to his feet. One jump—he slugged the third in the solar plexus and in the same instant kicked the fourth in the face—not with his toe, but with the whole big flat sole of his shoe. Four down and one to go. But this action had taken almost a second of time—plenty of time for Number Five to get organized. Maybe he was the boss, since he'd been smart enough to station himself well off to one side.

Number Two, who hadn't been hurt much, began to regain consciousness and to thrash around. Jules snaked belly-wise over to him, picked his stunter up, and tapped him on the jaw with its butt. Then Jules crawled noiselessly around until he found a place from which he could get a fairly clear view toward Number Five; who, although he did not seem to realize it, was making a lot of noise. The seeing wasn't good—the moon, while high, was only at quarter—but not much light is necessary to use a stun-gun at close quarters.

"P-s-s-s-t!" the hood said, finally. "Ed! Hank! Spike! Did you get 'em. What the *hell* goes on?" He put his head out from behind a tree . . . and what went on was a half-hour stun.

"Eve?" Jules asked then, of empty air. "Five here."

"Same here," she replied from across the road. "No sweat. Is there any clear space over there?"

"Yes—we'll lug 'em over here."

Yvette recovered her towering headdress and bag, then came across the road, dragging two limp forms by the collars of their leather jackets. In a few minutes ten unconscious or dead men—Jules was afraid that he had hit Number Three a little too hard—were laid out on their backs in a neat row.

Jules picked up a stunner, then paused. "Uh-uh," he said, "Better give 'em the talk-juice now, so they'll be ready when we get 'em out to the house."

"That'd be better." And Yvette took a hypodermic kit out of her bag and went to work.

VI

In two centuries the colonized planets numbered seven hundred, many of them having large populations. Interstellar commerce increased exponentially. Interstellar crime became rampant. The government of Earth, under a succession of strong and able kings, had been in fact an imperium for many years when, in 2225, King Stanley the Sixth of Earth crowned himself Emperor Stanley One of the Empire of Earth. (Stanhope, Elements of Empire, p. 539).

Storming the Castle

Jules and Yvette did not drive their car—which was of course the biggest and most expensive one obtainable—back to the hotel. Instead, they loaded their victims into the limousine like cordwood and took them to the "house" they had rented long since—an estate so big and so far away from anywhere that the nearest neighbors could not have heard a forty-millimeter Bofors working at full automatic.

They unloaded their freight, then listened to the nine surviving hoodlums tell, completely unable to lie or withhold knowledge, everything they knew about crime—and especially its biggest chief.

The gamble paid off. "Got it!" exulted Jules when they were done. "I knew our friends—whoever they are—wouldn't stay out of a heist with this kind of money involved. But who would have thought that it was the Baron of Osberg. . . ."

"You for one, brother dear," supplied Yvette. "And maybe me for another—at least we knew the boss traitor had to be *somebody* big—but tell me, are we going to sit here all night patting you on the back or are we going to *do* something?"

Jules grinned and gave her a mock-salute. Then they gave each of the men a twelve-hour stun and went elsewhere.

The castle of the Baron of Osberg was some seventy

miles away. They parked the car a good mile down the road from it and, after selecting certain items of equipment, went the rest of the way on foot, being very careful not to be seen. Then, very cautiously and keeping continuously under cover, they made their way around what was actually a fortress.

The two gates, front and rear, were built of two-inch-square bar steel, topped with charged barbed wire. Neither could be opened except by electronic impulses from inside the castle. The estate was surrounded by a reinforced concrete wall fifteen feet high, surmounted by interlaced strands of charged barbed wire.

The two grinned at each other and separated. Taking advantage of the high, thick hedges bordering the drive, they sneaked up to within six feet of the wall. Both squatted down. Eyes met eyes through the lower, leafless part of the hedges. Muscles tensed and, at Yvette's nod both leaped at full strength upward and inward. Each cleared the topmost wire by a good three feet, stunners drawn, and at the top of their silent flight they fired rapidly and precisely, stunning every guard they could see. Then, running around the main building, each taking a side, they stunned everything that moved. Yvette ran for the garage; Jules ran to the castle's back door. It was locked, of course! but a Talbot cutter burned the lock away in seconds.

Jules did not know whether that door opened directly into the kitchen or into a hall; but the fact that it did open into the back hall made the job easy and simple. The door to the kitchen was not locked. The dozen or so people in it slumped bonelessly to the floor before any one of them realized that anything unusual was going on. Through the kitchen Jules went, through the butler's pantry and the serving hall, and put an eye to a tiny crack between thick velvet drapes.

The "commons" room was immense. Its beamed ceiling and panelled walls were of waxed yellow-wood. It was furnished lavishly and decorated profusely with ancestral portraits. At the far end there was an antlered fireplace in which a six-foot log smouldered.

Eleven men were in that room; some sitting, some standing; smoking or drinking or both; talking only occasionally and mostly in monosyllables; glancing much too frequently at watches on their wrists. Jules brought his stunner to bear and all eleven collapsed limply into their chairs or onto the floor.

In a couple of minutes Yvette came in. "Okay outside." she reported crisply. "Now the big frisk."

"That's right."

They went over the castle from subcellar to garrets, and when they were through they *knew* that everyone else inside the wall was unconscious. Then, and only then, Jules went over to the communicator, cut its video and punched a number.

"This is the Service of the Empire," a perfectly-trained, beautifully-modulated voice came from the speaker. "How may I serve you? If you will turn your vision on, please?"

"Sote six," Jules said. "Affold abacus zymase bezant. The head depends upon the stomach for survival."

"Bub-but-but, sir. . . ." The change in the girl's voice was shocking. She had never heard any two of those four six-letter code words spoken together, and coupled with the words "head" and "survival" they knocked her out of control for a moment; but she rallied quickly. "He's home asleep, sir, but I'll get him right away. One moment, please," and Jules heard the strident clatter of an unusually loud squawk-box.

"Lemme 'lone," a sleepy voice protested. "G'way. Cut out the damn racket or. . . ."

"Mr. Borton! Wake up!" the girl almost screamed. *"Please* wake up! It's a crash-pri red urgent!"

"Oh." That had done it. "Okay, Hazel; thanks."

"You are connected, sirs, and I'm out. Signal green, please, when you are through." She would much rather take a beating than listen to any part of the conversation that was to follow, whether she could understand any of it or not.

"Praxis," Borton said. (Request for identification, symbol, or authority.)

"Fazzle and Fezzle." (Their own identifying numbers— Agents Eighteen and Nineteen.)

"Holy . . ." Borton began, but shut himself up. The very top skimmings of the very top cream of the entire Service! "Okay."

"Rafter, angles, angels. Angled. Suffer. Harlot static in-
247

vert, cosine design. Single-joyful, singer, status, stasis. Over."

"*My—God!* Okay, but you didn't say where you are."

"I don't know your code for local specifics, so . . . comprehend Old English ig-pay attin-lay?"

"Ess-yay."

"Tate-ess-ay aron-bay berg-oz-zay."

"Catch."

"Front gate. Douse you glims short-long-short. Over and out if okay."

"Catch. Okay," Borton said. And it *was* okay—perfectly so. If Agents Eighteen and Nineteen told any planetary chief of SOTE to go jump in the lake he'd do it—and fast. "Here's your green, Hazel. Thanks."

In the time that elapsed before Borton's arrival at the estate of Baron Osberg's, Jules and Yvette questioned the eleven men. They didn't get enough to give them a clear lead to the planet Aston and a general idea of what the mob on Aston would have to be like. Then Borton arrived and they let him in.

"You!" he exclaimed, looking from one spectacular agent to the other and back again. *"That's* a switch. You came in with bands blaring and pennons waving."

"Check. They would be looking for pussy-footers."

"Could be. . . . If I may ask, I suppose there's a good reason why I wasn't let in on any of this?"

"Very good. Come in and you'll see what it was." They led him back into the commons rooms and Jules waved an arm at the stupefied men who, glazed eyes unseeing, lolled slackly in chairs.

"You used Nitrobarb," Borton said. "And on the Baron of Osberg. Half of them will die. I see."

"They'll all die," Jules said grimly. "Especially the Baron. Those who live through this will live a few days longer than the others, is all. But you really don't see, yet. Keep on looking."

Borton's fast-panning gaze came to a burly, crew-cut man of thirty-odd and stopped. His face turned grey; he was too shocked and too surprised even to swear.

"That's Alf Rixton," he managed finally. "My first assistant. He's been with me over ten years! top clearance—lie-detector and hypnosis—every year. He's done splendid work."

"Yeah—for the other side," Jules said coldly. "The only ones he ever gave you were the ones they wanted to get rid of. Take over, Borton, it's all yours. We'll have to stick around for a while—it'd smell cheesy if we'd leave the planet too soon—but we don't want to appear in this. Not a whisper. Nobody around here got a glimpse of us, but there are nine men—" he told him about them—"who shouldn't talk."

"They won't. But listen! This mess here—I couldn't *possibly* have done this alone!"

"Of course not." Jules grinned. "Your assistant there cooked the whole deal up and helped you swing it. He was a tiger on wheels. Too bad the honors are posthumous."

Borton nodded slowly. "Thanks. One of our very best, he died a hero's death, defending gallantly and so forth— sob, sob—the *louse*. But this thing of me taking all the credit for an operation that. . . ." He broke off and grinned wryly. "Okay."

"Uh-huh," Jules agreed. Then he and Yvette said in unison, "Here's to tomorrow, fellow and friend. May we all live to see it!" And they strode blithely out. One nest had been cleared out—it was time to move on to the next!

Borton, motionless, stared at the closed door. He knew *what* those two were—Agents Eighteen and Nineteen—but that was all he knew or ever would know about them. . . . But he had too much to do to waste much time wool-gathering. Shrugging his shoulders, he called his office and issued orders.

Then he set up his recorder and began to ask questions of the hoodlums who were still alive.

VII

THE STANLEY DOCTRINE. Empress Stanley 3 also re-organized, simplified and in a sense standardized the there-tofore chaotic system of nobility. Her system, which has been changed very little throughout the years, is in essence as follows. Grand Dukes rule sectors of space, each con-taining many planets. Dukes rule single planets. Marquises

*rule continents or the equivalent thereof. Earls rule
states or small nations. Counts rule counties. Barons rule
cities or districts. Primogeniture is strict, with no distinction as to sex. Nobles may marry commoners or higher
or lower nobles; the lower-born of each pair being automatically raised to the full rank of the higher-born spouse.
(Stanhope, Elements of Empire, p. 541).*

The Switch

The news broke early the following morning. It broke with
a crash that was channelled to every planet of civilization.

Carlos and Carmen Velasquez knew nothing of it until
half past ten, when the eager waiter hurried in with the
breakfast they had ordered a few minutes before. He was
accompanied this time by his captain, who carried both
morning papers in his hand.

"Good morning, sir and madam," that worthy said.
"You have perhaps not heard the extraordinary news on
your receiver?"

"Uh-us." Jules covered a yawn with his hand and shook
his head. "We're hardly awake yet." He was wearing only
purple-and-gold pajamas; Yvette wore her fabulous headpiece and a purple-and-gold robe that, while opaque in a
few places here and there, was practically transparent
everywhere else. "Something happen?"

"Most assuredly! The most tremendous, the most sen-
sational of happenings, be assured!" He put the papers
down on a side table and helped the waiter arrange the
breakfast table most meticulously. "But you will read of
it later. You will eat your breakfast now, please, while it
is hot." And the two hotel men accepted gratuities and went
back downstairs.

After eating, Jules and Yvette went through the story
with interest—if with an occasional snort or giggle. The
official version was of course new to them. SOTE, under
the masterly direction and leadership of Planetary Chief
Borton, had been keeping this band of traitors under close
and continuous surveillance for over a year. They had
waited until they were sure that they had found every

250

member and connection of the band, then they had struck everywhere at once. They had made a clean sweep.

Faced with absolute proof of guilt, each traitor had confessed and each had been promptly executed, including the Baron of Osberg, who had been the leader. All had been cremated and their ashes had been dumped. The reporter was very glad to say that, since the Baron was the only member of his family involved in the crime, the Barony of Osberg would not revert to the crown. The Baroness Carlotta, who was very well known as a philanthropic clubwoman would succeed—and so on.

Planetary Chief Borton had had no help, not even from Earth. And there was no hint anywhere that nitrobarb— the mere possession of which was by law a capital offense— had been used.

"Nice," Yvette said. "That story is so tight I almost believe it myself. But you said we'd have to stick around. Why? The fact that we were here on the planet—coupled with the fact that those two Delfians had to be DesPlainians —would be plenty for people not half as smart as they are. Whether we stay here a month or leave today makes no difference—except perhaps as an exercise in the old guessing game."

"That's probably right, at that . . . Okay, we'll shoot in a call for the ship as soon as we're dressed."

Since the ship had to come from DesPlaines, it was eight days later that Carlos and Carmen Velasquez left the Hotel Splendide for the spaceport, scattering largesse from the penthouse to the limousine as they went.

It was good to feel real gravity again; it was vastly more than good, when, safely inside a private lounge of the big subspacer, they were met by three particular people— two of whom were very special people indeed.

"Jules!" a brown-haired girl shrieked, and took off at him in a flying leap from a distance of twelve feet.

"Vonnie! Sweetheart!" He caught her expertly, although her momentum swung him around in a full circle; and for a long, ecstatic minute they stood almost motionless, locked fiercely in each other's arms.

Yvonne pulled back a little, looked at him closely and shook her head. "I've got to have a picture of you. Both

251

of you. They told me, but *this* is a thing that has got to be seen to be believed. You always were a handsome dog, Julie, but now you're simply *beautiful!*" She kissed him a few more times. "But I *don't* like that moustache—it tickles! You know something? I asked the Council to let me be Carmen Velasquez—begged them, practically on my knees—but the old stinkers wouldn't. They made me take the thousand-point test, just like everybody else, and Gabby here beat me out."

Jules grinned. "Did you think they wouldn't?"

"Well, they certainly *ought* to've given me the job, since I'm engaged to the only thousand-pointer alive. Anyway, I speared second place. I got nine eighty-nine."

"That's mighty good going, sweet." There was a brief interlude, then Jules, with his arm still around his Yvonne's waist, turned to the two others, whom he hadn't even looked at before. The man was of his own age, size and shape, his hair, moustache, and eyebrows matched Jules' exactly. The girl, too, except for costume, was a very reasonable facsimile of Yvette, purple hair and all. The man had been embracing Yvette ardently; the girl, having taken the towering ornament from Yvette's head and put it on her own, was unblushingly admiring herself in a mirror.

"Hi, Gabby; hi, Jacques," Jules said, extending his free hand.

" 'Gabby,' indeed!" the girl said, tossing her head in fine scorn. " 'Grand Lady Gabrielle' to you, lout. I don't think I'll even speak to any of the common herd any more unless they come crawling, bumping their foreheads on the floor."

"Here, here!" "That's telling him, Gabby!" Yvette and Jacques said at once, and Yvette added:

"I *liked* wearing these jewels and that crown and stuff, darn it," she mourned. "They *did* something for me," and the conversation became general.

Jules and Yvette took off their spectacular finery and turned it over to the new Carlos and Carmen. They had their hair un-dyed and rebarbered long and plain; and Jules unwaxed and un-curled his moustache. They donned shapeless brown trousers and jackets of homespun and became in appearance somewhat unorthodox Puritans. The switch completed, at the next transfer-point a new Carlos and Carmen Velasquez, still tossing five-dollar Earth bills around like confetti, boarded the biggest and plushiest liner in port for a planet halfway across all explored space.

There wasn't room enough in Jules' cabin for him to pace the floor, so he stood still, with clenched fists jammed into his pockets. Yvette sat on his narrow bunk, frowning in concentration.

"It's like fighting a fog," Jules said, scowling. "And yet everything we find is just too damned pat."

"You just lost me. Fog, yes. But I haven't noticed any patness."

"Look. In sixty-seven years SOTE hasn't found any evidence that Duke Henry of Durward wasn't I, T, IT."

"Which goes to show that he was."

"Does it? He milked Durward of a staggering fortune, yes. Billions of bucks. But could he possibly have got away with enough to finance a project that big this long? And the others . . ."

"I see what you mean. Never mind the others, let's pursue this one. Either he had help from the start or he hooked up with some. He'd have to, to do what he did." ·

"That's sure. Yet nobody ever got a solid trace, ever. And the leads they did get didn't point to anything solid; just to nit-picking stuff. My thought is that every one of those leads was a trap—a trap that worked."

"And we weren't trapped because we made them come to us."

"I'm not even sure of that."

"My God! Surely you don't think *this* is a trap!"

"Not exactly. I just think it *may* be. We have to follow it, of course, but we'll follow it with our eyes wide open and everything we've got on the trips. And if what we dig up points to Durward—we'll go anywhere else in all space *but* there."

"So you think everybody's been barking up the wrong trees and all they've got is forty-seven reels of junk and . . ."

"I said *maybe!*" Jules snapped. "I don't *know* anything!"

"Which puts you one up on SOTE," Yvette said quietly. "That makes the most sense of anything I've heard yet. So we jettison the junk and start from scratch . . . the big

253

question being—how? You're implying a Grand Duke. We *can't* go running around sticking nitrobarb into Grand Dukes at random."

"How true; but you've read about how the old FBI used to catcch the top mobsters?"

"Uh-huh. CPA's."

"So look. Durward is in Sector Ten. Algonia is in Three, Aston is in Six, Nevander is in Thirteen and Gastonia is a rim-world clear to hellangone out on the edge of Twenty."

"How did Gastonia sneak into this muddle? It was muddled enough already, without another question mark."

"My own idea. Empress Stanley Five started exiling rebels there way back in the twenty-two hundreds sometime and they've been doing it ever since. What could be nicer for recruiting purposes? But to get back on the beam, the Head thinks this thing is getting ripe. If it is, whoever's doing it has had to do a lot of heavy work and spend an ungodly lot of money. You can hide a lot of building—armaments and such—even without putting it underground. But you can't hide big flows of money from experts who know how to look. So if you don't think I'm nuts, we'll message the Head tonight to check the growth curves of all the planets for the last seventy years and put the best CPA's he's got onto the top five or six."

She looked at him admiringly. "I'm for it; strong. And then we go to Gastonia, or wherever?"

"No. Then we go to Earth."

She looked puzzled for a moment, then her face cleared. "I see. It *would* have to be a Grand Duke, at that, to get an agent into—and especially out of—the Head's own office . . . and the brains *would* almost have to be on Earth. You *are* smart, Julie; maybe we're getting somewhere, after all."

The ship docked and the two, after killing half an hour— they expected real trouble, and preparations were being made to handle it—made their way to the middle-class dive that was the favorite hangout of the lower offices and the highest crewmen of whatever subspacers happened to be in port. That was all they had—the name of the dive and a cryptic recognition signal bought for them by nitrobarb at the cost of a man's life. But it was enough.

Since the latest ship to come to ground was DesPlainian, the six bouncer-guards of the place—it *was* a somewhat unusual fact that all six of them were DesPlainians—thought nothing of it when half a dozen leather-clad Des-Plainian spacemen came bouncing in, shouting for strong drink and friendly girls.

How could the guards have suspected anything? Or the brains, either, since the d'Alemberts had pitched them such a nice curve? There was no evidence that the Velasquez pair had anything to do with what had happened on Algonia. And if they had had, what were they skyshooting off into the middle of nowhere for?

The renegade Puritans came in—it was quite evident that they were renegades, since no Puritan in good standing would ever enter a bar—and looked unconcernedly around. Since it was early in the afternoon, only one bartender was at work and only a few waitresses and B girls were on hand. The two strolled up to the bar and Jules said, "I was told to ask for the Blinding Flash and say the Deafening Report sent me."

The entire room exploded. The six guards tried, but before any of them could get his blaster half into action he was struck by over an eighth of a ton of the hardest meat he had ever felt. In the same instant Jules put his left arm around the bartender's throat and, with the blaster now in his right hand, drilled a half-inch hole through the PBX operator's head. He then whistled sharply at the terrified girls and waved his weapon at a corner; into which they and the few noncombatant customers were very glad indeed to run.

In the meantime Yvette had dived at the PBX board. She snatched the single earphone off the man's head, put it on her own, let the body fall and sat at the board.

In two minutes the place was a shambles. When a five-hundred-pound pair of DesPlainian freestyle brawlers strikes furniture it is the furniture that breaks, not the men. Two tables and half-a-dozen chairs remained intact; one savagely warring pair had gone straight through the heavy yellow-wood bar.

And Jules, standing at ease with his blaster hanging at the loose, studied with keen appreciation the battles going on. He was not worried about the outcome. Only one result was possible. The guards were good, but they were not d'Alembert—and those six d'Alemberts were the pick of the hardest-trained troupe of no-holds-barred fighting wrestlers known to man.

In three and one-half minutes the place was practically a total loss, but the battle was over. The six survivors sported a few eyes that would soon be black, some contusions and abrasions, and several cuts, tears, scratches, gouges and bites that were bleeding more or less freely, but there had been no real damage at all.

"Nice work, fellows; thanks," Jules said, as the sixth spaceman came to his feet, grinning hugely. "Drink up. There'll be at least some ginger ale left in whole bottles—I think. And break out some champagne for the cuties. I wouldn't know whether they're still in the mood for fun and games or not, but at least we'll do the gentlemanly thing about the drinks. "Now, barkeep my friend—" he lifted that wight one-handedly over the bar, set him on his feet and put both big hands uncomfortably tight around his throat—"Do you want to tell me all about all the gizmos between here and the boss upstairs or do I wring your neck exactly like a chicken's?"

"I'll tell, I'll tell!" the man squawked. "Don't wring my neck—please don't! It's all on the board there—really it is—the whole works!"

"He isn't lying, Julie," Yvette said. "There's a whole row of special red indicators that doesn't belong on a standard PBX. It looks like the boss rings down and they set the traps from the board here."

"That's it, that's it!" the man babbled. "There are blacklight beams across the halls up there, set to trigger blasters and stunners. The boss calls down and the man on the boards sets up whatever he orders."

"Okay. What's his door like—wood or steel? Locked? And how about guards up there?"

"Wood. Not locked. No guards—no trouble ever gets to where he is, sir. He would've set 'em, of course—" nodding his head at the dead man beside the PBX—"but you blasted 'im too quick."

"Okay. Lead the way. That's so in case of trouble you'll get it first—from me, if necessary."

Nothing happened until they reached the Boss's door. The bartender knocked—no code, Jules noticed. A voice from inside the room called "Come in," and the pilot opened the door and led the way into the office. The man behind the desk was alone in the room. He gasped once, turned pale and reached for a row of buttons; but stopped the motion halfway as Jules' blaster came to bear.

"Go ahead, push 'em," Jules said, but the boss, except for twitching muscles, made no move whatever as Jules gave the bartender a tap on the jaw, taking a hypodermic kit out of his pocket, went up to the desk. The man's eyes widened in panic fear.

"Not that—*please* not nitrobarb!" he pleaded, desperately. "I'm allergic to the stuff—it'll kill me sure, my doctor says."

"What makes you think this is nitrobarb? It could be plain distilled water!"

"Don't mace me, mister! I think I probably know what you want . . . and you don't need to give me *anything!* I'll tell you everything I know without it, *honestly* I will!"

And he did, and once again the d'Alemberts listened to the secrets of a traitors' nest. And it was, as Jules had expected it to be, a clear, straight lead to one man in one city of the planet Durward.

"Okay," Jules said, finally. "I won't kill you—this time. Just tell your boss on Durward I'm coming; loaded to the gills with stuff he never even heard of."

Then the eight d'Alemberts went back to their ship; where Jules and Yvette spent all the rest of the day and almost all of the night in the control room, the most secure spot they could find, composing and encoding a long message to the Head.

When it was done, Jules rose, stretched and walked over to the galactic chart. His eyes brooding, he set it for maximum span and turned on the activating circuits. As the great wispy star-clouds of the galactic lens took form, each surveyed star positioned with minute accuracy, he keyed the index locators for Durward, the planet to which all their hard-earned information pointed so surely, and for old Earth. Quickly the taped data spools whined and spun and printed out course and the dizzying distance in parsecs between the two planets. He said slowly, "All the signs say Durward is where the action is . . ."

"I know, Julie," said his sister, covering a yawn. "So, of course we go to Earth. Well, what are we waiting for?"

VIII

All explored space was divided into 36 wedge-shaped sectors; the line common to all sectors being the line through the center of Sol perpendicular to the plane of the Earth's orbit. Each sector was owned, subject only to the Throne, by a Grand Duke. Earth, by far the most important planet, did not belong to any sector, but was the private property of the Throne. Each Grand Duke had a palace, several residences and a Hall of State on Earth. Because of these facts the nobility of Earth were far more powerful than their titles indicated. The Principal Palace, in which all Grand Imperial Courts were held, was in Chicago; hence the Count of Chicago had more real power than most Earls and Marquises. More, in fact, than many Dukes. (Manley, Feudalism; Reel I, Intro See viii).

The Massagerie

In his private office the Head was talking with a grey-haired man who, while old, was in no sense decrepit. Grand Lady Helena sat, shapely legs crossed, working on a twelve-ounce glass of cherry-ice-cream float.

"But what does it *mean*, Zan?" the older man asked. "Route the Circus to Durward—with instructions not to do anything whatever except circus routine. Carlos and Carmen Velasquez will not report and nothing they do, however wild, will be of any importance. And now this *beauty-parlor* business, right here on Earth! It doesn't make sense."

"Not a beauty parlor, Bill. A massagerie de luxe. Or rather, 'The House of Strength of Body and of Heart.' "

"But don't you *know* what they're doing?"

"Very little; and I don't want to know more. I give them a job; they do it their own way. I would hazard a guess that they have some reason to believe that a specific person they are interested in is likely to take an interest in bodybuilding. This, you will note, implies that they have reached the point of being interested in specific persons . . . but I don't know who. That is to the good.

"As a recent event proved, the less I know of detail, the better."

"That's true. No trace of your missing person?"

"None. There probably won't be any until the d'Alemberts crack the main case. While they're working on it they get anything they want, with no questions asked."

"As they should, especially since they want so little from us. I know that Circus taxes are rebated, but surely they spend more than that on Empire business?"

"My guess is, they don't. The Circus is so successful that its taxes are very high, but the Duke won't say *how* high. I asked him once if we didn't owe him some money and he told me if I wanted to count pennies I'd better go get myself a job in a dime store."

The old man laughed. "That sounds exactly like him. But DesPlaines is a rich planet, you know, and Etienne d'Alembert is a tremendously able man—as well as being one of my best friends. Well, I'll leave you to your work. I like to talk to you when I'm feeling low, Zan; you give me a lift." He raised his glass. "Tomorrow, fellow and friend. May we all live to see it." They drank the toast and Emperor Stanley Ten, erect and springy, left the room.

Helena grinned up at her father. "You didn't exactly lie, either; but if he knew as much as we do he wouldn't feel so uplifted."

"He has troubles enough of his own without having to carry ours. Besides, we don't know who they're after. It could turn out to be someone outside those six, as well as not."

The girl nodded. "If we had even a good suspicion, he'd get a shot of nitrobarb. All we *know* is that they haven't got a shred of evidence of anything. But how under the sun and moon and eleven circumpolar stars can this glorified gymnasium help solve anything?"

"I haven't the most tenuous idea, my dear—and just between us two, I'm just as curious as you are."

A ten-story gravity-controlled building in the Evanston district of Chicago had been remodelled from top to bot-

259

tom. All the work had been done by the high-grav personnel who now occupied the building. Over its splendidly imposing entrance a triple-tube brilliant sign flared red:

DANGER—THREE GRAVITIES—DANGER

and on each side of the portal, in small, severely plain obsidian letters on a silver background, a plaque read:

duClos

For weeks before the opening it had been noised abroad that this House of Strength would cater only to the topmost flakes of the upper crust; and that was precisely what it did. It turned down applicants, even of the nobility, by the score. Its first clients, and for some time its only clients, were the extremely powerful Count of Chicago, his Countess and their two gangling teen-age daughters. Since this display of ultra-snobbishness appealed very strongly to the ultra-snobbishness of the high nobility of the Capital of Empire, "duClos" raised snobbery to a height of performance very seldom seen anywhere.

"How're you doing, sis?" Jules asked, one evening. "I'm getting a few bites, but nothing solid. But there's a *feel* about Sector Twenty that I don't like—I'm sure we're on the right track."

"So am I, and I'm getting an idea. I wasn't going to mention it until I could thicken it up a little, but here goes. You know that Duchess of Swingleton? That snooty stinker that's supposed to be the daughter of the Grand Duchess?"

Jules came to attention with a snap. "*Supposed* to be?"

"Well, is then. Maybe I shouldn't have put it quite that way—but you know how I've learned to sneer, in my own inimitable ladylike way?"

"I wouldn't put *that* 'quite that way,' either. If it was me on the receiving end I'd sock you right in the middle of your puss."

"She'd really like to. I've been giving her the royal snoot all along and she's burning like a torch. But her mother, Grand Duchess Olga, takes it in stride. So why wouldn't

Swingleton . . . unless she's bursting at the seams with something she's bottling up?"

"My God, Eve! You think she's the Bastard's daughter?"

"I'm not that far along yet, it's just a possibility. Not daughter; sixty-seven he would be; she's only about twenty. Still in the silly age—which may account for her touchiness and everything. She's beautiful, athletic, rich, talented, noble and spoiled rotten. Her hobby is men. She works hard at it. So my thought is this: if she gets the idea from somewhere that duClos himself is the one and only Mister Big in this business I'm positive that she'll insist on you coaching her yourself—personally. You take her on, but instead of bowing down and worshipping, you act like and say that you wouldn't be caught dead with her at a cat-fight, to say nothing of in bed. If I'm right she'll blow up like a bomb and say something she shouldn't."

Jules whistled piercingly through his teeth. "Wow!" he said.

Three days later, Jules accompanied Yvette into the apartment of the Duchess of Swingleton, who proved to be a tall girl—two inches taller than Jules—beautiful of face and figure, with dark blue eyes and a mass of wheat-straw-colored hair piled high on a proudly-held. Jules, after being presented, walked slowly around her once, studying her from head to foot from every angle. He scowled and then said, "*Maybe* I can do something with this, but there doesn't seem to be much of anything there to work on. Peel, you, and I'll see."

"Peel?" The girl's head went even higher, her eyes blazed. "Are you talking to *me?*" she flared.

"I'm talking to a mass of fat and a little flabby meat that ought to be muscle but isn't, he replied caustically. "Do you expect a master sculptor to make something of a tub of clay without touching it? Wear a bikini or tights if you like—although how you can imagine that I, duClos, would get the thrills over such a slug's body as yours is completely beyond my comprehension."

"Get out!" Trembling with rage, she pointed at the door. "Leave this castle at once!"

He gave her his choicest top-deck sneer. "Madame,

nothing could possibly please me more." He executed a snappy about-face and made for the door.

"Wait, you! Turn around!"

"Yes?" he asked, coldly.

"I am the Duchess of Swingleton!"

"And I, madame, am duClos. There are hundreds and hundreds of duchesses, but there is only one duClos."

She fought her anger down. "I'll put on a swimsuit," she said. "After all, I *do* want to find out whether you're any good or not."

But when she came back, dressed in practically nothing, duClos was even less impressed than before. "Lard," he said, when his talented fingers had reported their preliminary findings to his brain. "Flabby, unrendered lard; but I'll see what I can do with it. We'll go to your gymnasium now."

"Why, aren't you going to take me to your place?"

He looked at her in amused and condescending surprise. "Are you *that* stupid? You'd fall flat and could hardly get up. It'll take a month of work here before you'll be able to work in the House of Strength. To your gymnasium, I say."

In the castle's gymnasium, he said, "First, we'll show you what we, accustomed to three Earth gravities, can do easily here on Earth," and he and Yvette went through a routine of such violence that the apparatus creaked and groaned and the very floor shook.

"Now what a fair Earth gymnast—such as perhaps I'll be able to make out of you—can do," and they showed her that.

"Now I'll find out what you can do—if anything. You can't do even fifty fast push-ups without going flat on your face," and of course she couldn't

He worked her fairly hard for half an hour, which was about all she could take, then said, "That's enough for today, poor thing." Then, turning to Yvette, "Give her a massage in steam, and go deep. After that, the usual."

"No, I want you to do it yourself," the girl said. "They say you're tops and I want nothing but the best."

"Okay," Jules said, in a perfectly matter-of-fact voice, and peeled down to his white nylon shorts. "That'd be better—I'll know more exactly how you come along."

262

The ladies-in-waiting were shocked—or pretended to be —as the three-quarters-naked man worked on their completely naked mistress; but Jules, alone, of all those present, was—apparently—not affected at all. He was a top-expert masseur working at his profession.

This went on for day after day. Since the Duchess was actually a strong, healthy athletic girl, splendidly built, and agile both physically and mentally, she learned fast and developed fast. But for the first time in her life she had struck a man and bounced. It was an intolerable situation —a situation that got no better at all as time went on.

He stayed coldly impersonal and more than somewhat contemptuous; he was and he remained a master craftsman wasting his talents on material entirely unworthy of his skill. He paid no attention whatever to any of the little plays she made.

One day, however, when she had become a pretty fair gymnast and was very proud of her accomplishments, all the ladies-in-waiting disappeared before the massage was to begin.

"We don't need them any more, I don't think." She posed, with her skimpy garment half off, and gave him an undereyebrows look that would have put any other man she knew into a flat spin. "Do we?"

"I don't, that's sure," he said, with the sneer that had become so maddening that she wanted to bash it back into his skull with a sledgehammer. "And if you're trying to seduce me you're wasting your time. You're a hunk of clay I'm trying to model into something halfway worth while, and nothing else. I'd not rather have you than any other mass of poor-grade clay—or a dime's worth of catmeat."

That blew it—sky high. "You low-born oaf!" she screamed. "You clod! You base-born peasant, I'll have you flayed alive and staked out on . . ." She stopped screaming suddenly and her eyes widened the veriest little.

"Stop running off at the mouth!" he rasped, timing it so perfectly that she *knew* he had interrupted her tirade. "My birth, high or low, has no bearing. I am duClos. I am trying to mold you into what our Creator intended you to be;

263

His instrument to produce *men*, not the milksops and flabs now infesting this sinful planet Earth."

"Oh? Don't tell me you're a *Puritan!*" she exclaimed, very glad indeed to change the subject. "I should have known it, though, by all that hair."

"An ex-Puritan," he corrected her. "I do not believe that everything pleasant is sinful, but neglect of the human body most certainly is. So get in there. And snap it up—before you cool off too much."

Work went on, exactly as though nothing had happened. She graduated into the House of Strength and, everything considered, she did very well there.

And she convinced herself quite easily that she had not revealed any tittle of the secret that had been held for sixty-seven years.

IX

As an example of the traditional loyalty of the Navy: When Empress Stanley 5, her husband and four of their five children were assassinated in 2229, their youngest child, Prince Edward, escaped death only because he, then an ensign in the Navy, was being guarded as no other person had ever been guarded before. Fleet Admiral Simms declared martial law and, in the bloodiest purge in all history, executed not only all those found guilty, including Prince Charles and Princess Charlene, but also their entire families. He then made himself regent and ruled with an iron hand for six years. Then, to the vast surprise of all, he relinquished his regency on the day that Prince Edward came of age and he himself crowned Prince Edward Emperor Stanley Six (Farnham; The Empire, Vol. 1, p. 784).

The Fortress of Englewood

Jules and Yvette deigned to accept six Grand Dukes and their wives as personal clients—among whom were Grand Duke Nicholas and Grand Duchess Olga of Sector Twenty —but that was all they would take. In that position of intimacy they dug up a few hints, but neither of them could lay hold of anything solid.

At every opportunity they planted Earth operators in the kitchens, in the garages and everywhere else they could. These detectives found bits and pieces of information, but they could not find any leads to Banion or to any of his blood; nor to the all-important Patent of Royalty.

"We've *got* to take this to the Head, Eve," Jules said finally. "I hate to yell for help on our first really big job, but he's just too damned big for us. And it's more than a possibility that it'd be the Head's head that would roll, not Duke Twenty's. We simply *can't* take the chance."

Yvette nodded. "You're right, I'm afraid. He's really big . . . but he hasn't got a drop of Stanley blood in him . . ."

"Which is why he's playing it this way," Jules declared. "The power behind the Throne. I'll set up a meet."

He set it up and they laid the whole ugly mess squarely on the line, and while they talked the Head aged ten years. When they were done he sat silent and motionless, in intense concentration, for a good fifteen minutes. They could almost feel the master strategist's keen brain at work.

Finally he lifted his head sharply and he said:

"I was hoping it would be one of the others, but you're right. We can't move against *him* without the genuine Patent actually in our hands."

Jules scowled. "That's what I was afraid you'd say. And that Patent must be in the solidest safe-deposit vault on Earth."

"It isn't," the Head said, flatly. "The Emperor can open any bank vault he pleases, with no reason at all. So it's in a vault as good as any on Earth, but in the deepest sub-cellar of Castle Englewood. I'd stake my head on that. Theoretically, the Emperor could open that vault, too, at whim. But trying it would touch everything off and Nicholas might win. So I'm going to stake all our heads. No matter how daintily we try to pussyfoot it, there's always the chance of our touching off the explosion. However, there'd be no point in his killing the Crown Princess as long as the Emperor and the Empress are alive, so what do you think of this?" and they discussed details for two hours.

Three days later, the news media announced that Emperor Stanley Ten had had a heart attack.

It wasn't too serious, as such things go, but a battery of specialists agreed unanimously that he had to have at least two months of carefree rest, preferably at his favorite summer place, Big Piney in the Rockies. Wherefore Crown Princess Edna was given the unusual title of "Empress Pro Tem" and her parents went, with no pomp or circumstance at all—not to Big Piney, but to an island in the Pacific that was guarded by every defensive device known to the military science of the age.

And Empress Pro Tem Edna announced a party—a getting-acquainted party that, beginning with a full Grand Imperial Court, would last for three days—to which all thirty-six Grand Dukes and their entire families were invited. And did any of the invitees even think of declining? Not one.

As that party began, Jules and Yvette and a regiment of experts went as insidiously as possible to work on Castle Englewood. Having free run of the place, as far as anyone now there was concerned, the two went first—with stunners in their hands—to visit the key personnel. They were followed by fifty cat-footed, fully briefed d'Alemberts, who took care of everyone else; particularly of the many-times-too-numerous Castle Guard.

Architects and engineers had detailed plans of the castle, but they were found useless. The actual details had never been registered. So electronic technicians unlimbered their most sensitive detectors and explored walls, floors and ceilings. They traced cable after cable, wire after wire; and section after section of the vast building went dark and powerless.

It had been clear from the start that this was no ordinary residence of any ordinary Grand Duke. It was a fortress; a fortress that, except for the Head's brilliant strategy and the d'Alemberts' ability to carry it out, would have been starkly impregnable. And, even so, the attack almost failed.

"How about this, Major?" Jules asked, as the company, after exploring all the other tunnels and corridors in the sub-basements, returned to a grimly thick steel wall.

"It opens from somewhere, somehow." The officer pointed out an almost invisible crack where steel butted against steel. "It'd probably take a week, though, to find out where or how, I *think* we cut all external leads to here, but they could have independent power in that section."

"We'll assume they have," Jules said. "And automatic blasters—or worse, stunners. Gas, maybe, or triggered bombs. But the Head gambled his life on a lot less than we know now, so bring up your shields and high-powers and burn the damned thing down."

When the eight-inches-thick mass of armor-plate fell inward into the brilliantly lighted room, revealing a squad of tremendously-muscled DesPlainians, it struck a steel floor with a crash that shook the very bed-rock upon which Castle Englewood was built.

One glance, however, was all Jules had; for even before steel struck steel he was smashed down flat by a force of twenty-five gravities; and the fact that the musclemen inside the room went down too was of little enough comfort. They were weight-lifters. He wasn't.

"Ultra-grav!" Jules gritted, through his clenched teeth. "Can you fellows do anything with it, Rick?" he demanded of the leader of the fighting wrestlers who had done such good work on Aston. "It looks like they've got me just about stuck down."

"We're working on it, Chief," Rick said hoarsely, and they were.

It was fantastic to see two-hundred-fifty-pound brawlers, muscled like Atlases, exerting every iota of their tremendous strength; first to get up onto their knees and then to lift, with the full power of both arms, a five-pound weapon up into some kind of firing poistion. Unfortunately, one of the guards—a giant even for a DesPlainian weight-lifter—made it first. His first blast went straight through the man in front of Jules; and Jules, who had managed to get almost to his knees, lost a fist-sized chunk of flesh out of his left leg and went back down.

Only the one guard, however, beat the d'Alemberts into action. In the ensuing awkward, slow-motion battle eighteen men died; eight of them being the Grand Duke's guards. Then slowly, ultratoilsomely, the d'Alembert found the gravity controls and restored a heavenly three thousand centimeters per second. And Yvette, who had been pinned down all this time, rushed over and first-aid-bandaged the ghastly wound in her brother's leg.

They did not try to unlock the vault. It was too late now for cat-footing. Demolition experts brought up their shields and sandbags and blew the whole face of it to bits. They removed the debris and ransacked the vault—and they found a Patent of Royalty.

Then, hearts in throats and scarcely breathing, they looked on while hand-writing experts and documentary experts gave the parchment the works.

"This is the genuine Patent," the chief examiner said finally; and in the joyously relieved clamor that followed even the dead were for the moment forgotten.

The rest of the project went smoothly enough. The full regiment of Imperial Guards sealed the Principal Palace bottle-tight. The Navy put an impenetrable umbrella over all Chicago. Fleet Admiral Armstrong himself led a company of marines into the Grand Ballroom and broke up the Empress Pro Tem's party by putting Grand Duke Nicholas and his entire retinue under arrest. And immediately, then and there in the Grand Ballroom, the Emperor's personal physician administered nitrobarb and the Court Psychologist asked questions. And Empress Pro Tem Edna, her face too stern and hard by far for any girl of her years, listened; and having listened, issued orders which Fleet Admiral Armstrong carried out.

Since it is much faster to work such an inquiry from the top down than from the bottom up, full information was obtained in less than a week. And thus, while the resultant vacancies in the various services were many and terribly shocking, the menace that had hung over the Empire for sixty-seven years was at long last abated.

And thus—a thing supremely important to Jules and Yvette d'Alembert—the Service of the Empire was at long last clean.

X

Because of their high intelligence, their super-cat agility, their hair-trigger speed of reaction and their enormous physical strength, DesPlainians had been the best secret-

service agents of, in turn, the Central Intelligence of Earth, the Galactic Intelligence Agency and the Service of the Empire. And of all DesPlainians, throughout the years, the d'Alemberts had been by far the best. The fact that the Circus of the Galaxy was SOTE's right arm did not leak from Earth because only the monarch, the Head and a very few of their most highly trusted intimates ever knew it. Nor did it leak from the Circus. Circus people never have spoken to rubes, and the inflexible Code d'Alembert was that d'Alemberts spoke only to d'Alemberts and to the Head (unpublished data).

Bill, Irene and Edna

Again it was late at night. Again the d'Alemberts Service Special slanted downward through the air toward the roof of the Hall of State of Sector Four. This time, however, the little speedster was not riding a beam and there was no spot of light upon the building's roof. Except for the light of the almost-full moon, everything was dark and still.

Yvette was the Yvette of old. Jules, again short-haired and smooth-shaved, looked like his usual self; but there was a crutch beside him and his sister was doing the piloting.

She landed the craft near the kiosk of the ultra-private elevator, opened up and leaped lightly out; Jules clambered out, clumsily and stiffly; and Grand Lady Helena came running up in a very ungrand-ladylike fashion.

"Oh, you're wonderful, Yvette—simply *marvellous!*" She put both arms around Yvette's neck and kissed her three times on the lips. "I'm awfully glad father let me be the one to meet you!" She turned and went somewhat carefully into Jules' arms. "And *you*, Jules! Oh, I just can't—but *surely* you can hug a girl tighter than *this*, can't you? Even with a bum leg?"

Jules, returning her kisses enthusiastically, tightened his arms a little, but not much. Then, lifting her by the armpits, he held her feather-lightly out at arms' length, with her toes ten or twelve inches in air. "Sure I can," he said, solemnly but with sparkling eyes, "but the trouble is, I never hugged an Earther before and I'm afraid of breaking

269

you in two. It wouldn't be quite *de rigeur*, would it, to break a Grand Lady's back and half of her ribs?"

"Oh, there's no danger of *that*. I'm ever so much stronger than. . . ." She broke off and her eyes widened in surprise as her hands, already on his arms, tried with all their strength to drive her fingertips into them.

"Oh, I see," she said quietly. "I never quite realized."

Jules lowered her gently to the roof and she led the way into the elevator. She did not tell them what the Head wanted of them and they did not ask. As the elevator started down she said, "Jules, I'm going to tell you something. I was all set to fall in love with you and make you love me whether you wanted to or not. But when I couldn't make even a dent in those muscles of yours . . . arms as big and as hard as those of a heroic-size bronze . . . well. . . ." Her voice died away.

"You couldn't, possibly," he replied soberly. "There's too much difference. Three of your gravities is a lot of grav, Helena. But we have your friendship?"

"More than that, both of you. Ever so much more. That, and admiration and esteem and. . . ." She broke off as the elevator door opened.

She stepped aside; motioned for them to precede her. They took one step into the Head's private office and stopped dead in their tracks, their eyes and mouths becoming O's of astonishment. For—

The big but trim old grey-haired man was Emperor Stanley Ten! The statuesque, regal, brown-haired woman was Empress Irene! And the beautifully built, prematurely stern-faced girl mixing drinks at the Head's bar was Crown Princess Edna.

The emperor stood up and raised a hand. "Do not kneel," he said—but of course, with their speed of reaction, Yvette was already on her knees and Jules, gimpy leg and all, was on one.

He raised them to their feet, kissed Yvette's hand and shook Jules' and said, "During this visit and here-after in private, my friends, to you two I am Bill."

"Oh, we couldn't, Your . . . Sire . . . not possibly," Jules said. "But we might call you 'sir,' sir?"

Stanley Ten smiled; and in that smiling shed a heavy load. "Oh? I understand. Many of the younger generation

270

are not so well bred. 'Sir' will do very nicely. I take pleasure in presenting you both to Mrs. Stanley . . . and to our daughter, Edna."

Introductions made, Edna Stanley went around with her tray, serving Jules last. As she handed him his glass of lemonade her dark, grey eyes, usually distant, were soft and warm. "It's a damned dirty stinking shame," she said, feelingly, "that we can't give you two, the two who saved our lives, at least a Grand Imperial Court channelled to every planet in space. And to cap it off we have to give that stuffed shirt Armsbold all the credit. The fathead! And he'll get another medal, I suppose—and compared to you two he positively could not detect a smell on a skunk!"

"Well—" Jules began, but the princess rushed on.

"Oh, I know that's the way it has to be, Jules, and I know why. And I know exactly how you feel about it. The Service of the Empire. The fine tradition of the finest group of men and women who ever lived. But knowing all that doesn't make it taste any better or go down any easier that all we can do is thank you for saving all three of our lives at such tremendous risk of your own, and that we have to do even that on the sneak—or cost you yours."

She threw her arms around Jules' neck and kissed him warmly. And, while he could not bring himself to the point of kissing the Crown Princess of the Empire as though she were an ordinary girl, his response was adequate.

Edna Stanley was not the crying type, but her eyes brimming as she drew her head back, looked straight into Jules' eyes and went on, "But we three will remember it as long as we live; and you two will have a very special place in my heart as long as I live."

Without giving Jules a chance to say anything—which was just as well, since he could not possibly have said a word—she wriggled free and embraced Yvette. "What did *you* expect. Yvette? And call me Edna; we're about the same age."

"I'd love to, Edna, it warms me clear through. What I expected was a pat on the back from the Head there and another tough job."

The Head laughed. "You'll get both, my dear." Then, turning to Stanley, "You see, Bill?"

"I see, Zan. D'Alemberts. Metal of proof. Wrought and tempered." Stanley turned to Jules and Yvette. "You young people don't realize that your lives are more important to the Empire than mine is."

"I not only don't realize it, sir," Jules said, doggedly, "but I don't see how it can possibly be true. You are the third and the greatest of the Great Stanleys. Eve and I are just two d'Alemberts out of over a thousand."

"Correction, please. As of now you are, and probably for the next two or three years will continue to be the two most capable human beings alive." Stanley replenished his drink and brought Yvette a small pitcher of fresh orange juice, while Edna waited on the others. "Let's examine this 'Great Stanley' business a little; it will be a good way to get better acquainted. I've studied the House of Stanley quite thoroughly; enough to have developed what is—to me, at least—a new theory. Has it ever occurred to you to wonder why the three so-called Great Stanleys happened to be the three who reigned longest? Empress Stanley Three, thirty-seven years; Emperor Stanley Six, thirty-six years; and I, who have more than either, and will probably—thanks to you—reign two more before reaching the age of seventy and abdicating in favor of Edna here?"

"N-o-o-o, sir. I can't say that I have."

"It's a highly pertinent fact. You know, I'm sure, that only one Stanley so far has died in bed."

"Yes, sir, but. . . ."

"And one died in a space accident. The other seven were assassinated, usually by their own sons or daughters or brothers or sisters."

"Yes, sir. I know that."

"They had too many children, too young. So Irene and I had only one child, and Edna wasn't born until I was forty-five years old. So as soon as she's able to carry the load we'll hand it to her on a platter and step out."

"Dad!" the Crown Princess exclaimed. "You know very well I'd never even *think* of such a thing!" And:

"William!" the Empress protested. "What a *nasty* thing to say!"

The Emperor grinned. "If you'll analyze what I actually said you'll see that you read that wicked thought of regicide and patricide into it—and you'll know why. Anyway, Irene, you helped plan it. And it's worked out beautifully for all of us. You've all heard the old wheeze that "Power corrupts; absolute power corrupts absolutely?' "

They all had.

"My theory is that only the first part of that old saying is really true. For, as a matter of fact, no human being ever had absolute power until King Stanley the Sixth crowned himself Emperor Stanley One and took it. He had the whole galaxy. Every other despot in history was always reaching for more; so the truth of that old saying was never tested.

"Indeed, there is much in preStanley history that argues against its truth. The worst gangsters and the most rapacious capitalists Earth ever knew, when they got old enough and powerful enough and rich enough, turned from crime and rapacity to something that was for the good of all mankind. And the entire history of the House of Stanley bears this out."

There was a short silence, then the Empress said, thoughtfully, "Well, it's something to think about, at least . . . and it *does* seem to make sense . . . but my dear, what has all that to do with the present case?"

"Everything," Stanley said, deadly serious now. "It shows why these two d'Alemberts—highly trained, uniquely gifted, innately and completely loyal to the Empire—are much more important to the Empire than I am. Not that they are indispensable. No one is. But they are at present irreplaceable and I am not. Any Stanley who is able to live long enough becomes a Great Stanley by sheer force of circumstance, and Edna will be one from the day she is crowned."

The Emperor turned to face Jules and Yvette. "Nevertheless, my young friends, my life is extremely important to me. It is also extremely important to Irene and to Edna, as are their lives to me. Our three lives are important to a few real friends, such as Zander there and your father the Duke; but you would be surprised to know just how scarce such real friends are. The life of any individual Emperor or Empress, however, is of very little importance to the Empire itself, of which its rulers are merely the symbols. The Empire endures only because of the loyalty to it of such people as you. Such loyalty can not be commanded;

273

it must be earned. The Empire will endure as long as, and only as long as, it continues to be worthy of such loyalty. Without that loyalty the Empire would fall. Instead of prosperity and peace there would be widespread and terribly destructive wars of planetary conquest. Our present civilization would degenerate into barbarism and savagery.

"We Stanleys do what we can; but in the last analysis the Empire rests squarely upon the arch of its various services, and your Service of the Empire is the very keystone of that arch.

"As Edna said, it is a shame that we three can give you only our thanks. It is not, however the thanks of only three people, I am speaking for the Empire when I say to you and through you to those who work with you. . . ." Emperor Stanley Ten took the d'Alemberts' right hands, one in each of his own:

"Thanks."

AFTERWORD

The Epic of Space

How do I write a space story? The question is simple and straightforward enough. The answer, however, is not; since it involves many factors.

What do I, as a reader, like to read? Campbell, de Camp, Heinlein, Leinster, Lovecraft, Merritt, Moore, Starzl, Taine, van Vogt, Weinbaum, Williamson—all of these rate high in my book. Each has written more than one tremendous story. They cover the field of fantastic fiction, from pure weird to pure science fiction. While very different, each from all the others, they have many things in common, two of which are of interest here. First, they all put themselves into their work. John Kenton *is* Abraham Merritt; Jirel of Joiry *is* Catherine Moore. Second, each writes—or wrote—between the lines, so that one reading is not enough to discover what is really there. Two are necessary—three and four are often-times highly rewarding. Indeed, there are certain stories which I still re-read, every year or so, with undiminished pleasure.

Consider Merritt, for instance. He wrote four stories—"The Ship of Ishtar," "The Moon Pool," "The Snake Mother," and "Dwellers in the Mirage"—which will be immortal. A ten-year-old child can read them and thrill at the exciting adventurous surface stories. A poet can read them over and over for their feeling and imagery. A philologist can study them for their perfection of wording and phraseology. And yet, underlying each of them, there is a bedrock foundation of philosophy, the magnificence of which simply cannot be absorbed at one sitting.

In this connection, how many of you have read, word by word, the ascent to the Bower of Bel, in "The Ship of

Ishtar?" Those who have not, have missed one of the most sublime passages in literature. And yet a friend of mine told me that he had skipped "that stuff." It was too dry!

These differences in reader attitude, however, bring up the very important matter of treatment. It is a well-known fact that many readers, particularly those whose heads are of use only in keeping their ears apart, want action, and only action. Slambang action; the slammier and the bangier the better. It is also a fact that some editors will either reject or rewrite stories which do not conform to such standards. Since it is practically impossible to read such a story twice, however, the type is mentioned only in passing.

Something besides action, then, is necessary. What? And how much? And should the characters grow, or not? Many writers—good ones, at that—do not let their characters grow. It is easier. Also, it allows a series of stories about the same characters to go on practically endlessly; being limited only by the readers' patience. Personally, I like to have my characters grow and develop; even though this growth limits sharply the number of stories I am able to write about them.

It would seem as though anyone, after a few days or weeks of study of any good book on "How to Write the Great American Novel," could emerge with a clear understanding of such basic things as plot, conflict, situation, incident, suspense, interest, treatment, and atmosphere; but unfortunately, I didn't. Authorities differ. I don't know yet whether there are three basic plots, or eleven, or whether an author has a brand-new plot when he changes his hero from a bright young lawyer to a brilliant young physicist, and his heroine from a wise-cracking brunette stenographer to a witty blonde stewardess. I don't know yet whether the incomparable Weinbaum's "Trweel," which—or who?—rocked Fandom on its foundations was a new plot, a new school of thought, or an incident. So, while I will probably use some of those words, I will use them in the ordinary, and not in the technical, sense.

Besides action, a good story must have background material and atmosphere to give authority, authenticity, and verisimilitude. It must also have characterization—character-drawing—to make its people real people and not marionettes dancing at the end of the author's string. To balance these factors is not easy, since they are mutually almost exclusive—not entirely so, since much can be shown in action sequences—and since the slower-moving material must not detract too much from that intangible, indefinable asset which writers and editors call "story value."

Nor does the choice lie entirely, or even mostly, with the author; for the public cannot read stories which editors will not publish. I wrote three stories (not scientific fiction) which were not slanted, but which were written exactly as I wanted to write them. I liked them; but editors did not. Hence they will remain unpublished.

Character-drawing, however deftly or interestingly it is done, does operate to slow down the action of a story. Background material and atmosphere are usually slower still. Philosophy, even in small doses, is slowest of all. Yet any story, if it is to live beyond the month of its publication, must be balanced. Hence the often-heard accusation of "wordiness" hurled at so many writers is almost never justified. I do not believe that any author writes words merely to fill up space. He uses words just as a mechanic uses tools or as an artist uses colors and brushes, and with just as definate an aim in view. The casual reader may not know, or care, what that end is, but in practically every case the author has known exactly what he was trying to do with everyone of those words. He may have been using them for atmosphere, for character-drawing, for a subtle imagery or philosophy perceptible only to the reader able and willing to read between the lines, or for any one of a dozen other purposes. Thus, the action fan begrudges every word which does not hurl the story along; and does not like Lovecraft, saying that he is "wordy." To the reader who likes and appreciates atmosphere, however, Lovecraft was the master craftsman.

Some authors are better than others, of course. There are poor mechanics, too; and poor artists. For that matter, I wonder if any artist ever painted a picture that was as good as he wanted and intended it to be?

Great stories must be logical and soundly motivated; and it is in these respects that most "space-operas"—as well as more conventional stories—fail. A story must have action, conflict, and suspense. An author must get his hero into a jam; and, whether not he really *must* marry him off, he usually does so, either actually or by implication. Now it is (or at least it should be) apparent that if the hero has even half of the brain with which the author has so carefully endowed him, he is not going to land his spaceship and, without examination or precaution, gallop heedlessly away from it, specifically to be captured by ferocious natives. Yet how often that precise episode has occurred, for exactly that reason! Similarly, if anyone connected with the take-off of a rocket-ship—especially an experimental model—had any fraction of a brain, there would be just about as much chance of a beautiful female stowing away aboard it as there would be in the case of a 500-mile racer at Indianapolis. Yet that atrocity has been used sickeningly often, to introduce effortlessly an interference with the hero's plans and to drag it by the heels a love interest that does not belong there.

Now sound, solid motivation is far from easy—a fact which accounts for the rather widespread use of coincidence. This dodge, while not as bad as some other crimes, reveals mental laziness—excepting, of course, when it is an element in mass-production methods of operation.

I have found motivation the hardest part of writing; and several good men have told me that I am not alone. It takes work—*plenty* of work—to arrange things so that even a really smart man will be forced by circumstances to get into situations that make stories possible. It takes time and thought; and many times it requires extra words and background material whose purpose is not immediately apparent.

To refer to an example with which I am thoroughly familiar, what possible motive force would make Kimball Kinnison, an adult, brilliant, and highly valued officer of the Galactic Patrol, go willingly into a hyper-spatial tube which bore all the ear-marks of a trap set specifically for him? I could not throw this particular episode into the circular file, as I have done with so many easier ones, because it is the basis of the grand climax of the final Lensman story, "Children of the Lens." Nor could I duck the issue or slide around it, since any weakness at that point would have made waste paper of the whole book. Kinnison *had* to go in. His going in had to be inevitable, with an inevitability apparent to his wife, his children, and—I hope and believe—even to the casual reader. That problem had me

278

stumped for longer than I care to admit; and its solution necessitated the introduction of seemingly unimportant background material into "Galactic Patrol," which was published in 1937, and into the two other Lensman novels which have appeared since.

Now to go into the way in which I write a space story— specifically, the "Lensman" series, since it is in reality one story. Early in 1927, shortly after the "Skylark of Space" was accepted by the old *Amazing*, I began to think seriously of writing a space-police novel. It had to be galactic, and eventually inter-galactic, in scope; which would necessitate velocities vastly greater than that of light. How could I do it? The mechanism of the "Skylark," even though employing atomic energy, would not do. There simply wasn't enough of it, as several mathematicians pointed out to me later in personal correspondence—and as both Dr. Garby and I knew at the time. Also, the acceleration employed would have flattened out steel springs, to say nothing of human bodies, into practically monomolecular layers. Mrs. Garby and I knew that, too—but since the "Skylark" was pseudo-science, and since it was written long before the advent of scientific fiction, we could and did use those two mathematically indefensible mechanisms. This space-police yarn, however, would have to be scientic fiction.

I would not use mathematically impossible mechanics, such as that too-often-revived monstrosity of a second satellite hiding eternally from Earth behind the moon. Since the inertia of matter made it impossible for even atomic energy to accelerate a space-ship to the velocity I had to have, I would have to do away with inertia. Was there any mathematical or philosophical possibility, however slight, that matter could exist without inertia? There was—I finally found it in no less an authority than Bigelow (Theoretical Chemistry—Fundamentals). Einstein's Theory of course denies that matter can attain such velocities, but that did not bother me at all. It is still a theory—velocities greater than that of light are not *absolutely* mathematically impossible. That is enough for me. In fact, the more highly improbable a concept is—short of being contrary to mathematics whose fundamental operations involve no neglect of infinitesimals—the better I like it.

Other great drawbacks, philosophical or logical rather

279

than mathematical, were the difficulties of communicating with strange races and the apparent impossibility of having my policemen invent or develop an identifying symbol which all good citizens would recognize but which malefactors could not counterfeit. The only emblems which I could devise led, one and all, to the old "deus ex machina" plot, which therefore was the one I adopted; with, of course, details tailored to fit the broad scheme I had in mind and to put in a new twist or two.

Having the Lensmen's universe fairly well set up, I went through my collection, studying and analyzing every "cops-and-robbers' story on my shelves: from Canstantinescu's "War of the Universe," which I did not consider a masterpiece, up to the stories of Starzl and Williamson, who wrote literature worthy of the masters they are. I then wrote to the editor of *Astounding*, describing my idea briefly and asking whether or not he considered it advisable to go ahead with it, in view of the good work already done in the field.

He wrote back one of the most cheering letters I have ever received. I will not quote it exactly, but its gist was that it was not the pioneers in any field who did the best work, but some fellow who, coming along later, could take advantage of their strengths and avoid their weaknesses —and he thought that I could deliver the goods.

Thus encouraged to go ahead (I always did do better work while being patted on the back than while being kicked in the seat of the pants) I drew up the preliminary, very broad outline. As fundamentals, I had inertialessness and the Lens. I had the Arisians and their ultimate opponents, the Eddorians. I had a sound psychological reason why the real nature of the fundamental conflict should never be made known to any member of Homo Sapiens; since that knowledge would have set up an ineradicable inferiority complex throughout the Patrol.

It soon became evident that the story could not be told in a hundred thousand words. There would have to be at least three stories; and when the outline was done, it called for four. The point then arose: how could each book be ended without leaving loose ends dangling all over the place? I have never liked unfinished novels—I fairly gritted my teeth when Edgar Rice Burroughs left Dejah Thoris locked up in a doorless cell while he wrote the next book!

By taking the Boskonians one echelon at a time, the first two years could be ended satisfactorily enough. The third, however, was getting so close to the ultimate conflict that I had to do one of two things, neither of which I liked: either leave loose ends or apparently use the ancient and whiskery device, of the "mad scientist." After some experimental writing, I adopted the latter course. Please note, however, that neither I as the author nor Mentor of Arisia ever said anywhere that Fossten was either mad or an Arisian; although I have had, time and again, to go over the whole episode word by word to convince certain critics of the truth of this statement.

From the first quarter of the broad, general outline, only a few pages long, I made a more detailed outline of "Galactic Patrol;" laying out at the same time a graph of the structure, the progression of events, the alterations of characters, the peaks of emotional intensity and the valleys of characterization and background material. Each peak was a bit higher than the one before, as was each valley floor, until the climax was reached; after which the graph descended abruptly. My graphs are beautiful things. Unfortunately, however, while I can't seem to work without something of the kind, I have never yet been able to follow one at all closely. My characters get away from me and do exactly as they damn please, which accounts for my laborious method of writing.

I write the first draft with a soft pencil, upon whatever kind of scratch-paper is handiest. This draft is a mess; so full of erasures, interlineations, marginal notes, and crossovers to the other side of the paper that I can't read it myself after it gets cold. The second draft is written, a day or so later, from the first—with variations. It is also in pencil, but isn't so messy; except when radical changes are necessitated by departures from the outline a few chapters later. My wife can read most of it, and she types what we call the "typescript;" in reality the third rough draft. This draft, in various stages of completion, is read and heatedly discussed by the Galactic Roamers; a fan club in Michigan —and Los Angeles. Comments and suggestions are written on the margins; on some hotly-contested points they cover the entire backs of pages. I accept and use the ideas which I think are better than my own original ones; I reject the others. By rights, these friends of mine should have their names on the title-pages and a share of the loot, but to date I have been able to resist the compulsion to give them their due.

From the typescript, after the last "final" revision, my wife types the "original," which goes to Campbell. And as soon as it has been shipped I always wish that I had it back, to spend a few more weeks on the rough spots.

I have already mentioned the Galactic Roamers as a group. E. E. Evans pointed out the fact that "Triplanetary," having been laid in the Lensman universe, should be, was, and MUST BE the first story of the Lensman series, instead of "Galactic Patrol." Ed Counts found flaws and suggested corrections in my handling of the Red Lensman in the grand climax. The planet Trenco was designed and computed, practically in toto, by an aeronautical engineer who was in part responsible for the *Lightning,* the *Constellation,* and the *Shooting Star.* Dr. James Enright, of Hawaii, psychologist and psychiatrist, solved some of my knottiest problems. Dr. Richard W. Dodson, nuclear physicist, helped a lot. So did Heinlein. So did many others, not only in the United States, but also in such widely-separated places as Australia, Sweden, China, South Africa, Egypt, and the Philippines. It is bromidic, but true, to say that two heads are better than one. It has been my experience that fifty are still better.

In conclusion, if you want to write a space epic, go to it. This is the way I do it. The remuneration per hour does not compare with what a bricklayer earns, and it's harder work—I have done them both, and know. However, I get a terrific kick out of writing; especially out of the fact that quite a good many people really like my stuff.

Besides, you may find a way that is easier or better than mine: maybe one that is both easier and better.

BIBLIOGRAPHY

Magazine appearances:

Catastrophe (non-fiction article), *Astounding Science-Fiction*, May 1938

Children of the Lens (Four part serial novel), *Astounding Science-Fiction*, Nov. 1947

Fall of Atlantis, The (short story), *Science Fiction Monthly*, No. 10, 1974.

Galactic Patrol (Six part serial novel), *Astounding Stories*, Sept. 1937

Galaxy Primes, The (Three part serial novel), *Amazing Stories*, Mar. 1959

Grey Lensman (Four part serial novel), *Astounding Science-Fiction*, Oct. 1939

Imperial Stars, The (novelette), *Worlds Of If*, May 1964

Lord Tedric (novelette), *Universe Science Fiction*, Mar. 1954

Origin of Life, The (non-fiction article),* *Luna* No. 7 1969
   *Transcript of speech presented at 12th World SF Convention, California, Sept. 1954

Masters of Space* (Two part serial novel), *Worlds Of If*, Nov. 1961
   *collaboration with E. E. Evans

Robot Nemesis* (short story), *Thrilling Wonder Stories*, June 1939
   *see also as What a Course! reprinted *Startling Stories*, July 1950

Second-Stage Lensman (Four part serial novel), *Astounding Science-Fiction*, Nov. 1941

Skylark Duquesne (Five part serial novel), *Worlds Of If*, June 1965

Skylark of Space, The (Three part serial novel), *Amazing Stories*, Aug. 1928

Skylark of Valeron, The (Seven part serial novel), *Astounding Stories*, Aug. 1934

Skylark Three (Three part serial novel), *Amazing Stories*, Aug. 1930

Spacehounds of IPC (Three part serial novel), *Amazing Stories*, July 1931

Storm Cloud on Deka (novelette), *Astounding Stories,* June 1942

Subspace Survivors (novelette), *Astounding (Analog) Science Fact and Fiction,* July 1960

Tedric (short story), *Other Worlds Science Fiction Stories,* Mar. 1953

Triplanetary (Four part serial novel), *Amazing Stories,* Jan. 1934

Vortex Blaster, The (short story), *Comet Stories,* July 1941

Vortex Blaster Makes War, The (short story), *Astonishing Stories,* Oct. 1942

What a Course! (Robot Nemesis) (short story), *Fantasy Magazine:* 'Cosmos' part 13, 1934

Magazine series stories, in sequence:

Lensman series includes:

Triplanetary
Galactic Patrol
Grey Lensman
Second-Stage Lensman
Children of the Lens

Skylark series includes:

The Skylark of Space
Skylark Three
The Skylark of Valeron
Skylark Duquesne

Storm Cloud, Vortex Blaster series includes:

The Vortex Blaster
Storm Cloud on Deka
The Vortex Blaster Makes War

Tedric series includes:

Tedric
Lord Tedric

Book anthology appearances:

Atlantis (short story: see also "The Fall of Atlantis" above; from chapter two of book version of Triplanetary). Included in *Journey to Infinity* (Gnome, 1951) edited by Martin Greenburg.

Epic of Space, The (non-fiction article on sf writing). Included in symposium *Of Worlds Beyond* (Fantasy Press, 1947) edited by Lloyd Arthur Eshbach.

Vortex Blaster, The (short story). Included in *Modern Master-pieces of Science Fiction* (World, 1966) edited by Sam Moskowitz; also in paperback selection from this volume, *The Vortex Blaster* (Macfadden, 1967) edited by Sam Moskowitz.

What a Course! (short story). Included in *Cosmos* (Ruppert, N.Y. 1934). The 17 episodes of the round-robin serial from *Science Fiction Digest* (later *Fantasy Magazine*) professionally bound by Conrad H. Ruppert. Edition Limited to approximately 50 copies.

Supplementary:

A biographical /bibliographical profile of Smith by Sam Moskowitz appeared in the April 1964 issue of *Amazing Stories,* later included in book *Seekers of Tomorrow* (World, 1966) by Sam Moskowitz.

Books:

Note: In all cases, the first publication in the U.S.A. is given, and all editions are hardcover, except where stated. All titles are now in print in the U.K. in paperback.

Children of the Lens (Fantasy Press, 1954)
First Lensman (Fantasy Press, 1951)
Galactic Patrol (Fantasy Press, 1950)
Galaxy Primes, The (Ace, 1965: paperback)
Grey Lensman (Fantasy Press, 1951)
Second-Stage Lensman (Fantasy Press, 1953)
Skylark Duquesne (Pyramid Books, 1967: paperback)
Skylark of Space, The (Buffalo Book Co., 1946)
Skylark of Valeron (Fantasy Press, 1949)
Skylark Three (Fantasy Press, 1947)
Spacehounds of I.P.C. (Fantasy Press, 1947)
Subspace Explorers (Canaveral Press, 1965)
Triplanetary (Fantasy Press, 1950)
Vortex Blaster, The (Fantasy Press, 1960; later paperbacked as *Masters of the Vortex*)

And:

Best of E. E. 'Doc' Smith, Ph.D. (Futura, 1975: paperback)
The *Skylark* series, in sequence:
The Skylark of Space
Skylark Three
Skylark of Valeron
Skylark Duquesne

The *Lensman* series, in sequence:
Triplanetary
First Lensman
Galactic Patrol
Grey Lensman
Second-Stage Lensman
Children of the Lens
The Vortex Blaster